*Stay tuned and stay
in touch?*

GODS
OF CHICAGO

AJ SIKES

To Dad, who gave me the love of stories,
and to Belinda, whose love helped me believe I could write one

AUTHOR'S NOTE

Certain characters in *Gods of Chicago* are real, historic figures from Chicago's past. Notably, Frank Nitti, aka "The Enforcer" and a key member of Al Capone's gang, the Chicago Outfit. Capone himself is referenced in the story as well, but the man doesn't get a speaking part. For Nitti's role in the story, I intentionally went with what Hollywood has typically done with the man (i.e., I made him a bit of a monster) because that fit my story better. In real life, Nitti was reserved, and avoided the violent aspects of mob life. He earned his nickname because of his preference for following rules and protocols during mob activities and meetings. Nitti was kind of the Roger's Rules of Order sort rather than a gun-toting maniac.

Slang in the 1920s was pretty much how you've heard it on radio shows or movies made about the era. Sometimes it's done over the top, with every fourth word pulled out of some palooka's mouth and jammed back in sideways. I tried to avoid that here. You'll see words like *bird*, or *chopper*, meaning "dude" and "machine gun," respectively. A handful of other idioms made their way in and I endeavored to keep them in context so you can pick 'em out easy. But if you get stumped, a quick search online should point you straight, hey?

All that said above, this is *alternate history*, with a capital *This ain't the Chicago you know*. We're neck-deep in Chicago City here, with airships and automata roaming the skies and streets. Hope you enjoy it!

CHAPTER 1

THIS IS WCDR 1430, BROADCASTING ON THIS *fine morning, the fourteenth day of February, 1929. Happy Valentines's Day to everyone out there in Chicago City. We'll have the morning stock report for you in a minute, but first a word from our sponsor, Brackston Manufacturing, the leader in automated manufacturing and production today ....*

Mitchell Brand lowered the volume on the squawk box and shook his head. It should have been his voice coming over the airwaves, but he had to be at the Early Bird Diner this morning. So he gave the mic to a new guy and told him to run as many ads as he could so Chief wouldn't catch him out.

So far, so good. Brand just got his cup of coffee and Chief hadn't come busting through the door yet. Across the table, Brand's pal, Skip, sipped his own cup of joe and flipped through yesterday's paper. Brand lifted his coffee just as a metallic clattering filled the diner. The mug flew out of Brand's grip and cracked on the table top, spraying Skip's paper.

"Knew I brought this old sheet for a reason," Skip said, closing the soggy paper and setting it aside.

The radio kept up its squawking from the speaker box on the table top, but Brand could ignore it now. He had more to worry about than what his boss would say when he heard a rookie newsie giving the morning stock update. Coffee dripped into Brand's lap and the remains of the mug he'd dropped sat on the table like halves of an eggshell. Skip let a smirk stretch his face sideways and clicked his tongue at Brand.

"That's one way to get a girl's eyes on you, I guess."

"Save it, Skip. You know what's what."

"Yeah, and I know you got a girl's eye on you anyway," Skip said, flicking his eyes up to Brand's left.

The coffee girl marched their way, weaving her legs between chairs and tables and bringing a storm with her. Brand let his eyes meet hers when she stopped at his side and threw down a towel. He winced and nodded his thanks for her not pitching the towel at his head.

"Buster, that makes five weeks in a row. Every Friday, like you're getting paid to do it. They pay me to clean, sure, but can't a girl get a break?"

"Sorry, sister. I—"

"Look, all I'm asking for's a fair shake. Or is this your way of wishing a girl a Happy Valentine's?"

"Told you, Brand," Skip said, chasing his words with a laugh.

The girl gave them both a set of stink eyes. Brand figured he should cool things down. "My friend here was just saying how he's looking at a lonely night tonight, and he figured I could maybe get your attention for him. Since he's such a shy guy. Ain't that right, Skip?"

Skip dropped his joker face, but Brand caught him tucking his left hand out of sight. Before he could get a word out the girl had her teeth in them again.

"If you've got something against this place, fine. But maybe stop taking it out on my shifts."

"It's not you, sister. And it's not this place. I said I was sorry, but I can say it again if it'll help."

Up at the grill, the cookie banged his spatula on a bell. "Order!" he said, shooting a look in the girl's direction. She wrinkled her nose at Brand and stalked off to grab the platter of hash. The snapping of metal on metal came to Brand's ears again and his heart jumped into his throat. Without any coffee to spill this time, he held onto the table until his nerves ratcheted back down. While the machine shop next door built up speed, Brand scooped the pieces of his mug together and wiped the table. Skip leaned over a bit to whisper at him.

"You've got it bad and gettin' worse, Brand."

"You're right, Skip, and I sure appreciate you filling me in. Now how about you ask the girl for a new cup so I can get my wake up juice?"

Skip swatted it aside. "Ain't it been ten years gone since the Kaiser's guns stopped firing? Me and the other fellas, you know, we just keep on doing what we're doing, hey? Maybe you should try a new gig, something that don't remind you so much about the war."

"Tried it," Brand said, putting the towel aside and looking Skip in the eye. "Desks don't agree with me. They all seem to have a bottle in the bottom drawer, and you know where that story ends."

"So why not get into the manufacturing business? Chicago City's where it's at for making anything and everything, hey? From the Eastern Seaboard, down to the Southern Territory, all around the Great Lakes up here. If it's something you can sell, you can bet it was made in Chicago City."

Brand had to chuckle at that. "Factory work. Like you and the other boys do… well wouldn't that be rich, hey? Me in there when the auto-hammers start up and I'm diving under a table so you can all share a laugh. Be a real fun time, I'm sure. Thanks, but no thanks."

"Hey, Mitch. I don't mean it like that, you know. I'm just sayin' maybe something like what you didn't used to do over there. It's not like me and the fellas are out shootin' at everybody with a German name. We just… well, I guess we just left the war where it was, you know? You should do the same is all I'm sayin'. Stop reporting about murders and gunfights. Maybe ask Chief if he can give you the sporting page or something else?"

Brand sniffed and went back to wiping the table.

"Hey, I know!" Skip said, slapping a hand on the table, just missing Brand's fingers. "What about the World's Fair they're building? Century of Progress, right? You can interview all them guys and dolls behind it, get the real nitty gritty. Remember there was that bird murdered all them people last time they had a fair here? He was in the papers and—"

Brand figured Skip got the message from the look on his face, but it wouldn't hurt to add a few licks.

"So I'll report about murders I think *might* be happening? Skippy, sometimes I don't know if I should kiss you or sock you in the jaw."

"Well, I'd take the second one, Mitch. Just between you and me. Hey, here's your joe. And I didn't even have to ask for it."

The coffee girl came back with a fresh cup and set it down with an exaggerated curtsey. Brand thanked her and didn't say anything about how she'd brought him a straw along with it.

"So, Brand," Skip said. "You sure you want to do this? Today I mean. What if it does go down like the guy says? Could be real ugly. And that bit with the coffee just now. You gonna be okay?"

"Yeah, I think so. Or maybe not. But how else is Chicago City gonna get back on top again? Capone owns the place. Lock, stock, and barrel. That's not gonna change until the people see what he really gets up to behind those closed doors of his."

Brand pushed the sodden towel to the table edge and turned his attention to the street, lifting his steno pad off the seat beside him. Outside a light mist fell on the people of Chicago City as they strolled, pedaled, and clip-clopped around patches of ice and low-lying snow drifts along Clark Street. For all the world they looked like free men and women going about their business. But everyone from the tramps to the World's Fair investors knew that Chicago City was Capone's town.

Across the street the Brauerschift garage waited like a reluctant dance partner, a plain brick building sandwiched between a fenced-in empty lot and a grocer's storefront. Brand's contact said the hit would be on a Friday, sometime after the New Year. So here he sat in a greasy diner on Clark Street, just like he had for the past month. The neighboring machine shop sent another series of *rat-a-tats* his way and Brand fought down the urge to duck under the table, keeping his eyes fixed on the garage across the way.

"Well, I can see you're serious," Skip said. "Go on and take this then."

Skip held a case out, a square of brown leather about the size of a camera, but it didn't have a lens that Brand could see. He took it from Skip and turned it around in his hands.

"What is it?"

"Stuff that dreams are made of, what else? Nah, look, it's something special me and the fellas rigged up. Mr. Tesla has us all making these radio devices right now. All on the QT, so don't go telling nobody about this. But this one here—" Skip paused and sat back with a self-satisfied smile pasted on his mug.

"Yeah? You gonna tell me or do I have to spill my joe again? Maybe it'll end up in your lap this time."

"All right, Brand. Don't get heated about it," Skip said, and reached for the box. Brand handed it back to him.

Skip opened a flap on one side, revealing a set of three knobs and a lever, like a breaker switch. He pointed at the biggest knob. "This one sets your frequency. You wanna use that first to make sure you're in the right band. Then, when the static cuts, you flip the switch here." Skip worked the switch and Brand noticed how stiff it was.

"Looks like you really have to put some weight behind it, hey?"

"Yeah, it's like that on purpose, so it don't go off without you bein' ready. Now here," Skip said, pointing at the other two knobs. "These focus the picture. One's for vertical hold, the other's horizontal."

"Okay, and how do I get the picture into focus if I can't see it?"

"Oh, yeah," Skip said, turning the box over. He opened another flap to reveal a square panel of glass. "That's the viewscreen there. You gotta hold the box so you can see the screen and work the knobs. Best if you can sit down, but if you gotta stand up, just tuck it into your stomach with the screen on top and the knobs underneath. You gotta work 'em both at the same time, to sort of bring the picture around. Kinda like when you got water going down a drain, right? The picture's like … Geez, I never thought about how to explain this to a guy doesn't know radio."

"Just talk slow," Brand said, smiling. "And use small words. I'll be fine."

"Yeah, hey, I didn't— Right, so you work both knobs here, like you're trying to get the drain under the middle of the water. But it shouldn't take long. Once you get the center point of the picture fixed, the rest kinda falls into place around it. Does that make sense?"

"About as clear as mud, but I think I get it," Brand said, reaching for the box. Skip closed the flaps and handed it back to him.

Brand took it and remembered he had one more question. "Where's the lens go? How do I aim it?"

"Oh, yeah. You don't. You just gotta get next to a crab for it work."

"Eh? You never said anything about the crabs. How's this thing gonna get a picture from one of them? They're all wrapped up by the Governor's boys."

"Well sure, but who do you think makes it so the Governor's boys can do the wrapping up? It's all out of Mr. Tesla's factory, made by yours truly. And it's all on radio. The crab snaps a picture, right?"

"Yeah, and then it gets picked up and the film—"

"Nope, stop the presses, Brand."

"What—"

"There's no film in those things. It's like a little typewriter in there, all keys and punches on these chemical cards. That box there has the same thing in it. All's you gotta do is get the picture from the crab's frequency. They'll transmit to the Governor's ships lickety-split, so you gotta get close and get there fast. Dial in the crab's frequency, snap the lever, and the box'll make you a copy of the picture."

"A copy? But you said there wasn't any film."

"Nope, just a special photo card. Uses the same chemicals like film, but it's all inside the box, and you don't have to wait for the gel to set like with film. That box'll get you a crime scene photo, easy as pie. Someday soon we'll have it rigged up so you can send the pictures by radio, too, just like the Governor does. That's what the plug's for."

"Eh, plug?" Brand spun the box in his hands until he saw the port on the side. A black cylinder stuck out of the box just a bit, like it would take a thick needle.

"Sounds like hocus pocus, but I'll give it a whirl," Brand said, doubting he'd end up with more than an earful of static from the box, his boss, and any coppers who hassled him on the street. And that's if the hit went down today.

Could be next Friday, or could be never.

"Well let me know how it works, okay? I'm mostly working on something else, but ol' Nicky doesn't mind when me and the fellas make up our own ideas and see if they work. He kinda likes it when we bring him stuff, even if it doesn't work like we figured."

"Nicky?" Brand said, knowing the answer but not wanting to miss a chance at ribbing Skip a bit more.

"Yeah, you know. Nikola-Nicky. But we don't call him that. Not in person anyhow. But hey, Brand, I gotta go. Time for me to punch in over at the factory. Mr. Tesla's easy about what we do at work, but he's a hardnose about showing up on time."

"He should be with a bunch of jokers like you and the fellas on his payroll," Brand said, waving goodbye as Skip slid out of the booth.

CHAPTER 2

B RAND WORRIED HIS LIP AS THE MACHINE SHOP
fired off another round of clacks and clatters. Then a series of
pattering taps came to his ears, but lower than before. Brand
turned to the window beside him. The taps came again, heavy and
low, like hammer falls on stone. Brand noted the time, yanked a
dollar from his pocket, and tossed it on the table. He grabbed up
Skip's camera box with the other hand.

People strolled by. Cyclists trundled along. A wagon came to a
stop by the diner.

Another series of taps like before. Soft, like muffled gunshots.
Brand stood.

And now a faint screaming.

In a flash, Brand made for the door. He dodged out past a
beefy farmer type who'd just hitched his wagon outside. The horse
seemed to know something was up. Its whinnies and stamping drew
the farmer back outside to calm the beast. Brand skipped around
the nag's muzzle and flew across the pavement in five long strides,
aiming for a patch of ice by the curbside. He just missed colliding

with a cyclist who had some choice words as he put out a foot to stop himself from falling. But the screams soon overpowered every other sound on the street.

Traffic stopped outside the Brauerschift building. Cyclists and pedestrians froze in place, wincing and cringing at the sounds of violence coming from the garage. Slow as can be, a few crept forward, encircling the entrance.

Howls of agony and horror came to everyone's ears in the chill early February air. A clanging. More screams. Gunshots now. Brand tucked Skip's camera box under his arm and scribbled on his steno pad as fast as he could, getting every bit of detail his mind could capture. Just like he'd done in the trenches.

The gunfire stopped. Another scream. One final blast from... a shotgun. Yeah. Shotgun. Now silence. A deathly, funereal silence. For the first time in all his years, Brand stood on a street in Chicago City listening to nothing happening.

A few whispers sliced into the icy air around the crowd. Mentions of the police. A shout from down the street, followed by a siren. Then he heard it. The clacking feet of the law man's crabs. All through the crowd, streaming out of their nooks and niches in the storefronts came an army of the tiny automatons, clicky-clacking like typewriters in a secretary pool.

With the murder rate beating the birth rate ten to one, the people of Chicago City knew the drill better than anybody. As the little machines approached, people stood still and looked down into the single camera eye mounted on each crab's body. A shutter opened and closed and the crab moved away, back to its hiding place to wait for the coppers' airships. Brand watched the little antennae on the machines, waving like masts on a fleet of miniature ships.

The crab at Brand's feet kept skittering left and right on the ice and aiming its single eye at his face. Brand had his hands cupped around a cigarette he had no intention of lighting. Not yet anyway. He had one eye on the door to the Brauerschift garage and the other on the traffic cops pushing their way through the crowd from the next block down. Finally he spied his chance and spun to his left, letting his hands drop just as his foot kicked out and spun the little crab on the ice. His picture would be taken, sure. But it'd be a blurry mess at best.

Holding Skip's camera box in one hand, Brand aimed himself at the garage and pushed through the crowd ahead of the coppers. They'd be here in no time, but he had at least a minute to conduct his business unmolested. While Brand was ice-skating with the crab, another one had worked its way into the garage. Now it was coming out. Sidling up to it, Brand opened the flaps on the box and tucked it against his shirt like Skip showed him. He watched the viewscreen and fiddled with the dial to catch the crab's signal. When the box stopped squealing, he worked the lever. After it snapped back into place, Brand fiddled with the other knobs to bring the image into focus.

At first he got nothing but blurry streaks of gray, but then a spot in the middle stayed put, and soon other parts of the picture filled in. Slowly, the camera box clicked and clacked, and Brand felt the tiny keys punching out details on the photo card inside. Brand kept his eyes on the crowd, watching for the coppers and anyone who might sneak up on him to see what he was doing. The box kept working, and Brand kept watching the street.

Finally the box stopped, but it had taken a half-second longer than he had to spare. The coppers blew through the crowd and jostled Brand as they passed him. He ducked behind a gang of kids who'd been playing stickball in the fenced in empty lot next door. They'd forgotten their game and come through the gate to ogle along with the rest of Clark Street.

"Go on," one of the coppers said to the youths. "Police business here. Unless you saw something, beat it, and fast." Brand watched the kids scamper off. Then the copper's words hit him in the back. "And you. Hey you!"

When the copper's hand landed on his shoulder, Brand closed up the flap over the view screen. He pressed the box against his belly as he spun around.

"What gives, officer? Can't the press get a few pictures?"

The copper looked him up and down, his eyes sliding over the camera box.

"Press, huh? Which outfit?"

"Chicago Daily Record. I'm—"

"Oh, yeah. I know who you are. Go on, Brand. Stand over there and keep out of the way. You'll get your pictures."

Brand obeyed, bending and scraping like it was second nature. He stood off to the side, leaning against the fence, but he jerked away when two of the three coppers came tearing out of the garage. Their faces were a mix of ash and snow. One doubled over and spilled his breakfast into the street. The other stood in front of the door, staring blankly at the crowd. People began to draw nearer now that the police were present. That usually meant the danger had passed. As the second cop followed the first and vomited into the street, people backed away again.

"What is it? What happened in there?" someone yelled.

"Are they okay? What's going on?"

"Is it contagious?"

The questions kept coming until the third copper came out. His face had the same look as the other two except for his eyes. Brand recognized the look right away. He and Chief had reported for the Observation Corps, flying over Skip and his pals while they ran through the mud. And died in it. Brand saw plenty of blood over there. The copper that came out and stayed upright carried himself like an old soldier who'd just been taken back to the battlefield to refresh his memory. He addressed the other two bulls when they stood up straight and had wiped their mouths.

"Nobody's going in there until the gurneymen get here. Get a cordon set up on this side of the street. No traffic along here. You two, split off. Each end of the block. Redirect traffic one street over."

The two junior officers nodded and set out to complete their tasks. Brand watched in amazement.

What was inside?

The sounds of it happening were enough to go on, but the coppers had seen the aftermath. It didn't take a genius to tell they wished they hadn't. The third copper had his hands in the air, waving like a signal man on an airfield. He shouted for people to stay back and move away from the area unless they'd seen something. Plenty stayed nearby, standing off across the street by the Early Bird. While the copper had his attention on the dispersing crowd, Brand took the chance to see what Skip's camera box collected.

When he opened the flap over the viewscreen, he slapped it shut and stowed the box under his coat. Then he lit the cigarette from earlier, finishing it in a series of fast drags. He pulled out his pouch and rolled up a second one. Brand raised the cigarette with a shaking hand. He flinched his head back when the strings of tobacco tickled his lips. After a deep breath, he lit up and pulled the smoke in deep.

He'd nearly finished the cigarette when he heard grunting and moaning from behind the fence. Brand peered over the top of the fence and into the yard. The boys' stick and ball sat on a crate in the far corner, mixed in with a few old cans. Next to the crate, a rusty bicycle leaned against the far fence. Springs stuck up through the bicycle's tattered saddle. Brand heard a scratching and scraping down by his feet, then a heavy impact, like someone had kicked the corner fence post.

The slats rattled and shook as another blow followed the first, and another after that. The grunts and moans kept up. Brand tried to get an eye on who was making all the racket, but he couldn't get a better look into the yard without making an obvious move to the gate, and he needed to keep attention well away from himself. He turned and saw that no one else had heard the noise. The crowd's attention stayed on the coppers and the garage. A patrol boat came down to a nearby municipal mooring deck. It's sleek gunmetal envelope glinted in the weak sunlight that pierced the clouds in places. Teams of uniformed men raced out of the gondola and down the gangplank to street level. The officers made their way around the area, collecting witnesses and gawkers into groups, clearing the roadway. Brand's attention wandered back to the noise behind the fence just as he spied the G-man.

Men from the Governor's office stood out like white elephants whenever they showed up. Nothing said *out of place* like the hats those birds wore. A thin visor hung down from the brim, leaving only the G-man's mouth visible. Brand had run into them at crime scenes before, but never this soon after the action. Somebody in a fancy house up in Detroit got word about the hit, too.

A dull impact on the fence snapped Brand's head around. He peered into the lot between the fence slats. A tramp stood in the corner, leaning heavily on the post; his stench came to Brand's nose on a zephyr. The man staggered a few steps from the fence until his feet took hold of the earth. He wore a long leather duster, burnt along the backside and ripped on almost every seam. The tramp limped and hobbled over to the bicycle. Another patrol boat came in overhead and cast a shadow over the lot. The tramp looked up at the ship and Brand saw the man's face. Thick, bushy eyebrows shrouded dark recessed orbits beside a bulbous schnozz that seemed almost too big to be real. A matted clump of hair hung off his chin, looking like an animal pelt that he'd tacked on with glue.

The tramp reached the rusty bicycle and lifted it off the fence. He straddled the seat and let the bike take all of his weight. Brand winced and gave a cry as the rusted barbs of the saddle springs pushed into the man's groin. The tramp glanced up and his eyes met Brand's. He pushed the bicycle along with his feet, coming up to the fence, close enough for Brand to smell him again.

"Hey there, Brand. How's things?" the tramp said, chuckling. He coughed a deep throaty rattle from his chest and spit in the dirt of the yard. His rheumatic eyes glowed like coals from between the fence slats. Grime coated his leathery skin. He wasn't anyone Brand had seen before.

"Not sure how you know me, pal, but I know I don't know you."

"Oh, c'mon Brand. That any way to treat a fella' what used to shovel chow for the boys over there? Before they put me in the lines with the rest of them muckers. Then… " The tramp coughed again and spit. "Well, I guess you know what happened next, don't you?"

He looked at Brand as if waiting for a reply. But Brand's tongue couldn't figure any path to an answer, so he stuck with his original statement.

"Like I said, pal. I don't know you. And if you were over there, I'd remember you."

"You sure about that, Brand? Weren't but three of us come out of them trees at Argonne."

Brand's head spun at the mention of the battle that ended the war for him and then ended the war entirely. He'd been sent with the soldiers who were told to flush the Germans out of the trees, send them running. And run they did.

After what the boys brought down on them, those Germans ran and wouldn't have stopped until they got back to the Kaiser's palace. But not a single one got a chance to get any farther than the next tree. They gave as good as they got, too. Brand had followed behind the onrushing soldiers, camera at the ready, note pad tucked into his pocket. After it was over, when only he and two other men stood in the smoke, smelling death all around them, Brand had gone back into the trees following the wailing and the tears.

He'd come across a dying German, a kid no older than one of Brand's newsboys now. The kid was trying to hold his life in with both hands over a hole in his chest. Brand added his own hands to the effort, looking the kid in the eyes and willing him to hold on. Brand cried with him and babbled English at him, telling him help was coming. But the corpsmen who came through only had bandages and morphine for the American and English and French boys. One of them had walked right by Brand and the dying German kid without batting an eye.

"If you were in those trees, you'll know what I did when it was over."

"Yeah, I would. That's true."

"So what about it?"

The tramp hesitated and his eyes flashed crimson behind the fence. He looked away, over Brand's shoulder. Brand turned around and saw a copper heading his way. He turned back and saw the tramp backing away from the fence. He lifted his feet to the pedals on his bicycle and the air around him shook and fluttered like cloth. "Got a story you'll want to hear, Brand. But it'll have to wait," the tramp said. Then he reached behind him and lifted the air aside like a curtain, revealing a city skyline glittering in the night. He ducked under the drape and vanished leaving only dust and snowmelt in his wake.

Brand reeled from the fence and spun on his heel. He got a few steps and drew up short when a man and woman stepped out from the crowd like they'd just dropped into the street from outer space. With memories of the vanishing tramp fresh in his mind, Brand wiped a hand across his face and closed his eyes.

"I'm going to open my eyes. If you're still here, I'm gonna need a drink. If you're not, I'm gonna need one anyway."

Brand opened his eyes. He stood face to face with a dolled up couple that looked like they'd fit in better on the silver screen. They simply stared back at him, and didn't seem to mind him giving them the once over. The fella even cracked a grin when Brand ran his gaze up and the down the lady at his side.

Her bright red hair hung down like rolling flames around her shoulders. She wore a black velvet cloche hat and a heavy wool coat to match. But the smile she had on could have cost more than the coat and hat together. Brand had seen makeup and finery on Clark Street before, but never as fine as this. The bird didn't disappoint either with his tailored pinstripes, a bowler, and a walking stick that probably cost more than a year of Brand's pay.

"You two get the word and show up special, or is this your Thursday's best for Clark Street?"

"Mr. Brand," the man in the hat said. "Allow me to introduce myself." He tucked a hand into his coat and Brand figured he'd be spending the last few seconds of his life staring down the barrel of a gat. But the fella just whipped out a card case and opened it. Brand reached for a card and the bird closed the case with a quick snap, then tucked it back into his coat.

"Professor Timwick Argot Cather," Brand read from the card.

"Says here you do lectures at the university. Sorry if I don't see the connection." Brand extended the card back. The man didn't reach to take it, so Brand twisted his mouth a sniffed out a short grunt. "Okay, so I'm keeping it. What's with the get up then, and the jack-in-the-box act? You know anything about that tramp back there?" Brand said, jabbing a thumb over his shoulder.

Around them, the crowd pressed in and backed away as the G-men and coppers made the rounds. The professor seemed to notice this and motioned for Brand to step backwards, to allow a copper to pass by. Brand expected the officer to hassle them, ask them if they'd seen anything, but the uniformed man stepped by quick as can be, like he hadn't noticed their little pow-wow at all.

The professor snapped his fingers in Brand's face. "I'm sorry if I cannot entertain your questions, Mr. Brand. But I have pressing ones of my own. For example, what do you know of the events that just transpired in the neighboring garage here? Were you able to ascertain who … or what committed the crime?"

Brand's head flipped a few circles and then one more for good measure. "Who … you know fella, for a bird just pops into the street the way you did, I'd have thought you had the answers already. I'm not cracking up, so don't try telling me I am. I don't know about what happened in the garage because I wasn't inside. But I do know I wouldn't be alive if I had been. And I know what I saw in that empty lot back there. That tramp just winked out of sight like a money card in a game of Find the Lady. Then you two peacocks pop up like daisies in springtime. So what's the skinny here?"

"Mr. Brand," the professor said, his voice dropping low enough to hit a few notes of menace. "We do not have time for your nonsense."

The woman seemed ready to add her piece, but she spun her head to the side and tugged on the professor's sleeve. "Time to go," she said. Brand put out a hand to slow them down, but they slipped between a couple of people in the crowd. Brand tried to follow but the crowd became a wall coming his way. Coppers and G-men had formed a phalanx outside the garage and people crushed together to get closer, wedging Brand up against the fence. He squirmed out and staggered a few steps backwards, coming up against a pair of hands that held him by the arms and spun him around.

Detective Tom Wynes stood there in a dark suit and hat. The thick-built pug smiled down at Brand. Wynes was one of Chicago City's finest if you only rated coppers by the hands they shook in the daylight. "You okay, Brand? Looks like you saw something you wish you hadn't." Brand swallowed hard, tasting bile and the burning remains of the meal he'd found in a bottle the night before.

"Yeah, Wynes. I'm fine. Just had a pink elephant show up to say good morning."

Wynes pushed his lips out and gave Brand a bent grin that quickly turned into a frown. The way the copper worked his face, it was never easy to read his next play. One minute he'd be on your side and the next he'd be feeding you to the wolves. "I know how that is, Brand. Probably your luck the G-men showed up when they did. The word is no pictures on this one. You got any film in that thing that I should worry about confiscating?" Wynes stabbed a finger at the bulge under Brand's coat.

"Didn't get any pictures yet," Brand said, shaking his head. "The boys who showed up first told me to step off, so I did. I'm halfway through with a pouch, and you mean to tell me I can't even get a photo for my trouble? There goes my tobacco money."

"Good thing the boys waved you off, Brand. Way I hear it from the G-men, you don't need to be seeing what's inside. Nobody does. But hey, at least you had time to work up that little speech for me. Now how about you move along." Wynes jerked a thumb in the air and smiled his thin-lipped copper's grin that told Brand the story was a bust.

Brand waved a hand at Wynes. The copper turned away and went back to helping with the crowd. Brand shuffled to the gate and pushed into the empty lot, not caring if anyone saw him now. He went to where he'd seen the tramp on the bicycle.

Sure enough, he spotted tire marks in the dust, and the man's smell lingered like death on a battlefield. Brand swiped a hand around in the air, trying to find the trick curtain the tramp had pulled. He came up with nothing, so he kicked at the dirt until he felt sure the empty lot was nothing but empty.

Brand scooted, making his way around the crowd just as a couple G-men came out of the garage to clear a path for the gurneymen who'd finally shown up. Leaving the scene behind, Brand stepped fast down Clark Street. Along the way he bought a new pencil from a vet on a wheeled board. The one he'd had earlier was on the sidewalk by the fence, snapped into three pieces by his nervous hands.

CHAPTER 3

LATER THAT AFTERNOON, BRAND SAT IN the cabin of his flying newsroom, the Airship *Vigilance*, while it bobbed on the mooring deck outside the Daily Record. He scratched a few notes about the Brauerschift hit onto the paper in front of him. He read his notes, watching his thoughts dance in confused circles, and ripped the page out of his steno pad. It disappeared into the waste chute beside his desk and he tried again. Scribble, rip, repeat. After the fourth page went down the chute he gave up and let his eyes roam the skyline out the cabin window. He couldn't shake the image of the tramp and his rusted bicycle.

Had he seen the guy before? Over there? And what about the bird and his doll with the red hair? Brand kept a bottle on board and thought about washing away the memories with a glass or two. He reached for the drawer and then remembered the three glasses he'd used to tuck himself into bed.

He had to feed three more pages into the chute before he got his head back on straight enough to write a bulletin about the hit.

He stared at the picture on his desk as he wrote, taking in all the bloody details and trying to imagine what could have happened in that garage. Seven men torn to pieces inside of two minutes, and not without a fight. Brand heard the telltale chatter of tommy guns and the heavy reports of shotguns in his memory. He remembered the screams, too. Whatever happened, Brand had the proof on the desk before him. Chicago City had a lot more to fear than Al Capone's triggermen.

Just his luck it was Wynes who told him no pictures. The G-men wouldn't have thought twice about snagging Skippy's camera box, and that'd be the end of Brand's hot story. He took a drag off his cigarette and looked at the photo once more before flipping it face down. A more poisoned prize he couldn't imagine. After another lungful he stabbed out the cigarette and switched on the mic.

Ladies and Gentlemen of Chicago City, this is Mitchell Brand aboard the Airship Vigilance with a special bulletin. Today, the fourteenth of February, 1929, our city was witness to one of the grisliest crimes in history. Seven men, slaughtered in the Brauerschift garage on Clark Street. It looks like Al Capone has upped the ante, and this reporter wonders what the next play will be.

A special afternoon edition of the Daily Record will have a full report on the Saint Valentine's Day Massacre. Stay tuned, Chicago. And stay in touch.

Brand shut off the mic and went to the cabin door. The Record's loader automatons moved stacks of the special edition out of the press room. Their little two cycle engines chuffed and rumbled as they carried the wrapped bundles across the mooring deck. Brand waited until the gearboxes were finished and then called to his three newsboys. They waited by their airbikes that hung off the deck like rowboats on a pier.

The newsboys played a game of knuckles, taking turns slapping hands back and forth, aiming fingertips at the spaces between each joint. After the required three rounds, the tallest of them, a dark-skinned boy named Ross Jenkins, held up a hand with only his index finger extended. He let his chin fall and then laughed before running over. Brand thought about the day he'd hired Jenkins on, and how his boss, Chief, gave him a funny look.

"Kid's a negro, Mitch. You sure?"

Brand had been sure, just like he'd been sure about the dark-skinned soldiers who'd saved his life in the Great War. They'd been sure Brand was on the same side as them, and he didn't see any reason to disrespect their memory. Even if they weren't around to thank him for it.

A dozen years ago, Brand had watched kids as old as his newsboys fall face down in the mud. Most of them would stay where they fell, just a few feet from the trench where Brand hid with his camera and steno pad, looking at the notes he'd made during their interview. Some of the fallen boys would squirm a bit before going still. And a few he'd never forget had screamed until their blood ran out. Brand felt his face tighten from that memory and he made a quick adjustment before Jenkins got too close.

"Yessir, Mr. Brand, sir!" the boy said with a smile. His big eyes brightened as he looked up at Brand. Like the whole crew of newsboys, Jenkins admired Brand and was ready to do anything he asked. They gave him the respect a soldier gives his sergeant. For Brand, it was like having a trio of sons he would never have to watch die, and that suited him just fine.

His mouth curled up in a grin as he looked at the other two newsboys. An Irish kid named Aiden Conroy, bright-eyed and ready as anything to try his hand tinkering with the Record's equipment. The kid liked to follow the gearboxes around the deck sometimes, just watching them move. The third newsboy was a kid from the streets named Peter "Digs" Gordon. They called him Digs because he followed his mother's work around the city and so never had the same house week to week. Jenkins stood waiting for his orders; Conroy and Digs went back to jawing. Brand greeted Jenkins with his eyes and the grin still on his face.

"Is it my day to try the mic, Mr. Brand, sir?"

"Slow down, Jenkins. Looks like you win, but it's still not the mic."

The kid's face fell into his shoes. Brand would have given them all a shot at airtime, but his boss, Chief, had put the kibosh on that idea. That didn't stop the newsboys from pulling Brand's ear every chance they got. He had fun with it and did his best to keep their spirits up about the possibility. It made him guilty, knowing Chief wouldn't cave anytime soon. But there was plenty of time to get his old war buddy to let the kids try the air.

"It's Thursday, Jenkins. So that'd put your beat …."

"I'm doing La Salle today, sir, up to Old Town, then down Division."

"What say we give you another beat instead. Where's Conroy today?" Brand knew their beats like he knew his own shoe size, and the kid knew it, too. He played along though. The corners of his mouth made a grab for his big ears.

"Conroy? He on Riverfront. Wacker between Lake and Adams, sir."

"Nice work if you can get it. And now you've got it. See that stack of papers? Grab a bundle and pave the streets."

"Yessir!" Jenkins said as he snapped to and threw Brand a clumsy salute. "Will do, Mr. Brand, sir."

Brand gave him one last order, his face going grim as he spoke. "Jenkins, don't open those papers until you hit the Street. When you see the front page, you won't take another step. Tell your pals, too."

"Yessir," the kid replied, pinching his face up like he was going to ask a question, but then skipping it and turning around. He nearly tripped over his own legs as he ran down the deck.

Brand grimaced when he saw his pilot, Archie Falco, coming up the deck then.

"Hey boss," Archie said as he scurried his wiry frame up the ladder. Archie's face was coated in stubble and his jacket was stained with coffee. It wasn't the worst he'd looked since he got out of the cooler and picked up this job at the Record. But it was a damn sight worse than he should look. If Chief hadn't held a soft spot for every Ob-Corps veteran in Chicago City, Archie would still be looking for work.

More likely back in the clink.

"Take her up, Archie," Brand said as he climbed in. He sat at the broadcast desk and punched the radio set over to play back. Then he inserted an ad card from one of the outfits that helped pay the Record's coffee bill. His own voice crackled into the cabin while Archie warmed up the motors and radioed for the mooring lines to be let go. As the ad played, Brand slipped out of his coat, feeling the warmth of the heater spread through the cabin.

Hello, Chicago City. This is Mitchell Brand. Say, it's been a cold winter, and I know one thing that's helped me stay warm. My new suit and coat from Sibley's Emporium. They've got everything a fella needs to look good and feel better. So do yourself a favor, and get dressed at Sibley's.

The speaker crackled with the Sibley's recording, and Brand sat at his desk to roll up a cigarette.

Gentlemen of Chicago City, are you wearing last year's suit to the Mayor's Gala tonight? Suspenders sagging? And what about casual wear? Is your eight panel looking like a six panel these days? Well, look no further. You've found the answer to all your wardrobe woes in Sibley's Emporium.

We carry a full line of gentleman's wear. From hats to spats and spit-shined shoes. In a Sibley's suit, they'll know you're a man who means business. Do you want to be the man to see on the street? Then find your fabric, and find your fit. Find them both at Sibley's Emporium!

Brand let the next ad run while he smoked and looked out the window at the automatons on the deck. They'd released the mooring lines and stood back from the edge like sentinels. A few paces from where the machines stood, the newsboys mounted their air bikes. Their coats, scarves, and gloves kept them from shivering off the seats as they started up the motors. The small crafts hung lower under the weight of their riders and the loads of papers in the cargo box behind them, but the slim envelopes under the seats still buoyed the bikes in the chill air beside the deck. Brand watched as each bike dropped from its trapeze to glide down to street level in the cold midday flurries.

He called to Archie while looking at the photo on his desk. "We finally got it, Archie."

"Yeah, boss? Got what?"

"The story that's gonna blow this city open."

"That guy worked for Mr. Tesla? Pretty grim, boss, but I don't know if it's the big knockover." Archie laughed while he maneuvered the *Vigilance* into the sky.

"Eh? What're you talking about?"

"Thought that's where you were. Coppers found him just this morning. Most of him anyway."

"Most of him. What's that about? He get chewed up by the street cleaners or something?"

"Maybe. Who knows? Coppers found his legs sticking out of a storm drain, still had his boots on but all this way and that. Skinned down to the bone from hip to ankle. They're still looking for the top half."

"So how'd they know it was him?"

"Found his head a few blocks over. Followed the blood."

Brand slumped in his chair. The details rang a little too close for Brand's comfort, but he filed the thoughts away. He'd ask Chief about it the next time they saw each other. Brand looked at the photo in his hands again. The photo that was on its way to the people of Chicago City. He finished his cigarette in two quick drags, put the photo down, rolled himself a new one, and lit up.

"You said we got something big, hey boss? What's the story?"

"Huh?" Brand startled. "Yeah, we got a story all right. Seven men … killed over—"

"Yeah?"

"Over on Clark Street. I was at the Bird getting my joe."

"Bet you spilled it when you heard the shots, eh?" Archie said, turning to look over his shoulder.

Brand sniffed. "Didn't hear any shots. Not at first anyway." He remembered the terrified shouts that preceded bursts from tommy guns. Brand knew how much those pea shooters could put out. Whatever had killed the men in that garage had to catch a lot of lead in the process, but the photograph—

"So when'd you spill?" Archie joked, jabbing a thumb across the cabin and aiming it at Brand's slacks.

"You're a riot, Arch. Should try that act down at the Mayor's Gala tonight."

Brand got up and walked to the cockpit. "G-men showed up before I could get the scoop from the coppers, but I got this from the crabs."

Brand lifted up the photograph. Archie turned to look at it and then turned away so fast Brand thought his head might spin off his neck.

"Sorry, Archie. I should have warned you."

Brand looked at the photo again. At first sight, on the street, he'd been too terrified to examine it. Just now, before showing it to Archie, his nerves still felt like high tension cables running through his limbs and down his spine. But with Archie's reaction, Brand knew he wasn't alone anymore. Someone else had seen it and wished they hadn't. Someone he could talk to.

Brand sat at his desk and stared at the image until he had every piece of it memorized. Every jaunty angle of every severed limb. Every ripple in every dark puddle and spattered stain that spread around the floor and walls. Every grimace of agony and death on the heads lying around the space. He'd pulled in crime scene photos before, and some of them had been bloody, too. But nobody had seen anything like this unless they'd been in the Great War. Brand shook his head as he thought that even the war had been kinder to its victims.

"This'll get the city talking, Archie. The Mayor will have to come clean, and—" Something in Archie's silence worried Brand.

"Say, you okay, Arch?"

"Me? Oh, yeah, boss. Little shook up is all. That's some bloodbath."

"Not the first time Capone's spilled blood in this town. Ask me, The Outfit's looking at numbered days."

Archie whistled high and sharp. "That's high-stakes, boss. I didn't think you played up there."

"Like I said, this is going to break the city wide open. Everything's going to be different now."

Archie stayed hush as he flew them across the city. Brand got his viewing glass set up and began scanning the streets. They circled the major commercial districts, high end neighborhoods, and the World's Fair site. Patrol boats sailed beneath their altitude, monitoring the same districts for the same reasons but with a different aim. After two hours of not much happening, Brand called it a wash and resigned himself to the stack of pages on his desk.

"What's next, boss?" Archie called back to him.

Brand flipped through his notes, skipping the pages about births, marriages, and funerals among Chicago City's elite. His unholy trinity of worthless information. Dropping the stack of notes down the waste chute, he gave his attention to an envelope full of photos.

"Maybe some of these pictures'll give us a story," he said, not really meaning to start a conversation with Archie.

"Thought you hated talking about those society folks."

"I do. The only people who care to listen were there already."

"So?"

"So why tell them a story about what they did last night? They know better than me who kissed whom and when."

"Ain't Chief gonna give you the business about this one today? You might give him a little of the stuff he likes, hey?"

"People in charge always go for the sure thing, Archie, even if they know it's the wrong thing. Chief'll chew my ear maybe. Won't be the first time."

"What if the man on the street starts asking for a piece? Like when we was over there?"

During the Great War, the brass said people complained about Brand's reports from the trenches. But those reports were cited by the commission that finally ended the war, and he hoped reporting on Chicago City's crime scene would have a similar effect.

"Maybe the man on the street will change his tune when he sees what his fellow men are doing to each other."

Archie made like he wanted to keep the conversation going, but Brand spun his chair and waved a hand to call it quits.

Maybe Archie was right though. Now and then, Brand would do a story on the society folks, just to remind them that Chicago City cared about their tribe even if he didn't. The only thing celebrity ever did for anyone was build a glass wall around them for other people to throw stones at. Flipping the photos in his hand, he stopped halfway through the stack and gave a grunt of surprise. He pulled out a photo and put it next to the crime scene shot from that morning. Then he went back through to double-check and pulled out two more pictures. The rest went into the waste chute beside his desk.

"Take us out to Farnsworth's plant, Archie."

CHAPTER 4

AIDEN DROPPED OFF THE DECK WITH DIGS and Jenkins, flashing a thumbs-up at the other boys and turning his airbike in a wide arc to round the Record's building and head over to La Salle, a few blocks up from Printer's Row. Digs was off to the Gold Coast, where Aiden knew he'd clean up pretty good. Jenkins sailed away without looking back at Aiden's thumbs-up, going straight down Harrison and shooting the corner to State. He'd be at the Riverfront and selling his first bundle by the time Aiden was halfway to Old Town, and probably raking in a fine pile by the end of the day. Aiden let a moment of jealousy twist his mouth.

It was a bum deal getting put off the good beat by Mr. Brand that way, but Jenkins won the knuckles fair and square. And Aiden knew that just meant he'd treat when it came time to hit the soda counter after the work was done. Even better, the lighter load on Aiden's bike meant he'd be finished up before Digs and Jenkins were half done, and that meant he'd have time to watch the gearboxes while he waited for the other boys to get back.

At the corner of Jackson and La Salle, Aiden dropped to the street and pulled the airbike into a turnout beside a bank. He unloaded a bundle of papers and slipped his penknife under the strings that held the thick brown wrapper around the papers. When it fell away, Aiden's mouth hung open and his knife dropped to the pavement by his foot. He'd never seen a picture like the one on the front page. Not even in his mind after listening to monster hunter stories on Dr. Macabre's Fright Hour. Aiden's knees trembled under his wool trousers and he felt himself falling before he knew what was happening. He spun and let the stack of papers catch his weight. Aiden shook where he sat, his breath coming fast and his chest feeling a chill despite his thick coat. As he brought his hands up around him, a man came up from behind and tapped his shoulder.

"Hey kid, got the special? I hear Brand got a photo from the scene and I wanna see it."

Aiden was about to reply, forcing strength into his legs and lifting himself up from the stack of papers when a hand pressed onto his shoulder, making him sit back down. He jerked around to look over his shoulder and saw a man in a suit being pressed back by another tough looking bird. The second guy wore a suit, too, under a heavy overcoat. Aiden just caught sight of the first guy's frightened face before the fella took off down the street, leaving Aiden alone on the sidewalk with a bundle of papers under his tailbone and two thugs from Capone's Outfit standing around him with friendly smiles curling up under their eyes. These eyes were full of everything Aiden had ever heard about The Outfit. Most of what he'd heard sounded like bunko, but he'd hoped he'd never have a chance to find out.

"So, kid," one of the tough birds said. "That's the special from the Daily Record. Yeah?"

"Ye—, yessir."

"And that's the first bundle you've opened I see," said the other one, stepping over to Aiden's airbike and patting the still-wrapped bundles with a gloved hand. Aiden stared at the clean dark leather glove and then took in its mate. He darted his eyes back and forth, landing on the first guy who spoke. He had the same gloves, rich as the Gold Coast and then some. Everything these birds wore, from their wingtips to their tightly knotted neckties, it was all finer than anything Aiden had ever seen in his or his dad's closet.

"So, kid," the first one was saying to him, nudging Aiden's ear with a gloved knuckle. "What's the asking price for the Daily Record special these days? Three cents? Four?"

"A n—, a nickel, sir. It's a nickel."

The second thug whistled loud and some people on the street stopped to throw a quick look in Aiden's direction before going back to minding their own business and walking away. "A nickel," the bird said, now leaning against Aiden's airbike. "I'll make you a deal kid," he said, pushing off from the bike and coming over to Aiden while his partner kept a firm hand on Aiden's shoulder, holding him in place.

"How about a ten spot for both stacks?" the fella said, holding out his left hand, curled up into a fist. The dark leather creased around the guy's fingers, making black ravines between narrow ridges that made Aiden think of the landscapes that Dr. Macabre's monster hunter crept through on the trail of ghosts and beasts from the dark. Then the thug opened his hand to reveal a ten dollar bill that he picked up with his other hand and dropped into Aiden's lap.

Aiden stared at the bill. His jaw fell open. He hinged it back up and it dropped again. The bird with his hand on Aiden's shoulder gripped him and urged him to stand. Still shaking, now more from wonder than worry, Aiden took the bill and stood. It wasn't until he'd finished looking at all the lines in General Sherman's face that Aiden came out of his shock enough to see the guys loading the bundles of papers into a sedan that had pulled up beside his airbike.

"Now spend it right, sonny, hey?" the first thug said as he swept into the back seat of the sedan. His long coat folded around him and was sucked into the back seat as the door closed like a raven's wing folding up. The sedan was gone and Aiden stood by his empty airbike, dazzled by his good luck. Ten dollars! He had enough to treat himself to the soda counter twice a day for two weeks easy.

Chuckling, Aiden stowed the bill, mounted the airbike, and kicked off to sail back to the mooring deck. Heck, he'd be there with loads of time to spare and watch the gearboxes at work. Maybe Old Mutton, the mechanic, would let him try a little wrenching when he came out to do the evening shutdown later on. Full of dreams enough to fill the day, Aiden soared above the heads of cyclists and wagon drivers, shooting the corner back to Printer's Row and doing a lap around the Record's first two floors for the fun of it.

When he reached the deck on the fifth floor and saw Jenkins was already there, his heart fell a bit. The guy looked glum. Worse than glum. He looked beat. Aiden's pa would've had him ignore the other newsboy, because he was a negro. But Aiden saw the way Mr. Brand talked to Jenkins, and how he shook the guy's hand and treated him just like he did Aiden and Digs and pretty much everyone else. Jenkins had dark skin, sure, but Aiden couldn't figure what was so bad about that.

Aiden waited for the trapeze to catch his airbike and for the gearboxes to do their trick with the mooring cable. Then he hopped off and made for where Jenkins sat against the concrete where they'd shoot dice somtimes.

"What gives, Jenks? Thought you had it good today, hey?"

"I did. Figure I get at least a fin with all them papers Mr. Brand loaded up on me. But these two heavies come by and toss change at my face. They walk off with the whole pile. I was ready to stop 'em, but ...."

Aiden knew what Jenkins was going to tell him, but he let his pal get it out on his own.

"I think they was Outfit toughs, you know? Real nice clothes, like you see way uptown. Mayor's Office kinda folks. Except these birds was rough. Kinda like they'd been told to pay me for the papers but really wanted to put me in the ground. Right there. But, hey, what you doing back up so quick? You didn't sell out did ya? Ain't that how it go? I get the good beat and can't even make enough to come out on top, and—" Aiden cut him off and told him what had happened on La Salle.

"Yeah? A sawbuck? Conroy, you know how to put a fella's nose in it, and that's no joke."

"C'mon, Jenks. I'll get the soda tonight, no joking. It's only fair."

Jenkins lifted his chin at that. He seemed ready to smile again but lost his cheer when Digs came up to the deck with his coat hanging half off him and near shivering off the bike. They ran to help the smaller boy get tethered and onto the deck with both his pins under him.

"What happened, Diggsy?" Aiden asked.

"Couple of torpedoes tailed me off the deck. I seen their sedan on the ground soon as we're splitting up. When I get to the street, it's tailing me but good. It followed me over the river and sped on by. But I get to my first drop and these two bird are waiting for me, like they know my beat and are just waiting there, you know? I get down and this one fella, built like a pug with these fists the size of bricks, he picks me off my bike and shakes me down rough, pulls my coat off and stands like he's going to paste me if I make any noise about it. People are walking around and just go right on by, so that's when I key in, these birds are from The Outfit, right? Then the other one, he lifts my papers, both bundles, and throws them in their sedan. Then the pug gives me a tap on the cheek, just with his fingers like he's slapping me and there's nothing behind it. But he wants me to know there might be. I get my coat half on then I see it's ripped, but good. So I just kick off the ground while they're driving off. I don't look back."

Aiden whistled low. Jenkins, too. Digs said he had to get home. See if his mom had enough to get him a new coat. He held it up, showing Aiden and Jenkins the torn seam along one side under the arm and down the sleeve.

"I'd sew it up, but we don't got no needle and thread around the place. Not since Ma's last fella threw us out. And she ain't found a new set up for us yet, so we're at the rooming place down in The Loop."

Aiden reached into his pocket and fingered the bill he'd been given that morning. He knew Jenkins was thinking the same thing he was, so it was easier to speak when the words finally found their way onto his tongue.

"Guess I'm treating us all today, hey?" he said, lifting the bill from his pocket and showing it to Digs. Smiles lit all three boys' faces. They stepped fast down the deck and through the print room. They raced to the lift and tapped the floor with their feet, willing the box to drop faster. In the lobby, the three boys dodged in and out around newsies and nearly toppled the mail cart.

"Now wait'll Mr. Brand hears about this," Jenkins said, clapping hands over Aiden's and Digs' shoulders as they exited the building.

CHAPTER 5

EMMA FARNSWORTH HALTED JUST INSIDE the door and took in the signs of destruction. Broken picture frames and accounts ledgers were strewn around the room. File drawers drooped open, their contents sticking out in disarray, spilling out onto the floor below. Her father slumped into his chair and held a glass in his right hand. His other hand held a bottle of Templeton Rye that had been left with his secretary. According to the girl outside, two men had dropped the bottle on her desk saying *"Mr. Capone sends his compliments."*

She hadn't asked for names and couldn't even remember what color hats they had on. Most people forget what they see and hear when Al Capone's name is mentioned. But Emma's father hadn't been in the mood to hear the man's name himself, so he'd snatched the bottle from his secretary and given her an earful of his best advice on how to keep her job. It had taken Emma fifteen minutes to calm the girl down before following her father into his office. The sounds of his temper came through the closed door loud and clear, and Emma had to steel herself before going in after him.

"Dad?" Emma ventured, winding a path through the mess of broken glass and splintered picture frames. Her heel caught on a split piece of wood and she almost toppled over. Straightening up, she brushed aside the lock of curled hair that fell in her face. Emma paused to smooth her skirt and sett her face. Then she addressed the man she'd known all her life and couldn't wait to forget. "Dad, you're drinking at three in the afternoon. You said we'd go over the books today, remember? We were going to look at the plant's earnings. The accountants are supposed to be here in ten minutes."

"I called 'em off."

"What? Dad, why? How are we going to stay in the game if we don't—"

"Shut up! You wouldn't be standing there in those fancy clothes if it weren't for this power plant. Don't give me any guff about how I keep it running."

Emma squared her shoulders. She'd spent her childhood cleaning up after the old man. Her youth had been spent growing more than tired of being his daughter. She was twenty-five now, and without a husband to make her into his jewelry rack, Chicago City didn't know what else to call her. The only ideas she had wouldn't play in the society crowd she had to run with. It'd be nice, she thought, if the life she wanted and the life society allowed her could agree on something.

"Dad, you need to clean this place up." Emma nudged aside the bits of wood she'd almost tripped on and stormed out, flinging open the office door and ignoring the sound of her father's voice behind her. She left the building without buttoning up her coat, but she stopped short outside. A long sedan pulled up and Frank Nitti, The Outfit's prince, got out shaking his long coat around him, revealing a crisp white suit beneath.

"Miss Farnsworth," the gangster said through a grin as he approached. Emma drew her coat closed as Nitti's eyes walked up and down her shape. "What a pleasure. I hope you are enjoying a fine afternoon."

"You've got a lot of nerve," she said, clasping her coat and showing her teeth as she spoke.

Nitti gave her that shot for free, but the pinched up skin around his mouth told her he wanted to show her the back of his hand. Instead, he stepped in close, so the toes of his shoes rested an inch from hers. Nitti reached up and toyed with the stray lock of Emma's blond hair and then tipped his hat as he brushed by, followed by two of his silent goons. Through the open entrance, she heard the men step through to her father's office and close the door.

Emma went back inside, giving her father's secretary a look that said *Keep hush*. The girl understood and went back to her paperwork. Emma moved to her father's door and listened. The voices were muffled, but she pegged Nitti when he spoke. Nobody else could sound so cheerful and so deadly at the same time.

The conversation rose and fell with her father's outbursts and Nitti's sing-song talking. She knew the gangster could be violent, and hoped her father wouldn't push him too far. The door opened then and Emma just had time to move away.

Nitti came out first and smiled at her. "Miss Farnsworth," he said in a softer and more precise voice than she had heard in her father's office. "You know, that shade of lipstick compliments your eyes quite nicely. The Mayor is hosting a dinner this evening. For Saint Valentine's Day. Would you accompany me? I would be most honored, and—"

"And I'll be going alone," Emma replied with more ice than the Chicago River got in January. Nitti simply sneered, pushing by without tipping his hat this time. His boys followed, their eyes lowered, watching the step of their boss's feet.

• • •

Brand watched out the window as Archie brought the *Vigilance* down to the mooring station at the Farnsworth plant. Two smaller ships hung off the deck, their skin crusted with ashen snow.

"Farnsworth's going to lose those pigs he leaves them in the sty like that, eh boss? They ain't made nice with the wind for a while."

Brand grunted and went back to staring at the photographs on his desk. He could swear one of the victims in the massacre had attended a party held last week at Farnsworth Wind and Water. Brand circled the man's face in the image, which showed a group of men and women standing around Josiah Farnsworth. The power plant owner sat on a stool in the middle of his factory floor. Brand set the photos aside and picked up the other two he'd pulled from the stack.

In one of them, Emma Farnsworth stood next to Frank Nitti outside the offices at the power plant. By the look of things, the photo was taken at the same party. Emma glared daggers at Nitti as he shook hands with Josiah Farnsworth. The plant founder looked pretty grim, which highlighted Nitti's shark tooth smile even more. In the other photo, Emma was hanging off the Mayor's arm at some party. Her curled blond hair shone out of the photograph as a patch of stark white. The room had been well lit with the new electric lamps coming out of Mr. Tesla's factory, and that meant the party was held in one of two places. Capone's Banquet Parlor or the Mayor's Office. Wherever it had been, Miss Farnsworth didn't seem to be enjoying herself. She stared straight into the camera with her jaw set and her gaze pinched like a vise.

The feud between Farnsworth and his daughter was well known in Chicago City, so it was a sure bet there'd be something to help Chief sell news. And Brand might find the next piece of the puzzle surrounding the massacre. He left the crime scene photo on his desk and pocketed the others, then released the ladder and climbed down to the mooring deck. Brand's feet hit the concrete deck as a long sedan pulled away from the power plant's office. It roared through gravel and snowmelt, tracking a path to the yard exit. The car screeched to a halt at the mooring station and idled while Brand made his way down the stairs. He eyed the car the whole time. As he approached it, a back window dropped. Frank Nitti leaned over to aim a finger in Brand's direction.

"You are the radio man, right?" Nitti's careful pronunciation gave a sing-song quality to his words that reminded Brand of the sound a knife makes as it slits your throat. "Mr. Mitchell Brand. I should tell you to be careful. What you say on the radio. You never know who might be listening in."

Nitti sat back and motioned to his driver, who sat rigid in the seat, his face a blank mask and his eyes nearly closed. Brand made for the office building and dodged aside when another car came racing through the yard in his direction. Emma Farnsworth stuck her head out to holler at him this time.

"Nitti already talked to him. You saw them leave. He's got nothing left to say to anyone now and he's too drunk to put more than three words together anyway."

"So I can't go ask him a question or two? Like why his—"

"So he doesn't need a newshawk giving him a headache. He can handle that just fine on his own." Emma sped away before Brand could get another word in her direction. He thought about the two cars that had just passed him and made a mental note to put out a broadcast as soon as he got back to the *Vigilance.*

CHAPTER 6

BRAND PICKED UP HIS PACE CROSSING THE yard. Yesterday's storm had blown itself out, but sudden gusts still rolled snow drifts across the cold earth. Beyond mounds of gray and white, the power plant crouched like a patient behemoth on the shore of Lake Michigan. A low building with a brick façade around the entrance stood in the shadow of the hulking concrete structure. Even with February's wind buffeting him as he walked, Brand heard the rumbling turbines that churned within the facility. On one side of the building, four sets of heavy rotors spun on their shafts and channeled the wind into Farnsworth's pipes and wires. On the lakeside, a massive concrete chamber jutted out into the water. Inside, there would be more rotors turned by the action of the waves. Chicago City owed a lot to the Farnsworth family for keeping the lamps lit and the heaters running.

Inside the offices, Farnsworth's secretary sat at her desk beside a low counter. She'd stacked files and paperwork along the counter and was sorting a pile on her desk when Brand came in.

"Can I help you?" the girl asked, hunching down over her work and eyeing Brand like she'd met him in a dark alley.

"Yeah, I'm just hoping to catch a few minutes of the old man's time. He in? And you don't have to worry. I'm not after any company secrets," Brand said, motioning at the page the girl had clutched against her chest.

"Yes. Yes, he's in, but I don't …."

"I'll just poke my head in," Brand said as he left the shell-shocked girl. He crossed the small foyer to the alcove in front of Farnsworth's office door. A chair leg was wedged between the door and the jamb.

Brand gave a knock and looked around the door as he pushed it open. The only furniture in serviceable condition was the heavy oak desk at the back of the room and the chair behind it. Josiah Farnsworth sagged back in the chair with a glass to his lips. Brand's nose told him bootleg sauce was on special in Farnsworth's office. The old man's wisps of white hair hung limp off the sides of his round head. With his long nose, the Farnsworth Patriarch had the look of a vulture left out in the rain.

"Morning, Mr. Farnsworth. Mitchell Brand, with the Chicago Daily—"

"Yes?" Farnsworth growled. "I know who you are. Come in here. What do you want?"

"Well, I was hoping to talk with you about the gentlemen who just left. Anything you'd like to share with the Daily Record and the people of Chicago City?"

Farnsworth looked at him, incredulous to what Brand was suggesting. "You rotten fink! Share with… you wander in here and ask me if I want to share? Who the hell sent you? You tell me that right now! Was it Emma?"

"Actually your daughter warned me off of coming in here. Said you'd got enough of a headache already. But I figure a man should get to do his own talking about how he feels."

That was a cheap shot at Emma's expense, and Brand knew it just as well as the old man did. But it did the trick. Farnsworth's wide-eyed disbelief slackened into drowsy resignation. He let his shoulders fall and his head hang down to one side.

"You try to do right by your family," Farnsworth said. "You try to give 'em something to come home to."

Brand waited for the old man to continue and drew his steno pad out of his coat.

"You said *gentlemen*, didn't you? Thick-headed little runt you are. You wouldn't know a gentleman if he kicked you in the tailbone with a steel toe."

"Fair enough, Mr. Farnsworth. Do you suspect Nitti and his boys are the ones who smashed up your office?" Brand looked around the room and motioned to the destruction.

"All this," Farnsworth said, swinging his index finger around his head to take in the remains of his office. "All this is just smoke and mirrors, boy. The real show is happening somewhere else now." He poured himself another glass from the bottle as he spoke. Brand let the man drink and decided to change gears. To get any questions answered, he'd have to let Farnsworth feel in control of the conversation. But he couldn't just wait for the guy to figure out which way to take things. Not in his state.

"Can you give me the name of the man here in this picture?" Brand held up the photo showing Farnsworth and his employees. He let his finger rest just above the man's face he'd circled. Farnsworth squinted and snatched the photo out of Brand's grasp. He fumbled around in a desk drawer and came up with a monocle.

"Yeah. Yeah. That's my new chief engineer, John May. Why d'you want to know about him?"

"John May," Brand said as he jotted the name down.

"I said why d'you want to know about him!"

"Well, Mr. Farnsworth, I might have to head straight to the precinct house after telling you this, but I think Mr. May was killed this morning."

Farnsworth's surprise came at Brand like a freight train. "You mean that business over in Clark Street you just blabbed about? *He* was there? Damn it!" The old man lurched up out of his chair and nearly fell forward across the desk. He steadied himself and reached a hand into the drawer again. Then he just stood there, leaning on the desk and breathing hard.

"You get out of here. You go now and don't you come back unless I say so. You hear? Go on! Get out!"

Brand didn't need to see the gun Farnsworth was tickling in the drawer. He'd made sure to walk straight in from the door and knew the path behind him was clear. Getting shot was getting shot, but Brand would prefer to know it was coming. He beat it without turning around, matching the path he'd taken when he came in, just in case Old Man Farnsworth got trigger-happy.

On his way back to the *Vigilance*, Brand spun the meeting with Farnsworth around in his mind. What had gotten him so heated about John May? He tried out a few theories as he pulled himself up the ladder to the airship cabin. At the top he paused and wrapped his arms around the ladder to steady himself while he jotted down a few notes. Then he shimmied up the last two rungs and bounced into the cabin.

Archie whipped his headphones off and spun around in his seat when Brand climbed in.

"It's just me, Archie. Who'd you expect?"

"Nobody, boss. I just didn't think— You got back quick, you know?"

"Well I'm back. Let's go."

"You get the goods from Old Man Farnsworth?"

"Nothing really," Brand lied. "But it's his daughter I want to talk to now. I'm betting she'll be at the Mayor's dinner tonight. That means double time over to Dearborn. I need to scrub up."

Archie got the *Vigilance* into the sky while Brand sketched up a few notes for a quick broadcast. He took some liberty, steering the gist down roads he felt sure were there. He hadn't got much from the old man, but he'd got enough to keep the wheels turning at least.

Ladies and Gentlemen, this is Mitchell Brand aboard the Vigilance. The Outfit's golden boy, Frank Nitti, was just seen visiting

Josiah Farnsworth in his office. We have to ask what those two men might have to discuss. Farnsworth isn't talking.

The massacre this morning took place in his competitor's repair shop. Could Al Capone be making a play to get into the power business? Either way, there's writing on the wall. This reporter spells it bad news.

Come back later for more on this story and on the Saint Valentine's Day Massacre.

Stay tuned, Chicago. And stay in touch.

Brand punched the set over to play back again and slotted another ad card to follow his broadcast. His weary voice came back at him from the speakers, and he wished he'd convinced Chief to let one of the cub reporters handle the ad segments. Maybe if these stories came together right he could persuade Chief to give his newsboys some mic time. They hounded him about it often enough, and he knew he should try and do right by them someday soon.

· · ·

Josiah Farnsworth put the empty glass down and turned his watery eyes to the empty bottle. His office stank. He punched the line for his secretary and the girl came in.

"Yes sir, Mr. Farnsworth," she said, wincing at the smell and hunching her shoulders even tighter up around her ears.

The plant owner motioned with a finger to the waste bin by his desk. "Take it out," he mumbled. "I was sick."

The young woman stepped through the debris to reach the desk and turned her head as she picked up the can. She hurried out of the office with her face wrinkled up and her free hand over her mouth.

Farnsworth thought about the money he owed Nitti. He'd needed that money to buy the new turbine fittings. His plant wasn't failing, but it wasn't in shape to compete against the new German operation, not without some upgrades. And now Tesla's radio power stations were about to change the game again.

He thought about the deal he'd worked out with Nitti to *make it all go away.* Then he thought about what that damn newshawk had told him an hour or so earlier. John May was in the garage that morning. He was torn apart with the rest of them. Those mob bastards got what they deserved and if May was pinching information and selling it to the Germans like Nitti said, then he got what he deserved, too.

But now Nitti wanted a new deal. And Josiah Farnsworth's days of making deals had reached an end. He slid open his desk drawer and took out the revolver.

CHAPTER 7

BRAND SHOWERED AND PICKED UP A NEW SET of duds from his rooms. It was a trick to clean up with nothing but his old razor, but a stop at his barber wasn't in the cards. He hopped out of the cab, paid the driver, and watched the horse trot down the street. Stepping over a low drift of snow, Brand walked up the massive stone steps to the banquet hall entrance. Under the portico, he showed his press card and camera to the heavy at the door before he went through, getting nudged aside by a drunk couple just as he passed into the doorway.

"Excuse me, sir. Madam," Brand said, tipping his hat and smiling as they staggered past and went off to find a quiet corner.

"Future leaders of the city, hey?" Brand muttered. The heavy heard it, but clearly knew where his paycheck came from. He didn't even lift the corners of his mouth to agree with Brand.

Inside, a negro quintet played the latest jazz numbers while streamers of smoke swayed above the crowd. Brand hadn't expected to see dark skin in the room tonight. It was out of line with the Great Lakes Territory's Segregation Act, though it wasn't unheard of for the Mayor to bend the rules now and then. Brand filed it away as he gave his hat and coat to a girl waiting inside. He showed her his press card before snapping her picture.

"Welcome to the Mayor's Gala, Mr. Brand. And happy Valentine's Day," she said, showing him a crescent of perfect teeth framed by a ruby smile.

"Thanks. What's good tonight?"

"I'm sure you'll find something you like."

Brand returned her smile and moved into the room, putting thoughts of dallying out of his mind. There was no quicker way to run afoul of Chicago City politics than to mix it up with the Mayor's Office Ladies Auxiliary. Brand nudged by a couple to get to the bar. He sat down and waved to the bartender.

While he waited for his scotch to make its way from the back room into his glass, Brand looked around the room for familiar faces. He scanned the swirl of females in slinky dresses hanging off of business owners and other men of power. The Ladies Auxiliary were out in force tonight, he saw. Usually the Mayor wasn't so free with his gifts. Something big brewing, Brand thought to himself as his eyes took in the crowd. In the middle of the tangle a throng of guests stood around the Mayor, who held forth with a glass of hooch in one paw and a thick stogie in the other. Emma Farnsworth sat off to the side at a table with a man and woman wearing dark clothes. Their outfits matched the dark looks the man kept casting around the room.

Brand moved through the crowd, quiet and humble, nodding and excusing himself for every brush of physical contact. He kept Emma Farnsworth in the corner of his vision and aimed his path to bring him by her table. He saw a spread of cards between Miss Farnsworth and the creepy couple. They weren't playing cards though. These were illustrated with symbols and images of monsters and mythical beings. He'd seen them before, at another of the Mayor's events. Some kind of fortune telling act the Mayor brought in to entertain his guests. Brand never gave them much attention, but with Miss Farnsworth involved, his curiosity bone itched like mad.

He walked up to the table and caught the gypsy woman's voice through the din around him.

"… we shall meet again, Miss Farnsworth. Answers then." The woman fell silent then and draped a scarf over the layout of cards. The man next to her looked up at Brand, who stared back at the gypsy couple. Where the woman filled in a firm but matronly shape that almost glowed, the man was a dull-tinted wisp of a human being, a skeleton in funeral clothes with a bowler on his head and a monocle dangling from his upraised fingers.

Emma turned to look at Brand but didn't say anything. He could tell she'd been crying though.

"Miss Farnsworth," Brand said, nodding a greeting at the couple. "I wonder if you wouldn't mind talking with me about this afternoon. When you're finished here I mean. I don't want to interrupt."

"Get lost, Brand. You already did interrupt."

"Maybe later then," he said, and walked away into the crowd. A couple of young men were leaving the dance floor, each with a girl on his arm. They'd seen the exchange with Miss Farnsworth and both gave Brand a questioning smirk.

"She didn't want to dance," he said, shrugging his shoulders and wishing he could send a fist into their beaks. Brand moved over to where he could hear what the Mayor was saying, but stayed out of sight behind a group of tall ladies sipping drinks and blowing smoke rings over the heads of two shorter men standing in front of them. A circle of the city's wealthiest surrounded the Mayor, including the four principal investors on the World's Fair project.

"Mr. Mayor," said the chief investor, "we can't expect average citizens to stand up to mob intimidation, and the police are at their limit."

"And what's this we hear about increased production quotas?" said another. "Are the governors really making Chicago City responsible for manufacturing like they say? We can't just produce like that without a significant increase in investment from each territory."

The third and fourth investors chimed in to concur and then the first piped up again. "Indeed! And we're dealing with a menace. Crime like no other city has ever experienced. Why this massacre business—and that's something else. Did you see that special edition of the Daily Record, Mr. Mayor?"

The Mayor balked, looking dumbfounded for a moment, and darted his eyes at the assembly around him. "I, um …."

"It's got me worried, Mr. Mayor," the chief investor said. "We all heard about it on the radio. That Brand fellow talked it up like it was bigger than the fire of '71. But I haven't been able to lay hands on a copy of that paper all day. And that's not for lack of trying." The crowd all nodded their heads in agreement, and Brand saw the Mayor's confusion reflected in every face. It figured that the special edition had sold out fast, but Brand had expected to hear it from a few people tonight for printing the photo.

Another investor piped up to break the silence, but his question didn't help lighten the mood. Not at first anyway.

"What I'd like to know is who's got the scoop on this monster business? First it was tearing up tramps, but this morning I heard they found the body of a man who worked for Mr. Tesla. And that report Brand gave makes it sound like the thing has a taste for gang-land flesh, too. What if it starts going for us next?"

A small group exiting the dance floor stopped their conversations and turned their path to join the gaggle around the Mayor. The Mayor's face had drooped with worry, like a kid with his hand in the candy jar. He shook out a breath between his heavy cheeks and puffed on his cigar while murmurs tumbled through the crowd around him. Brand listened, waiting for the Mayor to speak when a bird in a crisp suit and with glimmering teeth piped up. Brand hadn't seen the guy a second ago, but he'd seen him that morning over on Clark Street. His red-haired partner was with him this time, too.

"A monster, Mr. Mayor?" the professor said with a chuckle. "Do you mean like Dr. Frankenstein's creation?"

The crowd didn't miss a beat. Someone else joked from behind the Mayor, "I thought Lon Chaney was in New York this time of year."

"How can you tell with that guy?" somebody else said, getting in on the act. That was all it took for the crowd to go into high gear. A man yelled from over to Brand's right.

"He could be here in this crowd, right now!"

A woman nearby feigned shock and pretended to faint into her companion's arms, nearly spilling his drink.

Brand listened to the crowd laugh with his tongue clamped between his front teeth. The professor and his lady friend made their way to his side while the Mayor found his stride in the crowd's laughter.

"Friends," the Mayor said, turning in a circle with a relaxed look on his face. "It is true. We have a threat in Chicago City, one that seems," he paused, searching his thick head for the right words. "... beastly. But we cannot let panic rule our thinking. I'm certain that our city's finest," the Mayor used his cigar to indicate Detective Wynes, who Brand spotted just outside the circle. "I'm sure they will have things under control soon enough."

The crowd mulled that over, giving Brand time to whisper to the professor, who had come to stand right next to him. "Nice trick you pulled. Got him talking again anyway."

"Indeed, I did," the professor said. "And I would rather hear what he has to say than trade words with you at the moment."

Brand stepped a pace away, shaking his head. For good measure, he turned his back on the professor, but that just put him looking at Wynes, who had his eyes on Brand like he meant to pin him down where he stood. Brand shuffled in place and finally gave up, turning back so he could at least see the professor and the redhead. She stepped around the professor and came closer, winking as she came to stand next to Brand.

The people around them seemed about done talking up the

monster idea, and the Mayor had his glass raised, like he had more to say.

"More important than monsters … more important, my friends, we must remember that the real and very human source of all our trouble is The Outfit." The Mayor let his words hang in the air for a moment. Brand eyed the redhead first. She gave no sign other than a smirk that she'd even heard the Mayor. So Brand roamed the crowd with his eyes. Everybody stared at the Mayor. A few people traded whispers.

The redhead leaned over to say something, and Brand edged closer to catch it. "He's about to get himself in trouble, Brand. You might want to skip out in case it gets messy."

"Not a chance, sister."

"Suit yourself," she said, straightening up. Brand sent a look her way, trying to get a read on her, but all he got was the cold shoulder. She had everything a guy might want, but made it clear that whatever he had on offer, she wasn't buying.

The Mayor answered a few questions in confidence with one of the World's Fair investors. The man stepped back all of a sudden, with a look of shock on his face. "But what do you propose to do about The Outfit?" the investor asked, adding an extra helping of bluster. "I mean, really! What do you propose to do?"

"Quite simple," the Mayor said, letting the man's bluster just blow on by. "We shut them down." The Mayor let a few gasps fill in the pause before rolling on with his speech, right over whatever the loud-mouthed investor had wanted to say in reply. Brand had to stifle a laugh when he saw the investor stagger back. The Mayor actually put up a hand to shove the guy's words back in his mouth.

The redhead, on the other hand, stepped away while she darted looks around the room like she had the scoop on something about to go down. Brand tried to follow her eyes, hoping to catch sight of whatever she was after, but the Mayor bellowed just then, and let out a doozy of a line.

"The way to shut down Capone and his organization isn't to fight them. They make the rules in that game, so they've already won. If you want to beat The Outfit, you have to play by rules they can't change."

The group was listening now, even the loud mouth. It was ears open and mouths shut, and Brand couldn't help but play along.

"I mean take away their money," the Mayor said. "The source of all their power is the money they count on from their illicit enterprises. Why, just look at us, sipping from these glasses. And where do you think this lovely amber liquid came from?"

"Are you talking about ending Prohibition in Chicago City, Mr. Mayor?" Loud Mouth asked. "That would mean going against decrees signed by all four governors. Can we take that kind of risk?"

"The governors have made it clear they expect great things. And if there is a city in any of the four territories that can deliver great things, it's Chicago City! We can take that risk with Prohibition because we have to if we're going to deliver what the governors expect from us. And the same goes for gambling. Prostitution, too. Why not? If we regulate the so-called vice industries like any other, we can ensure the workers are treated fairly and the city can take its share in taxes instead of slicing off the top to pay Capone. With their funding cut off, those men will have to find real work, real jobs. And then it'll be our game, where we make the rules! As it should be," he finished by raising his glass in a toast and then emptying it in one swallow.

"Hear, hear!" shouted a few of the assembled guests in chorus. Most of the crowd threw back whatever was in their glasses and went back to dancing and cavorting. A few in the immediate circle stared down into their glasses in between exchanging looks of concern. Brand spun in place, trying to spot the redhead, but they'd pulled their magic trick again. He turned back, ready to ask the Mayor a few questions, but the man had already pushed his way through the group to come in Brand's direction.

"Mitchell Brand," the Mayor said, clapping a hand on the reporter's shoulder. "Here to cover the doings of Chicago City's most trusted and trustworthy no doubt?"

"That's a sure thing, Mr. Mayor. As you say," Brand said, still fishing around the room with his eyes for signs of the redhead or the professor.

"Good," the Mayor said "That's good, my boy. Now, of course, you'll refrain from mentioning anything else you might overhear tonight, as no official business can, indeed, should be conducted at a social gathering."

"Of course, Mr. Mayor. Like you say, nothing official about tonight."

"Well, that is good to hear, Brand. Very good to hear."

Brand was set to ask about the evening's entertainment, but before he could open his mouth a commotion rose at the entrance to the hall. A whole flock of tough birds in suits, hats, and coats marched into the room. Guests backed out of the way until the group reached the Mayor's circle. Frank Nitti strode out of the clutch and shoved aside two of the fair investors.

"Mr. Mayor," Nitti said, his voice heavy with a weight Brand hadn't heard before. It was the sound a mountain of steel would make as it fell on you. "There are times. Things happen."

The Mayor shuffled his feet once, casting a quick wary glance around the circle of guests watching the scene. "Yes, Mr. Nitti. I am aware that *things* happen in Chicago City. I am also aware that as Mayor it's up to me to make sure the wrong things don't happen. This trouble—"

"Nobody wants trouble, Mr. Mayor. But there are times." Nitti spread his hands and shrugged. "You know this. Right?"

"I know I'm enjoying the rewards of a friendship I didn't choose, if that's what you mean."

Nitti's face went slack and then sharpened in an instant. He grinned and threw a right cross like lightning, his gloved fist impacting low on the Mayor's cheek. The thick set man spit out his cigar and dropped like a side of beef, crashing to the floor. His empty glass flew out of his hands and sprayed across the marble in a fan of chips and shards. The Mayor lay lay there holding his jaw and looking up at Nitti.

The band stopped playing and the room went quiet. People

stood up and craned their necks to see the action. Brand flashed a look for the redhead and professor again, but came up empty. He spared half a thought wondering why he was looking for them now. Nitti's voice broke through his concentration.

"Mr. Mayor," Nitti said, leaning down to look the man in the eye. His voice still heavy but sharper now, like a blade that sliced every thread of conversation in the room. With complete silence around him, Nitti went on. "Mr. Capone offers his sincere gratitude, Mr. Mayor. For the valuable service you have *provided* to Chicago City." Nitti stood and caught Brand's eye. His manner loosened up and a weasel's grin curled onto his face.

"I believe we have already spoken. Mitchell Brand of the Chicago Daily Record." Nitti's voice softened further, but the knife edge remained. "I'll remind you. Watch what you say on the radio. Certain ears may take offense at your tone of voice." He gave Brand's cheek a slap.

Brand nodded and kept his face hard, but he saw something in Nitti's glare that made him take a step back. A golden glow flashed from the mobster's eyes, disappearing as quickly as it came. In that moment, Brand felt a weight, like he'd felt from Nitti's voice at first. It pressed against Brand's chest and threatened to knock him off his feet with the slightest effort. Nitti and his boys turned to leave the way they'd come and Brand got his composure as the gangsters showed him their back. Whatever had happened with Nitti right then, it was gone.

Nitti and his group marched straight through the crowd, heading for the front door. Brand watched the gangsters leave. He couldn't be sure because Nitti's thugs had surrounded their boss again, but it looked as if Nitti simply vanished, winking out of sight as the group drew abreast of Detective Wynes. The copper looked to the Mayor, who had struggled to his feet. The Mayor waved to let the gangsters leave unmolested. He dusted himself off before shuffling out through a door behind the bandstand.

CHAPTER 8

THE PARTY RETURNED TO NORMAL AFTER A bit and Brand circulated, chatting with guests about the special edition. Nobody in the room had seen a copy, which gnawed at him after awhile. His story had been hot off the press, but without the photo to back it up, he was just blowing hot air up the city's caboose. After nearly an hour of people telling him they'd sure like to see the evidence, Brand's dejection ate a hole in his gut and he left his half empty glass on a table. He was about to leave when Emma Farnsworth came at him from the direction of the powder rooms. At her approach, a faint scent of roses wafted between them. She looked cooler than when they spoke earlier, but still ready for war. "What did Nitti say to you?"

"What's it to you? Besides, a newsman never betrays his sources."

"Funny stuff. Look, Brand, Frank Nitti is putting the pinch on my father. If you know anything about it—" she let her eyes finish for her.

"That's the spirit. Why don't we sit down?"

"Fine," she said and walked to a corner table.

Keeping things private.

Good chance he'd get some dope he could use for a story, and the photos of her began to make some kind of sense in his mind. He still didn't have all the pieces, but the frame was coming together.

"So what's this about, Brand?" she asked after he'd sat across from her. "Why are you really here? What do you know about The Outfit and my father's plant?"

"How about one at a time? Why am I here? To get the dope on why the mob is interested in your father's plant when everyone knows the old man's betting low cards. And speaking of cards, what's with the gypsy act? I didn't know you went in for that sort of thing."

"It's none of your business, but I'll tell you that every man and woman in this room has sat down with Madame Tibor. Now what was that crack about my father? The plant's doing fine. Sure, Dad's not in the game like he used to be. But if anyone goes down first, it'll be Lane-Hartley. Gas is out. It's all wind, water, and radio-electricity from Mr. Tesla's operation now."

"Okay, that's a safe bet. But then why go after your old man? Why not try for the big fish, like Tesla? If it's protection they're running."

Emma seemed to size him up, as if gauging his worth and debating whether to end the conversation or not. Her face went slack and she let her eyes drift off to the side before replying. "You think it's protection?" she said, turning to look him in the eye again. "I don't know about that, but I know they wanted something from Dad. Nitti's been coming by the plant since Christmas, first with a basket of sausages, then a new coat. This morning somebody brought him a bottle of Capone's favorite hooch. They wanted him to do something, but I don't know what."

Brand connected the dots for her. "Sounds like a patsy play. It's a cinch Capone ordered the hit this morning and Nitti's been coming by to set your old man up as the fall guy in case the coppers got wise. Maybe they were working the competition angle. Brauerschift hasn't made things easy for the Farnsworth operation, and the hit was in one of their repair shops."

Emma put her head to one side and cocked an eyebrow. "Dad would never do something like that, not just because of competition." She righted her head and stuck her chin out at Brand, defying his suggestion. "Besides, he'd bought some new turbine fittings and handed out bonuses for Christmas, and he ordered a new set of regulators last week. He's been talking about getting some of the new Brackston auto-tools even, so he could save on labor. He'd be laying off a few men, but he was going to pay the others better and still—" She cut herself off and her gaze wandered to one side again.

"Don't worry, Miss Farnsworth. I won't be printing any of this in the paper."

"Oh really? I should have known better," she said, her brow crinkling up with regret.

"Hey, I mean it. You might not have the highest opinion of me, and I don't know why that's the case. But I'm good for my word to people. Unless I can prove any of this, we're just blowing smoke in each other's eyes."

"Okay, Brand. But …." She let her words fall to the table and followed them with her eyes.

"You're not happy about what I've suggested, I can see that. Maybe you know it's true though. Those tools and plant fittings sound expensive. Your old man has that kind of money?"

"I don't know. It was all supposed to happen after next season was in. Dad doesn't tell me about the money side of things, just how the plant works, the machines, that kind of thing. We were supposed to go over the books this morning."

"And?"

"And he called it off."

Emma's face went dark, and even though he didn't have much experience with them, Brand could tell he was looking at a woman scorned.

"You and your old man don't see eye to eye. Half of Chicago City knows it. What's the story there?"

"He isn't happy that his only surviving child is a girl. He's giving the plant to the foreman after he dies. He says he wants me to know how things work, but this girl's not dumb enough to believe she'll be the one to run the show."

"Well if Nitti was looking to make your old man the fall guy, there has to be something connecting him to The Outfit. Is he at home now?"

"I doubt it. He's probably passed out on his desk. He had half that bottle in him when I left this afternoon."

Brand let it go at that. They were getting close to what he'd learned from the old man earlier, and he had to keep that conversation on the QT. Unless he wanted to end up back in Miss Farnsworth's not-so-good graces again. They said their goodbyes and Brand put a few notes down in his pad while Emma walked over to the bandstand. A pretty-looking rich boy, a young fair investor, snatched Emma's hand as she walked by. Brand wasn't sure, but he thought Emma and the horn player exchanged a look as she followed Mr. Moneybags around the dance floor. Brand spun it around in his mind as he moved to the entrance. The girl at the door helped him back into his coat. He turned to leave and drew up short, face to face with the gypsy couple.

"Madame Tibor, at your service. Mitchell Brand," the woman said, holding her hand out as though she expected him to kiss her fingers. He gave them a gentle tug, like he would a lamp cord.

"A pleasure, Madam," Brand said, lifting his hat as he stepped to leave.

"You wait!" Madame Tibor said, her eyes rounding to wide-open white orbs with pinpoints of black in the middle. "You wait and you see now." She pulled her stack of cards from the folds of her dark shawl. She slid cards over and under the stack in a practiced shuffle, and Brand had to force his eyes away. He ended up staring at the husband.

"You'd be Monsieur Tibor, then? Is that right? Look, I'm a little busy right now. So maybe you and the missus here …."

"He does not speak," Madame Tibor told Brand while she kept

up her shuffle, looking him in the eyes. Her hands and fingers danced a cat's cradle around the deck of cards as she spoke.

"Men from hills and men from towns. You say … feuding, yes? They are feuding when my András was boy. He tells his father where town men are hiding. They are all killed. Then town men capture my András. He is only boy, so they let him live. Take his tongue."

The gypsy woman finished and pulled a card. She gave it to Brand. He let it rest on his palm, looking from the husband, András, to Madame Tibor.

"You are important, Mitchell Brand. This card. Pantheon Tower. House of Gods. See?"

Brand let his gaze rest on the card in his hand. A black pillar stood over a cityscape against two skies. To one side of the pillar, the city sat beneath a golden sun and a sickle moon, both orbs casting a glow onto the buildings below. On the other side, the image of the city flickered in and out of focus on the card. Buildings grew and shrank in place, as if the city were being constructed and demolished on the surface of the card in Brand's palm.

"Where gods live, power lives. You are powerful man, Mitchell Brand. Very powerful."

Brand smirked, trying to keep his head. But the dancing image on the card spun his eyes into orbit. He felt like his mind might follow and he pried his gaze out of the card, giving himself a moment of clarity. Around him, the room swelled with laughter and conversation. He stared at the gypsy woman and her silent husband. Madame Tibor drew a second card and gasped as she saw it. András changed his expression, too, widening his eyes in shock. This made his gaunt face look even more skeletal as the skin stretched over his high cheekbones. Madame Tibor placed the card face up in Brand's palm, laying it crossways over the first card.

"Changeling," she breathed out in a hush. Brand's eyes went to the card and he saw a creature of every imaginable type all stitched together. It had a man's hands, with extra long fingers ending in claws and talons. These were attached to a feathered arm on one side and a bear's furry arm on the other. The torso was lengthened, with a ribcage like a great cat. The thing had the haunches and legs of a goat on one side and a horse on the other. The head was a real winner though, with the beak and eyes of a raven, the ears of a rodent, and a snake-like neck.

Brand felt himself falling into the card, but Madame Tibor's voice anchored him in the room. "This is problem. This card never good, but especially not good for you, Mitchell Brand. Man of power crossed by Changeling is man under threat."

"Threat of what?" He hadn't meant to say anything, but his tongue had different ideas about who was in charge.

"We see," Madame Tibor said and drew a third card. When she saw the card, the gypsy threw her head back and bunched her face up in a spasm of agony. András reacted with a speed and strength Brand hardly expected from the man. Madame Tibor slumped to one side and her husband had his arms around her before she dropped to the floor. He held her upright until she was steady and kept one arm wrapped around her as she placed the third card on Brand's palm. He relaxed when his eyes took in the image. Whatever spell the gypsy had cast on him was broken. On the card was a simple image, one that Brand was more than familiar with. He'd seen enough death in his life to know it on sight, even in an archaic and fanciful illustration like the one he held in his palm.

"Like I thought," he let himself say between worried lips. Then he broke out laughing and slid the cards together and pitched them back into Madame Tibor's hands.

"That's a good act, sister," Brand said as he turned away. Looking over his shoulder he smiled and waved, then let his face go stony. "Keep it. I'm not buying any."

With that, Brand left the room, letting the crowd's laughter and the sound of clinking glass usher him outside into the frigid night. Outside, the doorman returned Brand's wave with a nod and went back to holding down the concrete patio. Snow flurries kicked up in a sudden gust and Brand lost his footing. He skipped down the steps in a quick shuffle, only just saving himself from falling on his nose.

At the street, he hailed a waiting cab, a sedan that had just dropped off another of Chicago City's wealthy drunkards. Brand stepped up to the car and noticed a shifty movement in the corner of his eye. He turned to see the gypsy woman and her husband descending the stairs. Halfway down, they drew up short and the air around them fluttered and shook. The fabric of the night whipped aside and a shivering tramp stood astride a rickety rusty bicycle, an old Boneshaker with metal wheels that took every bump and sent it straight up to the seat so hard it could rattle a man's spine right out of his skin.

The tramp flickered in and out of Brand's vision, like a candle flame in a draft. He seemed hollow beneath his skin, but gradually filled in as he stood on the steps, like he was the bottom bell of an hourglass. Brand's feet carried him up to the scene before he knew what was happening. He stopped a few steps below the trio. The tramp pulled a satchel up from inside his loose overcoat and reached into it. He drew out an envelope and held it out for the gypsy woman.

"For you, um, I guess … Ma'am. Is that—"

"Yes, is correct. For me. Ma'am," the gypsy said, letting a bright tinkling laugh follow her words into the night air. "Is okay. Ma'am or mother. I am called both." Madame Tibor took the letter from the tramp's outstretched hand and replaced it with two coins.

"What're … I get paid for this job?"

"Is for passage. You are messenger now; immortal. Still may need passage in future," she said. Brand caught a gleam in her eye as she spoke. "Coins are for that."

"But I—" the tramp spotted Brand and skittered down the steps, dragging his heavy bicycle as he came. "Mitchell Brand, I know you."

Brand's eyes rounded at the tramp. It was Old Man Farnsworth. No question. Same beaky nose. Same squinty eyes and tousled thinning hair like the man had been running his fingers through it non-stop for days on end. Brand staggered away, down the steps, nearly tripping over his feet. The tramp, Farnsworth, followed until they stood a few feet apart by the curbside.

The cab waited behind Brand, the door still open. Snow flitted down around the men and they stared at each other. Brand took in the old man's features more carefully. He'd filled in now, no longer a shell of his former self. But he looked a damn sight worse than the last time Brand had set eyes on the man. Farnsworth the Tramp stared back with a look of shock and wonderment. His eyes welled and his lip blubbered.

"It's me, Brand. It's Josiah Farnsworth." The voice cracked and rattled in Brand's ears, but it was the old man's all right.

"What the blazes gives with this?" Brand said.

"I— I didn't know it'd come to this, Brand. I just wanted to protect my little girl. She won't have to worry about Nitti or the Mayor or anyone coming now. It's all gone. I made sure of it. It's all gone and done without her. She won't have as much as if I'd been alive to give it to her, but she'll be okay. You'll tell her, won't you? Tell her for me."

Madame Tibor's voice came down to them. "Messengers should not spend time talking to mortals."

Brand sent a look her way. Her face seemed to glow a burnt orange against the darkness of the wintery night and her scarves had caught the draft to form a swirling aurora around her head. Brand had a reply on his tongue when the air shook around him. Farnsworth straddled his bike again and pulled the city aside. Like outside the Brauerschift garage that morning, Brand saw the twinkling of a city skyline appear as if behind a curtain. Then Farnsworth winked out of sight and the city draped back into place. Brand staggered another step back and fell against the cab. He searched the area, glancing in every direction, landing his eyes on the steps leading into the gala. Madame Tibor and her husband had vanished.

The cabbie's voice shook Brand from his vigil.

"You getting in, buddy? I can get another fare—"

"Yeah," Brand cut him off and slid into the rear seat. He gave the cabbie the address to his rooms and closed the door. Outside,

72

the snow stopped falling and the wind died down. The car sluggishly pulled away from the curb. Brand thought about what he'd seen on the steps and what he'd seen on Valentine's morning. Something bigger than The Outfit and the Mayor combined had come to Chicago City. Maybe it had been here all along, and this was Brand's first glimpse of it. Maybe he was finally cracking up, the shell shock catching up to him like it had so many other men. He couldn't shake the images from his mind. The tramp in the empty lot outside the Brauerschift building. The odd couple, the redhead and the professor, with their glad rags and high society language. Old Man Farnsworth dressed in filth. The twinkling landscape behind a curtain of … of what? The city itself?

Brand closed his eyes on the night and its mysteries and settled back, letting the cabbie carry him off to whatever was coming next.

CHAPTER 9

EMMA PULLED HER CAR UP OUTSIDE THE PLANT offices. She turned to her passenger and kissed him. He returned the kiss with hesitation, finally pulling away to look Emma in the eye.

"Lovebird, you took some kind of risk putting me in this car with you tonight. Front seat, too. What's got you so crazy you're breaking all the rules now?"

"It's nothing, Eddie. Just dad again. He's drunk and probably needs me to clean up after him, like always. I'll just be a minute in there. Lay low, okay? I'll be back and then we can get out of here and back to your place."

Eddie's dark skin reflected the light from a lamp hanging over the office entrance. Emma saw the worry in his eyes.

"Don't, Eddie. Don't worry."

"I'll be all right. You just be quick in there like you say. Coppers don't come around here at night, but just the same. Be easier to smile when I don't have to worry about a hangman's noose coming up behind me."

Emma got out and held her coat tight as she walked to the entrance. It was after two in the morning but sure enough, the light was still on in her father's office. Kicking snow off her shoes as she went, Emma wondered if this was the time to spill everything. She thought she'd made up her mind after talking with Brand, but standing in the snow outside the plant, her gut twisted and her tongue felt like it would do the same.

Eddie and his band were there at the gala, just like she'd asked. If the Mayor hadn't known before, he was suspicious for sure now. And that investor who pulled her onto the floor after she spoke with Brand. The man caught on when Emma couldn't stop looking at Eddie as they danced. After the dance, the young man snarled something about dark meat and the smell of smoke before he disappeared into the crowd, leaving Emma standing alone in front of the bandstand.

She shook off the memory and the fear it inspired as she unlocked the office door and stepped inside. Even with all the foyer lights off, Emma knew something wasn't right.

The secretary's desk was a mess, like she'd closed up shop and left in a rush. A waste bin dripped with water, lying on its side in front of her father's office.

Emma could hear Eddie's voice in her mind, warning her to watch her step. She had different ideas about what it meant to be careful though. She stepped over the waste bin and pushed the door open.

Her shriek came fast like a razor through the curtain of the night. Eddie was there in a flash, but to Emma it seemed like everything happened in slow motion. She stepped into the middle of the room, tears falling in sheets from her eyes.

Her father's right hand cradled the gun in his lap. Eddie came in behind her. The door creaked slowly open. Eddie let his shock out in a whispered exhale. Emma stepped forward, close to the desk, putting her fingertips in front of the brass nameplate that read *Josiah Farnsworth, Owner*. Emma moved to one side, careful to avoid brushing against the broken picture frames and scattered papers. She kept her eyes off the blood and focused on the gun instead. She gingerly lifted it from her dead father's fingers.

"What the hell you doing, girl?" Eddie gasped, looking more haunted and harried than she'd ever seen him. Emma didn't respond at first. Then time snapped back to normal for her. She took careful steps to avoid the debris around the desk, and marched for the door when she was clear of disturbing anything. Eddie followed close, ducking to hide behind her. They got back to the car and Eddie slouched in the front seat to completely hide from view.

"Lovebird, what…"

"Nitti did it. So I'm going to do Nitti."

Eddie stayed down on the drive over to his place. Crossing the Chicago River, they could both hear the hum of the police airships overhead. Emma drove a steady course through the city, weaving a path away from her father's plant and into the South Loop neighborhoods where Eddie lived. Airships circled the central districts and over the waterfront. Their searchlights cut through the small hours, slicing the darkness into curtains of night and shadow that threatened to peel back and release every one of their worst nightmares.

• • •

Brand settled himself back at his rooms. He kicked his shoes off by the door and enjoyed a few deep breaths in his favorite chair with his feet aimed at the radiator. The warm air just filled that corner and then dissipated into the surrounding cold of the room. He hunkered into the cushions, wrapping an old afghan around his shoulders and neck. As the first nods of sleep came on, he heard footsteps echoing in his mind as if in a half-dream, and then something heavy dropping to a wooden floor. Voices argued in Brand's drowsy thoughts. A frantic hammering on his door startled him awake and sent him lurching up from the chair.

Foosteps, real ones, retreated down the hall. Somewhere outside, Brand heard a car engine revving against the cold. He went to the window. Outside two men in dark coats got into a long sedan. The door snapped shut and the car pulled away from the curb pretty as you please, like nothing in the world could be wrong. Brand watched it go, reminded of how Frank Nitti's sedan had rumbled away from him in the yard outside of the Farnsworth plant. Was it Nitti's car? He couldn't tell for sure through the gathering snowfall.

The car slunk down the street, rounded a corner and was gone. Brand shivered as he stood by the window and moved to his chair. He'd lifted the afghan over his chest and then remembered the sound of something heavy falling to the floor. Muffled voices arguing, the pounding on his door.

A body lay on the floor outside his door, wrapped in an old threadbare coat. Peeling back the blood soaked fabric, Brand saw a young face bruised so badly it was almost unrecognizable. But Brand knew it, he knew the boy it had belonged to before The Outfit took it from him and made it into a message. Brand learned to shut himself off in the trenches. Too many times he'd been forced to look into the dead faces of young men only moments after they'd told him about the girl waiting for them back home, or the baby brother or sister they hadn't met yet. Just before they climbed over the trench wall and threw themselves into the arms of death. But they'd known what they'd signed up for. They knew the job could be deadly. Probably would be.

A newsboy's gig wasn't supposed to get him killed. It wasn't supposed to end with him being taken apart by the mob just for shipping papers around the street. Brand felt the tears start quickly, in a flood, and he felt them end quickly as he stood and went to the phone. He stared at the body in the hall while the operator connected him.

"I'm sorry, Jenkins. I should have given you the mic this morning after all."

CHAPTER 10

THE NEXT MORNING, EXHAUSTED FROM THE night before, Brand went into the Record offices early and made straight for the elevators. He got out on the fifteenth floor and stalked down the hall to Chief's office. The boss was running his hands through his thinning hair when Brand came in.

"Thanks for saving me the trouble of calling you up here, Mitch. Before you get started, let me tell you what you don't know and what you *aren't* going to do today. I wish it weren't like this, Mitch. I do. But dammit, you ruffled the wrong set of feathers yesterday. As much as I hate to say it, with this suicide we've got a way out of the mess you made."

Brand's head turned around and his body followed. He went out and came back in again. "Yeah, it's your office all right. But you lost me somewhere between the door and what you're talking about."

"Farnsworth. The old man. He shot himself last night. His daughter is missing, no gun found at the scene. But his secretary was there when it happened. She heard the shot, went to investigate, saw the old man's brains on the wall behind him. She ran off then, but locked up like always. So the coppers have her held as material for now."

Brand stood quiet for a moment. Should he say anything? Not about the ghostly tramp he'd seen on the steps outside the gala hall last night. No. Not a word about that. Or the crazy couple. But if there was a connection between the old man killing himself and the Clark Street hit, and the coppers found out about it and came sniffing around the Daily Record…

"Meant to ask you about Farnsworth this morning, Chief. Guess I don't have to now."

"What about him?"

"The Outfit might have been running a patsy on the old man. Frank Nitti was out there at the plant yesterday, Emma Farnsworth, too. I ran into both of them before I went in to have a chat with ol' Josiah. Didn't get much, but I got enough to make it clear there's more to find. Or maybe there was."

"The Commissioner called, Mitch. You're to cool it on the Clark Street thing. That's what I meant about what you're *not* doing today. Or any day. No more reports on the massacre, even if you think there's a connection there. And you know I'm ready to believe you that there is. Just let it go away."

Brand opened his lips to protest, but the look in Chief's eyes took them both back to No-Man's Land. Chief had been trying to get a wounded boy off the wall and back down into the trench. Artillery came in, just as a second line of boys was going up over the wall. Brand saw a lot of blood. Chief saw more, and too much more. His eyes now had the same look they'd had that day, and Brand got the message loud and clear. He took a deep breath and sat down in the chair beside Chief's desk.

"Just send out a story about Farnsworth in print and do a radio bit. Keep it short, and nothing about the Outfit. Not on this story, and—not anywhere, Mitch. When your newsboys get in, I need them up here. The Commissioner's on his way."

"The Commissioner? What's he want with the kids?"

"Got me. He says somebody higher up wants to personally debrief with them since they took the paper down to the streets."

"Somebody? Somebody who?"

"I don't know, Mitch. I've been on and off the horn with the Commissioner since yesterday. Way he tells it, somebody's worried about the massacre getting the city in a panic. I'm surprised he didn't have anything to say about the photo you grabbed, but maybe he's just holding that one to hit me with later. If you don't play ball, I mean. That's from the Commissioner, Mitch. Everything I'm telling you here. It's what he says."

"Yeah? And what do you say?"

"Me? Hell, Mitch. You know me better than that. Now c'mon and get in line with the rest of us joes, hey? Send the kids up when they get in."

Brand let it sink in. Sure enough, somebody wanted to scare the newsboys, and the same somebody wanted Brand to clam up, too. "You can have Digs and Conroy when they get here."

"Jenkins, too."

"He won't be in today, Chief. He came by my rooms last night."

"You telling me you got the kid sauced and left him in your rooms to sleep it off?"

"I'm telling you that he came by my place after an appointment with Capone's boys. They delivered him. Most of him. His left arm was missing and so were his legs at the knees. I'm betting you don't want Digs and Conroy seeing anything like that. I know I sure as hell don't."

Chief stared at his desk and then let his eyes flick up to meet Brand's.

"I'm ... I'm sorry, Mitch."

Brand let out the breath he'd been holding and clenched his jaw tight, forcing the tears and angry words back down his throat. All he could think about was Jenkins' bloodied face. Holding his head in his hands, Brand said, "You can tell the Commissioner or whoever it is that they don't need to worry about Jenkins talking to anybody."

Shaking himself to pull his heart out of his shoes, Brand stood to leave. Chief told him to wait. When Brand turned to look at him, he saw Chief's eyes flashing on that look from the trenches again.

"Something else you need to tell me, Chief?"

"Yeah," he said, the issue of Jenkins' murder apparently forgotten. He lifted a page of notes from his desk and handed it across to Brand. "Two more dead tramps last night."

"Where'd it happen?" Brand asked, feeling the room begin to spin. He fought to control the floor with his feet.

"Their camp. Over by the riverside. It isn't going to be a pretty story, not by a long shot. Keep the blood on the QT. Stick to the facts and only as many as you need to make it news." Chief was almost done, but then he let his fingertips rest together and brought them up to his lips.

"Just in case. I'd better get that picture box from you. No more nabbing shots from the crabs, at least not until things blow over a bit. It's too hot right now."

Brand felt the room settle around him. The spinning stopped. He looked Chief in the eye. "You're not bluffing." Brand passed Skippy's box through the stony silence. "So now that I'm toothless and hobbled, how about you let me do my job? Archie let on about a murder yesterday morning, happened about the same time as the massacre, and just as messy. He said it was a guy worked for Mr. Tesla's operation. I figure I can go hit up Skippy and the boys for the scoop, hey?"

Chief tucked the camera box into a drawer without looking at it, instead letting his gaze rest on the papers covering his desk while he chewed at the inside of his lips. Brand had seen Chief work his jaw like that plenty of times, and he knew it meant his friend had something else on his mind. Something that would stay unspoken if Brand didn't push.

"Hey. Chief. I'm right here, you know? Mitch. Remember?"

"Yeah, I remember, Mitch. I remember," Chief said, resting his head in his hands just as Brand had done a few minutes ago.

"What is it?"

"I gave the murder to one of the cubs, Mitch."

"A cub? I thought we agreed I handle all the blood and guts around town. Those kids haven't got the stomach for it. Hell, they were still messing their pants when we were flying over No-Man's Land. Chief—"

"It's Skip," he said. "Skip was the guy got murdered, Mitch. I'm sorry. I didn't want to tell you because I knew you two were tight. I figured I had enough bad news for you this morning anyway."

"Yeah?" Brand said, standing and shoving the chair out from behind him. "Yeah, you sure did." Brand spun on his heel and stormed out, heading straight for the lift. He needed the security of his office around him. Maybe he needed a slug from the bottle in his desk.

The lift stopped at the fourth floor and he got out, nearly running over the only two newsboys he had left.

"Mr. Brand!" Conroy piped up with a grin on his mug. Brand tried to match the mood, but his face didn't cooperate. Conroy's grin slid off his face and Digs came up behind him, wearing the same worried look.

"What's the story, boss?" Digs asked.

Brand chewed his lip, fighting the need to tell the boys about Jenkins but knowing if he didn't sit down in a quiet room, he'd probably crack up like a china doll dropped from a third story window. "Chief— Chief says you gotta talk with the Commissioner, boys. I guess the man wants to know if any riots started when people saw the front page," Brand said, turning to head back to his office.

"Well, hey," Digs said. "That's easy enough then, ain't it? We can tell him like it happened. Didn't one of us sell a single paper yesterday."

"How's that?" Brand demanded, rounding on the boy, who jumped back a step.

"Honest, Mr. Brand. I think Conroy here got the farthest of all of us, but, well you tell him," Digs shoved his friend's shoulder. Conroy gave Brand a sheepish look and then told him how it went down, how all three of them had been waylaid by teams of gangsters who picked up the whole set of papers and rolled off in their cars with them. The kid smiled when he got to the part about the bird handing him a sawbuck. Brand let him finish and ushered them into the lift for their meeting with the Commissioner.

On the way back to his office he promised himself a double from the bottle. Knowing that every copy of the special edition had been nabbed by Capone's Outfit gave Brand a sinking feeling. The mobster had it in for him on this story. Capone didn't want word getting out about the crime scene. Brand remembered the touch of Frank Nitti's glove on his cheek. The Outfit had no problem making more crime scenes for Brand, and if he kept it up they'd make him one special, all his own. At the door to his office Brand turned to watch the lift slowly rising away with Digs and Conroy inside. He hoped that whatever the Commissioner had to say it was short and sweet, but something told him the worst was yet to come.

CHAPTER 11

EMMA CLOSED THE DOOR BEHIND HER quietly and slowly stepped down the porch steps. Snow began to fall, dusting the heavy coat Eddie gave her. She tugged it on tighter and looked back at the house, knowing Eddie was sleeping upstairs, alone. Their conversation from earlier played over and over in her mind as she went to the car.

"I don't have anything to lose but you, Eddie. But I can't let them get away with this."

"You're talking crazy, Lovebird. Crazy as crazy gets. Come back in the house now. C'mon back inside before you give me the vapors. I love you, Emma. And you're wanting to go out gunning for Frank Nitti like that don't mean a thing, like I don't mean nothing to you."

She'd followed him back inside. Let him hug her. Hugged him back, tight and warm against him. *"You do, Eddie, you mean everything to me. You're the only thing I have left. But the Outfit took my family apart. Mom left when dad started drinking. He drank because he couldn't keep up with the loans he took from Nitti to keep the plant running. I was a dope for believing his story about how mom ran off to live in the Seaboard with some guy from New York City. She left because she was sick of watching dad drink himself to sleep every night, and watching me clean up after him."*

"Dammit, I know it means we wouldn't never have met, but what kept you from going with her?"

"She didn't want me to go. I remember the day she left. She just looked at me from the door and blew me a kiss. I could tell she'd been crying, but she didn't give me a chance to ask why. She just left me behind. She left me to make sure he had somebody to look after him."

"And you did, and what'd he give you back for it? Huh? A lotta lip and not much else, some nice clothes maybe. This car here. But—"

Emma had cut him off with a look. Her father may have been a lot of things, but he'd looked out for her, given her chances other girls could never hope for. And he'd let her make her own way instead of showing her around the set until some dope walked up and said he'd marry her. Maybe her father hadn't been able to love her enough to trust her with running the plant, or maybe he was just protecting her from Nitti's hooks.

"Maybe I did hate him, or maybe I didn't," she said to the night sky around her now, still feeling Eddie's hands caressing her shoulders, his breath hot on her neck. "Maybe I loved him like every girl loves her daddy, no matter how rough it goes on her to love him. And now he's dead because that damn rat named Frank Nitti got into my family's cupboards and chewed holes in everything we owned. He's going to pay for that, and I'm the debt collector. Then we can go somewhere," she said, letting her eyes rest on the window above. "We can leave, just me and you, Eddie."

She'd said the same thing to him earlier, after he'd got her back inside the house.

"Where we gonna go?" he'd asked and smiled like she'd told him the funniest joke he'd ever heard. *"A negro and a white woman in a car together? You gonna ride in back for the rest of your life?"*

"We'll go to New Orleans. You've still got family there, and

friends. Miscegenation laws aren't on the books there. People live separately, but you said they know well enough who loves who, and nobody makes a stink about it. Not at all if you stay out of the wrong clubs. Clara Lewis would still be alive today if she had just taken a riverboat out of town instead of stepping out a window in the Monadnock."

Eddie's face had gone cold. *"Don't talk like that, Lovebird. You talk about dying when you want to get me thinking you're coming back, and I just know you ain't if I let you drive off with that gun in your bag."*

Emma had kissed him, full and warm. She held him and let his arms encircle her, his hands sweep up and down her back, pressing her to him. The warmth of his body against hers was almost enough to distract her from her plan.

"Emma … I know The Outfit did your family a hundred ways of wrong, but you ain't gotta do nothing but stay right here."

She'd reached up to silence him with her fingers, but he caught them and brought his lips to hers. He held her hand tight, pulling her closer with his other hand in the small of her back as he stepped away from the window and to the bed. She fell with him, fell into the caressing and the squeezing, the fevered kissing and then the rhythmic movement of her body against his and his against hers, over and over in tandem with their heartbeats.

Eddie had dropped back onto the pillow when they'd finished, letting his hands fall to her thighs. She'd rolled to the side to lie next to him. She stayed there until he'd fallen asleep and then carefully stole back to the dressing cabinet where she stored a few changes of clothes.

Whispering through a blown kiss, Emma'd said, *"I'll be back, Eddie. And then we'll leave this town. I promise."*

Outside now, with the snow collecting in her hair, Emma turned away from the house. She slid into the driver's seat and started the car, casting one last glance back at the upstairs window. Eddie's frightened face looked back at her and she ripped her gaze away. If she looked at him for just one more second, she'd lose her nerve and

Nitti would get away clean as can be. And Emma Farnsworth had had enough of rotten men spoiling her life and getting away with it.

CHAPTER 12

BRAND SPENT SOME TIME IN THE PRINTING room, listening to the Brackston auto-press churn out the story on Josiah Farnsworth's suicide and the two dead tramps. Behind him, at the old hand cranked press, the cub doing the story on Skip rolled out the last few sheets and wrapped them up with twine.

"Hey, thanks," Brand said to the cub.

"For what?" the guy said, but Brand just waved him off. The young fella stepped through the press room doors and was gone.

Brand went back to watching the auto-press work. He'd kept both of his stories clean, just like Chief said. It was easy enough for the story about Old Man Farnsworth, so long as Brand didn't think about how he'd seen the man dressed like a tramp and talked to him a few hours after he was supposed to have died.

The piece about the tramps though … it turned Brand's insides to jelly. Two men, shredded in their sleep, pretty much like Skip and the guys in the Brauerschift garage. The cops who found the tramps said there was hardly enough left to make sense of what had been killed much less who.

A few minutes later, the print copy of the Daily Record was on its way to the people with news about Old Man Farnsworth. Digs Gordon and the Conroy kid came in and hopped on their airbikes waiting for the loader gearboxes to do their thing. Like always, Brand noticed, Conroy couldn't take his eyes off the machines. With memories of Jenkins' last request playing through his mind, Brand went over to the kid.

"Be quick with your beat today, Conroy, and maybe Mutton'll give you some grease time later. But no playing the smooth, hey? I want those papers sold, not made into a tramp's bedsheets."

The kid's eyes went round like Brand told him his ma had just died. "Hey, sure thing, Mr. Brand, sir. You know you can count on me and Diggsy to do right."

The two newsboys nodded together like a couple of carnival clowns, but Brand knew they were straight with him. They hadn't gone to the Commissioner's after all. Chief had called Brand up right after he'd put them in the lift. When he got to the man's office, his boss had him tell the boys about Jenkins. He did, but only just. They didn't need to know the details. The boys agreed to keep quiet, nodding their heads so fast Brand thought they'd spin their eyeballs backwards. They gave him the same look now, and he hated himself for scaring them like that. But the truth was, he was scared himself, and it didn't do anyone any good to pretend nothing had changed.

"All right, then. Go on and hit the streets, boys, but watch your backs. You double up on your beats, hey? And if you sell out on the first round, that's fine. Just come on back home and take the afternoon off."

Digs and Conroy gave him a thumbs up each and kicked off their trapezes. Their airbikes dropped a foot and then glided down through the mid-morning chill.

"Keep safe, boys. And come home," Brand said to the wind. He watched the boys until they were out of sight. With his heart in his throat, Brand shuffled down the deck to the *Vigilance*.

He felt like folding when he climbed into the cabin. His whole life had been preparation for yesterday's story. Getting the crime scene photo, putting out the news about Chicago City's worst killing. Grabbing threads that brought one of the city's oldest families into the picture. Nearly getting one of those threads connected for certain. And then watching the whole thing unravel in his hands.

He wrote up a quick radio spot on the dead tramps, knowing he should keep it clean like he'd been told. But Brand couldn't resist the urge to warn the people of Chicago City. The victims in the garage yesterday morning were top dollar, and today they were penny ante. If the killer was a monster and decided to go after folks in between … Brand winced as he read the descriptions of the two dead tramps. Even though there wasn't much left to describe.

Ladies and Gentlemen of Chicago City, this is Mitchell Brand with the Chicago Daily Record. Some disturbing news has come to us this morning. Two men, found murdered in their sleep last night. The men were among the noble class of residents who enjoy life by the riverside.

Down and out they may have been, but to die like … This reporter has been asked to keep the details under wraps, but for all our sakes a more thorough telling is called for. Be watchful, ladies and gentlemen. And be warned. Killers are on the loose in Chicago City, and we've all seen what they're capable of.

For the full story on last night's murders, catch a copy of the Daily Record. They're on the way to you on the street as I speak.

Stay tuned, Chicago. And stay in touch.

Brand knew the story called for more, but with his hazy head from last night's long hours he couldn't put his finger on what was missing. Just his luck, Chief knew exactly what was missing and rang Brand on the radiophone as soon as he'd shut off the mic.

"Brand, I said—"

"You said. And I heard. I also heard what you didn't say, but I didn't catch all of it. I've got the Farnsworth story to do, still. So unless you've decided to come clean, I'll get back to the news."

"Do me a favor, Mitch. I'm asking nice, but it's all I can do not to

say you're fired. Just keep it on the QT as best as you can. You and me both know there's more to say. There's always more to say about every story comes through our hands. But sometimes you gotta play hush. It's how the game goes, Mitch. You know that."

Brand did know it, and he knew it had to be something heavy weighing on Chief's head to make him bring that card into play.

"Okay, Chief. For you. For old time's sake." Brand let a little syrup coat his words, just so Chief knew he still wasn't happy about being muzzled. Chief cut the connection after a grunt, leaving Brand still wondering what had gotten into his old friend's head so deep that it would come to slapping a gag over Brand's mic.

Archie would show up in a bit, to get them into the sky for the afternoon. The only thing on Brand's docket until then was a radio report about Josiah Farnsworth. Thinking about that set Brand to grinding his teeth in frustration. If the old man had gone quietly in his sleep, it'd just be another society death. Brand could have dashed it off and forgotten all about it.

But the tramp on the Mayor's steps was real. He was there.

Brand swiped at the air to keep the pink elephants at bay. He couldn't tell anyone about what he'd seen or they'd think he'd finally lost his marbles. No dice. he was a newshawk, and newshawks reported about the news.

The Farnsworth suicide was a tragedy. Sure. A real blow the Chicago City's foundation. Brand scribbled in his steno pad as the ideas came faster.

Farnsworth's death spelled more than tragedy for the society folks. It was tied up in a mess of dirty dealings. And it wasn't the only one, Brand reminded himself, thinking about Jenkins. He wanted to mention the boy in his report, too, but Chief's last warning came through loud and clear. Brand scratched out the line he'd been writing about Jenkins and tossed the steno pad and pencil onto his desk.

He settled into his chair and finished a smoke. He rolled another and lit it before reopening the broadcast link with the Record's spire.

Good afternoon, Chicago City. This is Mitchell Brand again, with the Daily Record.

Today we mourn the loss of a city patriarch. Josiah Gabriel Farnsworth shot himself to death last night. He was a strong man. A powerful man.

Brand paused there, remembering the gypsy, Madame Tibor, and the cards she'd placed in his hand. Then he mentally kicked himself for letting hokum break his stride. He drew in a lungful and continued the report.

Josiah Farnsworth was also a man in a game with heavy competition. Maybe that tells us enough to understand why. We can only hope his surviving daughter, Emma Farnsworth, finds solace in her time of sorrow.

Brand reached to shut the mic off and then stopped. He saw the place where the crime scene photo should have been. He'd left it on his desk yesterday, standing up against the radio set and held in place with a magnet. Now it was gone.

Somebody's got it in for me on this story. Somebody that got Chief to put a hand over my mouth and probably the same somebody that made sure Jenkins will never speak again.

In an instant, Brand imagined the city under attack. Capone's Outfit swarmed the streets like the Kaiser's boys coming over the top, piling into the trenches and killing everything in sight.

Brand saw the men and women who slogged it out in the factories every single day, just to make sure they could pay their rent, or the protection money, or the ransom. People who worked for chump change and used it up in the speaks that were owned by the same thug who prevented anyone from earning a decent wage. After a long drag on his smoke, Brand stabbed it out and kept talking.

It remains to be seen whether or not Frank Nitti's visit to Farnsworth Wind and Water, which this reporter witnessed yesterday afternoon, is related to Mr. Farnsworth's suicide. If anything is revealed about Josiah Farnsworth's possible involvement with The Outfit, the Daily Record is committed to bringing you the truth about what happens in your city.

Stay tuned, Chicago. Stay safe.
And stay in touch.

Chief would eat him alive for that, but Brand had taken enough from the world in the past twenty-four hours. The story was there, and he would follow it to its end somehow. The weight of the past day and night caught up to him as he stared at the radiophone, willing it to ring. After fifteen minutes of nothing but the sound of wind outside the cabin windows, Brand scribbled a note and left it in the pilot's chair. Then he staggered aft, stopping in the washroom to splash some water on his face before going back to his bunk.

Sleep came quickly, and Brand felt like it left just as fast. He jolted awake to the ringing of the radiophone by his head. Brand looked at his watch, but his weary eyes couldn't make out the time. He grabbed the horn out of its cradle and grunted into the tube in the wall, ready to catch hell for his last broadcast. It wasn't Chief though.

"Boss! You gotta get up here. Capone was arrested and they just shot the mayor."

When Brand got into the cabin, Archie had the *Vigilance* over a municipal mooring deck. Fading light outside said it was late afternoon with a snowstorm blowing its way into the city. Flurries had piled up in drifts on the deck, and clouds lowered over the horizon like a falling curtain.

"Where are we?"

"Few blocks from an old machine shop. That's where I saw the shooter's car pull up."

"Coppers?"

"They missed out. Whoever's driving the car, he knows the streets like I know the sky. I had us overhead when it went down. Saw their car. Long sedan, like Nitti was driving at Farnsworth's yesterday."

"What happened with Capone; when'd it go down?"

"Like the Mayor said last night. He was gunning for Capone and his crew. They got him coming out of a warehouse full of hooch. Governor's boys were there, too. Lots of them."

"Why didn't you wake me up? We should have been on that story."

"I would've, boss, but sure enough the Governor's boys would have kept us off, hey?"

Archie was right. Except for the times when Brand had got there first, like on Valentine's Day, a G-man showing up meant that whatever story might have been there ended up being someplace else. And any story you did get from them wouldn't be worth printing on a three-dollar bill.

"Who told you to cover the Mayor's office?"

"Nobody. Got your note and figured I'd just circle around the hot spots like usual. Then I heard on the wire about Capone and I had us just a few blocks over. I got us overhead when the Mayor's on the steps giving his speech about Capone. He's talking big when this car comes up fast. Then it's *bang bang bang* and down he goes."

While Archie dropped down to mooring level and radioed the gearboxes on the deck Brand threw on his jacket, overcoat and hat. The city's automatons radioed back that the ship was secured.

"She's all set, boss," Archie said. "We're tied down nice and neat."

"Yeah, with a bow, I'm sure. Have the gearboxes get the Morse lines in, too," Brand said back. He'd send out a wire soon as he got the scoop on Nitti's whereabouts. Archie was on the horn and gave a thumbs up over his shoulder.

Brand opened the cabin door and dropped the ladder.

CHAPTER 13

EDDIE WAS RIGHT, AND SHE KNEW IT. WHAT was she doing driving around Chicago City with a snowstorm blowing into town? The coppers were still after her for taking her dad's gun from his office, leaving him there with an extra hole in his head. Somebody would spot her if she didn't play it careful. She tugged Eddie's coat closer around her, turning the collar up for warmth and to keep her face and hair hidden.

Down the city streets, around corners, down alleys. Where was she going? She had a gun in her handbag and a man she wanted to point it at, but she had no idea where to find him. Who could tell her where Nitti was hiding out? Who knew and would tell her without giving her up to the coppers?

Brand? That flea-bit newshawk couldn't find—maybe he could. But how could she get to him without being pinched for showing her face in public? And could she trust him to help her anyway? Not unless she gave him a story to blab all over town.

Emma kept half her mind on the road as she spun ideas around in her head, wondering who she could talk to, who might help her.

A cyclist came up alongside her when she stopped at an intersection. In the flurries, she could just make out the press badge on the man's hat. Dropping the window a crack, Emma called over to him, raising her voice above the gusting wind.

"Where's the story tonight?"

"Eh? Oh, thought you were a fella for a second there. What'd you say?"

The guy tried to get an eye on Emma's face, but she kept the coat collar up so only her eyes showed.

"I said where's the story? Nothing else gets a newshawk out on a bicycle in this weather, right?"

"Heh. Guess you haven't heard then either. Maybe aces up for me. Big news about Capone at the Mayor's Office right now, I'm heading over to see if I can get the scoop."

In the middle of the intersection, the auto-warden lowered a red paddle and raised a green one. The cyclist took off like a shot and skidded on the slick pavement. He got himself straightened out and Emma saw her chance. She followed after him and caught up quick enough. On an open stretch of road she drifted close to him and he wobbled trying to avoid her fender. He shouted something back at her as he went down in a heap. Emma got out, leaving her car idling. Before the newshawk could react, she'd snatched his press badge and bag.

"Hey, what the hell, lady? Hey, you're Emma Farnsworth. Coppers are—"

"You don't need to tell me about it," she spat back as she slid into the driver's seat. The newshawk's shouts followed her and she spotted a few folks staring after her as she drove away.

If the Mayor had big news about Capone, it was even money he'd have a little story about Frank Nitti, too. Emma could pass herself off as a newsie. Or maybe she'd get arrested the minute she stepped inside. But it was the only play she had.

She crossed the river and did a few switch backs to make sure nobody had tailed her from where the newshawk took his tumble. The road behind her looked clear, and she'd only spotted one patrol boat up above as she crossed the river. The Mayor's Office waited down the street, next to the ballroom where he threw his gala parties. That building had always been an eyesore for Emma, a place to avoid whenever she wasn't being forced inside with the rest of the duckies.

She looked across the street at the park and noticed a few men and women marching along the sidewalk. They crossed the street to join a crowd gathered at the steps to the Mayor's Office. Should she get out and join them? How could she hide from their cameras? They'd pick her out in a flash, even with her phony disguise. So that idea was out the window, and now she was sunk.

Disgusted with her failure, Emma pulled in across from the park and watched the snow fall on the car's bonnet, melting away into wisps of steam that turned to mist in the frosted afternoon air. The Mayor's Office loomed over the street, all hulking white marble and shimmering glass. Clouds shrouded the building, giving it a haunted look. It stood out from the dark background like a giant's face, the doorway an enormous mouth open in shock. Or hunger. Soot from the city's furnaces blackened the bell tower up top.

Emma felt a deep ache in her chest. If her family's plant had the money to really compete, the air would be cleaner. The whole city would be cleaner. But Capone saw to it that nobody enjoyed clean living except him. Even the Mayor's digs were tarnished.

"Serves him right," Emma hissed as she watched the Mayor, flanked by his aides, shift his porcine bulk out of the doorway and down the steps. A microphone waited for him, standing just above street level. The Mayor regarded the crowd before him and raised his hands as if in triumph. Whatever he had to say, it had to be big. The Mayor never made public speeches except after the election results came in. His voice boomed out into the street, too loud for the small speaker boxes off to the sides. Emma saw the megaphones then, two sets of bullhorns high up on the walls of the building that now stood above the steps like some lurking monster belching forth the sounds of its rage.

"Members of Chicago City's society, citizens, and ladies and

gentlemen of the city's journalism corps, thank you. It is with great pleasure, and not too small an exhalation of relief, that I announce to you the end—"

The Mayor paused, drawing out the moment with a shit-eating grin on his mug. Emma's stomach turned watching the spectacle. The Mayor was as guilty as the mob for making Josiah Farnsworth into a desperate drunk. And Nitti's words after he landed that punch the other night, about Capone thanking the Mayor, *for his service.* The man was a highbinder if ever there was one; the whole city knew it.

"The end, ladies and gentlemen. Tonight, the fifteenth of February in the year 1929, tonight marks the end of The Outfit. Just ten minutes ago, members of my police force, Chicago City's finest men in uniform, were joined by the Governor's marshals in a raid on Al Capone's hideout. In the raid, over five hundred gallons of bootleg liquor were confiscated."

The Mayor stepped back, reached into his coat pocket and withdrew a slip of paper, then stepped up to the mic again.

"Five hundred gallons, ladies and gentlemen. Also captured were fifteen members of Capone's gang, including… Friends it gives me great pleasure to announce that Alphonse Capone has been arrested by the Governor's marshals and is—"

A cheer went up at the news of Capone's arrest and Emma had to admit her heart felt lighter when she heard the words. But a screech of tires came to her ears, making her whip her head around. A long sedan fish-tailed around the corner behind her and roared down the street. The crowd of reporters turned as one to see the car, and they all fell together in a tangle trying to escape its path, stumbling up the steps, some slipping to land face down in the filthy snowmelt.

The car skidded to a halt and the sickeningly familiar figure of Frank Nitti leaned out of the back seat with a tommy gun that burped fire. The Mayor staggered, caught by the fusillade, his arms whipping up and backwards. Bullets picked at him, punched into his gut and his chest, flung him up the steps. He went over on his backside and jerked under the impact of more and more lead. Emma felt herself screaming for it to stop, but Nitti kept his finger on the trigger until the sound of sirens swelled in the gathering snowstorm. Then he disappeared into the back seat and the sedan roared away, turning at the next corner and heading for the river. Before she knew what she was doing, Emma had pulled away from the curb.

At the intersection, she whipped around the corner and slowed to a crawl. The mobster's car was out of sight. Had he turned here or up one block? Maybe he'd cut around to cross the river farther down. Was he headed for the waterfront? Traffic moved here and there, wagons and bicycles. Sirens gathered behind her. They were close. Somebody must have seen her leave the scene. They'd think she was in on it.

Not knowing where to go or why, Emma continued and crossed the river, her eyes darting around and up. She nearly slammed into a wagon when she saw the *Vigilance* hovering overhead, following a course away from the Mayor's Office.

Brand was on the hunt. Fine. She'd follow him to the scoop and write the final chapter in Nitti's life story.

CHAPTER 14

MEMORIES OF JENKINS' BLOODIED FACE played back through Brand's mind as he stepped around the piles of slushy snow. When he stopped across the street from an abandoned machine shop, Brand let memories of Frank Nitti take over the playback. Nitti'd used Jenkins to send Brand a message. Nitti'd set up Josiah Farnsworth as a patsy for the Valentine's Day massacre. Nitti'd punched out the Mayor and threatened Brand. And now Nitti had gunned the Mayor down for nabbing Capone.

If Brand could get sight of the gangster, maybe listen in on his crew's chatter, he could get the pieces that would put the story together for him. Then he could call the cops in and have the satisfaction of watching Frank Nitti try on the city's jewelry.

And the new chair they've got down at the pen. Custom made for rats like you.

Brand took shelter in the boarded up entry alcove of an old hotel. The neighborhood had been abandoned for a while. The perfect place for gangsters to arrange a hideout. Brand watched the shop building, dancing his weight back and forth to keep his feet from freezing up. The shop sat low on the old street, like a forgotten pile of bricks and lumber left to the elements. A line of barrels, like weary and fallen soldiers, stood along the shop front. Some lay on their sides, mouths open and showing small drifts of snow collecting like chalky grins. Next to the shop an empty yard stretched away into the gathering darkness of the stormed-over afternoon. Brand couldn't see a car anywhere, but someone was in the building.

A door opened onto the yard, sending an angled slice of warmth into the dusky light. A man in a dark suit appeared for a moment, looked into the depths of the empty yard and went back in. The door swung shut behind him and the metallic click of the latch came to Brand's ears. Should he try to get in that way. What if they spotted him? Would they gun him down? Of course they would. The abandoned area made a great setting for a murder that would never be seen. Brand gave himself a full ten seconds to worry and then remembered Jenkins' face one last time.

He dashed out to cross the street when two tramps on creaking rusty bicycles slipped out of the night to foul the air around him. Brand pulled up short at the edge of the sidewalk and stared into the rheumatic eyes of the dirtiest human beings he'd ever seen. Filth clung to them everywhere, like their clothes were made of waste. Even the muddiest soldier in the trenches had a clean face beneath the grime. These two were something else, like a pair of walking trash heaps. Even worse, Brand recognized one of them.

Josiah Farnsworth slunk along beside his younger and taller companion. Brand realized he'd seen both men before.

"That was you on Valentine's morning. Right, pal?"

"Yeah, sure enough it was me, Brand. Hey, I get you know my new partner here," the tramp said and leaned in close to whisper, "He won't shut up about some squeeze named Emma. You know where we can find her?"

"She's no squeeze. She's his daughter." Brand said, leaning back from the stink coming off the tramp. The old man had stayed back, huddling into his coats and shivering like he had nothing on.

"So, Brand, you want the scoop on the Bicycle Men or you just here for the show and tell later?"

"Eh?" Brand's mind raced and he struggled to keep track of the conversation and remember why he'd been standing on the sidewalk to begin with. Wasn't he supposed to meet someone? Was it these two bums?

"What'd you say your name was, pal?"

"Didn't. But I'll tell ya. Larson Combs, formerly at Argonne. Like I said yesterday morning. Remember that little hike we took through the trees?"

"I still don't think we ever met up over there, friend. You said something about a story?"

The tramp shot a glance over his shoulder at Old Man Farnsworth. "Probably better we wait until it's just us two, Brand. Company can ruin a good telling, and I want to make sure you get the skinny without none of this fella's moaning about his Emma. C'mon, old timer."

Larson lifted his feet to the pedals and grabbed at the night air beside his head. Before he pulled it aside he gave Brand a wink and a nod. Then he lifted up the city night like it was a blanket. Brand tried in vain to see what was back there, but the tramp blocked his view, sliding into the deeper black like shadow. Then he was gone. Old Man Farnsworth trundled up on his creaking bike.

"That you in there, Mr. Farnsworth?"

"It's me, Brand. Sure as anything can be sure anymore. This is me. Josiah Farnsworth." His face hung glum and stone drunk, and a tic quivered under his left eye. The old man held out a hand waiting for Brand to shake. Brand came closer, reached out and touched his fingertips to the old man's palm. Feeling real skin, he gripped the hand and gave it a squeeze.

"So that's squared. You're real, so that means your pal is real, too. Now how about the get up. Last time I saw you it was uptown starch even if you were three sheets to the wind. What's with the magic act?"

"It's like the gypsy woman said, Brand. I'm a messenger now. Work for them."

"For who? The gypsies?"

"No. The ..." Old Man Farnsworth looked off down the empty street, staring into the distant dark. "Hell, I never was a church going man. Never gave no thought to what came after it all. Thickheaded. That's what I was." He turned back to face Brand and his eyes stayed full of terror, but his mind had clearly moved on to something else. "You'll tell her, won't you? Like you said. You'll tell my Emma that I'm sorry. And ... and that I love her. Always loved her."

"Yeah, I'll tell her. But—"

The old man lifted a drape of the city just like Larson had, and Brand got a look in this time. He saw a cityscape, just like the one he stood in now, only it flickered like a candle flame, with buildings wavering and guttering in and out of focus.

"What is that place?" he said.

"Not now, Brand," the old man said.

Farnsworth stepped slow, half hauling the clunky bicycle with him because its wheels snagged on the icy pavement. Then the city dropped back down to cover his exit. Brand waited, willing the old man to pop back into existence so he could answer more of Brand's questions. Nothing happened. The night stayed still except for a sighing breeze and flutters of a coming snowfall.

Promising himself a double once he got back to the *Vigilance*, Brand stepped clumsily off the sidewalk. His right foot sank into a sodden pothole full of ice cold water. He leaped out of the hole and shook his leg to get some of the wet off him, but it was pointless. He'd have to peel off his shoe and sock and go back to the airship with one bare foot. He stepped carefully across the street, made it to the other side and tucked down by the barrels. Still on edge, Brand looked back across the still, quiet street to where he'd been standing. He tracked his focus through the air above the street, trying to zero in on any movement between him and the hotel entrance where he'd hidden a moment ago.

Nothing moved. No mysterious tramps on bicycles popped out of the night. For the second time in as many days, Brand felt reality going fuzzy around him. His flashbacks to the Great War had been worsening, going back to the first day he spent in the Early Bird waiting for the hit. Now, with the image of the tramp's haunting grimy face staring out from memory, Brand felt his gorge rise. He choked it back and stared into the street until his icy wet foot shouted at him for warmth.

Brand shook himself, focusing on the ground beneath him for balance. He went in a crouch, down the line of barrels to the tattered awning above the machine shop entrance. Voices came from inside, muffled and angry. Brand quietly slid up to the door and pressed an ear against the wood. He caught a few words about the Governor. Whoever was talking had a case of rage big enough to take on an army. Brand's foot felt numb, like it had iced up. He hopped on it and caught movement out the corner of his eye.

Something in the street or just more visions? Brand swiped a hand through the air and felt his fingers drag, peeling away the fabric of the city in thin streaks. Beneath these tears in reality, he saw the glimmering skyline of another cityscape. His breath caught in his throat and he jerked his arm down, bumping his elbow against the door. He held his breath, cursing himself for being careless and thinking he should run for it. But nobody came out. He let his ear rest against the wood of the door again and fell backwards as it was whisked open.

Dark shoes under starched white slacks greeted Brand's eyes, under a voice slick with venom that stabbed icicles into his ears.

"Mr. Mitchell Brand. Of the Chicago Daily Record. Won't you come in? You can rest your feet by our fire."

CHAPTER 15

BRAND THOUGHT ABOUT RUNNING, BUT decided to pass on getting shot in the back. The menacing .45 in Nitti's grip told him that was good thinking. Nitti motioned with the gun, guiding Brand through the foyer and into the shop room in back. Their path took them through bits of glass and scattered ledger sheets. In the shop room, a small furnace burned, giving off radiant heat. A stout chair was positioned facing the furnace mouth. Down to the right, the remains of a machining line sat like a rusting skeleton, draped heavy with cobwebs and blackened here and there by soot. One of Nitti's heavies stepped up to Brand and grabbed him by the lapels, lifting him off the floor. The thug slammed Brand onto the chair in front of the furnace.

In the firelight, Brand caught Nitti's face looking scared, saw the gangster's lips shake as he pulled up a chair and laid his .45 on his knee. His goons stood around them, one of them adding coal to the fire, making the air in front of Brand's face grow hot. The heavy behind him kept his hands on Brand's shoulders.

Sitting there facing his own death, Brand wondered which of the toughs around him had been responsible for Jenkins. With his heart heavy with regret and rage, Brand hoped he'd at least have a chance at getting a shot in before they put him down for keeps.

The thick-necked thug by the furnace put on a heavy pair of gloves and hoisted a metal rod to stir the coals, eyeing Brand with a nasty grin the whole time. Sparks rose up into the air above the furnace mouth. Nitti addressed him and Brand pulled his eyes away from the bird with the metal rod.

"I have spoken with you. Now three times. In just two days. You have a deficit. Do you understand?"

Brand wanted to make a remark about Jenkins evening the score, but Nitti's face told him to play nice if he wanted to play at all.

"Yes, Mr. Nitti," Brand said, his own lip shaking now and threatening to rattle his jaw off his face. "I'm into you for a day, I see."

"You are behind a day. You understand me, right?"

"Yes, Mr. Nitti. I understand. I'm behind a day. I should…"

"You should shut your yap and listen," Nitti shot back at him. Then he looked to the goon standing behind Brand. "*Mattone. Che fai?* Our guest is cold."

The bird pushed forward so that Brand's face was less than a foot from the furnace mouth. Then Thick Neck stuck the metal rod into the furnace again, stirring the coals and causing a spray of sparks and ash to fill the air in front of Brand's face. His eyes stung and watered.

"Mr. Brand. We. Mr. Capone and myself. We have been quite disturbed with your radio show. We find it lacking in certain qualities."

Brand felt Nitti waiting for a reply so he nodded, slowly raising a hand up to wipe the tears from his eyes.

"Of course, you must know. Mr. Capone was arrested this afternoon. This leaves me in a position I had not hoped for. As it means my employer is incapacitated. And so I find myself confronted with a difficulty. You."

Brand turned to look at Nitti and had to blink and shake his head to clear his vision. The gangster kept swimming in and out of focus, like he sat behind a film of quicksilver. Nitti's eyes ran with threads of glimmering light that split the skin of his face. His jaw stretched, lengthening until his narrow chin formed a knife point under his thin lips. He stood up with a rapid flex of his legs and Brand jerked backwards in fright. He fought to keep from screaming as Nitti towered over him. The point of his chin lowered to Brand's face and would stab the newsman in the eye if the mobster bent forward even an inch. In the corners of his vision, Brand saw images of Nitti's victims. The gossamer forms of their bodies swirled in the air, trailing away like embers and sparks rising from the furnace. Brand didn't see Jenkins, but he did see dead men from rival gangs. He saw coppers and business owners who didn't play by The Outfit's rules. He saw women who'd outlived their usefulness as playthings and whose children were nothing more than a burden to the man who'd sired them.

Murder and death swam around Brand's head, sneaking into his lungs with every breath of smoke and soot he drew in. He opened his mouth to say something. He wasn't sure what, but he felt a revulsion and rage at everything Nitti stood for and he had to get it out. As the words rose from his throat, Brand felt strong fingers pressing under his ears, forcing him up close to the furnace again. The heat stung his eyes and tears ran down his cheeks. Brand's heart beat a deafening cadence in his ears as he gulped down the words he'd almost spat out.

"Did you want to say something, Mr. Brand?"

"Mr. Nitti, I … I guess you think it's my fault Ca—" Nitti's fist connected with Brand's jaw.

"You will refer to my employer with respect."

Spitting blood from between his teeth, Brand corrected himself. "Yes, Mr. Nitti. I meant to say Mr. Capone. You think I'm the reason Mr. Capone was arrested. I'm just a newshawk, Mr. Nitti. The

Governor—" Nitti gave Brand another shot across the face, putting stars in front of his eyes. The gangster cuffed Brand behind the ear and tugged his face upward. "Mr. Brand. Who do you think runs this town?"

The mobster's question hung there like a clock ready to strike the hour. Brand wanted to turn his head away, but the heat from the furnace stung his cheeks and he didn't dare turn back to look into that hellish future. He let his eyes drift over Nitti's face. No knife points stuck out of the man's cheeks or jawline. No ghosts of those he murdered swam around his head. Instead of rage or even plain old anger, Brand saw what made Nitti's mouth shake before. It was fear, plain and simple. The gangster's eyes rounded as if terror hid somewhere nearby waiting to strike.

"I asked you a fucking question," he said, wrenching Brand's head and slapping him with his other hand.

"What—?" Brand said, before Nitti slapped him again and harder this time. Brand could still taste blood welling up from his lip and now had another flow coming from inside his cheek.

Nitti hit him again, just a light slap though. He grinned and asked "Who is it? Did you find out? Do you know?" The gangster's lips curled back turning his grin into a sharp-toothed sneer. He grabbed Brand's head in both hands and stared him point blank in the eye. "Who calls the shots in Chicago City?"

"I'm just a newshawk, Mr. Nitti. I'm a reporter. That's all. I don't—"

Nitti wasn't having any of it. He slapped Brand again and then gave him a shot straight across the face that sent the stars spinning off and replaced them with an empty suffocating black. Brand's head slumped forward. His ears filled with a ringing and his vision went blank.

Bombs and artillery shells had the same effect. It just took a few seconds to shake it off, check to make sure your arms and legs were still on right and you hadn't grown any new holes in your chest. Brand managed a weak shake of his head. His ringing ears made room for Nitti's voice and the sound of the shop door opening. A gust of icy wind blew across the floor over Brand's sodden shoes. He felt his toes curl by reflex and then a shiver forced its way up his legs and into the base of his spine.

Brand felt his head jerked back. His vision remained clouded, but he could see a hand moving in front of his mug and then felt a stinging cold all over his face. He smelled and tasted the ash and oil and dirt of the streets all in a wet mash that scraped his skin. A second handful of snow got shoved up his nose before he shook his head clear and had his vision back. Gasping, Brand looked up and saw Nitti smiling beside him and then reaching out to cup Brand under the ear. He gave a firm shake and dug his thumb into Brand's neck then let go. The goon with the gloves had the metal rod in his hands again. Then the one behind him pushed Brand's face at the furnace mouth.

"Mr. Mitchell Brand. I believe you are telling the truth. You know nothing." Nitti's lip had stopped shaking. His face was back to normal, feline and fierce with a set that spelled disaster for anyone who crossed him. "But I did not bring you here to discuss things …."

Nitti brought him here. What'd he mean by that?

"My problem with you is one of disrespect. When I am faced with such a problem. I am forced to provide encouragement. The offending party should not make the same mistake twice. For their benefit, I encourage them. You understand, right?"

Brand nodded slowly, thinking about Jenkins again and unable to keep his tongue this time. "Yeah. I understand you. I'm sure Ross Jenkins understood you just fine, too. You could have just told the kid to keep hush. He would've listened."

Nitti's face dropped from fear to confusion. "Who is Ross Jenkins? I do not know this person. Should I know him?"

"He was one of the kids that worked for me at the Record. Your boys here brought him by my rooms after the gala last night. I get it. You don't want me snooping around about the hit on Valentine's Day. So this is where I get mine now. Well?"

The gangster said a few words in Italian to his boys. They shook their heads, all of them. "Mr. Mitchell Brand, I am afraid you offend with your suspicions. None of these men are to blame for any dead children. I, on the other hand, am offended by your disrespect." Nitti motioned at the man behind Brand and said something in Italian again. Before Brand knew what was happening, the heavy behind him reached down and lifted the newsman's left arm, twisting it up and separating the fingers. The goon kept Brand's arm bent behind his back, holding onto it by the wrist.

"As I was saying, Mr. Mitchell Brand. Disrespect. I believe you understand. Right?"

Brand could only nod. His eyes swam with tears and his heart beat a double time tempo.

"You are behind a day. I encouraged you once yesterday afternoon. Then again in the evening, at the gala. I had nothing to do with this boy named Jenkins, but if his death has helped you correct your thinking, then I am glad for it. Either way. I am done encouraging. You are going to stop talking about The Outfit on your radio show."

Nitti pulled a sheet of paper from his pocket and gave it to Brand.

"Write."

"Write? Write what?"

Nitti slapped the back of Brand's head, pushing his face closer to the maw of the furnace. "You write a fucking goodbye letter." Nitti laughed like a rasp drawn across a chalkboard. Brand made to reach for the paper and instinctively tugged on his left arm. The bird behind him held on tight, squeezing his wrist so hard Brand yelled out.

"I'm left-handed! Goddamit!" he hollered, and then collapsed inside and began whimpering. "I'm left-handed," he sputtered through tears. Brand let his arm hang in the thug's grip and let his chin fall to his chest as he sobbed from the fear. Nitti was on his feet beside Brand, his hand on the newsman's right shoulder. He was talking to the bird behind him, whispers in Italian. Brand felt his arm drop from the thug's grip.

"You may now write the note."

"I'm supposed to write my suicide note?"

"Suicide note?" Nitti said, his face softening. "No. No, tonight you are going to say goodbye for The Outfit. For Mr. Capone and myself. He is indisposed, I believe is what you will say. I and the gentlemen here are leaving Chicago City. You need to tell the people for us. They listen to you for news. You will give them my news. From your airship radio show. And the people who run this town will hear it, too. I am sure of it."

Nitti told him that The Outfit was moving to where the violence of other parties would not intrude upon its legitimate business practices. Brand would also say how sad Al Capone was to hear of the Mayor's death. Between gasps from pain in his freezing foot and the fear that he would be shoved face first into the furnace, Brand got out a report that would cover everything Nitti dictated. He handed the paper to Nitti, who read it and gave it back.

"Now. You'll go back to your gasbag. You'll give that little sermon. And then, *te ne stai a cuccia,*" Nitti said and shrugged, dropping his chin down to his chest with a smirk. "You be a good little dog."

"That's it?" Brand asked. "You're not going to kill me?"

"No, Mr. Mitchell Brand. Somebody might kill you. But it won't be me. Chicago City. She has always been my city. Now, somebody else will own her. I never dance with a woman who has two partners. You understand?"

"I think so, Mr. Nitti. If I get it right, somebody else called the hit yesterday morning. Not Ca—not Mr. Capone. And you're wanting to be gone before that somebody shows up."

"Yes, Mr. Brand. And I want that somebody to know I am gone and to believe it. That is why you are alive. Now, I see that your feet are very wet."

Nitti motioned with his .45 and his goons grabbed Brand before he could make a move. They both gave him a shot in the gut and then a couple slaps around his face. Then Thick Neck held him tight while the other thug got Brand's shoes and socks off and threw them into the furnace. Together they held his feet up to the furnace mouth, making him squirm as the icy wet on his skin gave way to a searing heat. It didn't take long before the soles of Brand's feet were raw and stretched tight from the heat. A stinging pain cut between his toes and his heels felt like they'd been dragged over crushed glass. Finally, Nitti stood up and said "Let him go." He kept the .45 in his paw and waved it to his goons. "*Andiamo.*" The gangsters flung Brand into the chair and stepped away out of his view.

He slumped to the side, holding a hand over chest as he tried to follow his heartbeat back to some kind of safe haven, something like the shelters he found in the trenches when the shells came in waves. Pain radiated up his legs from the ravaged soles of his feet. His gut twisted with fear. He could hear the gangsters' footsteps, but couldn't see them. Brand risked turning his head to the side and saw movement out the corner of his eye. The goons had shuffled off to the foyer, leaving only Brand and Nitti in the open space of the shop floor. A sudden slap across his cheek sent Brand sprawling out of the chair. His hip and shoulder slammed against the cold concrete and he felt terror rising as Nitti's feet approached. The mobster stopped only a pace away. He was close enough to drive a toe of his fancy leather shoes into Brand's eye.

"So. Mr. Mitchell Brand."

The two men stared at each other, Nitti standing upright and looking as shell-shocked as Brand felt. The .45 came up until Brand could see into the hollow blackness of the muzzle. Then Nitti holstered the gun and stood with his hands at his sides, looking knives into Brand's gaze. The ghosts showed up again, spiraling around in the air above the furnace and dancing around Nitti's head like moths.

"You don't want to be one of them. Do you?"

"No. No, Mr. Nitti. I don't."

"Good," Nitti replied, glaring down at Brand. His face ran with quicksilver again and then it was just a face. Just flesh. A hissing like the sound of a tire going flat cut into the night air from outside. Brand heard the goons in the foyer stammering words in

Italian. Nitti shook where he stood. He opened his mouth and a black, oily smoke gusted out to swirl in the air before the gangster's face. Brand shuffled backwards a few feet, anything to put distance between himself and that threatening black cloud that seemed to drip with the purest evil. Nitti's eyes had rolled up in his head and he staggered away from the cloud. It swirled with violence and threat and then swept away into nothingness. Brand shuffled on the floor, watching Nitti. The gangster staggered and caught himself on the chair where Brand had sat. The hissing from outside grew louder. Nitti snapped out of his shock when his boys shouted in alarm. Their screaming filled the shop like glass breaking again and again.

Brand stared into the darkness of the foyer as time slowed down around him, just like it had in the trenches when the screaming had been twice as bad. Nitti reached into his jacket for the .45 and made a few steps toward the foyer. Howls of terror came out of that black pit, echoing around the high ceilinged shop space. The sound of something heavy slapping against something soft. Thick slaps, wet with gore, punctuated the air. Brand thought he heard bones crack. A choking gurgle.

Nitti remained frozen where he stood, pistol in hand, facing the foyer door. The mobster twitched his head back, throwing a glance behind him and into the space behind and above Brand. Nitti's gaze returned to the foyer as a deep, rasping *hhhhhisssss* slashed into the space of the shop. More sounds of bone snapping and flesh tearing came from the foyer.

"No! No, no, no! Non c'é!" Nitti chanted, backing away from the foyer, sending his eyes in every direction as he moved. His feline features contorted with rage and fright, making him look even more feral and vicious. "It's not fair, dammit! You said we'd be clear!"

Brand thought Nitti meant him, but he didn't dare speak up to object or question the mobster. Nitti's attention, and gun, were now aimed at the darkness of the foyer. Brand slid sideways, farther away from sounds coming from the foyer. He had to settle for rolling onto his back. His feet were useless, so he used his hands and scooted on his ass until he put a few more feet between him and the dark space at the edge of the shop room.

Nitti still had his pistol trained on the foyer and kept up with his chanting. Some of it reminded Brand of the Latin he'd heard in churches. Most of it he recognized from the time he'd spent in Chicago City's underbelly. Nitti seemed to remember Brand then. His eyes met Brand's and locked onto them. Nitti's cheeks bunched up under his eyes and his face fell as the hissing grew louder. Brand scooted away faster, turning to crawl, dragging himself along the floor. He got up onto all fours and raced a bumpy course down the length of the shop room, banging his hands and knees against cold concrete and bits of old metal. Behind him he heard Nitti's gun roar in rapid fire underneath a snarling and hissing violence that became a throaty roar. Brand risked a backwards glance and caught sight of Nitti lying on his back, pinned under thick sinew and bristling greasy hairs that hung like needles. That was all Brand saw of the beast. He crawled underneath the machine line and begged death to spare him.

More gunshots rang out, frightening Brand into nearly shrieking. He could hear the thing chewing into Nitti with wet sloppy snarls. At the end of the machine line, the exit door beckoned, taunting Brand with a promise he didn't dare hope would be fulfilled. In the background, the snarls stopped. Brand thought he heard the sound of the front door opening and closing. He risked a look out from his hiding place. Nitti was alone, lying in a mess next to the furnace. The monster was no where in sight. Brand's heart thudded like a gong and he held a hand to his chest, trying to keep the noise from echoing around the room, giving him away. He sent frantic glances in every direction. Where was it? Where'd the thing go?

A man's voice echoed from the other side of the room. Brand shifted his weight against the ironwork of the machining line and slid behind the boiler by the exit door. Brand crouched and dropped forward to let his knees take his weight. A man dressed in a sharp dark suit stepped from the entrance to the foyer. He walked over to Nitti's remains.

"I'm so sorry, Mr. Nitti," the newcomer said. "But, you did bring this on yourself. I recall we agreed to set you up with a safe location after you handled that business on Valentine's Day."

The man squatted down and looked at Nitti's face, almost like he was having a conversation with the corpse.

"Old Man Farnsworth made it easy for us, of course, and I recall you were to be paid for your assistance in that matter as well. What I don't recall is agreeing that you would threaten and then assassinate a public official."

Brand slapped a hand over his mouth when he heard a gurgling reply from the mobster.

"F— fuck you ... goddamned ... f— fucking rat." Nitti said a name, but Brand couldn't catch it.

The whole time Nitti spoke, the G-man held his mouth in a smirk. Brand knew in his gut that the man had to be from the Governor's office even though he didn't wear the standard issue headgear. As Nitti let his final curse out, the G-man stood, turned on his heel, and stepped over to the foyer, vanishing into the darkness beyond the shop room. Nitti gurgled some more and groaned. A moment later, the hissing sound filled the shop again and Brand slunk down to hide in the corner behind the boiler.

Brand stayed still until the slapping and crunching sounds stopped. Scratching sounds followed, then grunts and groans. Then a body falling and something heavy sliding or being dragged across the concrete floor. Brand stayed hidden. The sounds were still on the far side of the room and hadn't come in his direction yet. He waited until silence settled across the barren concrete, shrouding his thoughts along with whatever was left of Frank Nitti.

The room echoed with the soft crackling of the furnace fire. Brand shivered in his niche by the door and cried quietly from the pain, from having been so close to the beast, to have smelled its feral stink mixed with blood. His feet felt like they'd been hammered onto his legs with railroad spikes. He waited. His mind went in and out of dozy thoughts, half-sleep coming and going in his rattled mind. When he couldn't resist the pull of sleep any longer, Brand slid on his hip across the shop floor, back to the furnace.

To distract himself from the pain, he played back his conversation with Nitti. Who could be coming to Chicago City that would be bigger than the Outfit? The G-man? Brand tried to make sense of it, but he was too worked over to concentrate. He sat with his back against an ironwork frame and waited for his feet to stop cursing at him. Across the room, Nitti's shredded corpse filled the air with the stink of death. Wanting only to leave that den of horror, Brand stupidly tried to stand and fell to his knees instantly. He turned his head and retched before passing out.

CHAPTER 16

WHEN BRAND WOKE UP, HIS FEET YELLED at him to get them covered. His jaw yelled at him to get it iced. And his head yelled at him to quit while he was ahead and just wait for the coppers to show up or maybe eat a bullet from Nitti's gun, whichever was quickest. Sliding on his hip, Brand edged closer to Nitti's bloodied remains. The monster was gone, it's acrid musk nowhere that Brand could place. The shop door was open, too, a cold wind blowing in from the street. The G-man wasn't around. Nitti and his gang were ground beef on the shop floor. Brand was broken, scared, and scarred, but he was still a newshawk with a story to tell. After what he'd just seen, he wondered if anyone in Chicago City would listen. Should he mention the monster or not? At least one person in the Mayor's circle had heard of it. He corrected the thought as he closed in on his goal: *the former Mayor's circle.*

He made it to the first of Nitti's legs, near the furnace. The other was halfway to the foyer entrance. The gangster's shoes fit a little loose. Better than tight, Brand thought as he let out a cry of pain when his tortured feet scraped against the leather. He risked standing, holding the chair he'd sat in for support. Nitti's .45 rested against the chair legs. Brand reached down and picked up the gun, checking the chamber. It still had one in the pipe and two cartridges in the magazine. On shaky legs, Brand shuffled in a circle, scanning the shop room for any signs of the monster and doing his best to avoid looking at the rest of Nitti.

It was hard to do. Nitti was all over the place.

The room closed in on Brand, like the trenches had during the worst battles. Walls and floor and ceiling pinched together like a shroud over his face, blackening his vision. He forced his eyes to clear with a fierce shake of his head. That set his jaw to aching even worse. Stumbling in the too large shoes, Brand made his way along the room to the side door. He could have looked for the key, or just gone out the open front door. But he knew what was in the foyer. Brand had seen enough.

The side door creaked open after he'd blown the lock out. It took all three shots, and he held the gun with both of his unsteady hands. The gun fell into the oil-stained dirt of the yard beside the shop and Brand took his first halting steps to freedom and safety. Somewhere between the machine shop and the *Vigilance*, his feet went completely numb from pain or cold, maybe both. Coming to the shop, the trip had taken five minutes at a good clip. The return trip took nearly half an hour with Brand stopping to lean against buildings and lamp posts along the way, doing anything he could to give his dogs a break. Above him, clouds swelled in angry masses of dark gray and near black, reminding him of the roiling fog that blew from Nitti's open mouth before the monster appeared.

At the mooring deck, Brand struggled up the steps, crying out when his numb feet clumsily banged against the icy metal. The shoes helped, but his ravaged soles howled at him with every step. He stood at the base of the airship's ladder, gazing into the open cabin door. Something twitched in his mind, but the pain and horror of what he'd seen took over before he could make sense of his thoughts. His hands were numb, too, and he had to wrap both arms around the ladder to climb it. More than once he ended up pressing his cheeks to the stinging cold metal. Flopping into the cabin, he yelled for Archie to get them moving as he crawled to his desk. There was a smell in the air, something he recognized but couldn't place. He rolled a cigarette and then realized the ship hadn't moved.

Brand let the paper and tobacco drop from his hands. Archie sat in the pilot's seat with his head slumped forward. A dark stain covered the cockpit windows and the controls. Brand thought about tossing the hokum broadcast he'd worked up to satisfy Nitti, but he held onto the paper, dangling it above the waste chute by his desk. Someone was coming to replace Capone's mob. Somebody with a lot of pull and a lot more punch than Capone and the other gangs in Chicago City could ever hope to match. That G-man in the shop. He said Nitti did a good job and then flubbed it when he shot the Mayor. A bad hand played wrong.

Brand picked up the rolling paper and swept the spilled tobacco threads together. He thought about his next play. Everyone around him had bet big and bet wrong. So what should he do? The Mayor had taken down Capone hoping to find better digs. That meant a move to Detroit and to a chair that wasn't vacant yet. The Mayor was a sap, plain and simple. The Governor had contacts in every office from Green Bay around the bend to Rochester; he'd have known about the Mayor's game. Hell, the Governor's boys were at the bust. Taking out Capone might have netted the Mayor a new stenographer, a little extra juice come Christmas. But any gifts would have come with a message to stay put, cool his heels and enjoy the good life he had. Of course, Nitti had seen to it that those messages weren't necessary, and it had cost him big. So why couldn't he have held off on doing Archie?

Brand had promised Nitti the broadcast thinking it was a bluff. With the Governor in the shadows now, Brand knew the broadcast had to go out. It was hokum, but he needed to give the Governor a reason to ignore him. Making himself out to be snowed like the rest of Chicago City was the only play for a man holding a handful of junk.

Good evening, Chicago City. This is Mitchell Brand. I have just received formal notice that The Outfit is leaving the city.

Brand stopped to roll a new cigarette.

The Outfit leadership feels that Chicago City is no longer a place where they may safely conduct business. They have secured a new center for their operations, which, they are sad to announce, will prevent them bestowing any benefits upon our city such as they have in the past. Mr. Capone would also like to express his sadness...

Brand paused, lit his cigarette, and added,

and remorse, for the loss of his dear friend, the Mayor.

One more piece needed fitting in, and he couldn't let it go.

Since the events of yesterday morning, beginning with the Saint Valentine's Day Massacre, Chicago City has seen a lot of killing. A lot of death.

Why were those seven men torn apart in that garage? Why did Josiah Farnsworth take his own life? Why were employees of Mr. Tesla's operation and the Daily Record killed? Why was the Mayor assassinated tonight?

Questions. A lot of them. And this reporter thinks the answer is always the same. It pays to remember that the house always wins.

Stay tuned, Chicago. And stay in touch.

Brand let a few minutes of silence fill the cabin as he finished his smoke, then he thought about tapping out a wire to the police. Turning to stare at Archie again, Brand noticed the unmistakable outline of a revolver on the floor. As he moved to stand, he heard the click of the galley door and in that moment he knew what he'd smelled when he came in.

"Hello, sister."

Emma Farnsworth came a few steps into the cabin. Brand settled back into his chair and let the scent of roses fill the air between them. Her outfit was different than the one she'd had on last night. She hadn't been home, the coppers had checked. So that meant she had a safe place to stay somewhere in town. The way she looked now, Brand figured she'd like nothing better than to be in that safe place again. Her sleeve was torn and her hair hung out in tangles on one side.

"You're okay now, sister," he said as the story came together for him.

She pulled it in after a few more sobs and stood up straight. Brand met her gaze and watched her eyes go cold.

"Looks like I was wrong. I thought Nitti had his boys do Archie. But it was you."

"I was going to kill Nitti for what he did to Dad. When he shot the Mayor, I saw the *Vigilance* above. I got here right after you left. At first I waited, but you didn't show and I didn't want to lose Nitti so I came up. Your pilot let me in. He told me you were going to get the scoop on the Saint Valentine's Day killers. He said I could wait for you to get back, but first I had to give him a little sugar. He tried to kiss me and I turned away. So he got rough. He had me against the cabin door and said I could take a jump or give him a tumble."

Brand wasn't surprised Archie had done it. He had a dirty past and now Brand knew how dirty. He wasn't surprised she'd done it either. Nobody deserves being forced into anything. That didn't mean murder was the way to solve it, but some things can't be forgiven. And some things can force a person to do the unforgivable.

"Listen, sister. I don't make the laws, but—"

"I had no choice. He was calling his pals. He was on the radio."

Brand stood up and motioned to the door she'd come through.

"C'mon. We should get out of sight."

Brand struggled on his feet, sucking in air and staggering against the cabin wall. Emma recoiled when she took in Brand's condition, looking him up and down with a bent eye.

"I ran into some trouble on that last story. C'mon," he nodded at the doorway again and she stepped aside so he could go through first. She followed him a few steps into the darkened hall. Brand looked her in the eye.

"Tell me everything. Make it quick. Coppers'll be swarming this district before too long."

Her eyes shot open when he mentioned the law, but she pulled herself together and gave him the story. The first few lines of it anyway.

"It's like I said. I came out and he was calling his pals."

"Yeah, you said. How'd you get from Archie hanging you out the cabin door to being back here? How'd you get behind him with a pistol he didn't know you had? You played him, and it worked out in your favor. But now we're stuck unless you've got an ace up your sleeve."

Emma stood back from him. She looked at him hard, with eyes like ice. "I told him I needed to freshen up first, so he let me go back to the washroom. I had the gun in my handbag for Nitti. When I came out he was on the radio. He was talking to one of Nitti's boys and saying he'd take care of you after you gave that last broadcast. Then he said for the fellas to come over to join the fun. I knew what he meant. I didn't know what I was going to do next, but I knew he'd pay for whatever happened. He was laughing when I shot him."

Brand thought about what Emma had just told him. Now he knew Archie'd been playing both sides all along. He'd sold him out to Nitti. Archie had done a stretch for running liquor after the war, but he played it off like it wasn't him being connected. Brand never figured him for being in that deep. But just like Capone, the Mayor, and even Brand himself, Archie had bet on a losing hand.

A voice came from outside the cabin, pleading and half-hushed, like the speaker wanted to stay hidden.

"You expecting company?" Brand asked.

"It's …." She turned and went to the cockpit, scooping up the revolver and holding it down by her leg. "Go see who it is, Brand."

"You want to try that again, sister? I've had one too many gats pushed in my face tonight already. How about you tell me who you think is out there and then I'll see about saying hi?"

"It's Eddie. My …."

Brand figured it then. She had a man nobody knew about,

someone she wanted to keep hidden. Someone she probably made eyes at while he played horn on the jazz stage.

"Eddie'd be your negro then, is that it?"

"Eddie Collins," she said, lifting the gun to aim at him. "Now go see if it is him."

"And if it is?"

"Tell him to come in."

Brand let his mouth form a sneer to show how he felt about it, then shook his head and chuckled. "Well why not, right? It's everybody's day to point a gun at Mitchell Brand. Quick one-two and tell him what to do. Watch him jump, folks," he kept up his bitter muttering as he took halting steps to the cabin door, Nitti's shoes sliding around on his ruined feet. Outside, a dark figure hunched in the hollow of a covered waiting area at the edge of the deck. As Brand watched, the figure, clearly a man, poked out from hiding and cupped his hands around his mouth. A few plaintive words came into the cabin.

"... please, Lovebird ... gotta go ...."

"I'd say that's him, Miss Farnsworth. That is, if you go by the name of Lovebird."

She stepped closer, still holding the pistol at him.

"Tell him."

"Stop waving that thing in my face."

They held the stalemate, eyes meeting across the battle lines between them. Brand wasn't sure she'd shoot him, but he wasn't sure she wouldn't either. "I'll make a deal with you, Miss Farnsworth. You put that thing down, aim it somewhere else at least. Then I'll tell your jazz man to come up. Otherwise, fire away and tell him yourself. And have fun explaining it all to the coppers when they track you down."

Her face still burned with anger, but she lowered the revolver. It stayed in her hand, by her leg. Brand leaned out the door into the snowy night. The figure stepped out and then ducked back into hiding.

"It's okay," Brand called down. "She's up here."

Emma pushed to stand beside him. The man came out of hiding and darted looks to either side before launching up the ladder in a hurry. Brand helped him on board and stood back to give the lovers room to embrace.

"I don't mean to be rude, Miss Farnsworth, but we need to figure out what we tell the coppers. Then you and your friend might want to think about scooting, and pronto."

"Who's this?" the negro asked, eyeing Brand with a mix of fear and suspicion.

"His name's Brand, and he's nobody we need to worry about. Is he?" she said, looking hard at Brand. She still had the revolver in her mitt.

"No, you don't have to worry about me. The last thing you need to worry about is me blabbing on the radio about Miss Farnsworth and her negro."

"He's not just a negro," she said. Her face shifted from cold fire to burning rage. "He's a man and a musician. He's a woman's son and a girl's older brother. So he's dark skinned! What of it? We're in love and that's all you need to know about it. That's all anybody ever needed to know about it, but they're all too busy knowing that color leaves a stain that won't wash out."

Emma's eyes searched Brand's face. He kept his thoughts on the QT, letting her press her point as far as she liked.

"Now you know why I hate you and every newsman who ever stuck a camera in my face."

"Keep your fire for someone else, sister. You got me figured wrong if you think I have any beef with your choice of lips for kissing. A man measures up for me with what he does, not what he looks like."

"You expect me to believe this won't end up on the front page?"

Brand felt his own anger rising and let it out. "That's the problem with you society types. You grow up hearing you're the most important people in town and one day you start believing it. Then you can't stop believing it. Well believe this, sister. I wouldn't put a story about you on the front page if I owned the Daily Record."

"I should—"

The negro came to Brand's rescue just as Emma raised the gun. He put a hand on her arm and the other around her shoulders. The man turned to look Brand in the eye.

"Name's Eddie Collins," he said. "People ain't my friends call me Mr. Collins."

"Pleased to meet you, and thanks," he said and nodded at Emma. "If you're ready to play nice, we need to work out a story about what happened here tonight. Otherwise all of our names are going to be mud with a capital M for murder."

Emma and Eddie had no reply to that, so Brand went with his only idea.

"I can tell the coppers I came up and found him like this. Our one problem is that you used your father's gun."

"How did you—"

"It wasn't in the old man's office. And the coppers can add as well as anyone, including me. They'll match the slug they pulled out of the wall in your dad's office to the one that went through the cockpit window. We can hope they don't find it, and maybe they won't with all this snow on the ground and more coming. But the coppers know their stuff, and one thing they know best is how to find evidence that's just waiting for them to pick up."

"So what? They can't prove I took the gun."

"That's true. They can't, and I sure as hell won't help them. But we have to expect they'll be looking for you. You disappeared the night your old man cashed in, and his gun disappeared, too." For a moment, Brand thought about telling Emma he'd seen her father. But the tension between them kept his tongue calm. Now was the time for facts, not fairy tales.

"They're probably after you as a person of interest, and if they find you with that gat, they'll lay a charge of concealing evidence, which'll lead to murder once they match up the slugs like I said. Our one safe bet is this. The Outfit's done in Chicago City; they're over with and I know why. The game that's coming to replace them won't waste a chance to swat me like a fly if I connect them to this, but I can steer it so Nitti's crew takes the fall for you shooting Falco."

Emma's eyes rounded at his words. She stepped closer, her face half lit by a weak glow coming in from beyond the cabin windows.

"What are you talking about? Who's coming? Is it someone involved with Dad? What do you know?"

Brand weighed his options. She still had that pistol in her hand. A hand that had begun shaking while she made her demands. So he gave them both the story. How Archie had brought them in and sent Brand off on Nitti's trail. He told them about his conversation with Nitti, what he'd been put through, what he'd been told to put out on the airwaves, and why. He left out the part about the monster and the G-man though. Best to keep that under wraps in case somebody higher up got their hands on Miss Farnsworth and her jazz man and got them to talk about this little chat in the airship. Instead, Brand told them Nitti's boys had thrown him out in the snow after roasting his feet for him, that he'd passed out and, when he came to, that the gangsters were all dead inside the building.

"So that's where I was while you were putting Archie to sleep. I'll tell the coppers all of it, just like I told you, except I'll say one of Nitti's boys went out at the beginning and came back right before they tossed me out the door. That'll match up with my thinking when I got here, that it was one of them who did Archie. It isn't airtight, not by a long shot, but it's the best we can do, unless you've got—"

All three of them ducked down at the sound of a patrol boat sailing overhead. A searchlight cut across the street beside them and tracked down to the machine shop where it stayed, lighting up the building and the yard beside it.

"They're here. Go on. Get moving. Get out of sight and stay there."

Emma and Eddie climbed down from the airship; their feet hit the mooring deck as sirens whined from farther down the street. Brand watched them take cover as two police sedans raced past the mooring deck. In the coppers' wake, two figures sneaked down the stairs to the shadows below. Brand went to the telegraph at his desk. He waited for the lights of Emma's car to swing around before tapping out a wire. He hit the last stop as Emma and her lover rolled away down a side street, disappearing into the night.

CHAPTER 17

DETECTIVE WYNES REPLIED TO BRAND'S WIRE and showed up a few minutes later. A team of gurneymen followed to clean up the mess Archie left in the cockpit. Two uniformed officers popped in when they were done. Brand let out a breath he'd been holding when Wynes confirmed that no G-men were en route. "They're handling whatever happened in the machine shop down the way. You two," Wynes said to the coppers. "Take a look around." The officers set to inspecting the airship, starting with the quarters in back and the galley. Brand sat at his desk and let them work. He bristled when they asked him to stand so they could rifle his desk. But compliance was the only card he had left to play, so he stood on shaky legs and limped off to the side.

"What's with the gimpy act, Brand?" Wynes asked.

Brand took a breath and told Wynes he'd start at the beginning. "I was racked out in my bunk. Archie had us overhead during the Mayor's speech, said he'd caught news of Capone getting picked up and figured the news would be at City Hall. Then Nitti shot the

Mayor and Archie followed Nitti's car this way. That's his hideout in the machine shop, by the way. Or it was."

"And you didn't think to send word our way. You're looking at an obstruction charge, Brand."

"I would have called it in, but I like I said, I was asleep in the back when Nitti shot the Mayor. Archie didn't wake me up until we were docked here. I couldn't very well call in a story I couldn't prove yet, could I?"

"You mean you wanted to get the scoop first, and then you'd have the decency to inform the authorities."

Brand sniffed at Wynes' jab and reached for his tobacco and papers. Wynes let him roll one up and get it lit before working on him again.

"So what's the story here, Brand? Didn't like the way Falco handled this girl so you shot him?"

"Yeah, and then I called you and the boys here to come by and make sure I did a good job of it."

"Cut the funny stuff. That kind of talk'll get you locked up, Brand, and I'm still not ready to drop the obstruction."

Brand had another retort primed and ready to fire, but he held back and gave Wynes the story he'd worked out with Emma and Eddie. He got to the part about seeing the tramps pop in and out of thin air and almost slipped up, but he kept his cool and related his ordeal with Nitti.

"They tossed me out with the broadcast in my coat pocket and no shoes on my feet. I passed out for a bit. They'd worked me over pretty good. When I came to I went back in and—"

"You went back inside after they threw you out? What for?"

"My feet were freezing or on fire, I couldn't tell which. I figured they'd lit out of the place anyway when I saw the doors hanging open. When I got in there…" Brand shook his head and let his eyes drop the floor.

"Yeah? What'd you see, Brand?" Wynes had a sinister smile playing across his mug, and for the second time in as many days Brand wished he'd had more practice playing poker. Facing off against

Wynes had always been a trick. Brand steeled his jaw and let h
relax before saying, plain as day, "I saw something no man sh
ever see twice. I'd already seen it over there. Bodies in a tangle w
pieces missing from both ends and all points in between. It wa
worse than the hit on Valentine's Day."

"Oh, yeah. The hit on Valentine's Day. You know, every fella with a badge has a theory about that story you put out. Something about pink elephants stepping on your neck, making it so you can't see straight because you're too busy thinking sideways. Of course, the people trust you, Brand. You're always telling them what they need to know."

Brand felt the heat in his belly rising into his throat, choking off any attempt he might have made to reply. Wynes dropped the grin and got serious again. "So, you go in looking for some shoes. The crooks are all dead. You picked up Nitti's shoes?"

"Yeah," Brand said, unable to prevent the sneer from creeping across his face.

"And then you hot-footed it back here and found Falco shot. I still like you for it, but let's hear what you've got to say in your defense. Who did Falco?"

"Had to be that bird from Nitti's crew. The one who left when they started working on me. He came back just in time to pitch me out the door."

Wynes seemed to buy it, but he smelled something and let Brand know it. "All right, Brand. Stick around, and be ready to answer more questions. When we find the slug that took Falco's brains on a joyride, I'll be in touch. One'll get you twenty it's got a match somewhere, and my money's on that somewhere being somewhere you've been."

Brand sniffed and wiped a thumb under his nose. The two coppers finished searching the ship and reported to Wynes they'd found nothing, except for the bottle Brand kept in his desk.

"Contraband, Mr. Brand," Wynes said. "We'll have to take this back to the precinct and we might as well take you with it. C'mon." Wynes reached a hand to help Brand to his feet, lifting him by the

.n and helping him over to the cabin door. One of the officers preceded him down the ladder and the other followed. A patrol boat had come alongside the *Vigilance* and tow cables connected the two ships. The coppers released the mooring lines and took Brand off the deck to their sedan waiting below. Brand stared out the window and watched the *Vigilance* follow in the smaller patrol ship's wake. He wondered if he'd ever see her again.

CHAPTER 18

BRAND MISSED THE WEEKEND EDITIONS because he spent the days going in and out of sleep in between rubbing Novocream on the soles of his feet. And that was after Wynes grilled him so much that Brand thought he should be rubbing steak sauce on his feet instead of the cream. Even so, he thought he'd hear something that might explain what was happening in the city. The Mayor had been shot, Capone was under wraps. That sort of news should have made the rounds, but the street outside Brand's rooms stayed quiet through the snowstorm on Saturday and grew quieter still in the gray mists of Sunday.

When Brand stepped into Chief's office on Monday morning, he was prepared for a chewing he'd never forget. But his boss had nothing to say. He just handed over a bulletin without even looking up from a stack of papers on his desk. The papers all had a symbol at the top that matched the one on the bulletin.

"Every thirty minutes. That's all we got for today. Just keep it going. I'll let you know if it changes."

Brand didn't stick around to ask questions. He'd seen Chief in low moods before. This one beat them all, so he just made his way down to the broadcast booth, looking over the bulletin as he rode the elevator. By the time he hit the fourth floor his jaw and neck felt tight, clenched to contain his rage. The page had the Governor's seal at the top and bore the address *Ministry of Public Information, Chicago City.*

Brand stopped with his hand on the doorknob of the broadcast booth. The sound engineer stuck his head out.

"Mr. Brand? We're supposed to be on the air."

"Yeah? Keep the mic warm for me, why don't you."

The engineer sniffled and whipped back into his cabinet. The sliding door closed behind him with a sharp *click* and Brand saw the lights in the broadcast booth flicker twice, signaling everything was a go. He let them flash on and off again before going inside and taking his seat behind the mic.

Ladies and Gentlemen, this is Mitchell Brand with the ...

The page read *Ministry for Public Information*, but Brand couldn't get his tongue around those words just yet.

... with the Chicago Daily Record. Martial law is in effect in Chicago. I repeat. Martial law is in effect. The Mayor's assassination has forced the Governor's Office to assume control. This will ensure an orderly transition to new leadership. Curfew will begin at ten-thirty tonight. All citizens are to remain indoors until five-thirty tomorrow morning. That is all.

Brand shut off the mic and pitched the bulletin down the waste chute behind him. As he turned back to the mic, Chief slid the door open and gave Brand a look that told him he'd better stick to the script next time. He had a copy of the bulletin held out in his left hand. When Brand didn't take it right away, Chief tossed it at him and let it fall to the floor. Brand got the message loud and clear, but Chief wanted to make sure it stuck.

"The Daily Record doesn't exist anymore, Mitch. Got it?"

Before Brand could get anything out of his mouth, Chief turned on his heel and was gone. Brand snapped up the page from the floor and hit the hall in a flash, catching up to his boss at the elevator.

"What gives? The Governor's Office isn't here to help establish new leadership. They are the new leadership. You and me both know it. We've never heard of any Ministry of Public Information before because until this morning there wasn't any such thing."

"Mitch, this isn't coming from me. Just go back into that booth and stick to the page in your hand. Every half hour unless you want to try on the city's jewelry. They've got a set of bracelets for anyone doesn't toe the line like they're told. Chances are I've got a phone call waiting for me at my desk, and it'll be all I can do to convince the guy on the other end that you're ready to play ball." Chief snarled out the last few words.

Brand stared at his boss, his old friend from the trenches of the Great War. It never does to throw a punch at a memory like that, so Brand turned around and stalked back to the broadcast booth with the bulletin in his hands.

"Load of damn hokum," he muttered and took his seat behind the mic. He knew that for a fact even if he couldn't prove it. But what good would that do for people on the other end of the wire? They were ready to believe almost anything Brand had to say, and he was stuck with nothing to say but what was printed on the page in front of him.

That is all.

Brand knew the bulletins weren't all the Governor had to say. At the bottom of the page he read a warning in red ink. It ordered no transmissions or broadcasts other than this one and threatened the penalties of *sequestering* or *internment* for violation of the order.

Below that, Brand saw the words *Further instructions to follow.*

Chief came down an hour later with a fresh cup of coffee, spiked from his desk bottle. Brand still didn't have more than two words for his boss, but Chief quietly slipped away before Brand got the second one out, leaving the newsman sitting there with hooch and a curse burning his tongue. He swallowed both and gave the bulletin again a minute later.

After a day of this, Brand felt like he was just waiting for the moment when a G-man would come in to say he'd given his last ever broadcast. Late in the day, Brand got pulled off the mic, but it was Chief who did it. When he came into the broadcast booth at six on the hour, Chief looked like he'd gone a few rounds with a bottle in between bawling his life away. His eyes were red and puffy and his cheeks were slick with the stain of sadness. Chief's nose wrinkled and his bottom lip trembled with every word.

"I just got the order to stop the bulletins, Mitch. You can go home. If you want to."

Brand tossed the bulletin page down the waste chute behind him for the second time.

"What's this about? If you got the scoop, how about letting an old pal in on the joke. What does the Governor's Office know about the news?"

"Somebody thinks they know enough. They're replacing me tomorrow, Mitch. Some bird named Jameson Crane."

Chief turned away and walked a shuffling gait back to the elevator. Brand watched him go and then stormed down the hall to the washroom where he let a few tears out in between shouts of rage. Could this be happening? Chicago City turning into a jailhouse town? Sure there were no bars on the windows and you could walk free down the street, at least for now. But putting a muzzle on the news like this meant bigger changes than Brand had expected.

He'd got his questions answered though. The Governor's Office ran the show, and they'd planned every move with precision. But what did they want with the city? What would make the Great Lakes Governor want to take control of Chicago City when he already had Detroit under wraps?

Later that evening, Brand stewed on those questions while he emptied his own desk bottle. When that failed to improve his mood, Brand stormed out of his office and upstairs to the print room. He stood there, staring at the Brackston auto-press. The machine would never churn out news again. Just whatever the new leadership saw fit to pour all over the people. It took a while, but Brand managed to jimmy a printing drum loose at one end. The pin he'd removed fit snugly into a recess between the platen and ink rollers. As satisfying

as it was, the act of sabotage didn't cheer him up. Looki.
doors to the mooring deck, he saw the empty stretch of*lt the*
where the *Vigilance* should be tethered.   ete

"*She's a crime scene now, Brand,*" Wynes had told him
wanted to protest, but without a pilot what good was an aii
Brand could have flown the ship himself; he'd had some tim.
the helm over there. Not enough to qualify him for flying throu;
Chicago City's airspace though. Too many hazards: radio beacons
the lawman's silver pigs, and the few civilian craft that took the air
now and then. In his mind he imagined the shackled bulk of the
Vigilance swaying softly in the gathering flurries. His mind saw her
just as she had been two nights ago when Brand struggled up the
ladder, his feet half blistered and flopping around in a pair of shoes
taken from a dead gangster.

He thought about that night and how it ended. The ghosts of
Nitti's victims swirling around the mobster's head. The monster.
Nitti and his boys torn to pieces. Through the whole ordeal, Brand
had been helpless to change his circumstances. He bristled at the
same feeling of helplessness as it swelled in his throat. He wanted to
smash the Auto-press, but he'd have needed a bazooka to do more
than just dent the thing. And his fingers already ached from the
workout he'd given them monkeying with the drums and rollers.

Slamming the loading doors open, Brand stepped outside, letting the chill blow across his face, chattering his teeth. He pulled his
collar up and snugged his hat down. His eyes locked on the space
where the *Vigilance* should be. Brand stopped short and felt the cold
against his cheeks, felt his watering eyes sting in the icy wind. The
emptiness at the edge of the deck called to him. He took another
step and heard a scream on the wind. He looked up just in time to
see a dark shape plummeting down from above. Brand recognized
Chief's face in the seconds before jumping aside and clapping both
hands over his ears.

CHAPTER 19

THE LINES WERE TIED UP SOMETHING FIERCE, but Brand finally got a call through to the police. Detective Wynes came by with a small patrol boat. Then gurneymen came to haul away Chief's body. Wynes took Brand aside and got his statement before taking him down to the precinct anyway.

"New protocols, Brand," Wynes said as his eyes took in the heavy ink stains on the newsman's hands and shirtsleeves.

At the precinct house, Brand confirmed his statement about Chief's high dive while he and Wynes traded sips of the desk sergeant's best attempt at watery joe. Then Wynes asked about the night Archie Falco had been shot. Brand stuck true to his story, saying he'd arrived to find Archie's brains on display.

"Uh-huh. You know we found the slug, Brand. It had a brother in our evidence room. Any guess as to where the second one came from?"

Brand shook his head, using every muscle to hold his face up and keep it out of his shoes. Wynes stared back at Brand from across the desk.

"The wall in Old Man Farnsworth's office. Seems that the same gun has been used to redecorate the insides of two men's heads. That gun is missing. And so is Miss Emma Farnsworth." With each word, Wynes grew more wolflike, hunching in his seat, jutting his jaw. Brand resisted the urge to shrink back from the copper.

"So I'm wondering where Farnsworth's little girl is, and I'm also wondering if overnight maybe you decided it would be a good idea to give me a reason to forget the obstruction charge."

"You trying to strong-arm me, Wynes? You can't prove the obstruction any better than I can prove what I saw in that machine shop, and we both know it."

"Don't try that bet, Brand. You're holding junk. Your face told me the second you sat down. So I'm asking again. Where's the Farnsworth broad? Here's a hint. I get she's in with some smoke. I saw them together outside the gala the other night."

Brand wasn't ready for that and his face nearly split wide open, spilling out every detail of the conversation he'd had with Emma and her jazz man in the *Vigilance* that night. But he ran a thumb under his nose and pulled his thoughts in fast.

"I've never seen the guy. But I overheard Miss Farnsworth talking to some people at the gala. She mentioned an Emmett or Enos, something that sounded like her name."

"Emmett and Emma. Sounds sweet. Almost good enough to be true. Where are they, Brand?"

"I don't know, and if you think—"

"Yeah, if I think. Now try this. If you think you're off the hook on this, think again. This case is my way out of the bullpen and up to a chair in central. I'm not missing that train, Brand. I'm going to find her, and if I find out that you knew where she was, you'll get accessory to murder. Now what's with the dirty fingers tonight?"

"Eh?" Brand said, shocked by Wynes' sudden change in direction. "Oh, well," Brand said, rubbing his fingers. "I guess I got a little angry about how things are going at the Record now. Made a mess in my office. I'll have to clean that up tomorrow morning."

Wynes seemed okay with that story at least. Like clockwork, the copper shifted back to his earlier line of questioning.

"You know," Wynes said, "they're picking her old man's place apart. Saw it this morning. The plant's been shut down. Bet you didn't know that. Wonder why you're not freezing to death in here?"

"Yeah," was all Brand could think to say. Without the Farnsworth plant putting out steam, how was Chicago City still lit up and heated? The Brauerschift operation? Wynes had the answer, of course, and handed it over with an extra side of smug.

"Mr. Tesla's towers are up and running. Came online yesterday morning. Old Farnsworth left everything to his foreman, but he hasn't been located and is presumed missing. So it was a quick one-two and the operation is shut down. No need for it anymore. Got a wrecking crew coming in later this week I hear."

"What about the Brauershift outfit? They just opened last year and weren't doing too shabby. And Lane-Hartley's gas plant. What about them?"

"All of them, Brand. Shuttered or about to be. But that's on the QT and you didn't hear from me anyway."

Brand wanted to ask where Wynes got it from, but a stenographer trotted up and deposited a stack of reports on the copper's desk. As she turned away, Wynes reached for her wrist. She spun around and faced him, looking like hunted game and poised to backpedal as soon as he released her.

"What's this?" Wynes asked the girl.

She took a moment to get the words from her throat to her lips, and her mouth shook around the first few syllables.

"Re- reports. Reports for the Underminister. You're supposed to sign off and record them before he does."

Wynes let her go, sneering and then flashing a look of hatred at the stack of papers on his desk. The girl took the opportunity to flee.

"You know, Wynes," Brand said, unable to resist a dig. "You keep doing that with your mouth and your face will stay that way. Sage advice from Mother Brand herself."

"Yeah, I heard. I see you didn't listen either."

"Hard to listen to a woman who isn't around," Brand shot back, bristling.

"Uh-huh. Save your crying for someone else, Brand. I got work to do," Wynes said, lifting a page of notes and jamming them into a slot in a metal box on his desk. The machine *whirred* and then gave a short chime. Wynes pulled the page out and grabbed the next one on the stack.

"Say, what is that thing?" Brand asked.

"This?" Wynes said, jerking a thumb at the machine. "It's another one of Mr. Tesla's gadgets. One I could do without." The machine chimed again and Wynes yanked out the page he'd inserted. "Since it got dropped off this morning it's been my new partner."

He repeated the jamming in, waiting, yanking out procedure as he spoke. "It gets to sit here *jam* all day while I'm on my beat. Then I get to come back *chime* and make nice *yank* with it until it's time to head home. Problem is, *jam* by the time I'm done, it's time to get up and come to the precinct house again *chime*. So I'm thinking of setting up a cot *yank* behind my desk. That way *jam* I won't have to worry about the Underminister getting on my case." *Chime. Yank.*

Brand had watched the whole episode with disinterest, but his eyes snapped open when Wynes mentioned his boss' new title. The girl had said it, too.

"Underminister? You're telling me the Governor's getting into the police business, too?"

"I'm not telling you anything, Brand. And you got nothing I want to hear. Beat it."

Brand took a last sip of the coffee then put on his hat and stood to leave. Wynes had a few more words for him though.

"Curfew starts up in about twenty minutes. Doubt you'll find a cab around here this time of night, so make like the wind, hey?"

"Couldn't set me up with a police escort, could you, Wynes? I am here on official business."

When Wynes didn't bat an eye, Brand took a step forward. "I said—"

"Go on and blow, Brand. Fast."

Brand stood still, weighing a decision and the chance he'd make it to the door. He uncurled his fist and stepped as lively as his sore feet would allow. Brand made his way down the street, dodging slicks of ice and puddles on the pavement. The first patrol boats had already begun circling the precinct and surrounding neighborhoods. Their bullhorns hung heavy, like wasp nests, ready to alert Chicago City that curfew would begin soon. Brand knew it'd be a trick getting back to his rooms. Even without the searchlights that fell without warning, slicing the pavement into rafts on a pitch dark sea.

CHAPTER 20

BRAND SHOOK FROM THE COLD EVEN THOUGH he'd worn his overcoat. Snow flurries stung his cheeks as we went. His feet cried for relief after two blocks, so he stopped in an alleyway, slipped off his shoes and socks, and smeared more Novocream onto the cracked red skin of his soles. A few minutes later, Brand laced up his shoes and made for his rooms. The curfew bell rang out from the patrol boats above as he stepped out of the alley.

"Twenty minutes," Brand grumbled. "Wynes, you stinking rat." He picked up his pace, trotting and skipping when he could, dodging around the gas lamps on the street, but his feet screamed at him again after the third block. No way could he keep moving at this speed. He ducked into a side street off the main stem and grabbed another breather in an alley. He was almost out of the cream.

Searchlights stabbed down all over the city. Brand watched them snap on and off, giving away the position of patrol boats hidden in the cloudy night. He got his shoes back on and stood. "Slow but sure, Brand. Just keep out of sight," he whispered to himself as he moved. "Slow but sure."

He made it to Printer's Row by sticking to small streets and alleyways, and he thought his luck might hold after all. But at the station he had to pull up short and duck behind a trash barrel. A jeep blocked the roadway. Two guards stood beside it, holding rifles and smoking. They wore thick coats, gloves, and heavy boots against the cold. And they had a spotlight mounted on the jeep. Creeping back the way he'd come, Brand snuck down the last alley on his path. Which way to go? Back down his path or risk getting spotted by the soldiers in the street? Thinking of how warm his feet wouldn't be if he had to sleep outside, Brand figured he had no choice but to try for his rooms, and that meant the street. Maybe the soldiers would show him their backs if he waited long enough. After two steps toward the alley mouth, Brand caught a shuffling sound behind him. A foul smell of human filth came to his nose as the shadows breathed out a filthy tramp pushing a flimsy bicycle with two flat tires. The man muttered to himself and pushed the bike as if he'd walk right by Brand, and he did. As the tramp passed, Brand caught his mutterings.

"Storytime, storytime. Got no story, got no time."

Without thinking, Brand's hand shot out and grabbed the tramp's shoulder. The man startled and spun around to stare Brand in the eye. It wasn't Larson, but the only difference Brand could see was that this guy had a smaller nose and he kept his face shaved somehow.

"You…" Brand didn't know what to say to the man. Was he like Larson and Old Man Farnsworth? Would he pull the city aside and disappear where he stood?

"Got no time, Brand. No time. Sorry friend. It's the end."

"How do you know my name?"

The tramp moved to push his bike out of the alley and Brand tried to stop him, but his fingers were weak and stiff in the cold and he couldn't grip the man's grimy coat. The tramp went on, muttering to himself again in the same sing-song cadence, like he heard a jazz beat in his head.

Brand called after him in a throaty whisper. "Wait. There are soldiers out there."

The tramp turned to look at Brand over his shoulder. "And they can see me, they can? Think so, Brand? Think you can?" The guy pushed his bicycle into the night and disappeared around the corner. Brand rushed forward to follow. He stopped at the alley mouth and checked if the soldiers had their spotlight on. They didn't, so Brand ducked low and scooted down the street after the tramp. The guy was fast for a stumbling bum. He'd made it to the next block by the time Brand was close enough to smell him. The tramp slipped into another alley and Brand pushed himself to follow. He skidded to a halt when a scream cut the night apart, followed by snarling and roaring from the direction the tramp had gone. Brand shivered and knew he should run back the other way, leave the tramp to his fate. But the soldiers were back there, and they'd be coming this way soon enough to investigate. Another scream ripped Brand's attention from the street and back to the alley mouth. He felt his legs moving, taking him step by step closer to the alley, closer to finally seeing the monster that had haunted the city since Valentine's Day morning.

The sound of snapping bones came to Brand's ears. A gurgling followed, and then just a heavy panting, a throaty breathing like a rasp drawn across pavement. Brand stopped in his tracks when the breathing ceased. It must have smelled him. The thing was going to come out of the alley and tear him apart. He had to run, but how? Even if his feet weren't in tatters inside his shoes, how could he hope to escape the monster?

Brand had his mind made up for him when a roar cut the night and he heard the monster moving from the alley, knocking aside trash barrels that clattered against the alley walls. Brand turned and ran not caring anymore about patrol boats or soldiers with spotlights and guns. He ran, as fast as his tortured feet would carry him. For a short stretch of time, he thought he'd escaped. He couldn't hear anything behind him. Had he imagined it? Was he just cracking up? A roar from behind Brand told him all he needed to know. He pressed on, sliding around the next corner and nearly tumbling into the street. The roaring behind him turned to an almost feline hissing, as if the monster perceived a threat. Brand couldn't deny his urge to turn around. What he saw drew him up short and sent him skidding into a barber's pole.

A tramp on a bicycle slid around on the snowpacks a block behind Brand. The tramp shot frightened glances over his shoulder to the monster behind him. Brand could only see a large dark shape and patches of greasy gray pelt picked out in the dim glow of the streetlights. He got moving again, running and turning to watch his own path through the snow. He slipped leaving the sidewalk and went down on his hands and knees. As he stood, he felt the air shake around him. He dove to the left and crashed against a storefront as the tramp whipped out of the night air, throwing it aside like a curtain to Brand's right. The tramp grabbed Brand by the collar and pulled him like a rag doll onto the bike. Brand's heart thumped a drumbeat in time to their motion away from the monster.

They moved a lot faster than any bicycle Brand had ridden before. Looking down he saw they weren't on any kind of bike he'd seen before, either. They sat astride a gleaming ironwork machine. A thick chain ran from a bulk of shining blackened metal that Brand and the bum straddled. He figured it to be the motor. The chain disappeared into a metal shroud that concealed most of the rear wheel. The front wheel hung between two silvery rods that connected to the handlebars. As they flew, glinting sparks shot out from beneath the wheel. It spun like a dynamo above the surface of the street. He opened his mouth to ask a question, but swallowed his words when the tramp spoke close to Brand's ear.

"I'm getting you out of this, Mitch. Hold on."

Hearing Chief's voice coming from the filth and grime behind him, Brand decided now was as good a time as any to let the night have the final say. He closed his eyes and held on tight to the handlebars, putting his hands between Chief's greasy woolen mittens.

Behind them, the monster's growls and hissing faded and disappeared. After what felt like a few seconds, they'd reached Dearborn Station. Chief brought them to a crawl and stopped, the motor of the strange bike quietly humming down to a steady drone and going silent.

Brand turned in his seat to regard the man behind him. He took in the heavy duster Chief wore, the torn and lopsided hat, and the threadbare mittens. He would have taken in more details of his friend's appearance but the world around him got his attention instead. They'd pulled up outside of Brand's rooms sure enough. But the sky and city glowed like nothing Brand had seen before. The sky rolled in waves of black and reddened clouds, flames burst forth here and there, lightning, too. The streets were paved in layers of earth and cobble and asphalt. Brand knew the city had been around long enough to have multiple layers on each road, but to see them all at once like this... he struggled to take it all in. The whole city had the same layered look, like every building that had ever been erected still stood in place, even with others on top of it or surrounding it. Houses had skyscrapers and storefronts standing halfway through them. Dearborn Station's military foundation rippled out around them, barricaded and bristling with watchtowers and battlements.

"What the hell is this?" Brand said, his lips curling back.

"Let's get inside, Mitch. I'll tell you all about it. I promise."

Brand slid off the bike and staggered back a few steps, putting distance between him and his old friend. The instant he'd left the seat of the strange bike, Brand's world returned to normal. The sky was just the usual threatening dark cloudy gray of a Chicago City winter. The streets were dirty, dusty, and paved. The only buildings in sight were ones that Brand had always known to be there. And Chief was gone. Thinking he'd finally cracked up but good, Brand blinked and sent his eyes in every direction before closing the distance between him and where the bike had been. He stepped forward and Chief flickered into life in front of him, pulling aside a gossamer veil and letting it drop into place over the bizarre cityscape. Brand studied the face of the man before him. Same cheek bones, same thick lips and slender nose. Same scarred patch of skin under his right eye from where that piece of shrapnel had hit him. Same eyes that said they'd never forget what they'd seen and would always want to.

"Okay, Chief. That's you as far as I can tell it. In the past week I've seen plenty that would make any man question his sanity. I guess this is just the next step on the path to the loony bin. You're saying you've got the scoop. Let's go up and see if my bottle has enough to get it out of you and put me to sleep afterwards."

"No arguments from me, Mitch," Chief said. They walked side by side into the apartment house.

At the door, Brand remembered the bike they'd ridden on He turned around to suggest Chief bring it inside, but all he saw was a rusted and ruined bike with flat tires and a busted up saddle.

"We're on stage out here, Mitch. It's just a set piece like everything else."

Brand let it go and led them up to his rooms. They got settled in the corner by the radiator. Brand poured two glasses from his bottle and took his seat, propping his feet up on a stool. Chief settled into the chair Brand had pulled up for him.

"I'm not seeing pink elephants. Right, Chief? Just a dirty tramp with a fancy bag tucked under his coat. So what's the story?"

"I'm a Bicycle Man, Mitch. Same as the rest of 'em in this city. Any man tries to off himself in Chicago City ends up like this. Most of them are guys from our day, the war. Some are older."

Brand felt his chair falling out from under him. His vision stuttered a moment and everything was back in place, walls and floor and ceiling where they were supposed to be.

"Why'd you do it?"

"The news, Mitch. It's the only thing I've ever known, going back to before I met you in the Ob Corps. They took it out of my hands like it was candy and I was just a baby." Chief let out a sigh. "I got drunk enough to kill myself twice and then did it. I came to lying on the deck, watching the gurneymen haul me away. Then

I see I'm standing behind a screen or curtain, something you can't see or touch when you're on the other side of it, but I pushed and felt it give. Wynes came out and took you by the arm. I wanted to show him I was all right, but the blood in the snow told me I'd gone somewhere else. I wasn't really there with you and the flat foot, and then you were gone and it was just me out there in the snow.

'I had this coat on, and the bag. The bike was leaning up against the building, by the loading doors. I don't know how I knew it was mine or how to work it. I got on and then I'm racing through the city on a narrow strip of light under the tires. It was like a path that showed me where to go and took me there at the same time." Chief paused and shuffled the bag on his lap.

'Where'd you go?"

'Everywhere and nowhere. I just rode until it stopped. Goddamit, Mitch, I just want to go home."

Brand kept his hands tucked into his coat and let his friend have a good cry. When Chief was through, Brand asked the question that'd been on his tongue since he'd found himself on the back of that fancy scooter.

'I've run into a few of your pals since Valentine's Day. One guy, calls himself Larson, says he was over there with us. You seen him yet doing this new gig?" Brand said and waved a hand to indicate Chief's new clothes and the satchel.

Chief sniffed, wiped a grimy sleeve under his nose, and held his glass out for another slug from the bottle. Brand poured a healthy dose for each of them and raised his glass before he took a small drink. Chief lifted his, too, and then finished off the hooch in a single swallow.

"I don't know any of the others yet. Except the guy who showed me the ropes, and I think I've seen the last of him."

"How's that?"

"He was the one in that alley just now. He's still there I guess, but his insides are where his outsides are supposed to be. Not sure how the boss'll take the news."

"Who's the boss?"

"You won't believe it, Mitch."

"Try me. For old time's sake."

"I work for one of the Gods of Chicago City now. Calls herself *Propriety*. She picked me special because I was always so careful not to make waves with the news. Makes me wish I'd listened to you more back then."

"Your new boss likes an even keel, huh?"

"I think she's ten kinds of nuts. But the whole gang. They're the worst bunch of crackpots you've ever met. We used to joke, you and me, about what would happen if all the generals over there got in a room together and tried to run the war. The punchline, remember that?"

"We said that's just how they did things and that's why it was like playing pick up sticks with greased nails."

"This isn't any different, Mitch. The gods can't so much as look at each other without going berserk. They have to keep things running though, make sure they're where they need to be so everything goes smooth out here on stage."

"So they have you run messages for them?"

Chief nodded. "Just like the rest of the tramps out there freezing their pins off in the cold. We're their Mail Corps."

"Not how I'd like to end up after I've had my run, but I guess it's better than a lake of fire, right?"

"I guess," Chief said. He sighed again and held out his empty glass. Brand filled it and downed his own. They sipped in silence for a moment before Chief gave Brand the rest of the scoop.

"Some of the gods are good, Mitch. Maybe it's better to say some of them *can* be good. There's something big brewing back there behind the curtain. Something I don't like. When it finally gets going, it'll make the Great War look like a game of stickball. Two of the gods are in cahoots, setting things up for a big knock-over like you've never seen before. They're going for the whole city, Mitch. They want to take over, run the show by themselves without all the other gods getting in the way. And they can do it, too."

"How so? Can't the other gods stop them? What's the use of

being a god if you don't have the power to stop your enemies making a mess of things?"

"That's just it, Mitch. Power. These two have all they could want and more just waiting for them out here. All they have to do is give the people a reason to hand it over. Al Capone was small fry compared to these birds. Aw, hell …" Chief trailed off and looked away. "You must think I'm nuts."

Brand stared at his friend, wondering whether to trust Chief's words or the gnawing feeling in Brand's guts that said he really had cracked up.

"You are nuts, but that's all right. I'm nuts, too. Pleased to make your acquaintance." He reached his hand out. Chief moved to shake, but gave a start and dropped his hand into his lap. Brand followed his friend's gaze down to the leather bag and his eyes widened. The bag swelled in the middle as if something were growing inside it.

"Got work to do now, Mitch." Chief stood, shaking out his duster and tightening his belt before heading for the door. Brand fumbled with his coat buttons and followed.

"I'm coming with you. We gotta—"

"No, Mitch. You can't. Us guys work alone. I gave you a lift, and that's bad enough. They'll give me hell."

"You telling me there's something worse than what they've got you doing now?"

"I'm telling you." Chief's eyes had that trench-weary look to them again, and try as he might Brand couldn't argue with that gaze.

"Be careful, Chief. That thing you saved me from seems to have a taste for your kind. And look me up when you're off duty, hey? I want the rest of the story." Brand tried to put on a smile, but his face turned it into a grimace. The two men nodded at each other and went back to their duties, Chief down to his bike and Brand trying to get a clear look at the bottom of his bottle.

CHAPTER 21

A DRAFT CREPT IN FROM SOMEWHERE AND stung Emma's skin. She felt the cold like a threatening knife from every window in the upstairs bedroom. How long had she been lying there awake? What time was it? Two, three in the morning? Memories of what happened in the airship kept dancing up out of the darkness in her mind.

Most of all, she kept remembering the sound of Archie Falco's laugh just before she shot him. A high, thin laugh, like the giggle of a scheming child. Emma had heard that laugh all weekend while she hid out in Eddie's room.

He and the band had a gig to play Saturday night. She'd stayed in and cried in between staring out the windows at the gray skies that haunted her with visions of her father's face in the clouds. The law man's patrol boats would sail through sometimes, making the clouds dissipate into damp soot-stained halos, all too reminiscent of the spray that exited Archie Falco's head. Sunday hadn't been much different, except that Eddie'd been there trying his damnedest to coax her out of bed.

Now it was the small hours of Tuesday morning and Emma felt the beginnings of a will to act, her old fire burning again, lighting her eyes and fueling a steady beat in her chest. Eddie curled around her in the blankets and Emma's throat clenched. She clutched the grip of the revolver under her pillow and let a tremor of fear shake her from head to foot. What if Eddie and the band were with her when she got caught? Downstairs, the band slept under their coats, huddled around the radiator, snoring and probably dreaming about days and nights of stormy weather. Eddie'd told them about his and Emma's plans to go to New Orleans and they'd all agreed it was a good idea. They'd all feel better living in The South, even if they did have to take along Eddie's *white girl*. She wished they'd call her something else. Even moll or chippy sounded better to Emma's ears.

"You ain't slept a wink, Lovebird," Eddie said over her shoulder. He nuzzled into her hair to kiss the back of her neck, but she flinched away.

"We should go, Eddie. The van's all loaded up. It's just my bag up here that needs to be packed and we can leave. What's the use of waiting around for the coppers to find us?"

"Who says they're gonna? Ain't nobody know what happened in that newsman's pig but you, me, him, and the dead man. I know you don't trust Brand for being a newsman, but I got a feeling about him. He's all right, Lovebird. That means we're all right, too. Don't it?"

Emma nodded, but she couldn't shake the feeling that leaving sooner was a safer bet than leaving later.

Or not at all.

She slid out of bed, gently pushing Eddie's grasping hands away, and went to pack up her bag. Eddie sat up in bed and whistled low when she crouched in the weak moonlight that lit up the dressing cabinet. She smiled to herself and set to pulling her garments from the cabinet, folding them and tucking them into her travel bag the way she had when her father had sent her to visit relatives in Detroit.

That was just after mom had left. Then he'd sent her to visit other relatives over in Cleveland. Her first trip on a steam ship, through the waterways between the Great Lakes. She'd been so scared as a child, staring out the cabin window at all the water rolling by.

She stood and went to the bedroom window. Emma watched the snow falling to the ground. She watched a pair of headlights turn into the alley behind Eddie's house. Emma's heart rocketed into her mouth. Her guts nearly followed and she ducked down out of view.

"What is it, Lovebird?"

"They found us," Emma said. She went to the cabinet and pulled her coat on.

"Who's out there?" Eddie asked, still not moving from the bed. Emma didn't answer. She just kept packing, stuffing her clothes into the bag now, grabbing everything in a pile. Slamming the lid shut and heaving the bag up with both hands. She went for the bedroom door while Eddie went to the window. He kept out of sight and peered around the frame.

"Shit!"

"It's the coppers. Like I said, Eddie. I knew they'd find us." Tears dripped down her cheeks, but she kept her chin level and tugged the bag beside her. Emma had a hand on the doorknob. "I have to leave, Eddie. I can't stay here. They'll blame you or kill you, and they'll get away with it. I can't let that happen."

Eddie looked out the window again and he chuckled. "Ain't but one man out there, Lovebird. Just one man lighting up a cigarette. You sure he's a copper? Looks like maybe he's some fella just back from a speak, way he's leaning on his car." Emma left her bag by the door and joined Eddie at the edge of the window frame. She peered out at the man down below. Eddie was right. The guy had a hard time standing up and seemed to wish he could be anywhere but where he was. Still, his presence sent a stinging fear into Emma's ears and down her neck. After the man finished his cigarette he shook the snow off his shoulders and dusted off his hat, too. Emma couldn't be sure but she thought the fellow might be tipping his hat to the house. He got in his car and drove away, but Emma's nerves kept up a racket throughout her body. She only relaxed when Eddie's soothing basso voice came to her ears.

"See, Lovebird. Ain't but some sad fella got left behind at a speak. He come out here to smoke his last and tell himself he'll do better next time he's out with the good-timers. He ain't no trouble of ours."

Emma let Eddie draw her out of her coat and shoes and lead her back to the bed. After a few moments of fearful half-sleep the night crept around her vision and drew her eyelids shut. She let sleep come at last and woke to a charcoal-gray morning with a sky full of storm clouds heavy with threat. She and Eddie ate a quiet breakfast while the band got themselves together. The band left first, in the van. Emma and Eddie stayed behind to make sure the place was cleaned of anything that might put the coppers on their trail. Love notes and pictures of the two of them together, anything that could burn went into the grate. They'd packed clothes and Eddie's horn, plus a few toiletries. Nothing but the essentials, and nothing that could lead anyone back to the lives they'd lived in Chicago City.

In the alley behind the house, Eddie hefted Emma's bag into the boot. He took out the tire iron and held it close while he closed the lid.

"Why do you need that?" Emma asked.

"Just in case, Lovebird. Just in case. Let's get a move on."

Emma's fear had settled from the night before, but now, seeing Eddie shaking where he stood, she felt the worry and terror climbing back up her spine. They were on opposite sides of the car when a sedan pulled into the alley at the far end and roared up to them. Emma froze with one hand on the door latch and the other tucked into her coat pocket to clutch the heavy revolver. Eddie had ducked down beside the car and began moving around to Emma's side, but the driver stepped out of his car and called to him.

"That's far enough, boy," he said, reaching a hand into his coat. Emma had been ready though, and she drew first.

"And that's far enough for you, too, Detective."

Wynes stopped in his tracks, lifting his free hand palm out but keeping his other hand snug inside his coat. "Miss Farnsworth," he said. "I'm going to suggest you think twice about aiming that my way. We've already matched the slug from your father's office to the one that killed Archie Falco."

"So what's to stop me from adding a copper to the tally?" Emma said. She had a hand full of nothing, and she knew it. All the more reason to go out with guns blazing. Wynes had found Eddie's place, so even if she did get away, the law man would come back and hassle Eddie's neighbors. That would lead to his mother and sister in their house a few blocks over. Emma had stayed with them when she and Eddie had first met. She couldn't repay their hospitality that way, no matter how meager it had been.

"You're not going to shoot me, Miss Farnsworth," Wynes said. His right hand slowly stirred inside his coat and Emma could see from the bulge that he'd retrieved his gun.

"You don't think so? A good cop makes a pinch with back up. You're out here all alone. Like you were last night. I'm supposed to believe you know someone out here? Someone who's going to make noise about a copper getting gunned down in this neighborhood?"

Wynes stopped moving his hand. His eyes told Emma he bought her act, and she had to admit she halfway believed her own words. She'd shoot him down if she had to. If that's what it took to get away and make sure Eddie's friends and family were free from the law man's corrupting touch.

"Toss the gun over here," Emma said. It was the only play she had left. If he was armed, he was a threat. He could still follow her and Eddie, and they'd have to make a fast exit from the city. But at least they wouldn't have to worry about him shooting out their tires, or shooting them. Wynes hesitated and Emma could feel his eyes searching her face for cracks. She steeled her jaw from quivering and kept her eyes hard and fired for the task. Slow as can be Wynes drew his pistol and dropped it in the snow.

"Now walk away. Go on," Emma said. "We're leaving this city, so don't bother looking for us." Wynes cast a suspicious glance over

Emma's shoulder and she knew he was eyeing Eddie. "I said get moving. Beat it." She lifted the revolver to sight down the barrel into the copper's face, just like she had done in the airship when she'd been staring at the back of Archie Falco's head. This time though, she could see his eyes. The fear in them almost made Emma lose her nerve. Her hand wavered a tic, but she forced her arm to stay straight and kept the growl in her voice when she ordered Wynes to leave the way he'd come. He stayed put a few beats, shaking his head.

"You're in the soup, Miss Farnsworth," he said. Wynes stepped away from his car, still eyeing her and shaking his head. He backed down the alley, keeping his eyes on Emma the whole time. She waited until he was at the corner before putting a bullet into the front tire of his sedan. She ran quickly to pick up the copper's gun and then, stumbling, made her way through the dirty clumps of snow to her car. Eddie slid in beside her and flipped around to look out the rear window while she got the engine going.

"He's coming back, Emma. Get us moving on." Emma worked the clutch and whipped the car around in a tight arc to drive down the alley, straight at Wynes. He dove to the side as they roared by. Emma gunned the engine at the corner and slung them onto the street and away into the glowering overcast Chicago City morning.

CHAPTER 22

THE NEXT MORNING BRAND WOKE UP WITH his feet still in his shoes and frozen stiff. His head didn't feel too much different. He tumbled out of the chair and limped his way into the kitchenette to make some coffee. The sky outside looked pretty much the same as the night before. Brand let his mind wander while he poured himself a hot mug of joe and stared at the empty skies outside. Nothing but bleak, gray clouds and a light dusting of early morning snowfall. He was supposed to help stop some kind of big scheme. Chief gave him the scoop last night, right?

The empty bottle over by Brand's chair told him he'd earned the woozy head, and had probably dreamed most of what he did remember from the night before. He staggered over to sit by the radiator while the joe did its trick and his blood came up to temperature. Brand stopped short when he saw the ripped up hat lying beside a second chair over in the corner. The chair he'd pulled up by the radiator for Chief.

Memories of his conversation with Chief flooded into Brand's head and spun his eyes. Memories of the monster that had chased them on that electromagnetic bicycle that Chief rode behind the city. Behind … Brand peeled his feet off the floor and went back to the kitchenette. He snapped his eyes out the window, wanting nothing more than to see a single skyline criss-crossed down below by the only set of roads he'd ever known. When he saw the empty skies, the mug slid from his hands and landed in the sink with a dull *clunk*.

Every morning he'd had his coffee and watched the city's transport boats haul workers up from Dearborn Station and into the factory districts, the lakeside warehouses, the stockyards. Where were they now? The empty sky draped over the city like a funeral shroud, except for a few patrol boats that Brand hadn't noticed before. These were circling around the waterfront and moving north. Shaking off the sleep that still hung from his eyelids, Brand staggered into his washroom and cleaned up as best he could. He still hadn't picked up a new razor. Chief wouldn't knock him for coming into work—

No, Chief wouldn't knock him at all. Would he?

What about the new boss? Brand tried to remember the man's name, but his foggy head could barely remember how to knot a necktie. He did up the buttons on his shirt and shrugged into his suspenders. He reached into the closet for his coat. If he made double-time, Brand could get to his barber's for a quick shave. He checked his wall clock and put the idea of a shave out of mind. He'd slept later than he'd thought. It was nearly eight o'clock. Snapping up a half-empty pouch of tobacco, Brand scooted out the door. He had a new boss to meet, and it wouldn't do to show up unshaven and late to boot.

The streets clapped and clattered with traffic by the time Brand's feet touched pavement. The soreness was either retreating or his feet were numb from the cold. Either way, it was a little easier to walk and he took advantage of that, making time up from Dearborn to Harrison and then onto Printer's Row. The Record's building was across the street, and when Brand saw it he barreled into a couple of newsboys from one of the other outfits on the Row.

Banners hung across the entrance to the Record, proclaiming the building home to the *Ministry for Public Information, Chicago City*. But what had caught Brand's attention first were the two uniformed guards standing on either side of the entrance. They held some kind of fancy rifles and saluted as a group of men in suits strode into the building. The sedan that had let the men off slowly moved away. Its headlamps burned away the early morning chill in front of the car, and Brand didn't miss the two little flags flying on short posts mounted into the sedan's fenders.

The newsboys he'd knocked into brushed themselves off. One of them spoke up as Brand stood there.

"Hey, Mr. Brand, yeah? Huh. Hey, get this," the kid said to his partner. "We're giving the news to Mitchell Brand, eh, Robby?" The kid held out a paper. It fell open as Brand swiped it. Across the top, the now all too familiar sigil of the Governor's office stood out in bold red, black, and gold ink.

Just like it had on the flags on that damn car.

Beneath the symbol, Brand read a message that sent his gorge one way and his heart the other.

Citizens of Chicago City are advised of the implementation of Eugenic Protocol 421, which allows for the registration, relocation, and sequestration as necessary of affected individuals. All persons meeting descriptions of ancestry related to African, Irish, Italian, Balkan, Central European, and Semitic birth are advised to report to the nearest processing facility without delay.

Brand's mind whipped to what Chief had told him the night before. A play for power, and all it needed was for the people to let it happen. He shoved the ragsheet into his pocket and sneered, "Thanks, boys, but that's yesterday's edition."

The newsboys let their mouths hang open for a second before they shuffled off, looking like a couple of hunted dogs. Brand turned and saw another sedan pulling up in front of the Record. This one flew the Governor's flags on its fenders, too, but curtains darkened its windows. Only the windscreen allowed a view into the car, and Brand could see a partition between the driver's seat and where passengers would sit in the back. He dashed off the sidewalk and into the street ready to spit at whoever stepped out of the sedan.

Thoughts of impressing his new boss forgotten, Brand chewed on the pile of words on his tongue. It was big enough to fill a front page, and somebody would hear a few of them before the morning was out. Brand's feet hit the next sidewalk and two men exited the vehicle. The driver worked some lever from inside the car to close the door. Brand drew up even with the car's bonnet and stared hard at the men who'd emerged. One of them stood no more than five feet high if that, and nearly as big around the middle. The other stood just over Brand's sixty-six inches and probably weighed in a few pounds heavier. The taller fella spoke first, putting his hand on the squat fellow's shoulder as he spoke.

"Mitchell Brand. What exceptional timing. I do hope you can keep to a slightly tighter schedule in the future though. We need all employees in the building before I arrive. And …" the G-man took in Brand's scruffy appearance with a sneer. "There'll be time to discuss protocol later. First, I'd like to introduce you to your new colleague." The tall man slapped his squat companion on the back. Brand couldn't help but notice the pained look that passed across the little fat man's mug. "This is Franklin Suttleby."

Brand just stood there half gaping at them. The fat one, Suttleby, beamed under his boss's attention, the pain now gone from his face. Brand didn't know where he fit into the mix yet, so he held off replying with his signature half-sneer and swallowed his smart remarks. The tall one spoke up again. "Please accept my condolences for the loss of your former employer. I understand you knew each other a long time. This is probably quite a change for you."

The tall man paused, giving Brand a shot at some air time. Brand didn't buy any. He'd guessed the one doing the squawking must be Jameson Crane, the name coming up from the fog in Brand's head as he stared at the odd couple from the fancy car.

Whatever conversation Crane hoped for would have to wait. Brand wasn't about to get chatty with *the new leadership* until he could call their play for certain.

Crane piped up again. The guy seemed too busy to care about Brand's stonewall act. "Until new leadership is in place, Chicago City is under governance of the Great Lakes Territory. We have everything under control and are rapidly improving conditions around the city. You'll be working with Suttleby here on the hourly bulletins, scheduled broadcasts, and special reports. Of course, anything not strictly approved beforehand will need my say-so before it can be broadcast."

"Sounds all right," Brand said, hiding his true feelings with the calm of a boiler. "I guess you'd be Crane, then. Is that right?"

"Jameson Crane. Yes. My full title, of course, is Minister of Public Information, and you'll address me as Minister Crane from here on out."

Brand couldn't help but smirk at that, and he saw Crane's face darken in response. Before either Crane or his pet, Suttleby, could say anything else, Brand tipped his hat and stepped to the doors.

One of the soldiers moved into his path.

"Identification, sir." The soldier and his partner wore a new style of military uniform, black cloth with gold piping along the collar, crisp starched lines down each arm and pant leg. They each carried some new kind of rifle. It had a wide-mouthed barrel set into a metal box with a glass vial on the back end. The trigger was bigger than anything Brand had seen before, even on the shoulder rockets the army used. The rifle wasn't the only dingus these soldiers carried though. A visor extended from the lip of their helmets to conceal the top half of their faces, just like the G-men had. The soldiers also carried a metal baton on their belts. A coil of wire connected the baton to a small box on their opposite hip.

Brand had seen some fancy dressed soldiers in the Great War. These birds were something else. And they weren't patient either.

"Identification is required to enter this facility, sir."

"How about you tell me who's asking first," Brand gave back, resting both hands on his hips. "And since when did the Daily Record become a facility?"

"This facility houses the Ministry of Public Information, si- All persons entering through these doors must show identificatio■."

Brand spun around and looked at Crane. The man seemed content to let Brand sink or swim on his own, so the newsman tu-ned to face the soldier again. Then Brand spat out a few of the words he'd been chewing on.

"A man's not even cold yet and you come walking in here with your boots, a fancy pea shooter, and that pig sticker on your belt. You ever see any action overseas? No? Oh, I get it then. They picked you and your pal here special because you were so good at stan-ing around while everyone else climbed over the trench wall and into the meat grinder."

That last remark got the sentry's blood up. Brand could see his neck flush with anger and his lips had curled back. Through a growl, the soldier repeated his demand for identification, barely keeping the spittle in his mouth. Brand just smiled and then laughed. Turning around, he addressed Crane.

"Well, Minister Crane. It seems these two battle-hardened veterans need me to prove I belong in the building. Can you vouch for me, or should I go to the trouble of sneaking upstairs to get my identification from my desk? It's just that I'm not too good at climbing fire escapes these days."

"You're free to enter now," Crane said with a tone that fit the mask he'd let fall over his mug. "In the future, you'll be expected to show identifying documents whenever you enter or leave the facility. And you'll arrive in a timely manner, no later than zero seven-thirty hours on the dot."

Brand sniffed the air and decided the stink came from the goings on, not the usual soot and sulfur of the city's factory lines.

"Fine by me, *Minister*," he said, and pushed by the soldie- to go inside.

CHAPTER 23

EMMA FELT LIKE SHE'D DRIVEN DOWN EVERY street in Eddie's neighborhood twice and still hadn't found a safe place to hide. The neighborhood looked like a maze now, and every corner promised a dead end in handcuffs or a hail of gunfire from above. The only comfort Emma could find was the lack of airships. Then, realizing that was unusual, she felt her guts twist up even worse.

"They're just laying low, Eddie. Waiting us out."

"Gotta get us out this neighborhood, Emma. That man coming back, and you know it. And he's gonna have friends this time."

"Where do we go, Eddie?"

Eddie took a moment to reply. His face had gone slack and gray with anger or fear, maybe both. "Get us out to the village."

"What? Which village? Where is—"

"Ukranian Village!"

Emma recoiled from his outburst, shrinking against her side of the car. Eddie's face said he was sorry. Then he opened his mouth and made good on the promise in his eyes.

"I'm sorry, Lovebird. This ain't how I want to go out, running from the coppers. It's how I always worried it'd be for us, and I'm mad about that."

"I'm sorry, too, Eddie. Mostly I'm scared." Emma let a pause fill the close space inside the car and they drove in silence for a while. "We'll have to cross the river somewhere," she finally said, cruising along a quiet street at the edge of Eddie's neighborhood.

"Try up by the rail yard on the wharf road," Eddie said. "Always quiet there this time of morning."

At the riverside rail yards, Emma pulled into an empty stall beside a grain silo on the neighborhood side of the wharf road. Au up and down the road, deserted wharves extended like dead fingers into the waterway. Low sheds and stalls waited on every one, open to the cold morning air and hungry for purpose. Some stalls were fitted with racks to take clothing. Others held coils of rope and netting. Emma stared at the wharves as if seeing them for the first time. This musty, cold, gray environment was the first stop for products from the fish and garment industries of the Eastern Seaboard. Products that used to end up on her plate and in her closets.

Between the nearest wharf roads, a narrow bridge stretched across the river and into Little Italy. Greektown and then the Ukrainian Village were next, with plenty of routes through both. Emma put the car in gear and crept from the covered stall. At the opposite end of the bridge, a truck turned onto the narrow track and came across the river at them. They'd have to wait for it to clear the bridge before they could cross.

The truck crossed and pulled up by another silo down the road. Emma hesitated, wondering if the driver had seen her car and hoping he hadn't. Two men got out of the cab and went into a yard shack beside the silo. The driver got out and eyed Emma's car. The other men came out of the shack with a third and they all gathered around the truck. They held steaming mugs of coffee and blew smoke at each other. The one who'd stayed out motioned with a thumb and the group turned as one to look at Emma and Eddie sitting together in a car.

"Shit!" Eddie said, dropping to the floorboards. Emma gunned the engine and raced the car across the bridge, leaving shouts and curses in the air behind them. Whatever head start they'd had was gone now. It wouldn't take long for news to spread of a white woman and a negro driving out of the poorest neighborhood in town in the early morning hours.

Following a switchback route, Emma took them through Little Italy, dodging around horses and bicycles with carts, slowing for crowds of pedestrians making their way to the wharves. As Emma guided them on to the village, following Eddie's directions, a siren whined and faded somewhere far behind them. Emma stomped the accelerator and nearly crashed into the back end of a wagon loaded with coal.

'Just keep even on, Lovebird," Eddie said from the floorboards. He guided her by asking for landmarks. She said they were two blocks from where Ogden crossed Ashland. He told her to keep going and to turn at Lincoln Park, heading west into the village. She followed his directions and a few minutes later the sights and sounds of the village filled her windscreen.

Emma was amazed they'd survived the morning. Overhead, an empty sky hung above empty washing lines stretched between apartment windows. Emma drove at a crawl, marveling at the neighborhood she'd often heard about but had never seen. They moved past doorways that spilled children and bundles of bread, followed by worn down mothers and stooped over crones. Men strode through the streets leading livestock. Some hefted beams of wood between them. The long posts rested on the mens' shoulders. In their hands, the men carried wooden pails or boxes bristling with tools. Nobody looked at the foreign white woman in her foreign vehicle, but Emma knew they all had their eyes on her.

"This is gypsy town, Eddie. Who's going to help us here? I haven't got any real money on me. What I do have, they'll take and the car too. We'll be stranded. Or—"

Eddie shushed her and waved away her concerns. "Up a ways now, Emma. Go on until you see the railroad." They kept on like that, with Eddie asking for landmarks and calling out turns. At last, Emma pulled into an alley beside a cobbler's shop.

"Man's gotta a speak, downstairs," Eddie said. He sat up in the seat. "Boys and me played here Saturday night, and twice the month before. Gypsies got a taste for jazz, Lovebird. We get lucky, and I think we will, old man gonna let us hide out here for a bit. We get real lucky, they'll play some of their music for us. C'mon."

Emma reluctantly left the car, sliding over to leave through Eddie's door so she'd be standing next to him when she got outside. She followed Eddie around the bonnet to the cobbler's shop. Inside an old man crouched over a sheet of leather that he stretched and cut and stretched and cut again. Emma stayed so she could see out the window. She kept an eye on the car, worried that if she looked away, the next time she turned to look the car would be gone. Eddie put a hand on her shoulder and smiled, raising a finger to his lips for silence. Beside them, the cobbler punched holes in the leather for laces. He seated grommets in the holes. These he clamped down with a tool he gripped in both hands, closing the rough metal jaws over the eyeholes. When he finally put his work aside, Eddie greeted the man and introduced Emma.

"This is my Lovebird, Mr. *Naw-djee*. We need a place to stay, just for a short time. Just until tonight. I was hoping you might help us in exchange for some of my horn playing."

The old man's eyes twinkled and he laughed loud and booming in the close space of the low ceilinged shop. After he laughed, a look of concern draped over the man's face. "Why does Eddie Collins bring trouble to Nagy? Eh? Eddie Collins is always paid so well for making his jazz in Nagy's room. Making so the young people come and are buying Nagy's Zwack and beer, even the Ouzo from the Greeks that Nagy sells the young people for twice what he pays. Eddie Collins makes Nagy's life easy. But now he makes it hard."

"I'm real sorry, Mr. Nagy. I'm in love with this girl and she's in love with me. You can see plain as anybody that's not a good thing for us here in Chicago City. That's why we're going to New Orleans. First thing we can. But we just need a place to get our legs under us.

We won't make no trouble. I promise. If you want, I'd be happy to play my horn for them young people free of charge."

The old man blinked a few times, wiped at his eyes with a rag he pulled from his shirt pocket and tucked back in before speaking. "Eddie Collins is a crazy man. Is okay. Nagy was crazy man once, too. Nagy loved the wrong girl. That is how Nagy lost his tooth. See?" The old man lifted his cheek aside and showed a gaping space in his jaw. "Girl's father did not like Nagy's family, so he showed Nagy better way to live. Without girl. Also without tooth. But Nagy has other teeth. Can still chew meat," he said, and nodded at a picture of a woman hanging on the wall by the door.

"Eddie Collins has plan to go to New Orleans. That is good. Also foolish. But foolish and crazy make bed together, so Nagy is not surprised. Bring car to back." The old man finished speaking and stood, waving with two crooked fingers in the air. He left through a rear door while Emma and Eddie went out to move her car around.

Emma had watched the whole exchange in the shop with wonder in her eyes and a mix of fear and guilt in her heart. The old man's clumsy English and his twinkling eyes reminded her of her own father when she'd been a little girl. When her mother was still in the house. Back then, Emma's father knew how to laugh and he knew how to make other people laugh, too. He liked to play at being a gypsy, dancing like a buffoon and aping speech like the old shoemaker's. Emma had laughed at her father's antics. She'd laughed at how the silly gypsies talked. Coming face to face with the reality of these people, she wanted to apologize. For her father, but more for her memories of laughing at people she'd never known except through the pantomiming of a silly drunken old man.

Eddie showed her where to drive the car. A garage stood behind the cobbler's shop. Emma pulled in on a pad of concrete. Off to the side of the space, a set of stout wooden stairs led down to a well-lit cellar. The cobbler held open a trap door and ushered them down the steps. Eddie thanked the man called Nagy. Emma couldn't look the man in the face, but she nodded as she passed him and mumbled a quiet "Thank you," before following Eddie into the cellar.

Candles and gas lamps illuminated the room, reflecting off of wood panels that lined the space. A small bar stood in one corner. The glow of light bouncing back from assembled glasses and bottles warmed the chamber, and Emma couldn't resist the temptation to sit at the bar, despite the early hour. Eddie had brought his horn down and opened the case on a table at the side of the room. While he busied himself cleaning the instrument, Emma took in the space, pretending not to be searching for exits other than the stairs. A low stage sat at one end, framed by a circle of what Emma knew to be handmade chairs. Everything in the place had to be handmade. None of the new auto-mills turned out furniture like what she saw in the little downstairs speak, but how could these people afford handmade goods like this? Emma ran a hand along the bar and her eyes went wide. The surface was like glass, smooth and perfect as any piece of furniture she'd grown up with. In a second, she understood. The men with the lumber and toolboxes in the street.

"This is where it all came from," she said, half sure she was dreaming.

"What came from, Lovebird?"

Emma didn't answer. She stared into her reflection in the surface of the bar, then glanced up to the bottles arranged beyond. A woman's voice, full of authority and compassion, shook Emma from her tempting thoughts.

"Miss Farnsworth. Cards did say we would meet again. Did they not?"

CHAPTER 24

INSIDE THE BUILDING, BRAND MADE A FAST DASH for the stairs. Suttleby came in the doors after him and asked why he didn't want to take the lift. Brand couldn't resist the chance to dig at the little fat man.

"Figured a guy your size'd be up on the latest fitness techniques. Climbing stairs does more for you than standing in a box on a rope."

Suttleby grimaced as he stepped into the lift. Brand raced up the stairs but didn't make it to the fourth floor before his new colleague.

Just my luck.

Brand still had to make good on the story he gave Wynes the night before. And he was certain Crane would come storming in any minute, shouting about Brand's act of sabotage in the print room.

But the Minister of Hokum Peddling didn't show his face all day, and Suttleby had gone straight for his own office. Right next to the lift. Brand had plenty of time to toss a few bottles of ink on the walls and floor, making sure to keep his hands and shirtsleeves clean in the process. A few droplets splashed onto his pants, out they were dark anyway.

At a little before nine o'clock, Aiden Conroy and Digs Gordon came up to Brand's door, sheepish and scared.

"Mr. Brand, sir?" Conroy said. "You got ... you got a minute?"

"Yeah, Conroy. What do you need? Shouldn't you two be on your beats with the morning run by now?"

"No, sir," Digs piped up. "Minister Crane says we're off the job and to let you know. He says we got work today, but after today that's it. No dice and no pay. We're supposed to head down to some scrap yard with Mutton."

"Scrap yard?" Brand said. "Unless Crane wants to get into the junk business, why send Mutton to a place like that? You know that old wrench and bolts fella loves collecting left overs. You too, Conroy, isn't that right?"

The kid nodded. Brand immediately felt guilty when he saw a half smile die on the kid's face. "Hey, Conroy, chin up, yeah? You and Digs here, you've always done good work. I'll put in a word. Maybe Crane'll listen to me and we'll have you back on the payroll lickety-split."

"Is it true, Mr. Brand?" Conroy asked. "About Chief, I mean. We heard he quit and that's why Minister Crane is running the show now."

Brand barely kept his temper. For the boys' sakes, he had to find some way out of the black mood that had settled over his brow. He watched Conroy and Digs fidget some more and worked up the courage to respond. He had to choke down his sorrow first though.

"About Chief, yeah. He quit, and that's all you need to know about it for now. But don't worry. I'll square it with Crane about you two working here. You'd better be getting on. Go on down to the maintenance rooms and check in with Mutton on the gearboxes. They're probably the first thing headed to the scrap pile."

Digs cut in ahead of Conroy, "I don't follow you, Mr. Brand. If the gearboxes aren't going to—"

"Mutton likes to have the machinery working right no matter

what it's called up for, even if that's being laid to rest in a heap. I figure the old boy could use a hand keeping the metal men tip top until Crane gives the order to haul them out of here."

Conroy's eyes brightened up right away. The kid gave a quick nod and then one of the rusty salutes the newsboys had always kept ready for their boss. Digs shook his head but followed suit. Brand snapped his hand to his brow in return and ushered the kids out.

"Carry on, gentlemen."

After the two boys left, Brand set to clearing out his desk, fuming and muttering to himself the whole time. Talking to Crane on the way in, he'd seen the end of his job as Chicago City's top newshawk. And with what he'd just learned from Digs and Conroy … a gnawing in Brand's gut said be ready to skip out and not leave any trail if he could help it. Stacks of old notes went down the waste chute where they were shredded up and dropped on a belt headed for the incinerator. Brand tossed out anything that Crane and his toady might be able to use as they set about pulling the rug that much further up over Chicago City's eyes.

Brand spent the day in his office wondering when Crane would show, but the G-man never did come down from his lofty perch in Chief's old office. Twice, Brand thought about going up there and collecting what he could of his old friend's mementos and keepsakes. Hell, even his pen set would have been nice to have. But each time the thought came, it was replaced by the memory of his conversation with Chief the night before. That just sent Brand fumbling in his brain for something that smacked of reality.

Everyone around him seemed fine enough with what was happening. Change coming to Chicago City. Big change. Real change.

Around the noon hour that day, Suttleby came by with a document titled the *Dictates for Journalistic Etiquette*, which Brand accepted, glanced at, and tossed down the waste chute once Suttleby had waddled his porcine bulk down the hall. By half past four, Brand had a full pot of coffee souring in his guts and a mood to match. With Crane still a no-show, Brand locked up his office, skipped the lift and took the stairs back the way he'd come. In the corner of his mind where things still made sense, he half hoped that he'd emerge from the stairwell and find his old boss and friend waiting for him like he used to when Brand tried to leave early. He waited at the stairwell door. Took a breath and then another before pushing it open. The foyer stood empty except for the receptionist at her desk. Down the room from her position, the main doors waited for Brand like a pair of guillotines turned on their sides.

The girl at the desk nodded smartly at Brand, like she always had. He put a finger to his hat and mumbled something about a story on his way to the doors. She looked back down at her desk and paid him no mind. Brand pushed a hand against the door and crashed into it when his momentum got away from him. The door didn't budge. Brand turned to the receptionist. She'd lifted her eyes from her desk and smiled at him from behind a mask of curiosity and fear.

"They'll be unlocked at 1700 hours, Mr. Brand. Orders from Minister Crane."

Brand stepped over to a waiting bench and plopped down on it, too tired to get really angry and too angry to think straight enough to find another way out of the building. True to her word, half an hour later the receptionist removed a key ring from her desk and marched to the doors. Brand stared in disbelief while she undid the locks.

"Any chance of the employees getting a set of those keys, miss? In case of a fire, I mean."

"Minister Crane has entrusted me with a set, Mr. Brand. The soldiers outside have a set, too, and so does the minister."

Brand blew it off with a shake of his head. He blew the whole day off going down the front steps and kept it up as he crossed the street. At least four people stopped to listen to the blue streak he let out all the way back to his rooms. When he saw the empty bottle from last night waiting for him, Brand cursed some more and then threw a few things around the apartment before collapsing into his chair. Outside, night fell on Chicago City, drifting down like gossamer but landing like a lead weight when the curfew bells rang out. Brand stirred from a shallow sleep just long enough to curse the night and the patrol boats he could see outside. Searchlights stabbed down here and there, piercing the city's belly and making her curl into a ball. Brand followed suit and wrapped up in his chair. He slipped into a fitful sleep, dreaming of a knife he felt twisting in his guts. In the dream, Brand wished the knife would finish the job before morning, and at the same time he knew it would only cut him enough to leave a lasting scar.

CHAPTER 25

THE GLOW OF CANDLES AND GAS LAMPS illuminated the scarves around Madame Tibor's head. Light glinted from her earrings and from her dark eyes. Emma sat across the table from the woman, stealing glances at Eddie now and then. He stayed put on the side of the room cleaning his horn and sometimes blowing soft notes from it. Emma had asked him to join her at the table, but he shook his head and hugged her. While they embraced, Eddie whispered in her ear that he didn't trust gyspy magic.

Madame Tibor placed a card in the center of the table before Emma. "Is you," she said. Emma stared at the card. It was upside down. On it, a blue-tinted female figure held a sword in front of her with the point between her feet. Around the figure swirled balls of varying shades of blue. A balance framed the figure, with the two plates sitting evenly beside her hips.

"Card is reversed, Miss Farnsworth. Is sign of your struggle. You would see the world through eyes of fairness. But too much you are thinking you are right. So you struggle. World does not look fair to you."

Emma sniffed at that last and turned her eyes to Eddie. Was it fair that she and the man she loved would have been thrown in jail if they'd shown their affections in public? Was it fair that Archie Falco had been a filthy rat and she'd been forced to kill him to save herself from the unspeakable ordeal he had planned? And now she had to run away from the only home she'd ever known. With or without Eddie, she had to leave Chicago City behind.

"What kind of world is fair when every step you take lands you in the soup?"

"Ah," Madame Tibor said, smiling. "Is this world. Or other. All worlds are the soup." The gypsy placed another card on the table, directly above the first. On this new card, an indistinct figure stood in front of a field of colors bursting in a star shape. Madame Tibor tapped the card with a long-nailed finger. "The Eternal. Is your dark man," the gypsy woman said. "He lets much fall away to be with you. This card critical to you both. To dark man, is his place low. Place of change. Of endings, but also freedom that ending brings."

"And to me?" Emma asked, afraid of what *endings* the gypsy might be referring to.

"Is what you bring with you. Eternal is very powerful all in time of chaos. Will know when to act. When to rest. Now." Madame Tibor slipped three more cards from her deck and placed them on the table in a fan around the central cards. Two of the cards came down reversed. The last of them landed upright. Madame Tibor stared at the spread of cards and tutted. Before Emma could ask why, the gypsy lifted a card and held it up for Emma. The image was of a man standing on one foot against a background of stars and planets.

"Card is reversed. Is man who waits, not man who—" Madame Tibor paused and searched the air with her eyes, finally bringing them back to meet Emma's gaze. "Is not man who *lives*."

Emma took in the card's full image. The man wasn't standing. In the upright position, the card presented him suspended by one foot while the other foot and both hands were held fast by nails driven into cloud shapes. "So who is he to me?"

"In place here," the gypsy said, putting the card back on the table, "is one you will help. But reversed. Does not know you will help. Will not ask you to help. Next card though, is one you will save."

Again Madame Tibor lifted the card for Emma to examine. This one also sat reversed on the table. Emma studied the image this time, looking for details to help explain its meaning. A male figure stood central on the card. His hands and feet seemed to wave in the air around him as he stepped off the edge of a cliff. A discarded walking stick tumbled down into blackness before him, and at his heels a dog trailed happily as if to follow with no concern for the drop ahead.

"That's the Fool," Emma said, remembering the dog from a previous reading with the gypsy. That was the night of the Mayor's Gala. Who had the card been that time? Her father?

"Yes," Madame Tibor said, as if reading Emma's thoughts. "We see this card before. Reversed that time, too. That time was one you would think lost. But—" the gypsy cut off, seeming to wait for Emma's reaction.

"I'm listening." Emma said.

"Ah. This time then. Fool is one you will save but is reversed now. You wait, act later. Because you act here, or maybe there, card will move on its own. Fool saves himself." Madame Tibor set the Fool card down and spun it around so the figure stood upright. Her face darkened as she lifted the final card for Emma.

"Is your future."

At first sight, the image on the card seemed to present a threat, something to prepare for. But hearing the gypsy's words staggered Emma. She flinched away and had to force herself to stay seated. Madame Tibor put a hand out, clasping Emma's interlaced fingers. "Is not bad. My eyes scare you, Miss Farnsworth. I am sorry. Here." The gypsy pressed the card into Emma's reluctant hands.

"This is what's waiting for me?" she asked. A horned figure, half man and half goat, stared out of the card at Emma. Around it swarmed vaguely male and female figures of pale yellow and blue. The scene stood out from a background of swirling black lines and flesh-colored shapes that looked like viscera.

"Not waiting for you. Is future. It comes to you when it is time."

"But this looks horrible," Emma said, feeling a tear course down her cheek.

"Horrible," Madame Tibor scoffed at the suggestion, waving a hand as she said, "Horrible. No. Is beautiful. This card Lightbringer. One who knows risks, always sees darkness. Goes forward anyway."

"And that's me. I'm going forward into darkness. How is that anything but horrible?" Emma couldn't take her eyes off the card. The swirling black lines pulsed and coursed like snakes around the image. They intertwined and wrapped around the indistinct human figures as if to entrap them.

"I tell you this now," the gypsy said. "You or one close to you in future will bring light to darkness. Makes it so other people can see."

Emma set the card down, still unable to shake the sense of dread that made short gasps of her breath. Eddie's horn filled the low, close room with a mournful melody. Emma turned her face to him and saw the same fear and worry in his eyes that she felt clouding her own.

Madame Tibor drew another card and placed it across the first one she'd set down.

"Two of Lances. You have courage to fight. Will succeed if you trust yourself." She placed yet another card on the table, to the left of the stacked pair representing Emma. A second card went to the right of the stack and Madame Tibor smiled. "Ace of Medallions and Ten of Vessels. Yes. I think you and dark man will see freedom. And will help others escape, too."

The gypsy woman cleared the cards away, her face blank except for the glint of light reflected in her dark eyes. Emma stood on shaky legs and went to Eddie. "She says we'll be all right."

"I heard what she said, Lovebird," Eddie replied. He held Emma tight to his chest. "I heard she said you're going to make it so other people can see better. As if you and me didn't have enough trouble."

"What do you mean?" Emma said, leaning back to look Eddie in the eye.

"I mean we already got every copper in town ready to slip a rope around both our necks. You for that man you shot down and me for touching your hand. Won't help us escape the hangman's noose if you go shining lights where other folks want it to stay dark."

Eddie pulled her close and they held each other. Emma turned to thank Madame Tibor for reading the cards for her, but the gypsy woman was gone. Emma gasped, afraid again that they'd been left out to dry until the coppers could show up and collect them. She relaxed when the cobbler called down to them, asking if they needed something to eat. Eddie said that'd be fine and thanks. The cobbler brought cheese and bread, and a pot full of a thick stew. They ate from wooden bowls and drank a rich red wine out of glass jars the cobbler pulled from behind the bar.

"Eat. Then you rest. Nagy leaves soon. Will come back and put Eddie Collins to work." The cobbler laughed and Eddie let a smile curl his mouth. Emma smiled, too. This was the closest she'd felt to happy in a long time. She wondered how long it would last.

CHAPTER 26

AIDEN AND DIGS TORE DOWN THE STREETS. The curfew bells rang out all around them. Mutton had left them as close to Aiden's neighborhood as he could before turning back down the street to drive his old jalopy home. The clunking and sputtering of the steam car's engine still echoed in Aiden's ears.

'How'd we end up so late?" Digs said. His breath came easy. Aiden huffed and puffed to keep up with his friend, not used to running or being very active beyond hauling stacks of papers on and off his airbike.

"I don't know, Diggsy. Old Mutton. He had us at that yard for ages."

Mutton had dug into a few piles before the yard boys came around and hollered at him to clear off. Then he drove down to the other end of the long yard by the lakeside and waited. Aiden and Digs had been stuck in the back of the delivery van they'd driven over from the Record. Aiden still thought of it as the Record, even with the new signs hanging up everywhere. He even called it the Record when Mutton drove them back to return the van and collect his old steam car. The sun had long since set when they finally tootled out of the garage beneath the Record's building.

"Hey, Diggsy. Hold up a tic," Aiden said. They'd turned down yet another alley that Digs said he knew was a safe route, away from main roads and places the coppers were probably watching during the curfew. Digs knew the streets, Aiden had to give him that.

"We can't stick here for long, Conroy my lad," Digs said, pulling an impersonation of Mutton that included slumping over a bit and dropping one eye lid.

"Aw, go on, Diggsy," Aiden said and waved a hand at his friend. "We're in the soup because of that old fella. He's the reason we're so late and running from the coppers."

"Yeah, but he gave you Mr. Brand's camera box, didn't he? Guy can't be all that bad he hands you a parting gift like that."

Aiden hefted the small box in its leather case. The strap went around his neck and the camera dangled in front of him like the weight on a case clock. Mutton had handed it over after he'd dug it from a box in the van. It was a heck of a thing to hand a fella, Aiden had to admit. He also had to admit that he'd thought twice about trading it for safe passage home. Of course, the coppers probably wouldn't have much use for it and would be just as likely to haul him and Digs in for stealing it.

"Hey, Aiden. What's with the long face? It'll be jake. Don't you worry. Ol' Diggsy Gordon's in the lead. Now are you rested up enough or should I ask the next copper that comes by if he's got a pillow handy?"

Aiden swiped at Digs and then the boys were running again. Up fire escapes and into windows of abandoned flats or empty storerooms above shops. Digs knew plenty of routes to and from everywhere a guy'd need to go. They even passed right behind their favorite soda shop. At the edge of Aiden's neighborhood, the boys pulled up behind a stack of waste barrels and crates outside of a butcher's. The stink of meat and blood cloaked their hiding place and a swarm of flies buzzed lazily in the cold night air above the boys heads.

'Just up here and we're good as gold," Digs said. He motioned for Aiden to follow and piloted them along an alley that ran down one side of the butcher's. It opened to a wider street at the far end and branched in the middle to follow a narrow trail between the butcher's and a grocer's building.

'What's up here?" Aiden asked, worried by the narrow length of alley they had entered. A patrol ship sailed overhead somewhere. Its motor rumbled in the clouds, low and threatening. If a searchlight came down on them in this thin alley, they'd be sunk but good. Digs pulled up by a cellar window in the grocer's building. He prized it open with a length of wood that he'd slid from a hiding spot beside the window.

'Down here. We drop into McCoy's cellar, sneak an apple or two if you're hungry, and then it's two blocks to home."

'How you figure, Digs? You want us to detour into the cellar first? I don't follow you."

'No, you dunce. The cellar lets out into Old Chicago. Underneath, right? It all burned down fifty some years ago and they just went and built up on top of it. But a few spots like this one let you in. There's tunnels all around that get you everywhere in the city. You just got to watch out for them gypsies. They'll gut you and serve you up as breakfast if they find you in their clubhouse."

Now Aiden understood how his friend was familiar with so many places in town that Aiden had never been and figured a guy couldn't get without knowing the right people. The tunnels also explained how Digs managed to cop the sneak so easy after lifting food or clothing from a storefront. Aiden felt Digs nudge his shoulder and he returned the gesture, remembering his friend's last words and imagining nothing but evil grins and sharp knives waiting for them in the cellar.

'You know the way, Diggsy. Go on." Digs bent his head and shoulders into the cellar window just as a car engine rumbled from one or two streets over and came closer. Shouting echoed through the alleyway and was followed by a gunshot. A scream and a second shot followed. Then silence except for the rumble of the patrol boat somewhere above. No searchlights came down, so the boat's position was a mystery.

"C'mon," Digs said. "That was the next street over. Let's go see what's what."

Aiden balked, but his friend was intent and had already squeezed past him down the narrow alley to the wider branch alongside the butcher's. Aiden followed and caught up with Digs at the alley mouth. They hung back, behind the crates and waste barrels, peering into the street they'd been on earlier.

"I don't see nothing, Digs. Let's go on."

"You heard the shots same as me, hey? Bet there's some kinda mess out there. Let's go get a picture with Mr. Brand's camera." Before Aiden could stop him, Digs had the camera off his neck and was on the sidewalk. Aiden came up behind Digs and they duck-walked their way down to the middle of the block. Digs brought Mr. Brand's camera up and fiddled with it one of the flaps. Aiden snatched it away and looked for the lens and shutter switch.

"How's this thing get a picture anyway?" he said. Digs made to snatch it back but his hands froze midway when a car roared to life at the far end of the block. It came tearing around a corner and speared the butcher's window with its headlights as it made the turn. The car drove past their hiding place and down the next street. Aiden clamped Mr. Brand's camera to his chest.

"We're sunk if we stay out any longer, Digs. Let's get hid."

Aiden moved to go back down the street when the thrumming of an airship filtered down from overhead. The boys shuffled along the sidewalk, trying to find a hiding place. Aiden tucked into a doorway and called for Digs to join him, but Digs lit out for the alley, staying low and galloping. Aiden's eyes rounded in terror when a searchlight stabbed down from the clouds and picked Digs out on the sidewalk.

Digs bolted for the alley and disappeared around the corner. Aiden heard shouts. He waited for gunshots but none came. Then

Aiden heard a sound that sent his heart straight into his throat. It began as a low throaty rumbling and grew to a rasping hiss. The scream that followed had to be Digs. Aiden heard his own name in the middle of the storm of sounds, roaring and hissing and howling. Then silence. The hum of an airship motor faded as the craft moved away, trailing its searchlight like a knife through the night.

Aiden nearly shrieked when he heard a clicking sound from the street around him. A trio of crabs had emerged and made their way to the alley. Aiden didn't want to go down there. He didn't know what he'd see, but his imagination kept trying to fill in the blank spot. And he kept trying to will the blankness to remain so he wouldn't have to think about Digs in any way except as he last was: running for his life, but still alive.

The crabs made the alley and turned. Aiden stayed on their trail, hanging back. He had to put a hand out to steady himself around the corner. The smell of the butcher's waste barrels nearly emptied Aiden's stomach. He swallowed once. Twice. The crabs continued along the alley, so Aiden followed. His eyes were still half-closed, and he knocked his knees trying to move around the crates. When he heard the crabs stop moving, he staggered and ended up slipping in a patch of slick soil. His knee came down hard onto a stone and he bit his lip to keep from crying out.

The crabs clicked a few more times and then went still. They were in the narrow alley Digs had led Aiden into. One by one the crabs came out. When the first one got close to Aiden's feet it stopped and rocked back to aim its lens at his face. Without realizing he was doing it, Aiden held a hand up to block the crab's eye from focusing on him. He heard the machine's shutter click and figured it must have taken a picture of him anyway.

The crab wandered off then and Mr. Brand's camera box hummed and squealed like a radio. Aiden tucked it up tight against his stomach and turned his face against the butcher's shop wall, so the crab couldn't get another shot at him if it came back. He looked at the camera box and saw the flap Digs had started to open. A gray light glowed around the edges, so Aiden popped the flap open all the way.

Underneath was a square of glass that glowed like a light-bulb about to go out for good. The box had another flap around the other side, so Aiden popped that one, too, hoping he'd find the lens underneath it. All he got was a switch and some knobs. Figuring the switch must be what worked the shutter, Aiden put a thumb on it. He wedged the box against his belly and stuck his other thumb on the switch when he realized how tough it would be to move it.

The switch went back and forth pretty slow, and the glowing glass went brighter. Aiden could almost make out his shoelaces in the light aiming down from the box. He flipped it over and saw part of a picture, but like it was being shaken up inside the box somehow.

Before he knew he was doing it, Aiden had a hand on a knob underneath the box. He spun it one way, then the other, and the squealing went quiet. The picture kept shaking around, but Aiden noticed it mostly went side to side. He flipped the box again and saw the knobs had letters on them.

"*V* and *H*? What's—"

Aiden tried one and rotated the box so he could half see the glass. The picture shook up and down now, more than before, so Aiden slowly spun the knob back the other way. With a little back and forth on both knobs, he finally got the picture to sit still in the middle. The camera box made a clicking sound, kinda like the crabs and the picture filled in.

The image was dark, but it was shot through in places with streaks of light from the searchlight. The picture showed the narrow alleyway just by the cellar window where Digs and Aiden almost escaped a few minutes earlier. Now most of Digs was in a pile by the window. Aiden's stomach heaved and he spluttered a mouthful of bile onto the butcher's wall.

A grunt and moan came from down the narrow alley. Aiden finally screamed. And he ran. His feet carried him down the wide alley around the corner. Back down the street and over to the next block. The rumbling motors of patrol boats swarmed like hornets above his head and he ducked as he ran, holding his cap on with one hand and clutching Mr. Brand's camera to his chest with the other. After dashing along streets and down alleys, Aiden came up short against the fence behind his family's home.

His parents would eat him alive for coming in after curfew. He'd have to ditch Mr. Brand's camera box, too. If they caught him with it, they'd see the pictures on it, and then they'd know about Digs. Aiden couldn't tell them about Digs, but he'd have to tell them something. He stashed the camera box under the back steps and crept to the kitchen door.

When Aiden opened the door, his parents flew into the kitchen from the dining room.

"What were you thinking?" his mother shrieked at him. "Why were you out after curfew? Are you crazy?"

Aiden's pa went one better. "Did the men find you and bring you home?"

Men?

"What men, Pa?"

Soon as the question left his lips, Aiden wished he'd kept it in. His pa had every kind of mean on his face, and Aiden could smell the hooch on his breath as he go up close. "The men that came by. When the curfew bell rang. Said you were needed somewhere. Some ministry thing. You on the wrong side of this new outfit, son? Huh?"

"No, Pa. It's—"

Men were looking for him?

Aiden focused on the only thing that made sense about his day. He told his folks how him and Digs were put off the job, but first they got sent to the scrap yard with Mutton, and the old man kept them too late because he wanted to dig through the piles. Aiden got dropped off a few blocks from home.

He hadn't wanted to mention Digs because his parents didn't like him hanging around a guy who doesn't keep a regular address.

Sure enough, Aiden's dad went to work on him again, turning to his ma with that grin on his face that says he knows right.

"Figures he'd come home late, eh, Alice? Hanging around the Gordon boy. And what about Diggsy?" he said, looking Aiden's way again. "Where'd he end up? He's not out there begging food from the neighbors, is he?

Aiden shook his head. "Digs went home," he told them, feeling his bottom lip quiver. He heard the sounds from the alley echoing in his memory and did his best to see a picture of Digs still alive. Aiden imagined Digs standing next to his mother in whatever house they'd been living in lately. Aiden never knew where Digs lived from week to week. Digs didn't either.

"He went home," Aiden's father said in a huff. "Where's he at this week?"

Aiden's mind called up the sounds from the alley, and the smell of the butcher's shop. His stomach turned and Aiden felt like he'd need a pail if his folks kept grilling him.

"Over by some butcher's."

Aiden's dad nodded and crossed his arms.

"Digs went home," Aiden said again. His father grumbled something about looking guilty and told Aiden to go to bed. Digs went home, Aiden thought to himself as he went upstairs to his room, fighting against the images that kept coming back to him.

Digs went home.

CHAPTER 27

WEDNESDAY MORNING, BRAND STRUG-
gled to leave his rooms. The door opened just fine.
The hallway was where he'd left it the night before,
and the only fog in his head was from too much sleep instead of too
much booze. Even his feet felt better this morning. But his heart
sank and his insides twisted when he thought about where he was
headed. The ache in his gut grew worse with every step down the
sidewalk to the Record offices.

He still refused to think of the building as anything but the
Daily Record. Brand told himself the minute he called it the ministry of anything that would be the last time he breathed Chicago
City air. Until then, he'd go on sucking it in and blowing it out
with the rest of the saps under the thumb of the Governor's *new
leadership*. But that didn't mean he had to follow the rules like a
schoolboy.

Owing to a stop for a new pouch of tobacco, Brand got to the
building a little later than expected, just like yesterday.

Crane was going in when Brand reached the corner, so he hung back until the G-man was well inside. It wouldn't help having another ass chewing for breakfast, and especially when it would be his ass on the platter. Brand shot a quick glance at the mooring deck on the side of the building. The *Vigilance* was still gone and her absence made his guts sink even lower and twist even harder. The newsboys' airbikes hung off the trapeze, but Crane would probably have them towed out to scrap soon enough.

Brand went up the steps to the building and flashed his press badge at the soldier by the door. The other soldier dropped the barrel of his rifle across Brand's path and demanded a photo identification card. Brand dug it out of his wallet and held it up by his face. The soldiers nodded at Brand and stepped aside for him to enter. He went straight up the stairs to his office and plunked himself at his desk, wondering how long he had before Crane stepped in and gave him both barrels before telling him to beat it.

It was nearly eleven o'clock before the Minister of Hokum Peddling poked his head in. Brand's sour gut hadn't improved, and before he could think twice, he felt himself giving Crane a bent eye. "Yeah?" The G-man's face went dark, and Brand came up out of his shoes. "I mean, hello, Minister Crane. What can I do for you?" He stood and rested his fingertips on the edge of his desk.

"Briefing, Brand. I'm only coming to tell you personally because we haven't outfitted your office with a receiving unit yet."

"What's wrong with the intercom I've got?" Brand asked, nodding to the box on the wall next to his desk. He wondered if this *briefing* wouldn't turn out to be his dismissal.

"Old equipment," the G-man said, waving a hand at the intercom. "Come up to the newsroom now. We've received some disturbing information to process and distribute."

So maybe he wasn't being put off the job today. But *process* and *distribute*? Not exactly words Brand associated with the news. Of course, he didn't think of the news as *information* either. You had *truth* and *lies*, *facts* and *embellishments*. If you called something *information*, you might as well call it hooey. It certainly wouldn't get people tuning into Brand's radio broadcasts if he started off saying he had *information* to share.

All of these thoughts danced and argued in Brand's head as he followed Crane up the hall to the lift. They rode in silence to the sixth floor newsroom and when they emerged Brand almost threw up at the sight. On every wall a poster had been hung proclaiming *The Dictates of Journalistic Etiquette*. Suttleby came up to greet his boss as Brand and Crane stepped off the lift. "I just finished getting the posters up, Minister Crane."

While Crane and Suttleby flapped their jaws, Brand took in the first few lines of text on a copy of the poster Suttleby clutched with his sausage fingers. Brand hadn't paid much attention to the page the fat man handed him yesterday, but he'd seen enough to know that journalism, as Brand knew it, was a dying thing in Chicago City. What he read on the poster now confirmed that thought and then some.

All information is of prime importance.

The Ministry for Public Information is charged with filtering that information which can be detrimental to the public good.

The Ministry for Public Information is likewise charged with ensuring the efficient and accurate communication of that information which can be most beneficial to the public good.

Brand stopped reading at that point. He'd seen and heard enough. But what could he do about it? Crane called to the gathered newsies, many of whom were new faces for Brand. They all had the same crew cut and dark grey suits, making Brand think they must have been sent special by the Governor's office.

"All right, everyone," Crane said, calling the briefing to order. Brand noticed every face but his had already turned in Crane's direction. "Brand, that means you, too," Crane added.

"Oh, yes, Minister. Just acquainting myself with the new faces around here. I see I'm in good company, just not company I'm familiar with."

"Yes," Crane said, "and there'll be time for introductions after the briefing. Now," he continued, turning to address the room. "We have two reports that need distribution, and I want them handled by Brand here and ...." Crane paused, scanning the room. "Franks. Let's have you take this one. Some tramps found dead by the riverside. Seems they froze to death last night," Crane fired a quick glance in Brand's direction. Brand kept his face stony and focused his eyes on a poster above a desk against the far wall. He swallowed the bile that rose when he remembered it had been his first desk as a cub reporter at the Record.

Crane held out a sheet of paper with the now ubiquitous symbol of authority stamped at the top of it. One of the nondescript newsies marched up, accepted the page, and spun on his heel. Brand had to hold in a laugh as the guy tromped back to where he'd been standing.

What is this, the Governor's Color Guard?

"Brand," Crane said, holding a second page in Brand's direction but still looking out at the room. Brand stepped a few paces up, took the page and stayed put, reading the print while Crane went on about following *The Dictates* and *confirming all redactions, amendments,* and *clarifications* through him prior to broadcast.

Brand's hands shook as he read. A young man, aged nineteen, had been killed last night in an alley in the Old Town neighborhood. The young man's mutilated body was found by his mother, Lila Gordon, when she stopped by a butcher's shop in the morning. The page of notes included strikethroughs and annotations, and one line of blacked out text. Brand mustered the last of his restraint and fought down his gorge for the second time that morning.

"Hey, Crane," he said, moving to stand only inches from the G-man's left side. Crane rotated on his heel and brought his gaze around to Brand like a cannon.

"As I've already instructed you once, Brand, my full title is Minister of Public Information, and you will address me as Minister Crane, Minister, or Sir. Any of those will do. Anything else may result in your being sequestered."

Brand stood back, stunned at the vehemence of Crane's protest. He was going to challenge the G-man on the changes in the report, but decided to err on the side of leaving the building a free man. At least for now.

"Right. Minister Crane. I wanted to ask about the omissions in this page of notes here. Am I right in assuming I'm to broadcast a report based on what isn't struck through or blacked out? Because that doesn't seem like much. And these notes here on the margin. Looks like the news about a guy getting torn to pieces is being charged into a tale of a drunk woman seeing pink elephants."

"That's correct, Brand. I don't see what the problem is," Crane said as he bent his face into a devil's grin.

Brand felt he'd earned a turn at vehemence, but he held it in. He'd had enough and wasn't going to risk his only chance at a sucker punch. Probably the only chance he'd ever get. If the page he held was the news from here on out, then Brand was about to give his last broadcast as a newsman in Chicago City.

At least he'd be the one who made the call.

"Sure thing, Minister Crane. Just wanted to clarify. Like you said just now. I'll take this down to the broadcast booth then?"

"That's right, Brand. And then come up to my office. We need to discuss your role here now that we have a full compliment of staff. You won't be on the microphone as often as before, but the people still expect to hear your voice. We'll have to find a suitable place for you. Carry on."

Brand lifted a limp hand in mock salute and stepped into the lift, not bothering to see if Crane returned the gesture or had noticed it at all.

CHAPTER 20

EMMA SAT STILL WHILE EDDIE REACHED ACROSS the dark wood of the table, resting his hands on hers. Candlelight reflected around their clasped hands, like a halo within the table's surface. Emma let her eyes dance across the table, following the movement of the candle flames and gas lamps that flickered like a scattering of stars over water. She followed the light out around the room. It glowed in the wood panels that covered every wall, ringing the space in a thin golden band that resisted the darkness. Emma felt her shoulders twitch each time a candle flame wavered, as if the candle going out might let the surrounding darkness get that much closer, making the threat of it consuming her that much greater.

"Where do we go, Eddie? We can't stay here waiting for that old gypsy to come back. Who knows when he'll get here? The coppers—"

"The coppers are after us, Lovebird. They're gonna be after us just the same, whether we're down in this speak or up on the street. My money's on us being safer underground so long as it's daylight up top. We got a few hours until the curfew. Then we can see. Besides, you heard the man. Nagy gonna put me to work, like he said. Probably have me help him cut shoe leather like last time."

"I thought you played down here in the speak," Emma said, confusion wrinkling her brow.

"I do. But other times, like when it's daylight and Eddie Collins needs some spending money to buy something nice for his girl. Times like that, I come down and help around the place, maybe do a little work for Nagy's friends and neighbors."

Emma felt her thinking about Eddie shift as he spoke. He'd always been her jazz man, the horn player she'd fallen in love with. But she'd never asked him what he did during the day, or if he even had work other than playing gigs at speaks around the city.

"What kind of work, Eddie? What have you been doing?" Emma asked. Eddie's face twisted up in a defensive sneer and his eyes bent with hurt, so Emma tried again. "I mean, you said you did these things for me, so you could be good to me. But I don't need you to do anything but be the man I love. Eddie and his band and his horn. Eddie at night, with his arms around me. Eddie who doesn't need me to be a little rich girl like all the other rich girls. I just want to know what you've gone through. And to tell you that if you did it for me, and if it was tough on you, that you don't need to do that anymore."

Eddie's face softened while she spoke, and he stretched both arms across the table to clasp his hands over her shoulders. They leaned together and kissed and Emma felt her sorrow and worry dissipate in the heat from her lover's lips. Eddie leaned back and Emma wanted to pour herself across the table to follow him. Their eyes met and she knew her worry had been for nothing. Whatever work he'd done it hadn't been that bad. Nothing like the dirty and dangerous work in the stockyards, railyards, or factory lines where most of Eddie's neighbors made their pay.

Emma smiled at her lover and opened her mouth to speak when a shuffle of footsteps overhead broke in on their quiet tenderness.

"Guess old Nagy came back, hey?" Eddie said, shifting his chair back so he could stand. He froze in a half crouch with his hands on the table when gruff voices filtered down through the cracks around the trapdoor, invading their hideaway. The voices were muffled, but Emma knew well enough who was speaking. Only a copper's voice can cut the air like a gunshot, and especially when that copper is on the hunt.

"That's her car, all right," Detective Wynes said in the garage over Emma and Eddie's heads. "Radio in. We'll have it towed out of here."

Emma heard a second voice grunting in reply, then footsteps as someone left the garage. She stood, slowly, making sure not to jostle the table or chair. Even a scrape against the earthen floor might be heard through the trapdoor.

Wynes spoke up again. "You search the shop. I'll handle the car and garage."

A third voice replied this time before Emma heard the telltale footsteps of the speaker leaving the garage. Wynes was up there alone. She had his gun still, and her father's revolver. Could she take him before the other two coppers came back? Eddie must have guessed her thinking because he came to her side and clamped a hand over her wrist. Emma realized then that she'd already half-lifted the revolver from her pocket. She let the heavy object drop from her fingers and met Eddie's gaze. His eyes flared caution and begged restraint as he turned his head back and forth in a tight arc.

Emma felt her lip quiver with fear, and her eyes welled. The trapdoor had to be covered somehow, otherwise Wynes would be down here already. What would they do if Wynes found it though? She'd have to shoot it out with him. But he was a copper. She'd stared over the barrel of her gun and into his eyes just that morning. In that moment, with snow melting into her shoes and freedom waiting in the car behind her, Emma believed she could shoot Wynes down if she had to. Now though, with the cellar's promise of security rapidly peeling back and away, Emma knew she wouldn't get the gun out of her pocket before Wynes could plug her. This was the end of her run, and Eddie's, too.

From above them, the sound of Wynes opening her car doors came through the boards of the trapdoor like the normal noises of a house. Someone in another room opening a cupboard or closet. Sounds of domesticity, not of violation or threat. Wynes got into the car, his weight making the springs creak. Emma heard him rifling through the vehicle, getting out and walking around to the back. He popped open the boot and Emma heard her bag tossed onto the floor of the garage. A scuffling and shifting in the earth over their heads as Wynes kicked the bag open and threw their belongings around. Some muffled cursing.

"Where is it, Miss Farnsworth? Where's my damn gun?"

Emma clapped her hands over her mouth and bit back the scream in her throat. Did he know they were in the cellar? Was the trapdoor uncovered all this time? Eddie gripped her by the shoulders and slowly walked them both to the back of the cellar space, where they hid behind a heavy table. After a quiet moment with no further sounds from above, Eddie stood and made to lay the table down, shifting it against his hip and sliding its weight down his leg. Emma stared in wonder for a second. When Wynes cursed overhead again, Emma snapped out of it and helped Eddie put the solid block of wood between them and the cellar entrance.

Eddie crouched behind the table, his back to Emma while she folded herself into the corner. They stayed that way for a stretch of anxious, silent minutes. Emma expected with every breath to hear the creak of the trapdoor and the stamp of heavy feet on the wooden steps. Muffled voices came from above and Emma's eyes flashed on the ceiling. Wynes was talking to someone else again, but this far from the trapdoor made his words indistinct and all the more threatening, like night sounds in a quiet house.

A motor started. They were driving her car away instead of waiting for a tow vehicle.

"We're sunk," she said to Eddie, no longer worried about being heard. "Sunk, and it's all my damn fault. I'm so sorry, Eddie."

He turned to face her, warm eyes glowing in the dark cellar. She watched the glimmer of reflected flames dance in his eyes and felt the comfort of home and hearth warm her skin. "Ain't sunk anymore than we're caught, Lovebird. Not yet at least."

Emma would always remember what happened next as an act of divine intervention. The sound of wood scraping on wood came from across the cellar as the trapdoor was uncovered. Then the creak of the hinges followed by shouts for her to come out. She cowered in the corner, clutching Eddie to her side as he ducked below the table he'd overturned. Shouts from above mixed with a cry of alarm, and footsteps raced out of the garage. Emma's eyes rounded in terror as the panel beside her slid away to reveal a tunnel entrance.

Nagy's wrinkled face poked out from the tunnel. He waved them into the darkness beside him with one hand and held the other to his lips, cautioning silence. They moved fast, Emma keeping her eyes on the cellar steps as she followed Eddie into the tunnel. Nagy worked a handle set in the wall and the panel slid back into place, concealing the passage once more.

"We go to *Bee-rosh*," the old gypsy said. "Come." He lifted a crank torch from his belt and illuminated their earthen escape route. Eddie gripped Emma's hand and she stayed close to him, hanging her free hand on his shoulder.

"Who's Biros?" Eddie asked when they'd gone a few steps.

"Friend," Nagy replied and kept shuffling forward, cranking light out of the slender tube he held before him. The tunnel was straight, that much Emma could tell. But which direction they'd taken from the shop and how far they had to go were mysteries she had no answers for.

"Is it far?" she asked, hoping the answer would be **No**.

"Only far enough," Nagy said with a chuckle. "Biros is tailor. Across street from Nagy's house. Makes clothing for *Mawd-yars* and Roma here in Village."

"Who?" Emma asked without thinking. She realized her mistake as soon as Nagy spoke his reply.

"Us. Gypsies," he said, letting the last word fly from his tongue like a wad of spit. As if he noticed Emma cringe at the sound, Nagy laughed softly into the dark earthen passage. "Biros is good gypsy.

Good Roma. He make you new clothing. Replaces ones policeman threw around Nagy's garage."

The mention of the police brought Emma's mind back to their flight and the reason for it. She couldn't help but feel guilt and shame for putting Nagy in the copper's sights. His shop would be trashed, no doubt. Detective Wynes had enough of a reputation that Emma felt sure the man would do everything but set the cobbler's building on fire.

"Mr. Nagy," she said in a whisper.

"Yes," the old man said, drawing them to a halt and turning to face Emma and Eddie. The glowing filament in his crank torch stayed lit briefly and then died. He turned the handle to keep the space around them illuminated as he spoke. "What does Eddie Collins' girl, his Lovebird, want to say to Nagy?"

"I'm sorry, Mr. Nagy. I'm sorry for making trouble. For you. It wasn't Eddie's doing. He was just trying to help me out of a fix I got myself into. I don't know how I can make it up to you now and I'm sorry. You've been kind and—"

"Is no need for sorry. Not from Eddie Collins' girl called Lovebird. Governor maybe should apologize. But he won't. Nagy knows this. Nagy does not worry. Is the same in old country."

"What do you mean?" Emma asked.

In reply, the old man pulled a crumpled wad of paper from his pocket and handed it to her. He gave the crank torch to Eddie, who worked the handle to keep light on the page Emma opened up and read. At the top, the Governor's symbol reminded Emma of bulletins and orders that she had read in her father's office. The text below, however, sent an icy shiver through her chest and down to her gut where it wormed its way in and then through every bone in her body.

Citizens of Chicago City are advised of the implementation of Eugenic Protocol 421. Persons meeting criteria for internment under EP421 are advised to report to the nearest containment and dispersal facility immediately.

These actions are in accord with the Governor's Guidelines for Eugenic Enforcement.

Below these words was a list of the oldest neighborhoods in the city, including this one. Eddie's, too. Below the list of neighborhoods, and under the words *eligible for internment*, were groups of people living in those neighborhoods.

"What is this?" Emma asked. Her eyes welled as she read the groups named in the list.

Negro

Italian

Gypsy

"Is like in old country," Nagy said again, shrugging. "Government wants to change city. So government first removes unwanted parts. Then government builds new city on top of old one. New city brings new people. Government makes who comes, who goes. Who stays, who doesn't."

"But … I don't understand. Where are they going to build? Chicago City doesn't have that many abandoned districts. Maybe a handful, but—" The truth hit Emma in the gut and she nearly buckled under the strain of knowing what was to come.

"Nagy already says, yes?" The old man somehow managed a feeble smile, casting a hellish irony over his words. "First, government removes what government does not want."

CHAPTER 29

AIDEN DIDN'T SLEEP. HE COULDN'T. SO HE sat up on his bed letting a dim glow come into the window from the searchlights. Chicago City never looked so bleak and cold and dangerous to him as it did that night. Digs had been torn apart by a monster. Aiden knew it had been a monster. Not even a copper's ironwork hound would make the kind of noises he'd heard in the alley.

And the pictures he'd seen on Mr. Brand's camera box.

As soon as dawn broke, Aiden scampered out of the house to retrieve the camera from where he'd hidden it last night. He snuck back inside and was halfway up the stairs when his mother's voice came to him from the hall above.

"Aiden? Is that you? Why are you outside so early?"

She was coming around to the landing. Think fast, Aiden. Get your tongue working. Say some—

"Getting an eye on the street, Ma. Figured I should make a good start finding work again," he called up to her. Aiden turned around and went into the kitchen to get the coffee going. His father wouldn't be up yet. His job at the Field Museum didn't start until noon, but it went all the way through to curfew. Cleaning up the place took a lot of time. His mother would be out the door in a couple hours though, heading to her reception desk at the museum.

Aiden stashed Mr. Brand's camera box in the pantry, behind some cans, and grabbed the canister of coffee beans. He crossed his fingers that his mom wouldn't start thinking about dinner until after she got home. She came into the kitchen as Aiden was pouring the coffee.

"I'm glad you're taking this seriously, Aiden. Losing a job now … " She busied herself getting the cream and stirring it into the dark liquid in her mug. She looked around the table and sighed, then stood up. Aiden realized he hadn't put the sugar on the table and dashed for the pantry.

"Thank you, Aiden. There's no need to act like a servant though. Your father and I just need you to find work." She stirred sugar into her cup, sipped from it, and set the cup down. "We can't afford to send you to the university. The bank foreclosed on the Milton's place last week. And with the curfew, your father can't work the swing shifts he used to." Aiden's mother looked him in the eye. "You have to be helping out."

"I will, Ma. I promise." Images of Digs in the alley threatened to send Aiden crashing into his mother's arms, wrapping himself around her like a child instead of the young man he was growing into. One more year and he'd be old enough to enlist or maybe try for work with the maritime outfits. He could almost see himself on a steamship. Maybe even one of the new Tesla boats. He'd wear a thick scarf and cap like the guys he'd seen at the docks, a pea coat, too.

Even in these fantasies, all Aiden could hear were the sounds in the alley.

His mother went back upstairs to get ready for work. Aiden told her he'd be hitting the streets straight away. She said he should pack a lunch but he said he was going for a job at a lunch counter or grocer's because if he got one they usually feed you. Not much, but enough to keep you going for your shift.

"That's good thinking, Aiden," his ma said from the upstairs landing. He waited until he heard the bedroom door close before grabbing Mr. Brand's camera box from where he'd stashed it. His ma probably wouldn't be in the pantry until later, but it'd be just his luck that today she decided to check how much lard they had stored up.

· · ·

Later that day, Aiden left yet another grocer's with his hands still idle, bringing the day's tally to eight lunch counters and five grocers without a single bite. He trudged through the wet streets, kicking at low drifts of snow and wrapping his coat tighter around him every time a gust came up. Aiden carried Mr. Brand's camera box under his coat so that his anxious fingers wouldn't be tempted to fiddle with the knobs and dials again. He'd thought about going by the Record to see if he could catch his boss there. But Aiden remembered how that G-man told him and Digs never to show their faces around the place again.

Digs wouldn't be. Aiden knew in his gut that he shouldn't either.

He stepped into a soda fountain and spotted a couple of birds in dark suits standing at the counter. Something about the two birds gave Aiden the willies but good. He backed out of the place quiet as a mouse and hot-footed it over to the next block.

The streets felt quiet for a midday hour. Wagons rolled by. Bicycles zipped past. But fewer than usual. The last few days really put a clamp on Chicago City's mood. The city had been under the weather since Valentine's Day. That massacre business over on Clark Street. People were talking about it like it was a phony story that Mr. Brand cooked up to sell papers. But those guys in suits had bought every copy Aiden had. Same as happened to Jenkins and Digs that day. Aiden's heart skipped a beat.

Jenkins and Digs were both dead. He hadn't got the skinny on what happened to Jenkins, but Mr. Brand had said it was bad news. The Outfit was involved; they were sending a message. Aiden had heard what those guys would do to a fella when they wanted to send a message, and he'd seen what happened to Digs.

Was he next on the list?

A few blocks farther along and the stabbing fear in his belly turned to hunger. He hadn't eaten anything all day and regretted not taking his mother's advice. Could he keep anything down? It was worth a try.

Better to eat now than to go home with no job and an empty stomach to boot.

At the next corner, Aiden stepped into another lunch counter. He didn't bother asking about work and ordered an egg salad sandwich with the change he had left over from the sawbuck he got on Valentine's Day. The chilly coins in his pocket stung his fingertips, and Aiden couldn't help but think the sensation was from the coins being the Devil's own money.

His sandwich came and he forced himself to take a bite. He had to eat, otherwise he'd be a shivering wreck when he got home. The guy at the grill switched on a radio set and told Aiden to eat up. He tried to return the smile, but Mr. Brand's voice crackled out of the squawkbox on the wall and Aiden nearly spit out his first bite.

… of ill repute. That's what you'd all call a whorehouse. Mrs. Gordon was a prostitute who used to work for Al Capone's Outfit. It seems—

When Mr. Brand's voice cut out, Aiden set his sandwich down and stared at the radio set, willing it to come to life, for his old boss to come across the airwaves and tell him the scoop. Give him something to go on. A second later, a whiny voice that sounded like it was coming from inside a tin can squeaked out of the set.

This is Franklin Suttleby, with the Ministry for Public Information. Citizens of Chicago City are asked to disregard that last broadcast. It was unauthorized and contained no factual evidence or details. We now return you to a repeat broadcast of last night's episode of Flatbush Ranch, which will be followed by a repeat of your favorite drama, Uptown Rooms and Downtown Dollars.

Aiden nearly choked on the food in his mouth when the door opened and two birds in suits came in. They looked a lot like the fellas from the last joint. These two had the same tight suits, tailored up nice, just like Outfit torpedoes. They went straight to the cook and started asking questions.

Aiden played it cool and finished chewing. As he swallowed, he caught the words *kid* and *newsboy* from the guys talking to the cookie. Aiden put a hand on his coat to hold Mr. Brand's camera box and slowly got off the stool. He backed up one step and made a dash for the door.

The suited guys gave a yell and came after him, but he had the jump on 'em and made it away clean. At the first corner, Aiden went right, slid into an alley behind a drugstore and came up against the grill of a delivery van. The driver braked hard and shouted from inside the cab, shaking his fist. Aiden made his way past the van and grabbed at the door when he got around the back. The driver slowly edged into the street. By the time he got moving, Aiden was tucked in the back of his box and holding the door closed.

He rode in the van for what felt like a dozen blocks, maybe more, until the crunch of gravel told him the driver had pulled up along the riverside. Aiden decided to hop out as soon as the van stopped. He popped the door and nearly hit someone who had been reaching for it. Following his momentum, Aiden tumbled from the van box and came face to face with a surly looking guy in a flat top bowler and heavy coat. The guy smelled like moneybags and looked the part, too. He shouted something at the driver, who had come out of the cab.

"That's the kid tried to get run over. Hey, kid!"

Aiden hot-footed into a maze of houses facing onto the north side wharves. His neighborhood was only a few blocks over. He'd make it home. He kept saying it over and over while he held the camera box tight to his chest under his coat.

Gonna make it home. Gonna be okay.

Aiden did make it to his street and had his home in sight, but he didn't like what he saw at all. He stooped behind a neighbor's fence and moved up to get a clear look at what was going down. A long black sedan was parked in front of his house. Two men in suits came down the steps. Behind them another man led Aiden's mother and father out of the house. That bird had a fancy looking rifle and wore a uniform, just like the soldiers standing out front of the Daily Record now.

The soldier bundled his parents into the sedan while the suits stood around like they expected someone else to show up. Another soldier came out of the house and stood on the porch. "Kid's not here," he said to the suits by the car. "I checked the whole place. He must still be on the street."

"Wait here," one of the suits said. "He might come back." The first soldier went back to join the other one. They both went into Aiden's house while the suits drove away with his parents in the sedan. Aiden stayed down until the sedan turned at the corner and drove out of sight.

His parents were being arrested. Those guys weren't with The Outfit. None of them were. Not the guys at the sandwich counter neither. Even the tough birds who bought the papers on Valentine's Day. They were all G-men. Had to be. Nobody else had pea shooters and soldiers with 'em like the guys inside his house.

What should he do?

Like an answer to his silent question, the curfew bell rang out through the cold afternoon air. It couldn't be time yet. The sun was still up, even if it was hidden behind a heavy dark cloud. It had to be a mistake.

Aiden searched the sky. Patrol boats circled the neighborhood. The silver pigs passed through thick blankets of white smoke from nearby chimney stacks. Aiden risked a glance at his house. The front door stood open and a trail of cigarette smoke filtered out and he caught muffled words and laughter. The soldiers were right inside the door. Tucking Mr. Brand's camera box tight under his arm, Aiden buttoned up his coat and moved out of his hiding place.

With some careful duck and dodge tricks he'd seen Digs pull, Aiden made his way around houses and yards until he was on a dirt track between the two oldest homes in his neighborhood. The Miltons had owned one of them. It was still empty. Should he try to hide out here? Would the G-men start searching for him? Would the monster that killed Digs come after him at night?

Every car that went down the street put a knife in Aiden's gut. He forced himself to move along the track and onto the street at the other end. The thought of what he would do once darkness fell nearly paralyzed him, but he kept on, making for the quiet roads far away from his Old Town neighborhood.

He'd made it a few streets from his house when a metallic clicking startled him. He ducked into an alley behind some waste barrels. He had to squat in a snow drift, but the barrels were the only cover he had. Two crabs scuttled along the pavement, heading in the direction of his street. A clanking followed them and Aiden squeezed himself tighter behind the barrels. He held his breath and prayed the ironwork hound wouldn't come down the alley. The machine clanked along the sidewalk and stopped at the mouth of the alley.

Muffled voices carried down to him and Aiden stayed still. His feet grew numb in the snow drift. An icy chill crept up his pants. He wanted to move like nothing in the world could be better, but the fear of getting caught kept him frozen like a statue. Aiden's heart thundered, and he shrank down when he heard the crackle of a bullhorn echoing from above.

"Citizens, curfew under Civic Order one-one-three-eight is now in effect until oh-five-thirty hours. Officials from the Ministry of Safety and Security are searching for known fugitives. Citizens are advised not to interfere in official actions. That is all."

The ironwork hound clanked away and the muffled voices followed. Aiden risked a glance and immediately ducked back behind the barrels. A G-man stood at the mouth of the alley holding one of those fancy rifles. The sound of a car motor put Aiden's stomach in a knot. He remembered his parents being put in the car and taken away Would the guy arrest him, too, or just kill him? Like Jenkins and Digs had been killed? A car door opened and closed then the car drove away. Aiden peered out and saw an empty sidewalk.

Running down the alley, Aiden kept throwing looks over his shoulder in case they'd been waiting him out. But nobody came tearing after him. Overhead, patrol boats kept circling. Every so often the ships broadcast the same announcement about curfew and fugitives. Aiden slid into a narrow alley that branched off the one he'd been in. He made it a few steps before he drew up short and nearly flew back out the way he'd come.

He was in the alley where Digs got it. The cellar window seemed to wait like the mouth of a waste chute. Aiden went stiff like an icicle when a car motor roared down the main alley. A sedan raced past where he'd been standing moments ago. The car stopped at the far end of the alley, then drove away with a squeal of tires.

Seconds later, the car pulled up at the other end of the narrow branch where Aiden hid. Just the end of the bonnet stuck out where he could see it. Doors opened and closed and feet crunched on gravel. The G-men seemed to be heading back to the street along with their ironwork hound. Its clanking steps echoed into the narrow alley and sent tremors of fear into Aiden's throat.

He edged deeper into the alley, moving fast and stepping in the line of snow that ran down the length of one building. It froze his feet even more but kept them from scraping in the gravel. The sedan hadn't moved. The clank of the hound came closer. At the window, Aiden pawed through the snow. The stick came out in his shivering pink fingers. He worked it against the window frame like he'd seen Digs do. The window gave a creak as it opened. Aiden looked up and down the alley at the slivers of light at either end. No movement. No shifting shadows or bulks of men and ironwork hounds coming into the space. Up above an airship flew by, broadcasting the same message that spelled doom for Aiden. He slid into the cellar and closed the window behind him. He couldn't latch it, and he knew the G-men would be there soon enough.

Aiden looked around the cellar. Crates of apples and shelves of root vegetables lined the space. At one corner a short flight of wooden steps led up to a door. A band of light glowed from beneath the door. In the opposite corner, another door was set into the wall. Aiden went to it, remembering what Digs said about the tunnels in the old city. The door was barred with a thick wooden timber set in two hooks. Aiden struggled with it but got it loose. He lifted one end, until the other end touched the wall. Moving slow, Aiden let the timber slide down and lean up against the corner, out of the way.

He tried the handle but the door wouldn't budge. Footsteps overhead told him that McCoy's Grocery was still open. Probably the old man himself since the curfew was on already. Maybe he'd come downstairs? Aiden ran his hands around the door in front of him, feeling for anything that might be holding it closed. His fingers brushed across a notch in the doorframe and he pushed at it. Something clicked in the wall and the door popped open a bit. He pulled it the rest of the way against old hinges that squeaked and groaned in protest.

The footsteps overhead grew rushed and Aiden heard shouting. A low voice gave orders and then Aiden heard the *thump-clank* of an ironwork hound. He jumped through the doorway into the darkness beyond and pulled the door shut behind him.

CHAPTER 30

IN THE BROADCAST BOOTH, BRAND PICKED OVER the page Crane had given him. He saw where someone had numbered the sentences, apparently ordering the statements into a neat and tidy pile of information. Thinking about that word, Brand pinned a mental badge on Crane as the author of the *redactions, amendments, and clarifications* in this report.

The lights flashed on and off in the broadcast booth and the 'On Air' sign by the door flickered to life.

"Ladies and Gentlemen of Chicago City," Brand read from the page before tossing it down the waste chute behind him and picking up his broadcast without missing a beat.

"'Last night, February nineteenth, a young man was murdered in the Old Town neighborhood. This wasn't just any young man, but a former employee of the Chicago Daily Record, now the Ministry for Public Information.

"'It seems this information, however, is too hot for some ears, so this reporter has been advised to offer you other information regarding the death of one Peter "Digs" Gordon.

"I'll let you decide which is bunko and which is the truth.

"According to a report written by the Minister of Public Information himself, one Jameson Crane, it seems that Mr. Gordon's mother returned home from a night of debauchery at a local house of ill repute. That's what you'd all call a whorehouse. Mrs. Gordon was a prostitute who used to work for Al Capone's Outfit. It seems—

Brand stopped talking as the *On Air* light went dim and the broadcast booth door slashed open. Crane stood in the doorway, full of bluster and clutching a few pages that he mashed in his grip as he stabbed a finger in Brand's direction.

"The Ministry of Safety and Security has been notified of this breach of the public trust, Brand. You are under arrest. Officers are on their way. And in case you get any ideas about running, I'm about to inform the soldiers outside that you're a threat to public safety and a fugitive. They'll have orders to shoot you if necessary."

Brand gained his feet when the door opened. Now he stepped toward Crane, who hadn't moved from the doorway. Stepping forward with his left foot, Brand let his right hand hang loose. Images of Digs Gordon blurred in his mind until all he saw was violence against a night sky. He took another step and was in reach of Crane. The company man stood there fuming.

Brand balled up his fist and slammed it into Crane's gut. The man toppled over and coughed all the air out of his lungs. He followed this by coughing up whatever he'd eaten for breakfast. Brand darted a quick look into the hallway and saw no one. At his feet, Crane slumped on his knees and struggled for breath. Brand's foot connected with his ribs. Crane fell face forward into the broadcast booth, crumpled and wheezing. Brand slid the door shut. Still thinking of Digs, and Jenkins, too, he went to the desk and grabbed the microphone, ripping its connections loose. Crane struggled to stand as Brand whipped the microphone down and across the man's jawline. Crane went slack and hit the floor in a heap.

Brand grabbed up the pages that Crane had when he came in.

"Important information in here, Minister Crane? The kind the people need to hear?" Brand spun to toss the pages into the waste chute, but his eye caught the first line of text and he paused. Hardly believing what he read on the page, Brand stuffed the clutch of papers into his pocket and pitched the microphone into the waste chute behind him. The sound of whirring gears and clacking blades gave way to a grinding noise and then an alarm sounded, alerting the maintenance room. Brand hot-footed over Crane's limp form and cracked the door open.

The sound engineer stood in the lift and shouted an alarm as the door closed on him. Brand watched the numbers light up, showing the lift climbing. He shot down the hall to the stairwell door and was two flights down before he heard shouts from above. The stairwell let out into the basement. Down a dim corridor, Brand saw a figure turning a corner. He had the gimpy gait of an old man who'd left the better part of a foot in a trench. Mutton, the Record's trusted wrench and pliers man. Brand let him go and snuck down to the workrooms where the old man holed up every morning.

Mutton kept a tidy workspace. Shelves lined with machine parts and tools stood out from every wall of the cramped little cupboard. Brand quickly tossed through the tools on the bench. He grabbed a hand cranked filament torch and went to shove it into his pocket. Remembering the pages he'd scooped up, he took them out and gave them a quick scan. He had to be sure of what he read.

The Governor's seal marked each page as official. The text on the page was something else. Brand had seen orders for military operations before. He understood words like *mission*, *perimeter*, and *enemy*. What he hadn't seen before was a bulletin about Chicago City that used those words. Crane had his fingers in some kind of pie, and it looked to Brand like the kind you'd pass on eating unless you weren't given a choice. The date on the bulletin read February 21st, meaning whatever events were being reported on hadn't happened yet. It also meant that the people of Chicago City would be served a heaping pile of bunko unless Brand could figure out Crane's scheme. And a way to pull the lid off it.

Brand stuffed all three pages back into a pocket and tucked the crank torch into the other pocket. He slipped out of Mutton's cupboard. The back stairs were deserted and Brand didn't wait around for that to change. He launched up the first flight and kept the heat on as he climbed. At the third floor, he fought down the acid burning in his gut. When he heard a door open below and the voices of soldiers, Brand pushed on to the fifth floor. He didn't give his mind a chance to imagine what the soldiers would do if they caught sight of him. Those rifles they carried were made for getting the last word in.

"He's up here!" one of the soldiers shouted down below. They must have been on the first floor. Still, Brand pushed himself up the last flight of stairs as though the soldiers were right on his tail. At the door to the fifth floor, he paused and let himself breathe a second. Then the sound of boots clomped behind him, forcing him through the door and into the hall. It was empty, but Brand knew it wouldn't be for long. He'd hoped they would fall for his diving act and spend more time in the basement. But these were the kind of soldiers you wanted on the battlefield: full of know-how.

"Just my rotten luck it couldn't be the birds on the front door instead."

He reached the door to the print rooms, slipped in and held the door closed then pivoted and went to the loading doors. Brand counted three and stepped onto the mooring deck, hoping Cane hadn't followed through on his promise. The airbikes still hung on the trapezes. Thanking his luck, Brand hopped onto the closest one, fired the motor, and kicked loose the tether arm.

The bike dropped fast until the motor came up to speed. Brand turned the little craft down and in a tight arc so the mooring deck would cover his descent. Then he drove it forward in the chill air, aiming for the houses on the neighboring block. If he could make it to the back of the first house, he'd have a shot at getting away in the alleys. Unless the soldiers figured out where he went and followed him on the other two bikes. Brand cursed himself. He should have cut the other bikes loose before taking off.

Fearing the pain of a bullet in the back, Brand piloted the

airbike through the chilly air. When he reached the alley behind the first house, he thanked his stars for a second time and wove a path through the quietest streets he could find, always aiming at the river. Two blocks from the riverside, a metallic scuttling came to his ears. Brand cursed and urged the bike forward. From all around him, crabs poured out of their nooks in the sidewalk and foundations of buildings. Adding trouble to trouble, the rumble of patrol boats came from a few blocks away, drawing curious crowds to a halt on the streets.

A trio of heavy wagons crossed his path up ahead. Behind the bulk of the wagons followed a long school of cyclists. Brand guided the airbike into the mass of bicycles, ignoring the shouts of alarm and cries to *"Watch it, buster!"* An opening came as two lead cyclists split the school into lines on either side of Brand's path. He opened the throttle and used the bicycles as a screen. When the last bicycle passed him, he turned the airbike down a side street and along an alley that he knew let out at the river's edge.

Crossing the river would be a trick. Brand chose the last alley because it was midway between two bridges, and so far his plan held up. The soldiers on the roadblocks hadn't spotted him yet.

Dropping in and then out of a wagon's shadow, Brand took the airbike down to the riverbank. He coasted to a tree by the water's edge and checked he still had the crank torch in his pocket. He did, but the focusing lens was busted. Figures he'd pick up the one tool on Mutton's workbench that was down there for repairs. It'd light his way though. He hoped. Brand's destination didn't have much going for it by way of illumination, at least not if he could figure out how to get in.

Looking back at the bridges, he saw the soldiers on alert. They stood stiffly around their jeeps like watch dogs on a lead. Across the river, the opposite bank provided less cover, and it was an open stretch across the water, too.

With one foot on the ground and the other ready to pop the clutch, Brand sent his eyes around the riverbank. Down to his left a crew of tramps sat around a fire. One of them looked in his direction and lifted a cup in greeting. Brand's eyes glazed for a moment and he shook his head.

Was that—?

The tramp eyed him up and down and lifted a stiff armed salute. That's when Brand spied the rusty bicycles lying around the edges of the encampment. Two of the tramps got up and lifted their bicycles after some discussion with Chief. By the time they'd vanished, Brand had thanked his luck a hundred more times.

Chief's ghost winked out like the others. Brand blinked and forced his foot to stay on the clutch. He wanted to fly away, go anywhere but there on the riverbank. Then his old boss appeared beside him and Brand relaxed his grip on the throttle. He'd nearly opened it up and zipped out across the river. Tossing a look at the roadblocks, Brand was glad he hadn't moved. The soldiers had their eyes on him already. If he'd bolted, they'd have picked him off like a fish in a barrel.

Chief clapped a hand on his shoulder then, breaking Brand's concentration on the soldiers and their fancy electric peashooters.

"How's things, Mitch? See you got yourself in a jam you can't get out of. Again."

"Yeah, and thanks for the pep talk."

"Least I could do."

Brand sniffed at that and changed course, still keeping both eyes on the soldiers down the way. "You hear about your pals last night? Three of 'em supposedly froze to death. I'm betting it wasn't like that. Am I right?"

Chief's face fell into his shoes. If a tramp could look lower than he already did, Chief was giving it a try. "Yeah. We all heard about them. They didn't freeze to death, Mitch. They—"

"They got ripped apart by a monster. I know. Hell, I was in the room with it when Nitti got his. I'm betting it's responsible for Jenkins and now Digs Gordon can be added to the list. Conroy's next unless I can stop it."

"How are you going to do that, Mitch? Do you have any idea what that thing is?"

"All I know is what I've seen, pal," Brand said and pulled the pages from his pocket. "That power play you told me about the other night. I think this is connected. Something about a military operation over in Old Town and the Village."

Chief took the pages and gave them a quick glance before shoving them back at Brand.

"That's something else, Mitch. Has to be. Not even the gods would go that far—"

The curfew bell cut into their conversation. Brand couldn't believe his ears at first. Then a bullhorn crackled to life from a nearby patrol boat and the soldiers on the roadblocks went into action, pulling people to a stop on the street and lining them up.

Chief slapped a hand on Brand's shoulder again. But this time he used his other mitt to draw aside the city like a curtain. He let it drop and the world changed. Brand was still sitting on the airbike, but every layer of Chicago City's life spread out all around him. Skies rippled and roiled with clouds, thunder and lightning, blazing sunlight, and misty rainfall. The river ran around them, swollen in flood, and it sat still, frozen under a bed of ice. Buildings wavered and shimmered, like a thousand giant candle flames.

"Where the hell are we?"

"Behind the city."

Brand stared at his friend letting his confusion ask the question.

"It's memories, Mitch. Memories of all the people who've ever lived here. That's what makes a city what it is. Without people and their memories, you've just got concrete, steel, bricks, and asphalt."

"You learn all this in your first day on the job?"

"Comes with the territory, yeah. I don't have to wonder about anything back here. Ask me a question. If it's about this place or my job, I'll tell you true."

"What about the night you saved my hide? You said the other fella was showing you the ropes."

"He was, but that just means putting on a show for the people out there to watch. You know how it is. You see a couple of bums dancing down the street together, you don't pay them any mind.

But one tramp? You might see him in the morning over by the station and then you're across town and there he is again with nothing but a bicycle with two flat tires to get him there. Maybe you start to wonder about him a little."

Brand stared into Chief's eyes like he'd never seen the man before. "Am I cracking up?"

"No. Now where am I taking you?"

"Village," Brand said, shaking himself out of the stupor he'd let fall over him. He held in the shiver that crawled up his legs when he thought about his destination. "The curio shop."

Chief balked. "You sure, Mitch? I can take you someplace else."

"I can't think of any place safer," Brand said. "Up here the lead makes a hole that stays made. Down there it's just ghosts."

CHAPTER 31

NAGY LED THE WAY THROUGH THE DARK tunnel, keeping the crank torch going for the rest of the journey. Emma felt the cold earth biting into her, and imagined the icy ground overhead would collapse any minute, crushing her into the floor under tons of rock. She couldn't think of any better place to be. Not after reading that page the gypsy—. No, his name was Nagy. He was a shoemaker. He'd helped them and he had a name. And now his whole community was being rounded up like cattle and taken to some facility. The word made Emma shudder.

All she could think about were the people she'd left behind. Her family and friends. They weren't being rounded up, losing their homes, their cars, their lives. They were sitting pretty, just like she should be doing right now. Only she'd never be sitting pretty again. Not in Chicago City anyway. Not anywhere if she couldn't get out of this fix.

Nagy held up his hand and let the crank torch go out. Emma heard a knocking, like a hand on a door. The darkness in front of them turned to light and the tunnel flooded with the sounds of a meal in progress.

Emma followed Nagy and Eddie out of the tunnel and into a low ceilinged room. Three women sat on benches around a rough wooden table. Each woman ate soup from a wooden bowl. The spoons they held looked heavy and solid. Like they'd been pounded out by a blacksmith. The women briefly glanced at Eddie, their faces showing wonder, admiration, and fear. A man on Emma's right held open the door to the tunnel. He ushered everyone into the room so he could close it.

Nagy and the man exchanged some words in a language that enchanted Emma with its rhythms. The men spoke and phrases danced in the air around Emma's head, musical syllables singing to her of hard work and fierce passion. She understood at once why these people liked to hear Eddie play his horn. His notes flowed as freely and with the same strength as their speech. But the lilt and drawl in their voices told her that Eddie's music gave them something they missed, or at least didn't have enough of in their lives.

A woman at the table smiled, stood and came over to Emma, reaching to hold her by the shoulders and kissing her cheeks.

"Go with her," Nagy said. "Go with *Ess-ti*."

Emma followed the woman up a set of steps and into the back room of Biros' shop. Bolts of heavy wool and tools were strewn about on thick tables. A single set of garments was draped neatly on top of a pile of fabric. They were men's pants and a thick coat, and a heavy shirt of cotton. All appeared to be smaller than average for the men she'd seen in this neighborhood.

Emma let Eszti guide her to a chair and remove her coat. The cold air quickly pierced every opening in her clothes and Emma clasped her arms around her. Eszti draped her coat over her, but let it hang loose. She took a strip of terrycloth and wrapped this around Emma's collar and neck, making sure no hair was trapped beneath.

Then she lifted a pair of heavy shears and lopped off a thick lock of Emma's hair. Blond curls fell all around her as Eszti worked, cleanly and evenly removing her hair down to a neat close cropped style that matched most of the men Emma had seen since coming to the Village with Eddie. Next, Eszti took some charcoal and smudged the terrycloth with it. She used this to darken Emma's face around her eyes, daubing lightly. Emma spotted a mirror on a far wall and went to it. Without any facial hair she couldn't pass for a man from this neighborhood, but she might be mistaken for a youth.

Emma resisted the urge to paw at her hair, try to make it take an attractive shape. She had to keep up the charade until they were somewhere safe. Until then, she'd have to look like the common people in the city, just a laborer, someone with a job and aches and pains.

Only she and the people here would know how much of a sham it was. The aches and pains she felt were real, but they'd been caused by a lack of work, not too much of it.

"Where will we go?" she asked Eszti. The woman smiled and shook her head. Eszti went into the next room and came back with a thick woolen cap, which she placed on Emma's head. The gypsy woman stood back and smiled, like she approved. Emma tried to smile back, but heard footsteps on the cellar steps and turned to see Eddie and Nagy coming up to join her and Eszti.

"Is time to go. Past time," Nagy said. "Wagon is outside. Come," he motioned to Eddie, who followed quickly but not before draping a thick coat around his head and shoulders. He crouched as they left the building through a back door. Emma stayed behind with the women while the men arranged things outside. Nagy poked his head back in and muttered something in their language. The women ushered Emma out with them and they all climbed into the wagon, taking seats on benches against the sides. Eddie was nowhere to be seen, but Emma found him when she put her feet against the bundle of fabric beneath her bench.

The street out front bustled with activity. Wagons and carts, pedestrians leading livestock, all clattered and rumbled down the roadway. Shouts and commands from a megaphone broke the chilly afternoon air and Emma cringed as the bulletin Nagy had shown her was repeated twice.

The wagon rolled out from behind the shop and merged with the line of traffic on the street. Emma cast a worried look at Nagy, who sat across from her. He patted at the air in front of him as if to say *Don't worry*, and gave her a smile, too. But his eyes told her to stay alert and stay in character. She was a man now, a gypsy man, like him. She'd seen Eszti display the inability to speak English, so she could always do the same if pressed by a copper.

Glancing around the crowds, Emma saw a few men in uniforms. Coppers stood on the corner outside a restaurant. Mingled in with the crowds though were soldiers in jeeps and on foot, all of them carrying rifles that looked like nothing Emma'd ever seen. These men had visors covering half their face, and they moved with assurance and command, brushing past the people near them and not caring if they jostled anyone as they moved.

Emma saw one soldier threaten a young woman after he bumped into her and she fell against him to keep her balance. She carried a basket against her hip and Emma saw a small hand and foot extend from one side. The woman frantically wrapped her child against the cold once more and did her best to avoid the soldier's shouted violence. Emma's heart caught in her throat as the wagon trundled along.

Overhead, patrol boats sailed in a formation. Two small observation ships and a larger gunship moved in tandem across the neighborhood. The ships soared smoothly through the darkening afternoon skies. Watching them, Emma remembered the cards Madame Tibor had shown her. She would leave the city by flying. And she would help others escape, too. How could she—

The curfew bell rang out, shattering Emma's thoughts, leaving only the broken hope of escape. At the reins, Biros pulled the horses to a stop as a soldier advanced on them through the thinning crowd. Emma hadn't noticed before, but people were being taken off the streets and lined up against buildings where teams of coppers put them into shackles, making chains of prisoners. Possessions and livestock were left in the street like signs of a rushed evacuation, only the people those things belonged to were just a few feet away, looking at the remains of their lives standing in the street.

The soldier had reached their wagon and shouted for Biros to dismount. Another soldier came around to the back and ordered everyone out.

"Is early," Biros protested. Nagy's eyes flared with concern.

"Is curfew, Pops," the first soldier said, yanking Biros from his seat. "Now get over there with the rest of your family."

Emma flinched as the second soldier grabbed at her and yanked her off the wagon seat. The soldiers searched Biros and Nagy, then the women. Emma patted her pockets, feeling for the guns and then remembered she'd left them in her coat back in Biros' shop.

The soldier searched her next and Emma cringed, fearing he'd feel her woman's body beneath the heavy wool clothing, but the man only dug into her pockets and checked her belt before pushing her along the street. Emma caught up with Eszti and the other women, doing her best to act like she meant to protect them. She'd seen a few men in the crowds, all of them shielding their women from the soldiers as best they could. Emma and her band drew up against a house with its door standing open. She could see furniture and clothing tossed around inside the house.

A soldier came out of the house and stared directly at Emma. His visor made it impossible to guess his reaction. Did he recognize her?

"C'mon, you," the soldier said, pointing a finger at Emma. "Get the broads over there and stand with them. Which one's yours? This one?" the soldier aimed his finger at Eszti now. Emma nodded, forcing herself to stare at the soldier's visor as if to meet his gaze. She'd seen other men on the street doing the same, and she had to be a man now. For her sake, for Nagy's and Eszti's sake, and for Eddie's.

The thought of Eddie nearly put her in a faint. The wagon remained where they'd left it. And Eddie was still wrapped in the wool under the bench. Emma couldn't go to him. If she made any move to go to the wagon, the soldiers would search it to see what she was after. Emma swallowed hard, forced her tears to dry before they spilled, and stayed close to Eszti and the others.

Soldiers came by the group and put shackles around their ankles. Seven of them stood there, chained together. Biros was at the front of the line. Emma stood in the middle, behind Estzi. The other woman was chained behind her, and Nagy was at the end. Emma watched as soldiers herded other groups out of the neighborhood.

One soldier to a group, no group larger than a dozen people.

She wasn't sure how she and the others would escape, but something had to happen. Somebody had to do something. A distraction? What could she do?

Nothing, and she knew it. At least not yet. Maybe if they got into a place with just the one soldier by them. Maybe she could get word to Nagy somehow and they could make a plan together.

Soldiers kept moving lines of prisoners down the street and out of the neighborhood. Emma would cough to get Nagy's attention. That was it. She'd wait until the soldiers told them to move and would cough, turning her head to see if she could meet Nagy's eyes. The soldier was ahead of her, nudging Biros and yelling for them to move it. Emma got ready to cough on the next shuffling step. Instead, she dropped all thoughts of escape and focused on the terror in her chest when she heard the unmistakable voice of Detective Tom Wynes.

"Go on and join the house-to-house teams, soldier. I'll move out with your bunch."

CHAPTER 32

AIDEN SPUN AROUND AND PUT BOTH HANDS out, feeling his way down an earthen tunnel. He could only see a few inches in front of his nose, but the menace of the voices he'd heard forced him onward. Aiden kept his palms on both sides of the tunnel and counted his steps, like he'd been taught during a cave walk one summer. The scout troop leader had all the boys line up and walk through an unlit tunnel in a cave. It turned out to be only twelve steps from entrance to exit, but Aiden remembered feeling like it took half his life to walk through that pitch dark passage.

Now, with his hands rubbing crumbs of dirt from the tunnel walls, he stepped slowly and kept his breathing quiet. Up ahead a light flickered in the darkness. After five steps, Aiden saw it was a candle. He picked up his pace until he stood below the wiggling tongue of flame that grew from a yellow stub stuck into a wad of wax drippings. Aiden thought the candle was floating in the air until he saw the stout wooden sconce jutting from the tunnel wall. The candle guttered, dripping fresh melted wax onto the ground by his feet. A small mound of accumulated drippings sat in the dirt like the leavings of some underground animal.

Aiden stretched out a hand. The candle cast enough light for Aiden to see just beyond his fingertips. He shivered and kept moving into the tunnel. He passed from the glow of the candle, leaving it behind him. His palms instinctively found the walls to either side and he pressed on, forcing each foot in turn to lift from the ground, step forward, and find safe purchase on the dirt floor. One step. Two.

Another candle lit the path father ahead. Once he saw it, Aiden made for it as fast as he could. Five more steps and he was there. He reached it just as a man's voice broke the silence of the tunnel. Aiden waited, frozen in place with his hands against the walls. The cool earth made him feel safe and the silence settled in around him again. He let it be a blanket, something to hide under as he moved. One step forward. Nothing. Two steps. Three.

The man's voice came again. Another voice followed the first, and then the clink of a bottle against a glass. Laughter. Aiden's chest almost warmed to the cheer the sounds grew from, but his fright and tension won out as he remembered what Digs had told him about the tunnels.

Gypsies hid out down here. The kind who'd cut you up if you wandered into their territory. Aiden fought back a cry of fright. With his lips tight and eyes open wide, he stepped through the light cast by second candle. The tunnel around him looked no different than before. So where were the voices coming from? Above him maybe?

Aiden took a careful step and passed out of the glow of candlelight. He took another step and toppled forward, his foot catching on a cable stretched across the tunnel floor. Nearby, a bell jingled, but the sound was quickly drowned out by the scraping of wood on wood and a metallic click that Aiden recognized as the hammer of a revolver being cocked.

Shivering with his palms pressed against the dirt floor of the tunnel, Aiden waited for the gunshot. When nothing came he shifted his weight to his knees and made to stand. Aiden cried out when he felt thick hands drag him to his feet and grab the front of his shirt, pressing him against the wall. Dirt crumbled from the surface and fell into Aiden's hair and down into his eyes. He lifted an arm to brush it out but the hands on his chest shifted. One moved to his collar and the second brought a cold metal blade against Aiden's throat.

In the weak fringes of candlelight, Aiden couldn't see the man who held him, but he guessed enough about the fella to know he meant business. His hands were rough and calloused against the skin of Aiden's neck, and the blade had come out of nowhere.

"You don't move," the man said.

A lantern flared from down the tunnel and Aiden gasped when he saw the man's face. Bushy brows lifted over two angry eyes. Below them a sharp nose and flaring nostrils. At the bottom a quivering mouth with the lips curled back showing a fierce grin of rage.

"Still don't move," the man said.

Aiden grunted, "Uh-uh." No, he wouldn't move. Not even enough to shift his head side to side to show he understood.

The hand on his collar snaked around his shoulder and neck, pressing him into the ground where he stood, then pulling him away from the wall and shoving him into the lantern light. Aiden froze when he saw a doorway set into the earthen wall to his right. Through the door was a small room with a table and two chairs. Floorboards had been spread out to cover the bare earth, but it showed through in places. A tall thickset man with a fat drooping black mustache stooped in the tunnel. The guy was wide enough to fill the passage and prevented Aiden from even thinking about making a run for it. That and the knife the other bird still had poking at Aiden's back.

The big man held a bullseye lantern in one hand. The glare blocked Aiden's view of his other hand. Then the man turned the lantern aside, and Aiden saw he had a pistol in his mitt. Running was not in the cards. Not a bit. The man beckoned for Aiden to follow and stepped through the doorway.

The guy with the knife nudged him gently and Aiden stepped forward, following the other man into the room.

"Sit here," said the man with the lantern, motioning with the pistol at one of the chairs. Aiden heard the second man close the door and stand against it. The room had a higher ceiling than the tunnel, and the tall man could stand upright here. It was still dark, but the enclosed space was warmer. Aiden felt his ears and fingertips tingle as blood moved more freely under his skin.

The taller man spoke again. "You are boy. Only boy, not policeman. Right?"

Aiden nodded, and when it seemed that wasn't enough to satisfy the man, he said "Yeah. I'm—. Mister, I'm scared," he said. Aiden's chest bucked and shuddered as he sobbed. He let loose the tears he'd been holding back since he saw the G-men putting his parents into a car, leaving soldiers in the house armed with electric rifles.

The men blew air between their teeth. The one with the knife said something fast and the taller man barked a reply, cutting off any objections. They went back and forth, each speaking too fast for Aiden to follow, but he caught the mood of what was said. They weren't going to kill him. At least not here. Whatever they had planned, he'd live to see it.

The one with the knife came around to where Aiden could see him, his bushy eyebrows casting shadows in the lantern light, making his eyes that much more threatening and large as he stared down his nose at Aiden.

"You come, he says. Come to house. Stand."

The knife had been put away, but the man had no sheath on his belt that Aiden could see. His face was threat enough, so Aiden stood. The man extended a hand.

"*Lahz-low,*" he said "Other man is *Mee-hawl-yee.*"

Aiden wiped at his eyes and rubbed his fingers dry on his pants before shaking Laszlo's hand. He turned to Mihalyi and they shook as well. Before Aiden could thank them for not killing him, Laszlo put a hand on Aiden's chest.

"Open coat, please. Here," he said, patting the bulge over Mr.

Brand's camera box. Aiden did as he was told, even as his mind raced with thoughts of how he could escape and protect the camera box from discovery. Laszlo lifted the strap from around Aiden's neck and hefted the box. He passed it to Mihalyi who turned it in his hands in the light of the lantern.

Aiden opened his mouth then. "It's my boss—"

"Is camera," Mihalyi said, his mustache twitching over his mouth as he regarded the device and brushed his thick fingers across the viewscreen. Aiden wanted to say *Stop touching the box*, but his lips and tongue weren't in the mood to play ball.

"Professor's house," Mihalyi said, stabbing a finger at the ceiling. "We go."

Aiden cursed himself for being weak, and then remembered where he was and feared what would come next. He followed the men out of the room and into the tunnel. They put him between them and moved deeper into the earthen shaft. Aiden kept his hands out like before, touching the walls. He heard Laszlo chuckle behind him and almost pulled his hands in. But the thought came that he should act strong. Make up for the weakness he'd shown in the little room, crying like a child. He was scared still, but he was alive to be scared and that meant he might still get out of whatever trouble was coming his way.

CHAPTER 33

BRAND HELD ONTO THE AIRBIKE. CHIEF gripped the handlebar and rode them both through the city's memories. Flashes of light pockmarked the surfaces of buildings that rose and fell around them. Indistinct glimmers made the gossamer cityscape into a projected image rather than a reality. Brand knew what he was seeing couldn't be real, but the feeling in his chest told him it was.

Passing through the street he grew up on, Brand confronted his own memories. His family home stood down the block, flickering against a backdrop of blackness shot through with star points of light. Brand couldn't take it and shut his eyes against the scene, against the memories of his childhood and everything he'd thought forgotten and buried.

"Hang on, Mitch. We're almost there."

Chief veered their course around the stockyards, over the rail lines, and finally into the Ukrainian Village. They pulled up beside the looming mass of an enormous home, larger than any other on the street. A collection of newer homes and a few apartment blocks hovered like supplicants around the larger house.

"Even back here this place looks like a palace," Brand said.

"We both know that's not true though, don't we?"

"And how, brother," Brand agreed. "Let's get me out of here and into there," he said, jutting his chin at the building. Chief breathed out and gave Brand a look. Brand gave him a look back.

"You can't hang around here all day, Chief. Any minute your boss'll be sending you on a delivery, hey? So just let go and I'll get out of your hair."

Brand couldn't explain the change in his mood. Maybe it was where he was headed. He'd grown resentful during the ride. Something loomed over Chicago City's future, and it wouldn't do for Brand to just sit around waiting for it to happen. But that didn't mean it should fall to him to make things right. Chief lifted his hand off the airbike and Brand couldn't hold back the shiver that rippled up his spine when the city fell back around him like a drape.

He straddled the airbike and hovered behind an evergreen tree by the front steps, his head just level with the porch. Chief's head appeared in the air beside Brand, only long enough for the man to sigh at him and shake his head.

"Good luck, Mitch," Chief said before he vanished behind the curtain.

Shouting and the sounds of vehicles came from down the street. Brand almost edged the airbike forward, but thought better about it. If the Governor's boys had followed him somehow, he'd be a sitting target out here. Nobody in the Village had as much as a bicycle. They all used wagons, horses, or their own blistered feet to get around Chicago City.

"I'll take any kind of luck right now," Brand muttered to himself. He slipped off the airbike and stepped out from behind the tree to examine the street. The Village was in full uproar a few blocks away and the commotion was heading in Brand's direction. Not wanting to get caught on foot either, he slipped back into hiding and searched for the escape route he hoped was still there.

The house next to him stood as it had the last time he'd seen it this close. Heavy and dark with peeling paint and cracked basement windows. But it was still the biggest, sturdiest building on the block.

Brand felt around the clapboard siding of the porch until he found the catch, his fingers lifting it slow and careful just as they had a year ago when he'd come here chasing a story about bootleggers. Chief had word from the Mayor's office about Capone's crew using old cellars and a tunnel network to run their hooch around the city. The cellars and tunnels were supposed to be closed off to prevent that very thing from happening. But somebody had gotten in, and now Brand was here again, following in their footsteps.

The side of the porch swung in on well-oiled hinges, not making a sound, and the tunnel entrance showed signs of use. Footprints and freshly tracked snowmelt marked the earthen floor of the passage. Brand went really slow, letting the door stand open behind him to give him light as he stepped deeper into the space. Three steps in and he lifted the crank torch from his pocket and spun the handle a few times to get a weak glow going in front of him. The stairs were still there, concrete steps, six of them, leading down to the basement below the manor house.

Brand waited and listened for movement or voices from below, in case anyone was there and had seen his torchlight. After a few quiet, deep breaths he moved to the steps, turning the torch handle and following the watery glow it let out. Even without its focusing lens, the filament's glimmer still helped Brand make out shapes in the darkness, but only just.

He slipped at the top of the steps, nearly missing the handrail in the dark. Brand's feet hunted for purchase on each step and finally he felt the soft earthen floor of the cellar. Remembering the space from when he'd been here before, Brand felt to his right and found the light switch. Should he hit it?

He heard noises from outside, shouting and the tooting of horns. Someone out there had a megaphone. Brand was probably safe down here. Anyone in the house would be watching the street.

He slapped his right hand against the button, letting his body sag against the wall in relief at finally getting a moment of quiet safety.

Light flickered on overhead and a single bulb glowed bright and clear in the cellar space. A set of steps descended into the space from across the room. All around the room shelves stood against the walls, packed full of items. Brand stood away from the wall and took it all in. Old picture frames, tools, lamps, cups and saucers, a doctor's bag and even a few pistols. On one shelf near Brand's head a small box held a collection of eyeglasses like a tangle of golden spiders with eyes the size of silver dollars.

Brand shook his head, recalling the story that had brought him down here before and the sense of failure he'd taken back to Chief's office along with the truth about the tunnel network. It was supposed to be Capone's liquor operation, his smugglers' corridor. All it turned out to be was a neighborhood full of immigrant gypsies who knew better than to let anything go to waste.

The tunnels went down into the ruins of Old Chicago itself, the city that had burned to the ground in 1871. For a few years, while the city rebuilt, tunneling was encouraged. People went down to collect mementos and lost possessions. After a time, the tunnels were forgotten, and the old city along with them. When they first discovered the tunnels under the manor house, the people living in the Village thought the Mayor had built them, so he could sneak his spies and police into their homes. Then the first kid had come back from the tunnels carrying a golden necklace, and then it was worse than the rush out to California.

Every gypsy in the neighborhood had gone down into those tunnels, and the things they'd brought back were put up for sale in the manor house above. There wasn't much to find, but they found enough. The manor house became Chicago City's most infamous curio shop, with belongings of the deceased up for sale alongside fakes the gypsies had made. Brand had to give it to them, because nobody had ever made the rich folks in Chicago City look so damn foolish before. They'd pile in from the Gold Coast neighborhoods, driving up in their cars and carriages, stepping lightly through the mud and beating a path to the shelves, fighting with each other for a chance to get the only remaining porcelain dish from this or that potter's shed, or to maybe find great old Aunt Doreen's cherished silver hairbrush.

Brand had been sent to get a story on Al Capone's hidden stash of booze and all he'd come back with was a dirt-encrusted beer bottle that some kid had dug up. It was that kid whose ghost haunted the space around him now. When the Mayor found out Capone wasn't using the tunnels, he quickly made sure the mobster wouldn't get any funny ideas. Teams of coppers went around the Village neighborhoods dynamiting any tunnel entrances they found. They hadn't bothered to check if anyone was in the tunnels before setting off the charges though, assuming the people knew well enough not to interfere with police business. It wasn't until the boy's mother came calling at the Mayor's office with her son's body wrapped in a sheet that anyone knew different.

The gypsies kept the manor house from harm because nobody ever found a tunnel connection in the building's cellar. Not even Brand, and he'd had a full day and night to search the cellar. The gypsies offered him the chance to find *the secret tunnel*, and laughed long and hard when he came up the stairs with nothing but his hat in his hand. The kid gave him the bottle and headed back downstairs to disappear in the cellar.

Standing in that space now, Brand still couldn't see anything that looked like a doorway. If there was a secret door, it was hidden but good.

A shuffling in the room overhead put Brand on alert. If the gypsies' reputation was to be trusted, they wouldn't take kindly to a nosy newshawk poking around in their cellar without permission. Before he had a chance to move into hiding, the shelf with the box of eyeglasses swung out into the room, knocking him across the brow.

A section of the wall followed the shelf. As Brand collected himself, a short man with a round face and weasel's eyes stepped out from behind the wall holding a pistol. Brand reacted fast, putting his hands up and giving a look of surrender as best he could. They might gun him down right here, but if they had arms out and at the ready, they were probably on the run from something. Brand's mind flashed on the sounds from outside, the horns and the megaphone. He figured he knew what it was the gypsies had behind them.

"I'm not a copper," he said, hoping that was enough to stop the little round-faced man from shooting him.

"Aw, sure enough you ain't," the man said, grinning like a fool and laughing out loud. "Hey, get this," he said over his shoulder. "Guess who's in our basement again. Mitchell Brand!"

CHAPTER 34

EMMA SHUFFLED ALONG WITH THE OTH-
ers, keeping her face half-turned away from the street. She
couldn't let Wynes see her, but she had to keep an eye on
him. He walked ahead of her, beside Eszti. Biros turned to regard
Wynes from time to time as they moved, and each time the detective snarled for the gypsy to keep his eyes on the road.

"Can't have you tripping, can we, Rigo?"

Eszti caught her breath and drew up short at the last word. Biros
halted, too, and Emma heard Nagy grumble from behind her.

"Don't like it?" Wynes said, staring Biros down. "Rigo?"

Emma eyed both men, worried that the standoff would end in
tragedy for them all. She wanted to stop it, tell Biros to let it be. She
understood *Rigo* had to be an insult. Her ears had caught plenty of
insults in the past, and even though this was the first she'd heard
that wasn't aimed at a dark-skinned man or woman, she knew well
enough how much weight the insult could carry. Biros' face shook
with anger and his mouth worked around words Emma hoped he
knew better than to let out.

A soldier approached from across the street, asking Wynes if he needed help with the line.

"No, I've got them," Wynes said. "Rigo and I were just having a chat here. Isn't that so, Rigo?" The soldier turned away and went to join his two comrades by a jeep. Emma hardly saw Biros' hand move, but she heard the slap of his palm across Wynes' cheek and saw the detective spin aside only to right himself and whip a gun out of his coat. The soldier came back with the others in tow. They held their rifles on Biros and yelled for him to stay still. Wynes came close to the man and gave him a smack across the face and then another. Emma barely kept her tongue, wanting to scream murder at Wynes, holler at him to lay off and pick on someone who wasn't chained up and held at gun point.

A soldier slapped a pair of bracelets onto Biros' wrists and looped a length of rope around them and the chain between his feet. If he wanted to raise his hands now, he'd have to upend himself to do it.

"Go on," Wynes said, poking Biros in the shoulder. "Lead the way, Rigo."

Eszti shouted a curse then, drawing Wynes' attention. He stepped closer and lifted his hand like he'd slap her. Emma stepped forward as far as the chain would allow. She put a hand up to cover Eszti's face and stared daggers at Wynes. For a moment, she forgot about being anything but a young man from the neighborhood. She bent her face into an angry glare and held her lips tight together. Wynes stared back and turned as if he'd let her have the smack instead.

"Is her brother," Nagy said from the back. "Hit me if you want to, but leave boy alone. Please."

Wynes looked to the old man and sniffed. He dropped his hand and then brought a finger back up to aim at Emma's nose.

"Keep a cool head and I might leave her be. Give me any trouble and a smack'll be the last thing your sister here has to worry about." With that, Wynes spun on his heel and addressed the soldiers. All but one went back to the jeep. The soldier went to the back of the line with Nagy and Wynes stayed up front by Biros. They moved again, shuffling along with chains dragging on the pavement, a steady cadence of rasping and grating.

After several blocks, too many for Emma to count, they reached the edge of the neighborhood, apparently the last of the prisoners to arrive. The street behind them was empty now. A roadblock had been set up at the last intersection before they left the Village and stepped into Chicago City proper. Two jeeps crossed the roadway, preventing anything bigger than a bicycle from getting through. Soldiers stood in the jeeps holding their ominous rifles. One soldier held a megaphone and shouted commands.

Wynes went up to this man and they exchanged a few words. The copper left then, stepping away from the jeeps and getting into the cab of a nearby police van. Lines of gypsies stood to either side of the roadblock waiting for trucks and police vans to drive them away. Line by line the neighborhood's residents were carted off, taken to the facility, a word that still burned like an electric shock in Emma's mind.

Their line was next up for transportation when Emma saw the air around the jeeps shimmer and flutter. The soldiers seemed to notice it, too. The one with the megaphone paused mid-sentence. Before the soldiers could react, the air whirled and whipped aside, revealing a man straddling an old metal bicycle on the street between the jeeps.

The man, a filthy tramp if ever Emma had seen one, laughed and bellowed at the sky. In one hand he held an empty wine bottle, which he threw at the nearest soldier, hitting the man in the face. The soldier's visor cracked and he went down in his seat, holding his hands to his eyes and howling. The other soldiers reacted then, drawing aim on the tramp, but holding their fire. The tramp took advantage of this and flung his arms out to either side, pushing at the soldiers nearest him.

Where the tramp found his strength, Emma had no idea, but the man knocked one soldier right out of his jeep. The other kept his balance and seemed to get his wits about him, setting his rifle aside and moving to grapple the tramp. Another soldier from the other jeep did the same. When they both had their hands on the man, the air shuddered again, like a fierce and purposeful wind had chosen just that spot to exercise its power. In an instant, tramp, bicycle, and soldiers vanished.

In the chaos of the tramp's appearance and vanishing act, a few lines of gypsies turned on their captors. They surrounded the soldiers tasked with keeping them in line and held them fast. Some soldiers were beaten to the ground. Emma looked to Nagy and then Biros, but neither showed any sign of wanting to fight. Biros couldn't anyway. The soldiers in the jeeps abandoned their posts and went to help their comrades, firing warning shots from their rifles into the ground. Emma's ears rang with the blasts as electric bolts seared the air and scorched the ground. Men and women who had overpowered the soldiers beside them quickly relented and went calm.

Emma waited for the worst. The soldiers couldn't let the revolt go unpunished. They were no different than the coppers who broke up speaks in Eddie's neighborhood. Somebody had to be an example. Emma shouted with Eszti and the others in her line when she saw the soldiers select a youth for their display of dominance. The young man couldn't have been any older than Eszti, maybe not even of age. As the rifle was raised, the youth quivered. He dropped the rage and fury from his face as tears fell down his cheeks.

Before the soldier could fire, the air shook around him, and again the tramp and bicycle appeared out of thin air.

"Boo!" the tramp shouted, grabbing the would-be executioner by the collar and vanishing from sight once more. The tramp flew in and out of view again, performing his trick twice more before the remaining few soldiers backed away from the roadblock and took up positions beside a waiting police van. The tramp whipped into view again, this time beside Emma. He stood with his back to her and yelled at the soldiers.

"Go on you damn worms. You damn rodents. Crawl back home where you belong."

The tramp's stink nearly made Emma retch into the street. He turned to face her and lifted a ring of keys from his pocket, stuffing them into her pocket.

"Go on, girl. Go on and get yourself out of here."

"Dad?" Emma's eyes swam and she felt the ground coming up to meet her. She fell into the tramp's embrace, felt his greasy hair and threadbare clothes smearing and scratching against her face.

"Go on, I said. Get yourself free and save what people you can."

The tramp whipped away from her and hollered at the soldiers again before vanishing one more time. He reappeared behind the police van and knocked two soldiers' heads together before flickering out of sight. Emma felt her knees buckle and her hands hit the dirt, catching her weight. She slumped forward onto her arms until Eszti reached to help her up.

"He gives you keys," Eszti said. Emma patted her coat and felt the key ring.

All around the roadblock was pandemonium. Lines of prisoners shuffled together, looking for hiding places and piling into nearby houses. Some headed back down the street, ignoring shouts from the soldiers. Only four remained, and of these only one had his rifle trained in the direction of the prisoners. The others darted their eyes this way and that, looking for all the world like frightened mice watching for the cat to return. The one eyeing the prisoners jerked backwards and Emma saw the tramp holding him by the throat. Seconds later both men vanished and the final three soldiers rushed away from the neighborhood.

Emma didn't waste any more time. With Eszti's help, she got their line out of sight behind a wagon. Eszti undid the shackles on Emma's feet first, then handed over the keys. Emma released Eszti and went to Biros. The man regarded her with suspicion.

"You know a messenger and do not tell us."

"A what?"

"Messenger. The Bicycle Man."

Emma shook her head and went to work unlocking the man's bonds. "I don't know what I know anymore. That tramp? Whatever he was, I don't know him. He couldn't have been my father. But that's who he sounded like and that's who he looked like." She stopped when the last chain fell from Biros' wrists. "Only my father never dressed like that and sure enough he never knew any magic tricks either."

Emma felt her stomach rising into her throat and fought it back. Whatever she'd just witnessed it had ended with her being free. At least as free as possible in this new version of Chicago City where soldiers marched entire neighborhoods off to jail. She handed Biros the keys. "Get somewhere safe, okay? I've got to get back to Eddie."

Shouting from the direction of the police van got her attention, and Emma stepped from behind the wagon to see what was going on. The tramp was back, and so were the soldiers. One of them had the man in a choke hold and two others had their rifles trained on him.

Emma didn't wait to see what happened. She got away quickly, moving off the main stem on a neighborhood street and stepping fast. Two blocks along and houses stood open and empty all around her. She thought about entering the nearest one when a soldier appeared in the doorway. He faced into the house and called for his comrade to join him. Emma kept out of sight until the two men had moved down the street to the next house.

She remembered what Wynes had said. They were searching the entire neighborhood. House by house, making sure nobody was left behind.

How many teams were there?

She'd have to risk finding out. The evening sky darkened above her and she slinked around the neighborhood, ducking into hiding every chance she got and watching for soldiers before moving again. Eddie may have been found already, or maybe he hadn't. But Emma wasn't leaving the Village until she knew for sure either way.

CHAPTER 35

AIDEN LET THE GYPSY, LASZLO, PUSH HIM forward, out of the tunnel and into the cellar of a nice home. He could tell it was a place for uptown living from the quality of dry goods and wine bottles all around him. The fancy looking jars, bottles, and dried meats were like something he'd seen in a dream or the stories Digs used to tell him about Gold Coast houses and the fellas who owned them. His mom found work there sometimes

Those were the best of times for Digs.

Aiden kept the tears in this time, but he couldn't stop his lip quivering. The gypsies waved for him to follow and the three of them climbed a set of carpeted stairs leading into a washroom off a kitchen. The house was arranged like Aiden's and for a moment he let himself feel that familiar safety. But the interior was different in so many ways that Aiden didn't for an instant think he'd just been through a bad dream. The gypsies led him through the kitchen and into the dining room, then out the other side and into the front parlor.

A warm light blanketed the hardwood floor and the dark wood of nicer furniture than Aiden had ever seen much less been close enough to touch. Light glowed from countless candles, and reflected in starlight, coffee, and amber from nearly every surface. Aiden wanted to reach out and touch the sideboard to his right, then the end table and chairs in the middle of the room. He wanted to touch everything, it all shined so beautifully. All polished wood and gleaming jewel-like glass. A man stood in the middle of the parlor regarding Aiden with gray eyes that smiled out from beneath a deeply furrowed brow. Aiden spotted the front door, across the room and behind the man. He couldn't run for it, no chance The guy would stop him.

He motioned for Aiden to take the nearest chair and Aiden sat, flinching upward as he touched the fine fabric. He worried that he might have tracked dirt in from the tunnels and would smudge the chair cushions. The man tutted, motioning for Aiden to resume his seat. He then resumed his observations. Aiden felt like he was being studied and examined, not watched for suspicious moves. All the same, he didn't like being watched this closely so he gave it right back, examining the man's face, looking for indications of intent.

The bird was no G-man or copper. He wore a tweed suit and dark leather shoes. Leaning against a chair opposite Aiden was a long black stick with a silver head and tip. A pair of fine leather gloves sat on the chair back beside the stick. The man's squat, slight figure seemed to hang in the air next to the chair, as though his feet merely rested on the ground and didn't support his full weight.

Aiden knew how to size a man up, at least enough to know this fellow was bad business in a fight. Unless you had him on your side. The man spoke in a language Aiden recognized from Mihalyi and Laszlo's conversations, though it wasn't until he heard it spoken here that Aiden knew it as a language. Before, in the tunnels, he'd been so scared he'd only caught sounds and mutterings, assuming the gypsies spoke too fast or low for him to make anything out. Mihalyi set Mr. Brand's camera box onto the end table beside Aiden, nodded to him, and patted him on the back before turning to leave. Laszlo followed him out.

"You may stay here."

Aiden whipped his head around from watching the gypsies leave and focused on the man again. He'd taken a seat in the other chair "If I may amend my statement, you may stay for as long as I am here. I will be stepping out rather shortly, I'm afraid. It seems those who would upset the balance have taken matters further than I had anticipated, and so I am forced to act without the privilege of preparation."

Aiden couldn't make half sense of the man's words. "Th—, thanks mister. I don't know but I'm in your debt I guess. I don't want to be a burden though, so I'll shuffle along soon as you tell me I gotta."

"My good fellow, I wish nothing of the sort. But come, let us use this brief time we have to prepare as we may. The Governor has crossed his Rubicon, and so should we two do the same."

Before Aiden could muster up the know-how to respond to the part he understood, the man stood and stepped over to a bookshelf on the far side of the room. Two more of his fine upholstered chairs sat with their backs to the bookshelf, and in between them, on the shelf at about chest height, was a Marconi box. Aiden's jaw fell open. An honest to goodness, real as you can get Marconi radio set. Inside a house.

Inside this fine as fine can be house. In this old neighborhood.

"Ain't nobody this side of the river and this far from the lake got a Marconi box, mister. Nobody but ...." Aiden thought better than to say the words he found on his tongue, but judging by the way the man's eyes glinted in the candlelight, it seemed clear enough he knew what Aiden had in mind.

"I am not now, nor have I ever been a member, beneficiary, or otherwise involved with the organization known as The Outfit. Please forgive my failure to introduce myself earlier; my name is Professor Timwick Argot Cather."

"Professor? Like in the university?"

"Yes. Like in the university. Rather, exactly in the university. I am head of the Department of Information Sciences."

Aiden screwed up his face and his tongue struggled to form the right question, but the man, the professor, responded again to Aiden's unspoken thoughts.

"I am the librarian. The Chief Librarian, if you wish to know my official title. While it would please me no end to entertain the other questions I see behind your eyes, I am afraid time is not on our side. Please understand that nothing pains me more than to put off the idea of dialogue over *Inquiry*." The man said the word like it tasted sweet to him, and he turned his face up like Aiden had seen guys do when they sipped hooch. He heard the word like a sigh of pleasure escaping the professor's lips.

Turning to the bookshelf, the professor fiddled with a knob on the Marconi box. Static hissed out over a low hum.

"This is no good," he said, and dialed in another frequency on the box. When he settled himself in the chair, the hiss and hum were gone. Aiden heard voices, too. After listening to the first few words, he wished the professor had left the box tuned to static.

"*—the Conroy kid got away. They got his folks though.*"

"*Why did they let the boy go?*"

"*They didn't, sir. He wasn't there, they said. But a team on the ground say they spotted him over by the barbershop. It doesn't matter though, does it? Brand's not with the kid.*"

A long silence followed, interrupted briefly with a grunt and the sound of distant machine gun fire. The voices returned and Aiden's heart leapt into his throat.

"*So, uh, sir ... we're to drop the Conroy angle? Is that correct?*"

"*Yes. We drop it. Unless the target makes contact with the boy—*"

Static washed across the airwaves and Aiden found himself about to paw at the dial, try to fiddle it into focus, clear the channel. The professor reached out a hand and touched Aiden's wrist with his fingertips.

"It is all right, Mr. Conroy. You are in no danger."

"How——, how'd you know it was me they were talking about?

Are you with them?" Aiden was standing before he knew it, backing into the dining room, glancing over his shoulder and flicking his head back around to keep the professor in view.

"Mr. Conroy, were I as sinister as you now fear me to be, you would be in no position to flee my abode. As it stands, you are free to go, though I do wish you would reconsider and stay here a moment longer. There is much you do not know about that *broadcast*." He said the word like it was acid on his tongue.

Aiden stopped with his hand on the wall by the dining room.

"What'd they mean? Conroy angle. What's that mean?"

'It means that as in all wars, those in power would see the young made pawns when battle is joined. Now I will ask a question. Were you not unceremoniously removed from your position of employment not two days prior?"

'How'd you know? That wasn't on the radio, too, was it? Jeez, how'd—"

'Not on *the* radio, Mr. Conroy, but on *this* radio. Don't you want to know whose voices we heard just now?"

Aiden had to admit that he did want to know who'd been talking about him like he was a loose end to be tied up. Or cut off. Like Jenkins? Like Digs Gordon?

"Was it The Outfit?"

"Goodness, no. That organization, I am pleased to say, is no longer a threat to Chicago City or her people. No, the voices we heard belonged to a much more deadly foe."

"Who?"

"The Governor and his Minister of Public Information. Your former employer. Jameson Crane."

Aiden let that sink in for half a second before the questions came spilling out. He wanted to know why the Governor was involved in kidnapping his parents, and what Minister Crane was doing. Why were they interested in Mr. Brand *making contact* with him? And what did the professor mean about wars and battles?

"I will answer those questions as best I am able, but not now," the professor said as he tucked a pocket watch back into his waistcoat.

"Time has run its course, Mr. Conroy. We must be off. If you will collect your observation equipment."

The professor aimed a nod at Mr. Brand's camera box. Aiden crossed the room and snatched it up and draped the strap around his neck as he turned back to face the professor, who now stood and shrugged into a heavy coat he pulled from a peg on the wall by the front door. His cane he tucked under his arm as he pulled on the gloves. A second coat hung on another peg and this he offered to Aiden. Putting it on, Aiden found his tongue again. "You said battle. We going out to fight now?"

"Not if I can help it, Mr. Conroy. But as you already know the battle has been joined. You can still hear the machine guns."

Aiden listened and sure enough he heard the *rat-a-tat-tat* of machine gun fire.

"The bombs will begin falling soon enough."

"Bombs? Jeez! What's happening, mister? What's this about?"

"As I said before, Mr. Conroy, what *it* is about is power. The obtaining and possession of power. I see you looking disturbed but not yet truly concerned. I would caution you to wear a more thoughtful grimace. Your future is out there, Mr. Conroy."

"All them words sound important, but I can't follow you. What's this got to do with me?"

Shaking his head slightly, the professor regarded Aiden through narrowed eyes. He seemed ready to holler at Aiden, but good. A blast echoed from outside, shaking the neighborhood and rattling the glassware and cabinets in the room. When gunfire split the night on the street outside, the professor seemed to reconsider giving Aiden the business and instead took him by the arm.

"We must depart now. But I will answer your question first. You wish to know what tonight has to do with you, is that correct?"

"Yeah. And what's going on out there? That sounded like—"

"War? Yes, Mr. Conroy. As I told you, the events of this evening are undertaken by those in pursuit of power."

"But what's that got to do with me?" Aiden hollered back,

half-fighting the professor's grip on his arm as they moved through the house to the basement.

"Mr. Conroy!" Professor Cather shook Aiden, nearly sending him sprawling. For his size, the man had a lot of strength packed away somehow.

"Lacking the wherewithal or any real means of providing an outlet for youthful vigor, those in power are always ready to see battle joined. What better way is there for them to enjoy the benefits of power whilst simultaneously avoiding concomitant responsibilities?"

Aiden let the mumbo-jumbo roll off his back and got to the point. "What's there to fight about? It's been aces up all over since the Great War. And that was the one to end them all."

"It pleases me not one bit to remark on your naiveté, Mr. Conroy, nor to inform you of this most dastardly truth: Where there exists no reason for war, those whom war benefits most will find one."

The professor led Aiden through his kitchen and washroom and stopped. He pulled aside a curtain over the washroom window and looked at the neighborhood outside. Flashes of gunfire spattered in the dark clouds overhead as airships fired down into the neighborhood streets. Aiden jerked aside when a burst of light a few blocks over was followed by a rumbling that rattled the house and turned Aiden's legs to jelly.

"What's happening, mister? What's going on out there?"

"Battle, Mr. Conroy. It begins now," the professor replied, still looking into the neighborhood. His words left a thick silence that quickly filled in with the sounds of gunfire and shouts of alarm. Aiden followed the professor's gaze into the tangled maze of houses and storefronts. Another building exploded on the next block, sending Aiden to his knees in fright. When he stood, he saw firelight flicker to life all around him as screams and gunshots echoed against the ink dark night.

CHAPTER 36

BRAND KEPT HIS HANDS IN THE AIR WHILE the round-faced man stepped forward, making room for another gypsy to step out from the hidden doorway. A taller man emerged from behind the trick shelf and the two gypsies exchanged words in a language Brand had never heard before. While they talked, the gun was put away, along with a knife held by the taller man.

"I'm Steven," said the round-faced man, turning back to face Brand. "Call me Stevie Five Sticks though." The man stuck out a paw and Brand held off taking it until the little man's round face bent with confusion. If they meant to help him, he'd need more than a handshake to believe it.

"This isn't where you gun me down?" Brand asked. His suggestion shocked the gypsy. His face twisted up and he gaped.

"Huh? What do you mean, Brand? Gun you … Didn't know you'd be down here, but ain't nobody around here doesn't know Mitchell Brand did a little story on Al Capone that turned out to be a story about an old beer bottle from a basement over here in the Village. And that breakout you just now pulled, it's all over the street you know.

"Out there? Coppers and soldiers aplenty, rounding folks up and questioning them. Seems more than enough if they're just after one guy, if you ask me. But what do I know, hey? I'm just another Rigo." The guy let out another chortle. His pal behind him looked at Brand through narrowed eyes and a scowl crept up the sides of his face.

"*Yo-seff*," he said to his pal, "this here's the guy on the radio."

The tall man simply nodded so Brand picked up where he'd left off with Stevie Five Sticks.

"Are you the only one who knows English or is Joszef here working on his dummerer act?"

"Aw, nah. He's just over from the old country, like a lot of the folks around the neighborhood. Especially all the gray hairs in the crew. They're all original from Hungary. Joszef here, he came on the last boat a year back. Didn't need to pick up much English, see? His cousins gave him a job in the stockyards. Doesn't matter what language you use. You speak cowpoke, you can do the job, hey?"

The little man set himself into a fit of chuckles and his pudgy round face opened up with a funny grin. Something about the guy rankled Brand. His talk, his shifty eyes. When he saw Stevie pull a knife from his belt, Brand went into a fighting stance and backed up a step.

"Hey, hey!" Stevie said, putting his free hand up, palm out. "Just figured you'd want to have something you can use if we end up in the soup."

"Thanks, but I was never much good with a shiv," Brand said. The gypsy tucked the blade back into his belt.

"Hey, no sweat, Brand," Stevie said. "But out there. What gives? They said all about you knocking out that G-man and sabotaging the joint. But that's a lot of muscle to take down one angry newsie. No disrespect, Mr. Brand."

"How many are we talking about? I heard some jeeps and a megaphone."

Stevie answered by moving to the steps and motioning for Brand to follow him. They went up to the passage beneath the porch and carefully stepped out to where Brand had left the airbike.

"Better get this somewheres else," Stevie said. "Hey, Joszef."

Stevie waved for his pal to join them outside. The tall man had been hanging back, but he came forward now. The two gypsies talked in the punchy musical language they had and Joszef got on the airbike. He kicked it into gear like he'd done nothing but ride the things since he was born. Before Brand could object, bike and rider had soared around to the back of the house and out of sight.

"Rides those things around the stockyards," Stevie explained. "Good thing we had him here, hey?"

"Good thing, yeah. What's happening on the street?" Brand moved to stand in front of the gypsy, trusting him now but not wanting to get his information through him if he could avoid it. Pushing through the branches of the tree, Brand got an eye on the street. Traffic moved slowly along the roadway, with pedestrians leading wagons and horses in a long line. Here and there, Brand spied a man in uniform wearing a visor and carrying a fancy rifle, just like the boys outside the doors at the Daily Record.

"So the Governor's getting into the relocation business. Listen," Brand said, turning to face Stevie Five Sticks and stare him in the eyes. "There's more going on than just evacuation, if that's even what this is. My money's on it being something worse. But even if it isn't, you and your people, Joszef and anybody else you can get to, you have to get out of here and to someplace safe. If you can take me with you, that's fine and I'll appreciate it. If you can't, that's fine, too. I'll make do on my own."

"See, now, that's just the thing, Brand. We spotted this action down the street and were coming to get everyone out so we could cop the sneak. Shouldn't be more than two people in there anyhow. Just the lady of the house and her daughter. They run the shop."

Brand nodded and moved to go back into the cellar when the clomp of boots sounded on the front steps. A soldier rapped on the door with a gloved hand and held his rifle up at the ready, tucked under his other arm. When nobody answered the door, Brand and Stevie both let a breath out slow and quiet. The soldier pulled a sheaf of pages from his pocket and slapped one against the door. Using his rifle to hold it up, he dug a pin from his shirt pocket and tacked the page in place. Then he banged on the door again and retreated down the steps. Brand watched the man rejoin the line of citizens and soldiers marching out of the neighborhood.

"What do you suppose that was?" Stevie asked.

"Let's find out," Brand said and ducked back into the cellar. Stevie followed. They came out in the kitchen and spotted the lady of the house and her daughter hiding in the breakfast nook off to one side. Stevie came out from behind Brand and greeted the women, speaking to them in their language.

Brand moved out to the foyer and cautiously cracked the front door open. The line of people continued to wind along the neighborhood street. Wagons and horses, livestock. Brand saw mostly women and children, but some few men mingled in with them. He wondered if the men were absent because they'd stayed behind or been taken elsewhere. Brand snaked his hand out and snatched the page tacked to the door. He closed the door and rested his back against it while he read the page.

He recognized the symbol at the top. He'd spent an entire day reading from a piece of paper with the same markings.

Citizens of Chicago City are advised of the implementation of Eugenic Protocol 421. Persons meeting criteria for internment under EP421 are advised to report to the nearest containment and dispersal facility immediately.

These actions are in accord with the Governor's Guidelines for Eugenic Enforcement.

That is all.

A list of ethnic groups followed, beneath the words *eligible for internment*. Brand's breath came in gasps in between snarls. Stevie Five Sticks came into the room with the women and they all drew up short when they saw Brand fuming by the front door.

"What is it, Brand?"

"It's war. That's what it is. The Governor isn't satisfied with a little friendly neighborhood relocation. No. He's taking the whole city. By force. By storm. By god, if he thinks he's going to get away with this he's got another thing coming."

Brand flung the page away from him and stormed around the room some more, shouting until he was hoarse. He finally collapsed into a chair by the hearth and let his head hang onto his chest.

"I can't stop it," he said.

Stevie came over to him; the women hung back. "Let's go to the safe spot, Brand. Some folks there I think you'll want to meet."

Brand let himself be led back downstairs. He walked in a half daze, unable to believe what he'd read on the page, but unable to deny the truth of what he'd seen on the street. Stevie led him and the two women into the hidden tunnel he'd emerged from. Candles lit their way, and Brand got his crank torch working. His mind walked away from him at times, and he'd stop turning the crank. Eventually the daughter took it from him.

After that, Brand retreated into his mind and mentally tore the Governor and Crane apart with a tirade of accusations; he watched the two men cower in fright as he excoriated and vilified them relentlessly. Finally, Brand had to admit his powerlessness in the situation. If he would be remembered for more than finding an old beer bottle, he'd need to find a way to stop the Governor or at least fight back.

He'd need to tell the real story, loud enough to reach the ears of people who were too comfortable to lift a finger against the tyranny and terror that had come to Chicago City.

"Hey, and here we are," Stevie said while Brand leaned against the wall. The tunnel ended in a stout wooden door with a catch set into it. Stevie worked the catch and the door popped open. Light flooded into the passage from a cavernous space beyond.

Brand followed the gypsies into the larger room. They were in some kind of basement, maybe an old root or cider cellar. It had been turned into an underground speak. Lamps hung from the ceiling and off of posts that stood in a grid and supported a wooden floor above them. Off to one side a wooden ladder was mounted into the wall beneath an open trapdoor.

Around the space, gypsies sat at tables alongside negroes, some sharing bottles. A crew of people worked in one corner, digging into the earthen wall.

"Hey, Five Sticks." Brand nudged the younger man. Stevie turned to face him, his old twitchy glee back on his face.

"Yeah, what's the news, Brand?" Stevie let out a laugh. Brand spied a few of the people nearby cast tired looks in Stevie's direction.

"Think it's a good idea to dig into a wall like that when there's a building on top of us?"

"Oh, it's all right. Just a short dig through and we'll be on the railroad." Stevie said it like Brand should know what he meant. Since he didn't, he asked.

"It's how we're getting out of here. The niggers are helping out because the Governor's after them same as us. And, hey, extra hands make for easy work. You know?"

Brand knew. Stevie had said it all.

Through the trapdoor Brand heard the familiar sound of glass against glass. Someone laughing. A piano tinkling and then going silent. Then the crackle of a radio and Franklin Suttleby's voice filtered down from the room above.

… are advised to remain indoors. Patrols from the Ministry of Safety and Security will be sweeping these areas, and citizens can rest assured that the criminals will be captured and prosecuted for—

"Someone turn the damn radio off," a woman's voice said from the room upstairs. The radio crackled into silence. Brand crossed the cellar in a few strides and put a foot on the ladder. At the top, the warm light of a speakeasy settled Brand's nerves. The cigarette someone handed him went a long way to settling him further, but the drink he reached for really did the trick. He had a second for Jenkins and a third for Digs.

Brand took in the room, the olive and coffee mix of gypsy and negro faces. Some stood in exclusive clutches, but musicians from both groups gathered by the piano and took turns tickling the teeth.

Against the far wall a lone woman sat draped in a heavy wool blanket. She sipped wine from a glass and held a book open on the table beside her. Her red hair stood out in the flickering candlelight, the only sign of color in the otherwise drab space of the speak.

Before he could ask Dana Reynolds what she was doing there, Brand caught a fluttering movement out the corner of his eye. Madame Tibor emerged from a crowd of gypsies by the bar. Her scarves danced in a slight draft as she approached with a mixture of disappointment and hope on her face.

Brand set the glass down on the bar and turned to meet the fortune teller as she approached.

"Where's your husband?"

She put up a hand to stop him. Her eyes confirmed what Brand feared.

"I'm sorry," he said. She brushed a hand at the air and moved away, motioning for him to follow. They went into a back room where men, negroes and gypsies alike, worked in a fevered rush packing items into boxes and barrels.

Brand stared at the scene. Cases and bags were strewn amidst the people packing dry goods and perishables into crates. The personal bags sat like they'd been discarded, spilling their contents onto the floor. Pocket watches, picture frames, knives, letter openers, tea sets. Bits of lace and fabric. Some old tools rested on a shelf in one wall. Hand planes, hammers, chisels. A long saw. A shorter one hanging on a peg beneath the shelf. A man went to the tools and removed them. He packed them with care into a long wooden box at his feet.

"You see us preparing," Madame Tibor said. "For danger. But danger is already here."

"When did this start? The Governor hit town two days ago—"

"Is long time coming, Mitchell Brand. Is not beginning. Now is end. Is what happens when criminals own city and people are made slaves who think they are free."

Brand could barely have put it better himself.

CHAPTER 37

MADAME TIBOR MOTIONED TO BRAND again and he followed out into the main room of the speak. The piano was quiet and the musicians were going down the ladder to the cellar, carrying their smaller instruments close to their chests and helping one another hand the larger cases down.

"Where are they headed?" Brand asked.

"To railroad. In tunnels. Old city lines are buried after fire. We find them, rebuild them for exploring old city. Now we use them to escape."

'Are we joining them or do you have an airship hidden in those scarves?"

The fortune teller turned dark eyes on Brand and he felt regret rise in his chest.

"Come, Mitchell Brand. Is now you see what your story is really about." As she spoke, her scarves lifted away from her neck and swirled around her head like the arms of a marionette. Brand could see no strings, and the shuddering air around her head gave him a good idea of what would come next. He held his booze through a force of will and let the room lift aside like a curtain, revealing again a thousand memories on top of a thousand more. Furniture and firelight swam in and out of focus around indistinct figures, then the room itself faded from view to be replaced by stretches of farmland and cattle.

Madame Tibor reached for Brand's elbow and took a step to the side. In the space of that step they crossed the city, her stride covering miles in half a second. Brand's vision blurred and his head spun. He only kept his liquor down this time because he'd forgotten he had a body to be sick with. All sensation and sound was reduced to a single feeling, a calm like he'd never felt.

Then Madame Tibor let go of his elbow. He came to a sudden halt in a top floor hotel room downtown, far from the old Village neighborhood. Brand's vision came around to register a tall white-haired man standing by a window, looking out at the city below. A satchel hung off his left hip. The man turned around as Brand's gut caught up with him and sent him stumbling for the washroom. He came back out when he was finished and looked the tall man in the eye.

"You're Tesla. Aren't you."

"Yes. And your surprise is not unexpected, Mr. Brand. That's, if it is surprise and not revulsion that is responsible for your nausea."

Brand took it all in. The hotel room, the gypsy fortune teller who'd just spirited him here from a speak halfway to the other side of the city, and now Tesla. Old and withered after years of proving to the world what no other inventor had dared try. Brand had heard the stories, about the man who never slept or took companionship, despite the many offerings he'd received. Brand knew what the man could do. Without Tesla's radio power station and the devices he'd rigged up, Brand's old pal Skip and the other vets wouldn't have had work after the war.

But this man, this frail and almost quaintly pathetic old man with a wispy voice and frills of white hair sprouting from his liver-spotted scalp. This was Tesla.

"No, it's not revulsion. I wouldn't call it surprise either, but then I don't know what to call it when a gypsy hauls me off my feet and flies me across the city in one step. What would you call it?"

Tesla seemed taken aback, but then chuckled softly through rounded lips.

"What do you know about gods?" he asked.

"Gods? Not much. They're good for when you need to ask someone for help. They're better when you need someone to point fingers at for not helping you."

Tesla barked a short laugh and his smile widened, though his weathered and wizened face drooped around his mouth, betraying his disappointment. "Your opinion may change shortly."

"I'll lay even money you're wrong, but go ahead. Try to win me over."

"Mr. Brand, certainly a man of your skepticism can agree. Humanity can be its own worst enemy."

"Certainly. So why do we need gods in the first place when it's all on us to make things better or worse?"

Tesla kept hush, seeming to consider Brand's question before speaking again.

"Mr. Brand, humanity needs the gods as much as the gods need humanity," he said, warming to the conversation now and stepping away from the window, coming into the the room and closer to where to Brand stood by the washroom door.

Tesla moved his hands as he spoke, seeming to grasp words from the air around him. "Gods and humanity. Each is beholden to the other for existence, and for influence."

"Influence? I think you mean power. That's how it's been told to me by your mailmen anyway."

"Yes, Mr. Brand. Power. The power to act without restraint, to see one's influence expressed in the world, widely and with purpose. With results."

"So where do I fit in here? I'm guessing the gypsy didn't fly me here to show up the air transport service."

Madame Tibor spoke then and Brand turned to face her.

"When gods find mortals who match influence, then gods emerge." Her scarves swam around her head in a whorl now violent ripples of burnt orange, deep passionate red, blazing sunlight yellow, a swirl here of emerald or sapphire. In each band of color, Brand saw tools and around them the products of their use. Hand tools intermingled with utensils. Around these were pieces of furniture, then rooms to house the furniture, then houses full of rooms. Outward the scarves spun, creating an aurora behind Madame Tibor's head. Beyond the houses grew cities, and then roads connecting these, forming a web of human activity that stretched into infinity as Brand stared, and wondered.

"God comes out from curtain. Possess the mortal and live on earth."

Tesla picked up the thread now, leaving Brand to stare between them. "On earth, in possession of a mortal, the gods may act on the world however they so choose. It is the most powerful position a god may claim. It is as close to immortality as either human or deity may ever know."

Brand stood frozen in place between Madame Tibor's and Tesla's words. Nothing they'd said rang true in the way that a gunshot told you a bullet was on the loose. But the gypsy's scarves kept up their light show, and as the inventor stared at Brand, his face took on a haunted look.

Tesla's eyes burned with a blue fire. Images floated in the air around his head. Spiraling conduits of electricity orbited the cross hatch of schematic diagrams. Ghostly machines operated and revolved around one another, performing anonymous tasks in a smooth cadence, all in time to their movement. Formulae spun about as well, the numbers and symbols danced as they were calculated and recalculated time and time again. At the end, Tesla faded behind the curtain, flickering like a gas jet and then re-emerging, his figure filling in like an electric lamp ablaze with the warm glow of light. Madame Tibor did the same, emerging from the curtain to stand before him with a potency Brand could not deny.

"*Ingenuity*, Mr. Brand," Tesla said.

"And *Necessity*," the gypsy added.

"The gods guide and advise us these many years," Tesla went on.

"How long?" Brand asked.

"Since last World's Fair is held in Chicago City," Madame Tibor replied.

"The fair? What's that got to do with it? And why here? Why not Philly or San Francisco? They've hosted fairs before."

"Chicago City is the natural seat of this nation's power," Tesla said. "This city is centrally located on all major shipping and transportation lines. It is the heart of manufacturing and production in the American Territories. Chicago City *is* the nation with its mix of peoples and enterprises. Raw materials are funneled through her port and along her rail lines. When people do travel across the territories, they must pass through Chicago City. To control the city is to have every branch of the nation wrapped up like a bundle of sticks held tightly in one's fist."

"And one of these— One of *you* wants to do this, is that it?"

Tesla and Madame Tibor nodded.

"Which one?"

"*Hubris*," the gypsy spat.

"His influence is legendary in Chicago City," Tesla said. "He aims to have his insulating self-righteousness invade every heart. Worse, we have learned he is in league with another member of the pantheon, a god whose influence is unmatched by any other in your city or in any of the American Territories."

"Who would that be?"

Tesla answered. "*Industry*."

"Sounds like they want to take us back to presidents and vice-presidents. Somebody should tell them that didn't work out too well. Lincoln was the last president this country had, and he didn't exactly leave office. Not on his own."

"There are not so many of us here beyond the curtain, Mr. Brand. The reach of the gods extends only as far as humanity allows with their worship and reverence. You can no doubt appreciate that our colleagues, for better or for worse, are willing to do anything for the freedom to walk the earth as we have. Many of them, like *Vice* and *Corruption* already enjoy a degree of freedom. Others, like *Pride* and *Shame*, would see themselves exalted higher even than *Industry*. And if he succeeds ....”

“Succeeds at what? You still haven’t told me what we’re up against, and what I saw back in the Village didn’t look like the greatest scheme on the books. What good is a war to a god of indu—” Brand stopped himself as his mind filled the picture in.

Tesla nodded again. “It is *Industry’s* wish that the entire nation be devoted to the cycle of production and consumption. Even when a need is lacking, the people will consume. Even when resources have been exhausted, they will produce, sacrificing what they truly need. They will sacrifice even to obtain what is wholly unnecessary. But they will believe otherwise, and so they will exhaust their very lives in the pursuit of falsehoods.”

“Is *Industry* out here? Like you?”

“Yes. The Governor. His army has taken over my factory. Stolen my designs and my inventions. All for his little game of soldiers.”

“Can’t you get it back? You’ve got to have some way of—”

“Of what? Fighting a war? That has never been my concern. *Ingenuity* will leave me soon. He will find another host, or he will wait behind the curtain for the next opportunity to spread his influence among humanity. Society is run amok with wealth and power now. Humanity has too little time for a man whose truest love is for the power of having ideas, rather than what can be done with them.”

Brand wanted to sniff at that, but he couldn’t deny the inventor his due. “I’m sorry, then. You deserve better after what you’ve given the world.”

Tesla acknowledged this with a nod.

“You said there were two gods working this play. What about the other one? *Hubris*? Who is he?”

“I do not know, but it would be someone able to command the sway of the people through coercion, force, or deceit. He will promote his ideas as undeniably just while being, in reality, nothing more than a braggart making a prideful attempt at gaining power."

Brand's mind called up what he'd seen on the street. Soldiers marching lines of helpless citizens like cattle to the slaughterhouse. Bulletins notifying the people. Bulletins marked with a seal like the one he'd read in a broadcast booth the day the Governor came to town.

"So what's the play? Where do I come in and how do I help?"

"You must again be the voice for Chicago City. You must speak for the people, tell them the truth. Tell them what the Governor's airships and soldiers are doing while the people hide inside their homes. Insulated. Believing themselves unaffected. Believing lies."

Tesla reached into the satchel hanging off his hip and pulled out a microphone rig. A coiled cable linked the square mic to a small box mounted on a thick leather belt.

"This microphone is connected to the transmitter on top of the building you used to work in, Mr. Brand. You may use it to give your broadcasts. I have configured it to interrupt any signals being sent from the building itself, so you may rest assured you will be heard tonight."

"How'd you manage that? This thing's smaller than my shoe shine kit. Where's the power come from?"

"My Wardenclyffe towers, Mr. Brand. The Governor may have stolen my factory from me, but the knowledge of how my inventions work remains mine."

Brand weighed the device in his hands, then slipped the belt around his waist and fastened it. The mic dangled from the cable until he lifted it and hooked it onto a clasp hanging from the belt. The power box sat at the small of his back and forced him to stand upright with his back slightly arched.

"Didn't think about comfort when you made this, did you?"

Tesla chuckled and placed his hand on Brand's shoulder, then removed it and clasped both hands in front of his belt. Looking the inventor in the eye, Brand nodded and gave a quick salute. Tesla smiled in return before fading out of sight, leaving only a thin veil of darkness to fall closed behind him.

A rolling thunderclap shook the city, sending Brand diving for cover by the bed. Madame Tibor instead walked to the window and stared into the gathering night.

"It starts now."

Brand moved to join her, caution and fear sending his every nerve into a riot of alarm. Outside the hotel the streets were quiet. The city had gone indoors in the middle of the afternoon because of the early curfew. Across the river, in the old neighborhoods they'd just left, Brand saw a burst of firelight, and then another. A stippling of gunfire peppered the sky and Brand saw gunships convening on the old neighborhoods. Fireballs blossomed up from the ground moments later as more gunfire punctuated the darkening sky with deadly starlight.

CHAPTER 38

AN ENGINE CRANKED TO LIFE NEARBY AND Emma's heart jumped. She tucked tighter into her hiding place by a porch while two soldiers kicked in the door to the house and hollered inside. Emma caught a meek reply that was drowned out by more hollering from the soldiers.

A jeep came around the corner and pulled up in front of the house. The driver hailed the two on the porch.

"Just got word. It's time to clear out."

The soldiers gave one more shout inside before they stepped fast down to the curb and climbed into the jeep. The driver worked the gearshift and the jeep peeled away with a roar and burst of smoke.

Emma's ears rang with dread. The quiet streets, the hushed voices of people too frightened to come out of their homes. Soldiers talking about orders heavy with the promise of portent. She had to find Eddie. Whatever was coming next, she had to be by his side when it happened.

Stepping as fast as she could, Emma left the porch and the side streets, making straight for the main stem where everyone had been marched out of the neighborhood. She could follow the trail of belongings and carts back to Biros' shop. The wagon would still be there. Eddie would still be there.

He'll be there. He has to be.

Emma let her eyes roam over porches and windows along her path. Here and there a curtain would drop into place just as her gaze passed over the house. But she saw nobody on the streets, neither soldier nor citizen. Overhead the dark clouds threatened rain or snow, but no airships sailed in menacing circles. At the street that led to Biros and Nagy's shops, Emma halted and caught her breath while she examined the neighborhood around her. The street had been cleared a bit. Wagons were pushed off to the side. The livestock were all gone though. Emma saw tire tracks in the slush. Trucks and jeeps had driven through here.

The thought of driving reminded Emma of her car. Would it still be at Nagy's? If it was, then maybe she and Eddie had a way out of this fix. She saw the wagon they'd been in, only two blocks away. Fighting the urge to charge down the street, she kept close to the storefronts and houses, ready to duck into hiding if she needed to. Before she knew it, she stood beside the wagon where Eddie was hidden, wrapped in heavy wool and tucked beneath a bench.

He wasn't there now.

The wool was gone, too, making Emma feel hope and worry at once. Had he waited until the street was quiet and then fled, keeping the wool around him for concealment and warmth? Or had soldiers found him and used the fabric to wrap his body before dumping it in an alley?

Emma followed a stumbling path back to Biros' shop. Her coat was still there. At least she hoped it was. And that meant her father's revolver and Wynes' pistol were still there, waiting for her to claim them.

• • •

Biros' house looked different now. The whole neighborhood

did, quiet and abandoned as it was. But Emma knew it wasn't empty. She knew people hid in their homes still, and she worried for them. On her path from the wagon to the house, she'd heard the heavy thrumming of airship motors, and the repeated alerts about curfews, fugitives, and internment protocols. Emma cast a final glare at the sky behind her before stepping into Biros' back room.

The first thing she noticed was that her coat was gone. She let it be a blessing. Guns hadn't helped her avoid trouble so far, just escape one kind and get into another that was worse.

She stared around the room, looking first to the chair she'd sat in when Eszti had transformed her into a member of Biros' family. Emma's curls had been swept up and put in a pail beside the bench in the center of the room. She let her eyes roam the bench and then the others around the room. Spending only seconds on each item, Emma forced herself to remember the scene, to take in all the possessions Biros and his family had left behind. Bolts of fabric, tools, scissors, measuring tapes and sticks, a dressmaker's dummy standing in the corner. Beside the dummy, a low bench was piled with cut out pieces for coats and pants and shirts. The uniform of the Village residents. Plain and gray, but made to withstand the harsh weather and the hard work these people performed every day. Emma lifted a section of a skirt, the needle and thread still in it where Eszti or her sister or cousin had left it.

When they stopped working. Right before the soldiers came.

Emma heard a shuffling sound from the cellar and her ears grew hot with alarm. She stepped slow and careful to the nearest bench and lifted a long pair of shears, maybe the ones Eszti had used to cut her hair. A gunshot exploded in the small space and Emma cried out as the bullet whipped by her head, embedding itself in the rafters above her.

"Don't shoot! I'm not a soldier."

"Lovebird? That you up there?" Eddie's voice came to her. Then she saw his face, worried as sick as she felt, and she fell into his arms and cried. Eddie let out his own set of sobs. He pawed the hat off her head and she felt his hand roam around her scalp, brushing the tufts of blond hair this way and that. She crushed herself against him, held him close and shook the tension from her body in the safety of his embrace.

"Thought you was gone, Lovebird. Thought they took you and Nagy and them. All of you gone."

Emma let her tears fall and listened to Eddie tell her about how he'd stayed put until all the soldiers had left. When the street was quiet, he'd snuck out of his hiding place and come back here to get her guns, then hid in the cellar, wondering if he should go after them or go back to Nagy's or someplace else.

Eddie handed her one of the guns and tucked the other into his belt.

"Didn't know if you'd be coming back. I didn't know a damn thing and truth is I didn't care to know. I just wanted to get out of here. Get somewhere felt more like home. If a man's going to die he should do it at home."

Emma pocketed the gun Eddie had given her. It was her father's revolver, the only thing he'd ever passed along, even if he hadn't meant to. She stared around the room again at all the tools and fabric.

"We should take them. Take their things so they can have them again."

"How we going to do that? You hear that man talking out there, don't you?"

The bulletin had been broadcast repeatedly since Emma got back to Biros' house, and if anything had changed it was the urgency of the speaker's voice.

"My car might still be at Nagy's. Do you think—"

"I think you got the same idea I did. Might be a long shot, but it's the only one we've got. Let's go."

They took the crank torch and made their way back through the tunnel to Nagy's basement speak. The room had been ransacked and all the booze from the bar was gone. Emma knew she owed these people a debt that may never be repaid. For now, she'd remember the help they gave her and the kindness they'd shown her.

Eddie led the way up the cellar steps and through the trapdoor. Emma's car was still in the alley outside Nagy's house and shop. Her bag and clothes were strewn about in the slush and mud next to the garage. She picked up the bag, now scuffed, stained, and torn, nothing like the fine piece of luggage she'd bought at Macy's a year ago. The clasp still worked, so she brought it inside.

She and Eddie picked out some shoes from Nagy's supply, and grabbed as many extra pairs as they could carry, in case they did meet up with the other Villagers or anyone else running from the soldiers. Emma stuffed her case with extra lacing, grommets, and the tools Nagy was using. They went to her car and checked it over. One of the tires had been shot flat.

"Wynes getting his revenge," Emma said. "I doubt we'd get far anyway."

"Where we going to, Lovebird?"

"Someplace with a way out. Someplace … I don't know, Eddie. Madame Tibor said we'd escape by flying. Where are we going to find a safe airship in this city now?" Emma's tears fell slow and steady, in time to her heartbeat. Eddie put his arms around her.

"I heard them soldiers talking about a yard. All the stuff they took from around here supposed to be going out by the lakeshore. They said cars are out there, too, and airships. All the private ones, even that one the newsman had, where you—"

"Where I shot Archie Falco and got us into this mess," Emma said, feeling the weight of her failure like a leaden blanket. Remembering the night she shot Falco put Emma's mind into thoughts of escape again. The fortune teller may be crazy, or maybe she really could read the future with those cards of hers. The idea of flight and escape tugged at Emma's gut and lit a fire inside that she was surprised to find couldn't be stopped.

"What else did the soldiers say about that yard, Eddie? Did they say why everything was going out there?"

"Yeah. They said it was the fair site."

The day's events added up in Emma's mind. An old neighborhood evacuated and probably not two days from being put to the torch. Livestock, private cars, and airships, all hauled away to the World's Fair marshaling area. It was four years off, but the Governor had pushed hard for Chicago City to stay on the ball and churn out the goods for the Century of Progress. Emma's father had been in on those talks not more than a year ago, when the Eastern Seaboard Governor had nearly convinced the fair committee that New York should have the honor of hosting the event.

Now the Great Lakes Governor was here, and he was going to make sure Chicago City lived up to his expectations. He'd start by giving the city a gift. A new neighborhood, shiny and clean and fresh as can be. Emma and Eddie turned their faces to the sky at the first sound of gunfire. He dropped the shoes he was carrying and she set her case down. Explosions sounded in the near distance and the neighborhood shook beneath their feet. Eddie grabbed Emma's hand and they ran, darting between houses and always moving away from the oncoming airships.

As backdrop to the sounds of war, a bullhorn continued to broadcast alerts about fugitives and vandals, and cautioned all citizens to remain indoors.

"They're doing it now," Emma said.

"Doing what?" Eddie asked, panting as they ran.

Emma forced him to halt. "They're demolishing this neighborhood. The Governor wants to build a new one in its place, to make sure Chicago City looks good when people come here for the World's Fair."

"That's what the old gypsy said. I know. Now come on."

"No, Eddie. No. This neighborhood isn't empty. There are people still hiding in their homes. Families with children."

Eddie stared into her eyes, and she knew he understood what she was asking. She also knew he didn't want any part of helping people escape unless their names were Eddie Collins and Emma Farnsworth. She begged him with her eyes. Eddie gripped her hand and shook his head. He turned and pulled her to follow. She let him lead her along, the two of them fleeing the neighborhood by the quickest route they could find. Off the main stem, down a quiet street Emma forcing herself not to look at the windows, to ignore the curtains that dropped into place as she and Eddie swept by in the growing night while machine gun fire and explosions crackled and roared behind them.

At the neighborhood's edge Eddie pulled up short and stepped into hiding beside a house. He yanked Emma to his side. She peered into the dusk and saw soldiers standing across the street. Teams of two and three stood with rifles at their sides, their visors reflecting pinpoints of firelight.

Emma reached a hand into her pocket, feeling the gun. Her fingers curled around the cold metal as she stared at the soldiers. "They're waiting for something," she whispered.

"I see that," Eddie said. "But what?"

A whistle sounded from somewhere in the line of soldiers. As one they lifted their weapons and stepped into the street.

CHAPTER 39

THE AIR AROUND BRAND'S HEAD SWIRLED AND shook. He batted at the visions of gossamer and lace until the room settled around him and he saw they'd returned to the speak. Madame Tibor stepped away from him, leaving go his hand.

"What the hell is this?" Brand asked. "They tell you to leave town and when you don't they bring in the bombardiers?"

"I tell you, Mitchell Brand. Your Governor, for a long time he makes ready for this war. This eugenics. Now you see what he wants with city."

'He isn't my Governor. Not sure he ever was and he sure as hell isn't now. Why'd you bring me back here?"

"Escape. To railroad."

"Rail—?"

"We are making ready for long time, too."

The gypsy led Brand into the cellar. Where before there had been gypsies and negroes resting and working, now there were only foot tracks and scuff marks showing the passage of multiple people and their belongings. The barrels and crates from the room above had been hauled through the room and out the hole in the wall. Brand heard an insistent squeaking from that corner, like a hinge being worked back and forth. Madame Tibor went to the hole and he followed. She stepped through first and Brand heard voices raised in surprise and delight on the other side.

A short passage of a half dozen feet had been cut into the earthen wall. Stepping through, Brand saw the passage connected the cellar to a wide tunnel with a set of tracks running down it. The fortune teller stood on the tracks talking to another gypsy, a tall man with a heavy mustache. Next to him, Dana Reynolds leaned against a barrel, still holding her wine glass in one hand and a book in the other. Madame Tibor caught Brand's attention and introduced the pair in the tunnel.

"This is *Mee-hawl-yee*," she told him, indicating the tall man, who reached out a hand the size of Brand's chest. They shook and swapped smiles.

"And this," the gypsy woman paused, letting her tone suggest she didn't know the nicest way to introduce the redhead.

"We've met," Dana said, tucking her book into a pouch on her belt. She threw the glass at the wall behind her where it shattered and left a dark stain pooling on the earthen floor. She wore heavy black skirts and carried an honest to goodness sword in a scabbard at her side. Brand spotted a cable connecting the pommel of the weapon to a pouch on her belt. Topping it off, Dana wore a thick jacket of brown leather over a white blouse that peeked out from her collar. A series of straps and belts were slung across her chest under her jacket.

"You look surprised to see me, " she said to Brand. A self-sure smile curled her lips while she waited on his reply.

"Try again, sister. This is my *disappointed* look. I save surprise for people I'm glad to see."

"Why so rough, Brand?" she said, resting her hands on her hips.

Brand felt the words hit his tongue in a rush, and he didn't bother putting the brakes on any of them. "Any dope knows you're mixed up in whatever's happening in this town. You've been here since the beginning on Valentine's Day. Then at the Mayor's gala before Nitti showed up, but somehow you knew to cop the sneak right then. I'd lay even money you knew about Nitti and these gods, and you were probably there when Nitti put the Mayor down for keeps, too.

"I don't see your fancy cat, the professor, hanging around, but five'll get you fifty he's not too far away. So you'll excuse me if I don't have too many kind words for you, but you've been a mystery since day one, and you're showing no signs of coming clean. I'd stick around and ask my questions, but right now I've got more important things to do than go chasing after ghosts."

To punctuate his words, a burst of airship gunfire echoed into the tunnel from outside the speak. Brand heard the bullets spray against metal like a drum roll announcing the end of the show. Another volley came and Brand felt the microphone weighing on his hip.

"I'd better get moving," he said to Madame Tibor and Mihalyi. Putting a finger to his brow he nodded at Dana Reynolds. "Little Red—"

Brand's next words died on his lips. The redhead drew her sword faster than Brand could blink. The gypsies didn't even flinch and let their grins tell Brand he'd played the wrong card. Not that he needed convincing. The blade hovering in front of his throat was proof enough.

"One thing first, buster. My name is Dana Reynolds. You ever call me *Little Red* again and I'll carve that name on your backside." She dropped the point, aiming it below Brand's belt.

"And if I run out of room back there, I'll just work my way around to the front."

The blade vibrated with a threatening hum and the pack on the woman's belt emitted a low buzz.

"What is it with the fancy pig stickers in this town," Brand said, shaking his head. "Okay, Miss Reynolds—"

"Dana. I don't miss."

Brand noticed her patting a shotgun that hung down by her other hip, hidden in the folds of her skirts. Before he could try a third time, Dana had sheathed the sword and clapped a hand on Brand's shoulder.

"You'll get used to me, Brand. Watch the name calling and we'll be jake."

"We go now," Mihalyi said, motioning to his right. Brand followed the gypsy's finger and saw a lantern light glowing down the dark throat of the tunnel. The squeaking sound from earlier grew louder as a handcar came into view. Two negroes operated the car and a trio of gypsies sat on the low wooden benches to either side. The two gypsies at the front were covered in sweat and the negroes looked fairly fresh.

Brand said to Madame Tibor, "Glad to see your pals take turns doing the work on this line."

"Governor hunts us, treats us all like animals. We should prove him right?" she said and jutted her chin at the handcar, urging Brand to follow Mihalyi and Dana who had already climbed aboard. Brand got on and turned around to help the fortune teller. She waved to him as the air in the tunnel fell across the space where she'd been standing. Brand stared at Mihalyi and Dana. Seeing no sign of surprise, he figured the gypsies were all in on it together. The gentle giant confirmed it with his thickly accented words.

"Comes and goes. You don't know when. If needed, always she comes."

The negroes did their bit and got the handcar rolling again. None of them seemed fazed by the gypsy's disappearing trick either. Brand stayed silent, watching the dark tunnel give way to the lantern light. Mihalyi lifted a heavy great coat from the floor of the car and offered it to Brand. He accepted it and draped it over himself, nodding off almost instantly. The first fingers of a dream reached for him in his sleep, and Brand let himself slip into the welcoming embrace of slumber. He jerked awake when the handcar came to a stop.

Lanterns came to life all around them and Brand rubbed at

his eyes to clear his vision. They'd reached a wider section of the tunnel. To one side was a large space piled full of crates and barrels. On the opposite side, the tunnel wall opened into darkness. Brand shrugged into the great coat before grabbing a lantern and aiming it at the opening in the wall. Through it he saw several sets of tracks, all heavy with handcars on them. Negroes and gypsies worked side by side, handling parcels and crates and loading them onto the handcars. Behind each handcar, flat cars were loaded with metal cans steaming with the scent of hot chow. Crates and baskets held loaves of bread and jars of preserves. A small barrel on each car dripped water from a wooden tap. Women and children were given the seats. Men stood or waited off to the side, apparently ready to walk the length of the tunnel if there weren't enough seats.

Brand stared and marveled at the sight. Traded laughter came from somewhere in the throng, distinct deep guffaws mingled and mixed with throaty chuckles and higher pitched cackling. Brand followed as his traveling companions dismounted their handcar and moved to join the bustling activity. Mihalyi turned to him at the edge of the crowd, a smile of pride and approval creasing his face.

"You see?"

"I see. Yeah. Where does this track lead to?"

"Edge of city. Close to edge. Railyard. Trains there to take us out of city."

"And how about the soldiers?"

"Governor has not soldiers there. All are here," the gypsy said, pointing a finger at the roof of the tunnel. "I leave now with my people. Good luck, Mitchell Brand. We count on you."

'Eh?"

The gypsy motioned for Brand to turn around. He did and saw Dara Reynolds stood on the handcar they'd taken. She smiled and lifted her eyebrows at him, drumming her fingers on the lever arm.

Brand watched the gypsies and negroes load their cargo and began their departure. Handcars rolled in a steady stream down the tunnel, their lanterns glowing like fireflies until they winked out of sight.

"Nuts to this," he said and stepped back to the handcar where Dana helped him aboard. Maybe he'd get those questions answered after all.

• • •

They pumped the lever arm in a rapid cadence to move the car down the tunnel. The squeak of the wheels against the rails gave Brand the distraction he needed. Overhead, the bombs continued to fall around the neighborhood. Brand was sure the roof would crash in on them in a shower of rock and flame. When the squeaking of the handcar wasn't enough to keep him from tumbling into memories of the trenches, he gave conversation a shot. It worked well enough, he found out, but he wasn't too happy with what Dana Reynolds had to say.

"You'll need protection out there, Brand. Besides," she said, "I'm not letting the Governor get off easy on this."

"You think one girl with a sword and a shotgun is enough to send the Governor's boys running?"

"I think somebody needs to fight back, yes. And it's more than just one girl with a sword. There's a resistance up there. Right now. Trading shots with those soldiers. Men and women who stayed behind."

"What the hell for?"

"Because they didn't want to give up so easily. Maybe they wanted to help their friends in that tunnel behind us. Make enough ruckus. Slow the Governor down. They think that train will get them out. But I'm not convinced."

They kept up their conversation while they pumped the handle and rode the track further away from the speak. After a while, Dana paused and caught her breath while Brand did the lion's share of moving the handcar. She gave him a breather a few minutes later.

After two more stretches of tunnel with breaks for each of them, they pulled up to a platform set into the wall. Above the damp wooden structure, the roof had been hollowed out, allowing for one or two people to stand level with the floor of the handcar. Dana stepped from the car to the platform and reached a hand over to help Brand. He nodded, but made it across on his own. Dana spun on her heel and stepped to the tunnel wall. Brand saw the outline of a door cut into the earth. He lifted the lantern from the handcar and saw a heavy layer of burlap and canvas had been draped to conceal the door.

"Who're we hiding the door from?" he asked.

"If the Governor finds these tunnels, he'll probably just dynamite them. Like the Mayor did. But if he sends his boys down here, and I think he might, we wanted to have as much protection as possible."

"You've been in with these gypsies how long? Seems you're part of their crew, but I don't get that you're one of them. Not properly, at any rate."

"No. I'm not a member of their community. I work for them. Same as I work for anyone who's got the right color money."

"Does that include the Governor?"

Brand knew he shouldn't have asked. The woman's tough girl act rankled him though, and he didn't know how else to play his hand. She stepped close and looked at him hard.

"If the Governor paid me to stick you in the eye, I might take him up on it. Otherwise, it'd be no deal. Any more funny stuff, Brand?"

He sniffed and gave her his smile that was half sneer. "No, Mis—I mean Dana. No more from me. Lead they way. Please."

She pushed the door open and they entered a tunnel with a concrete floor. Brand's feet were unsteady at first on the foreign stone surface. Two short lengths of tunnel later, they emerged through a second entrance to the curio shop cellar.

Outside, the bombs had stopped falling. At least for now, Brand thought. Gunfire crackled and popped still, echoing into the cellar through the doorway that led to the street.

"We should close that up," Dana said and went to the door. The secret shelf that Stevie Five Sticks had come through was closed. Brand went to it and tried to find a hidden catch that might open it.

"Don't bother," Dana said. "It can only be opened from the tunnel side, just like the one we came through. "Let's get an eye on the street, hey?"

They went upstairs and into the front parlor where Brand had stormed around the last time he was in the house. The soldiers had come through and left their mark. The chair was upended and much of the furnishings showed signs of being kicked or struck with rifle butts. A glow radiated through the cracked windows and Brand went to examine the street outside.

His jaw hung open as he took in the damage. Across the street, burned out husks of houses and shops stared back at him like a forest of corpses. Overturned carts and wagons filled the roadway. Brand went to the foyer and pushed aside the shattered door and went onto the porch. Down the street, moving away from the curio shop, teams of soldiers continued their trail of destruction. They went into homes, lighting fires and smashing windows before moving on.

"There aren't any bodies in the street," Brand said. "Where'd the people go? They weren't all taken out in that march earlier."

"You saw them down there, Brand. In the tunnels. Most of them. Hell, almost all of them. Nothing but a gang or two left up here, like I said. Trying to fight back. Buy their comrades some time."

Brand was angry now. Angry as hell that it had come this far and that he'd been powerless to stop it. He knew, reading that bulletin the soldier tacked to the door. He knew and he raged, but he couldn't think of a way to prevent it from happening. Still, seeing it now, on the street in front of him, in the splintered bits of wood hanging in the doorframe at his back—fury burned in his gut and sent a haze of blood over his eyes.

"Who's up here? Do you know who they are? I mean names, sister."

"Your pal, Stevie Five Sticks and his friends. A few others. What's—"

"Where are they?" he cut in, growling and barely keeping his voice down. The soldiers might hear him. So what. Let them.

"Follow the bullets, Brand. Like you used to do," Dana said and moved away, going down the first two steps before Brand caught up to her and put a hand on her shoulder.

"Hey. I'm here to get a story and to get that story to the people who need to hear it. Now how's about you make nice and lend me some help. I thought that's why you came along, isn't it?"

Dana knocked his hand aside. "I came along to get back to where the action was, Brand. You can follow and get your story in my wake, or you can take your chances looking for Five Sticks and his bunch. Make your choice whenever you like, but I'm leaving before the soldiers come by to break up our lover's quarrel." She gave him a salute and he felt his hand snap to his brow in reply. Then Dana Reynolds and her sword disappeared into the night while bullets peppered a wall nearby and someone screamed.

"Like I used to do. Dammit, sister, you know me too well," Brand said as he ran toward the gunfire and shouts, following the sounds of war.

CHAPTER 40

AIDEN AND THE PROFESSOR WATCHED THE gunfire rain down into the neighborhood. On the ground, bursts of flickering light swelled into blossoms and receded, leaving only the heavy dark shapes of gunships soaring overhead.

"What do we do, mister? Ain't there a way out of here?"

"Indeed, as I said. We must leave, and our departure is now overdue. Come."

Aiden followed the professor down the steps, through his cellar, and into the tunnels once more. He accepted the crank torch the professor handed him and kept up a steady glow of light to illuminate their path. Explosions overhead knocked earth and dust from the tunnel roof. Aiden's heart stuck in his throat. With every step, he feared the tunnel would fall in, trapping them in a grave no one would ever find. His parents would never know what happened to him.

"Mister?"

"Yes, Mr. Conroy?"

"Some G-men took my folks away. Do you know what happened to 'em?"

"I can surmise where they may have been taken, but I cannot say for certain."

More explosions and the sound of gunfire came to Aiden's ears.

"You think they're still alive, mister? Not out there getting ...." Aiden couldn't bring himself to say the words. He could barely manage to think of his parents because his mind wanted to tell him they were dead. He knew that wasn't a sure thing, but not knowing felt worse somehow, like a weight that would crush him into the ground. That dread grew unbearable as he moved through the darkness with only this strange man who called himself a professor for company and protection.

"I gotta find 'em, mister," Aiden said as they turned a corner. The tunnel ended in a wooden panel with a catch on one side. Before reaching to open the door, Aiden turned around and faced the professor. "I gotta find my Ma and Pa. If you got any ideas for where to start looking, I'd be obliged to you for sharing."

"Through that door, Mr. Conroy, is a place where you will find safety and, if we have arrived in a timely manner, perhaps even one who might help you in your quest to find your parents."

"Talk straight with me, okay, mister? I can't half follow you when you—"

"Mr. Brand. Your former supervisor. He should be on the other side of that door, or not too far from it. He will need that device you have tucked into your coat."

"How do you know all this? What gives?"

The professor went on, like he hadn't even heard Aiden's questions.

"Together, the two of you stand a greater chance of success than if either of you were to spend this night acting alone."

"What is this, mister? What are you talking about and how do you know Mr. Brand is out there?"

"I have said before, Mr. Conroy, that I am loathe to dismiss with *Inquiry*. No truer statement could I speak. The god lives within me and I within him. And now, I must depart for a more appropriate setting."

The professor brushed a hand through the air beside his head and stepped out of the dim light from the fading crank torch. Aiden's mouth fell open as the darkness surrounded the professor and seemed to swallow him whole.

"Mister, wha—"

And then the man was gone, the darkness falling into place where he'd once stood. Aiden stood shivering in the black, afraid and alone. His fingers coiled around a handle and he realized he'd stopped working the crank torch. With a shudder of fright, Aiden spun and aimed the torch light at the door behind him. With a touch of his hand, a simple catch to one side let the door fall open.

Aiden stepped out of the tunnel and into a dimly lit cellar lined with shelves full of household items, tools, and bits of fabric and leather. A single light bulb warmed the space, but only just. Aiden roamed the shelves with his gaze, looking for something he could use as a weapon. His eye fixed on a shelf on the opposite wall that had two pistols on it. Aiden darted across the room and snatched up one of the guns. He'd fired a revolver before, just like the one he now held. Next to the guns was a box of bullets.

He put the crank torch down and went to load the revolver, dropping the first two bullets he picked up. Aiden breathed deep and settled his shivering hands. With the gun fully loaded and a handful of cartridges in his pocket, he turned to regard the room. The cellar was empty. A door set into one wall was closed and barred. Across from the door a set of steps led into the house above. Aiden slowly moved to the stairs.

He thought about going back for the crank torch, but decided he'd rather have at least one free hand. The pistol weighed down his wrist and arm like a hunk of stone. He fought to ignore the feelings. Aiden tried to hold the weapon like his radio heroes would, but the cold metal and rough wooden grip made the gun feel too large in his hand. He pocketed it. The gun's weight sank in next to the bullets, dragging his coat against his shoulder.

Aiden put a foot onto the bottom step and waited there, ready to run back into the tunnel if he heard anything like a threat from upstairs. He heard nothing and put his foot on the next step, and the next. He reached the top and peered into the dark corners of the house. To one side was a sitting room where a chair was turned over and the other furniture looked beat up and ruined. To the other side was a little breakfast nook. The table top had been smashed and broken glass littered the kitchen floor nearby. A cold wind blew through the house, followed by the sounds of gunfire and shouting from outside.

Staying low, Aiden crept further into the house, going for the overturned chair. Outside the house, to the front, he heard voices. Angry voices, a man and woman arguing. Gunshots rang out from behind the house and a man shouted in pain. Aiden flinched and tucked himself into a corner beside a cracked up side table. He fished the gun out of his pocket and aimed it at the front door.

More gunfire and shouting filled the night air outside and seemed to surround the house. Aiden's lip quivered and he squeezed off a shot from the pistol. The loud report scared him and he dropped the gun between his feet. Picking up the gun, Aiden remembered what the professor had told him before he disappeared into the darkness. Aiden had to find his folks, and Mr. Brand was supposed to be up here. He could help. Mr. Brand could help him find his parents, and maybe Aiden could help his old boss somehow.

Creeping out of his hiding place, Aiden moved to the front door and looked outside at the ruined street. Blackened, shattered buildings looked back at him. Voices came to him from about a block away, and more gunfire from almost right overhead. He heard the bullets hitting the ground and kicking up chips of stone and dirt. A team of soldiers came into view from the right, moving low and staying close to the porch. Aiden ducked inside and begged, silently, for the soldiers to keep moving.

He heard footsteps on the stairs. Aiden bolted, running through the house, into the kitchen and the washroom beyond, to the back door. He drew up at the door, snuck a glance outside. Silhouetted figures struggled against the wall of the next house. A flickering firelight cast a glow around them that made Aiden think about stories of damnation and torment. The awkward angles and violent movement put a lump in his throat that no amount of swallowing could dislodge.

Mr. Brand's voice broke through the sounds of fighting and Aiden moved to open the back door. Another voice came to him then, from inside the house.

"I know you're in here, kid. I saw you run."

CHAPTER 41

EMMA WHIPPED HER HAND OUT OF HER pocket, feeling the cold metal of the revolver like a bee sting in her palm. She and Eddie darted from their hiding place and tore across pavement and muddy earth to the next block. Emma saw only one shot for them. Go back, deeper into the neighborhood. Things seemed quieter now. No explosions rocked the night or shook the ground beneath their feet. Emma searched the sky. The gunships were still there, circling. But they weren't firing. At least not now. This was their one chance.

They could stay in the shadows. They could find Nagy's cellar again. Maybe get lucky enough to find another way into the tunnels.

At the next house they pulled up beside the back stoop. Across a wide alley, gates stood open along the length of a fence. Emma shot her eyes up and down the alley. When she saw nothing but snowmelt and the pitch of night, she stepped out of hiding and ran through the mud to the first gate. She halted and turned. Eddie hadn't moved. She cursed under her breath before running back to Eddie.

"What are you doing?" she demanded.

"Staying hid. The hell are you doing running around like this? Where you think we're going to anyway?"

"The tunnels. It's the only place we'll be safe. Those soldiers—"

As if on cue, a man's voice broke into the quiet around them.

"*Over here!*"

Eddie and Emma moved as one, her hand in his, across the alley, through the gate and into the yard beyond. Eddie pulled the gate closed and they stood with their backs to the fence. Emma held her breath until she heard the soldiers in the alley.

"*I heard voices.*"

"*Go left. I'll take right.*"

Emma waited for the sound of footsteps. When none came, she turned her frightened eyes to Eddie. His eyes were rounded and just as full of fear. The soldiers had to have seen the closed gate and figured their hiding spot. Why hadn't they kept moving, gone into the house instead of staying put. Emma feared any second a bullet would break through the fence and go into her back or Eddie's. She twitched her head to show him she meant to make for the house. He nodded and they stepped slow as can be, placing each foot with care. Emma reached for Eddie's hand and found his outstretched fingers. They held on, keeping their arms a taut cord between them for balance, and for the safety of each other's touch.

They were halfway through the yard to the house when Emma heard a man cough beside the gate. Then the sound of glass on metal. What could that be? Emma heard the sound over and over in her mind as they moved up to the back stoop.

The house was one of the larger ones in the neighborhood and had seen far better days, even before the Governor's airships attacked the neighborhood. Windows were boarded up on the ground floor. The cellar door stood open beside the back stoop, which drooped to the side like a ship listing in the mud and snowmelt. Eddie motioned with his free hand, pointing at the cellar door. Emma nodded. They made it to the cellar steps, slow but sure through the mud.

Emma heard a whispering, like a flag fluttering in a slight breeze.

A crash of glass and a gust of flame followed. Then another fluttering and Emma turned in time to see a bottle with a flaming rag stuck in it. The bottle struck the side of the house and exploded into a fireball, joining the flames licking the wood where the first firebomb had hit.

Eddie pushed Emma down the cellar steps and raced after her. They fell together, landing on the earthen floor in a tangle. Shouts and laughter followed them in from outside, but quickly dissipated as the crackling of the fire grew louder. Emma held her lover and he wrapped his arms tight around her. They stayed that way until their terror faded, listening to the fire grow above them and watching its glow frame the cellar door in angry orange.

'C'mon, Lovebird. Ain't out of this yet. Got to be a door up into the house."

Emma let Eddie lead her again, feeling less sure of herself after landing them in this mess. They could have stayed hidden outside somewhere. They could have run down the street instead of deeper into the neighborhood.

The sounds of shuffling feet and shouting came through the floorboards overhead. A man cursed and stomped his feet on the back stoop, yelling a litany into the night. His footsteps went back inside and followed a path to a set of stairs. Emma and Eddie listened to the man's approach, afraid that whatever freedom had awaited them was about to vanish in a series of gunshots or worse.

Emma pulled out her gun and nearly let off a shot when the dark of the cellar was split by the glare of a lantern. The man holding the lantern froze when he saw the two intruders in his basement. He fumbled at his belt and came up with a pistol. He shouted at them both, rambling in the language Emma had heard before. This time the tongue felt sharp in her ears, like a sword thrusting and slicing.

"Nagy! Biros!" Emma shouted, dropping her gun and holding

her hands out to fend off the man's verbal assault. He stopped shouting and narrowed his eyes, examining Emma carefully. Her voice betrayed her sex, but she still wore the garments Biros and Eszti had given her. The man eyed her, then Eddie. When the lantern glowed off her lover's dark skin, the man resumed his attack, but lower this time, and deeper. His guttural accusations echoing off Emma's eardrums like hoofbeats through mud.

From behind the man, a girl's voice interrupted the scene. "Papa, no." The man stepped aside and turned to face a young woman who had come down the stairs. She wore a heavy coat and had a scarf around her hair, half-shrouding her plain face and sad eyes. She looked like any other woman Emma had seen in the neighborhood, but a deeper sadness came off of her, like a cloud begging for a chance to rain.

"We're friends," Emma said to the girl. "Of Nagy and Biros. We tried to help them. To help you all, but the soldiers—"

"I don't know from soldiers," the man shot back, turning again to stare Emma down. She gave back as good as she got, keeping her eyes firm and fixed on him as he spoke. The man was heavy around the middle, pillowing inside his coat. His limbs stuck out of his mass like stunted branches on an old tree, and his face was a goblin's mask, all bristling hair, thick lips, beady black eyes, and bulbous nose.

"I know my house is on fire. And my daughter tells me she knows a dark man. This dark man, who you bring to my basement when soldiers make my house to burn. So tell me, woman who looks like a man. What do you know about this?"

"I know we were here when the soldiers came and took everyone away. I know they helped us. Biros, and his daughter, Eszti. They dressed me to look like I belong here, and they helped hide Eddie," she said, putting a hand on her lover's shoulder.

"Eddie," the man said, looking at him now. "And what does Eddie know? What does Eddie know about my daughter?"

"Sir," Eddie began. Emma heard steel on his tongue and hoped he wouldn't go too far. "I don't know your daughter, though I seen her plenty of times before. Maybe you don't want to ask how she knows me, but I'll tell you it's because she's been to Nagy's speak. You can see my piece is still where it belongs, so I'd be much obliged if you could wave yours in another direction. That's what I know."

The man chuckled, but kept the gun level with Eddie's navel, eyeing the butt of the pistol that stuck out above his belt.

"The damn shoemaker and his room for drinking and dancing. My girl," the man said, turning to his daughter. "you told me you would not go there. Your friends go there, but you say you will not. Now I find you have lied to me."

The girl's face fell. Her father's disappointment worse than any bullet from his gun. He put the pistol into his belt again and went to her. holding her close and whispering comfort before turning to face Emma and Eddie again.

"I am Peter. Biros I know. He is a good man. I would trust him. My house is burning. We must leave." He handed the lantern to Eddie and motioned for him to shine its light to the left.

Peter went to the wall. The lantern illuminated a set of shelves there, and beside them a stack of crates that stood floor to ceiling. Reaching behind the crates, Peter fished out a key. He inserted it into a slot in one of the crates and twisted it, then pulled on the edge of crate. The whole stack swung out slowly, scraping the dirt floor. Eddie passed the lantern to Emma and lent his hands to the task.

The tunnel waited for them, cold and silent and so very different from the world outside. Flames crackled and roared from upstairs and the structure shifted as a floor or wall collapsed somewhere above.

"I would have my stick with me," Peter said, looking at the steps leading into the house. His daughter moved as if to go fetch what her father wanted, but he put a hand on her arm. "No, girl. Let it be. I can find another stick."

Emma bent down and retrieved her father's revolver. Peter watched her as she dropped it into her pocket. The old man's face curled into a grim smile and he motioned for Emma to give the lantern back to Eddie and for the two of them to enter the tunnel first. They did and moved into the darkness, the lantern casting its glow ahead of them.

Peter and his daughter stayed close behind, giving directions when they came to intersections and branches. They moved fast, down the dark passage on a twisting course under the neighborhood. Their path crossed another tunnel that was much wider. After his first step into this new passage, Eddie stopped moving.

"There's tracks down here. Like an old railroad."

"Is an old railroad," Peter said, moving past Emma and accepting the lantern from Eddie. The old man shined the light on four sets of tracks in a tunnel that stretched out in front of them and away into darkness on either side. The ceiling was higher, too, at least twice that of the passage they'd followed to this point.

"Is from old city," the daughter said.

"Where do they go?" Emma asked.

"To where it is safe," Peter said and moved down the tracks, waving for the others to follow.

CHAPTER 42

BRAND SKIDDED TO A STOP BESIDE THE CURIO shop's back stoop. He put his back to the wall of the house. Its bulk loomed over him in the night. Firelight flickered beyond his position and horrific shadows danced on the wall of the next house. A gunshot sounded and a man howled in pain. Brand darted out when he heard laughter. What he saw made him nearly bellow with rage.

Behind the curio shop, in the glow of a burning woodshed, Steve Five Sticks and two other village types had a soldier pinned to the ground. Five Sticks held a pistol aimed at the soldier's leg. Brand saw an angry wound there in the fire's crackling glare. Before he could shout to stop the execution, Five Sticks lifted the gun and shot the soldier in the chest. The man heaved once and went still.

Brand quietly moved back into hiding before hailing the gypsy.

"Hey, Five Sticks. It's Brand. I'll come out if you promise to keep that pistol pointed at the ground."

'Sure thing, Brand. Hey fellas," came the reply. Brand didn't bother listening to the rest. He stepped out and moved fast to close on the trio of men standing around the dead soldier. Five Sticks had his pistol aimed at the ground all right, and Brand didn't miss a beat before bringing his fist up and into the gypsy's cheek. Five Sticks saw it coming just the same and rolled with the punch. He jumped back a step and held his free hand to his face. The pistol hadn't moved, but Brand noticed the gypsy's grip tighten around it.

"What gives, Brand? Don't tell me you're working both sides here."

"I'm only working one side, and that's the side that knows when a prisoner of war has earned an execution and when he hasn't. But it doesn't matter what side a man's on when he's been shot in the leg and is lying there unarmed. Who the hell gave you the right to kill a man like that?"

Five Sticks stepped slow and easy, wiggling the pistol in his hand now but still keeping it pointed down. His voice rose as he spoke.

"We're not like the gray hairs in the neighborhood, Brand. We're from here. This is our home. You hear that? Our home!"

"And so you'll do what you like, when you like, and how you like. Is that it? Well—"

A gunshot from inside the curio shop broke in on their argument. Brand whirled to see the door to the back stoop bang open and a kid come rushing out holding a pistol. A soldier appeared in the doorway behind the kid. Brand winced as a shot cracked the air by his head and the soldier fell backwards into the house. The kid fell down the steps, landing in a heap in the mud.

Brand rushed forward to the kid, hearing Stevie Five Sticks and his pals laughing behind him.

"See the way that fella toppled back, Brand? Wish they didn't have them masks on. Would've loved to see his eyes just then."

Spinning on his heel, Brand hollered blue murder at the gypsy. "How about the kid here? Want to see his eyes, too? Go on and look!"

Brand reached down and lifted the kid by his arm. The pistol he'd been holding tumbled to the ground. A whimpering plea came to Brand's ears and he paused. He knew the voice.

"Conroy?" he said, lifting the kid by both arms now and looking him in the face. It was Aiden Conroy, all right. He wore a great coat that was two sizes too big and ten kinds of fancy too much for his family's wardrobe. Brand knew the kid lived in Old Town. He'd dressed the part everyday since getting hired at the Daily Record.

"What gives, Conroy? Where'd you get the duds here, and what's with the gunslinger routine? Didn't your folks tell you right about guns?"

From across the frozen ground, Stevie Five Sticks wished Brand a farewell and waved goodbye.

"Be seeing you, Brand. If you and your little brother here aren't too scared, the show's over by Humboldt Park."

"What show?"

"The big one. That's where it all ends tonight for the Governor. C'mon fellas," the gypsy said to his pals. They sauntered off between the nearby houses and disappeared in the darkness.

"Nuts," Brand said, turning back to Conroy. The kid had his legs under him again. He opened his coat and brought out the camera box Skippy had given Brand on Valentine's Day.

• • •

Aiden held the camera box out, but his boss told him to keep it tucked into his coat.

"We might need it, or we might not. I don't know. We'll see when we get to the park."

"The park? But I thought you weren't in with those guys. You gave 'em hell after they—" Aiden felt his voice cut out, so he pointed to the dead soldier on the ground. He'd heard the whole exchange after the gunshot that killed the man. Even though the gypsy had saved him by killing the soldier coming out of the house, Aiden felt worse about it than if he'd shot the man himself. He kicked at the gun on the ground by his feet, sending it sliding into a pile of muddy snow.

"I did," Mr. Brand said, breaking in on Aiden's thoughts. "I'd give 'em hell again if I had the chance. But the gypsy is right. This is going to end for the Governor over at that park, only it won't be Five Sticks and his gun that ends it."

Mr. Brand reached into his coat and lifted a square microphone that was hooked to his belt.

"We're going after the story, Conroy. You ready to do the news?"

Aiden flinched as gunfire crackled across the night. He felt his stomach roll over on itself, but he still couldn't help the grin that stretched over his face.

• • •

Aiden followed his boss through the neighborhood, in and out of hiding around the broken up buildings. Small explosions kept sounding in the deadly night, threatening to end their journey at any moment. Each blast made Aiden's stomach quiver. He thought about going back for the pistol he'd dropped, but he hadn't liked the way it felt in his hands. The heaviness frightened him, like he might drop it on his foot and shoot off a toe.

"When's it gonna stop, Mr. Brand? Been going on all night, since …."

His boss pulled up by a bombed out house and turned to look at him. Mr. Brand's questioning eyes roamed over Aiden's face, and he felt the memories welling up in his throat.

"You all right, Conroy?"

"My folks, Mr. Brand. Some G-men took 'em away." Aiden blubbered while he told his boss about seeing his folks pushed into the sedan and the soldier staying behind to wait for him. Mr. Brand moved them deeper into hiding within the ruined home.

"What else happened? How'd you get out here anyway?"

Aiden explained about finding the tunnel Digs showed him, and getting caught by a couple gypsies. He told about the professor and his radio, too, and about how the guy led him back through the tunnels after the shooting started.

"Then the guy just up and vanished. Like the tunnel swallowed him. He was there and then he wasn't."

"Well that settles one thing."

"What's that?"

"Eh?" his boss said, shaking his head like he was waking up from a dream. "Oh, you don't have to worry about that bird. He's with the good guys. At least I think he is. C'mon."

They kept moving through the neighborhood, aiming their path toward the sounds of fighting. They crossed a wide street with shattered homes and shops facing onto it. Firelight glowed from the next block.

"That's the park up ahead, Conroy. Let's get—"

An explosion shook the neighborhood and then another. Aiden held his hands to his ears when a whistling pierced the night and before he knew it Mr. Brand had him pressed against the ground in front of a still burning storefront. The flames waved in the nighttime breeze and cast shadows over them as earth and wood and stone rained down. When the clumps of mud stopped falling, Aiden shook his head free from his boss's hands and rolled into a ball.

Mr. Brand slid forward on his belly and put a hand on Aiden's shoulder.

"I know what you're thinking right now, Conroy. I thought it myself when I was over there and the Kaiser's boys kept up the mortar fire day and night."

"Ain't going to see my folks again, am I?"

"Eh? Oh, sure you are. I mean, I hope like hell you will. It won't be on account of me letting you buy it at any rate. But I need you on your feet, Conroy. Your folks want to see you just the same as you do them. It won't do them any good you lying on the ground like that."

Aiden struggled into a sitting position. He dusted his palms on the heavy coat the professor gave him. The bullets rattled in his pockets and he fished them out, both hands heavy with little pills of lead and brass. Aiden let them fall into the snowmelt and ash.

"I'm ready, Mr. Brand. Just needed a good cry is all."

"Attaboy, Conroy. We need to get the story now. That's our job. Like before, only now we're on the ground and in the soup. Look, I'd better show you how to work this," Mr. Brand said, lifting the microphone off his hip. He held the device out and pressed a switch on the side then released it.

"That's to transmit. You have to hold it down if you want to be heard. And don't pull this cable out of the bottom. That'll cut your power and then you're just talking to yourself."

Aiden was still in a daze, but he tried to focus on what his boss was telling him. Mr. Brand seemed to notice and gave Aiden's shoulder a shake.

"You have to know how to use this, Conroy."

"Why?"

"Because if I get mine out here, it's up to you to tell the people what's happening."

The weight of it settled into Aiden's stomach like a ball of lead. He couldn't move to join Mr. Brand when he stood and looked around the corner.

"The park is down the street. That's where we have to be." Mr. Brand looked down on him and seemed ready to shake his head. "C'mon, Conroy. Get up. I'll pour you three fingers when its all over. Right now, we're on duty."

Aiden took his boss's hand and stood. Then they moved out.

CHAPTER 43

EMMA STAYED CLOSE TO EDDIE AS THEY followed the old man and his daughter down the tracks. The rails stretched forever into the darkness, pushing the edge of Emma's vision deeper and deeper into the black but never showing her a destination other than the pitch ahead of them. To the side, she would see bits of old sidewalks, the planks and trestles rotten or showing burn marks from the fire that swallowed Old Chicago and spat it out a charred and blackened husk. Just like the neighborhood behind them.

Their path reached an incline and Emma's legs felt like stone. Her steps faltered as the long day's fatigue settled in. She fell against Eddie and he caught her.

"Keep on, Lovebird. We're almost there. See?" He pointed up ahead and Emma could make out a circle of paler darkness, a slight shade of gray brighter than the surrounding tunnel. Through the opening, she saw the promise of freedom leading away and into the night, but it was a promise soon broken. They emerged under the canopy of a deserted train shed. The tracks were empty but for two old handcars off to the right.

"Trains have gone," Peter said, dropping the crank torch into the gravel at his feet. His daughter turned on him and spoke fast and sharp in their tongue. The squat little man recoiled from the abuse and held up his hands, defending himself with cries of shame and regret. The girl gave up and went to Emma with great streams of tears pouring down her cheeks.

"The soldiers, they take my mother. Take her with the others. He says no, that she came with others, that she will be here waiting for us. But I know better. They are at the camp. She will be made to work until she is dead." The girl collapsed against Emma and clung to her shoulders for support. Emma found her legs, but was thankful for Eddie's hands on her waist.

"What camp? What's she mean about a camp?" Emma demanded of the father.

"Is by lakeshore. For the fair they build. All the Rigos are taken there to work. To make fair happen. My daughter fears her mother will die there. Will not be first time our people are made to work like slaves. Will not be last."

"And that's all you can say about it? Your wife is there with the others, all those people from your neighborhood, and you're just going to stand here?"

"What should Peter do? Eh? Peter should fight soldiers? Should take his gun and shoot at men with rifles and bombs and airships? Peter should die like other Rigos who fight for neighborhood that is already lost? Ah," the old man's voice cracked. He shook his head and turned away.

"What does that mean?" Emma asked. "That word. I know it ain't nice, so why do you keep saying it?"

The daughter piped up. "It means blackbird in our language, but is used to call us *gypsies*. Person with no home. Person who doesn't belong anywhere. But we are not Rigos!" she shouted, whirling to face her father. His grief had passed and he stood with his hands by his sides, defeated but not dead.

"No, my girl," he said, coming close and putting his hands on hers. "No, we are not Rigos. We are Kertész, and I would see your mother, my Katarina, again before I die."

Emma stepped forward, leaving the support of Eddie's hands. She went to the handcars. Both had been loaded with cargo recently. Fresh scrapes in the deck showed where heavy objects had been dragged and shifted. One of the cars had a broken handle, making it next to useless unless they wanted to pump and lift from one side only. The other car's handle was fine though.

"How far do these tracks go?" Emma asked, turning back to Peter and his daughter.

"To river, but—"

"So we'll need to find a way across the river and out to the lakeshore. Let's go."

Peter and his daughter hesitated until Eddie came up and put his hands on their shoulders. "She's right. We can't hang around here, and Misses Kertész ain't going to like it if we're late picking her up, is she?" He looked into Emma's eyes as he spoke and she saw that old fire again, the embers that glowed in the heart of the man she loved. She smiled at him and moved to help Peter and his daughter over to the handcar.

• • •

They took turns pumping the handcar down the tracks. Peter's daughter lit the way with the crank torch. Emma and Eddie worked the lever arm for the first leg of their journey. Peter spelled Emma a bit and then she gave Eddie a break. The car squeaked and squealed along the tracks as they made the quickest pace they could manage. They kept on this way, rotating shifts on the lever arm, until they reached the ruins of a depot house from the old city. The musty smell of sodden wood mixed with charcoal filled the tunnel around them. Emma climbed off the handcar and helped the girl down behind her.

They stepped aside to make room for her father and Eddie

to dismount the car. "What's your name anyway?" Emma asked.

"Marta. Your name really is Lovebird?"

Emma laughed. "No, that's what Eddie calls me. My name's Emma."

The girl's eyes rounded and Emma felt a tension forming in the air behind her. Peter spoke up then and confirmed her fears.

"Emma Farnsworth," he said. "Rich woman who murders man in airship and runs away with dark man." The tension between them grew so great Emma feared she would have to draw her father's gun. An instant later, Emma felt the thickness in the air dissolve amidst the old man's chuckles. "Peter chooses good company tonight."

Emma looked into Marta's eyes and saw friendship there still, but her sadness remained and a ring of worry creased the skin around her eyes now. Not knowing what to say, Emma simply nodded, admitting her identity, and waited for the girl or her father to respond.

"Is okay," Peter said. "My daughter and I do not believe all the news government says is fit to print. Come."

He ushered them up a set of crumbled stone steps and to a door that was set into the tunnel wall. Working a catch on one side, he pushed the door open slowly and Emma felt the chill of a Chicago City night rush into the tunnel. They stepped out at the back of an open shed that sat at the mouth of a wharf. Stacks of lumber and rope filled the shed, and they moved through them carefully. Emma kept her eyes darting around the wharf area. Across the pier was another set of sheds, their far sides open to the river.

Silos and half-filled lumber yards waited across the river, expectant and hopeful for the next day's shipments from the Eastern Seaboard. Emma spied the narrow bridge she and Eddie had driven across the previous day. It was two piers farther along the wharf on this side. Across the bridge, the silos and shack stood ominous in the dark night, and she couldn't shake the fear that coppers or soldiers would come rushing out of the shadows at any second.

"Let's get moving. That bridge isn't guarded."

They moved as fast as they could, staying low and shuffling

between piles of cargo, coils of rope and netting, and stacks of lumber. Within minutes, they'd reached the near end of the bridge.

"We're almost there. Just a—"

Emma swallowed her words and pulled up short when a jeep engine sounded from farther down the wharf road. A set of headlights flashed across the wall of the silos across the bridge. The vehicle came slowly along the road and for a moment, Emma hoped it would pass by. But a searchlight stabbed out into the darkness and swept the area. Emma and her companions dropped to a crouch behind a stack of railroad ties.

The jeep pulled to a halt at the opposite end of the bridge and the engine cut. The headlights dimmed but the searchlight stayed lit and continued to sweep like a blade against the curtain of darkness.

"What is Emma Farnsworth's plan?" Peter asked, making no effort to hide his disappointment.

"Father!" Marta hissed.

Emma put a hand up to silence them when the searchlight sliced in their direction and hovered off to the side of their hiding place. A bullhorn crackled to life and they all pressed their backs tight against the railroad ties.

"Citizens, curfew is in effect until oh-five-thirty hours tomorrow morning. Anyone on the streets is subject to internment."

The four of them stayed put. Emma drew her dad's revolver and saw Eddie palm the pistol they got from Wynes. Only Peter kept his gun tucked away. He shook his head at Emma and Eddie, muttering something under his breath. Emma ignored the old man. If the soldiers were coming for them, they'd have to take them with a fight. She hadn't gotten this far just to throw her hands up in the air and waltz off to a cold cell and a jailer's leers.

Shouting from across the river came to her ears. At first she feared it was the soldiers yelling for them to come out, that they'd been spotted somehow. But shouts of fright and anger cut the night air. When a sharp, final silence fell again, Emma risked a look. She couldn't see any soldiers, and the searchlight wasn't moving anymore either. It was still lit, but had been aimed farther away from the bridge, leaving the passage across shrouded in shadow.

"Let's go," she said, stepping fast to the next pile of lumber along their route. She turned to see Eddie following her. Peter and Marta came next, the old man shaking his head and showing more distress than before.

"Is no good. No good," he kept muttering, twitching and whipping his goblin head side to side like he expected a threat to emerge from every corner. Emma wanted to calm him down, quiet him for fear he'd give them away, but the air around them fluttered and shook, reminding Emma of her escape from the prison chain earlier. An instant later, her fears were made real as the ghost of her father stepped out of the night beside her astride a rusted old Boneshaker bicycle.

His face was stained with filth and his wispy white hair stuck out in all directions from his scalp like whorls of spider silk.

"Emma. My girl, I'm so sorry."

"Dad?"

Tears fell in rivers that froze on her father's hobo face. He wiped at them and dirt smudged across his cheeks, showing a patch of clean skin. In a flash, the edges of the clean area grew inward like a fungus until a layer of grime had coated Josiah Farnsworth's face again.

"Can't tell you how sorry I am, my Emma. My only ...." He trailed off, and his eyes blinked fast, like he'd heard or seen something in the distance that scared him. "We gotta move on now my girl. Time to go," he said, taking her free hand and leading her out from behind the lumber pile. She went with him, unable to deny the pull to follow, just as she was unable to deny the feeling of horror that rose in her chest and throat.

"Time to go now. Just like when you was a little tot and your Momma and me used to put you on the trains to New York to visit your Grandmother. Time to go, Little Emma."

Her father had been walking backwards, pushing the bicycle along with his feet. He paused and glanced over Emma's shoulder.

"They with you, Emma? That nigger boy there and them two—what are they now, some of them gypsies? They your friends now?"

Fearing the vulgar names escape her father's lips, Emma broke from the spell and ripped her hand from his. "Yes, they're my friends. His name is Eddie, and he's not just a friend. He's the man I love. And they're not gypsies. They have names. Peter and Marta. She's his daughter, and at least he has enough sense to stay by her side and see her through the worst of times instead of taking the easy way out like you did."

"Emma, I—"

"Shut up! Just shut up," Emma hollered at him, her anger and fury unstoppable now, even though the threat of discovery still hung heavy in her mind. Whatever this tramp was supposed to be, wherever he'd come from, he'd earned an earful, and she was going to give it to him.

"What the hell are you? I saw you in your office. I saw what you did. With this," she said, lifting the gun between them. The tramp recoiled in fright, putting his hands up and begging her to remove the weapon from his sight. She pressed forward, holding the gun on him now, and backed him into a corner between two stacks of lumber.

"I'm your daddy, Emma," he said, broken and defeated. "I'm the same as ever I was. A good for nothing drunk. I helped you as best I could back on the street this morning, and I did the same just now. But it's going to cost me, my girl. It's going to cost me more than you can know."

"What do you mean? What's left to pay? There's nothing left of the Farnsworth name in Chicago City, nothing but a—"

A rabid hiss split the night around them and Emma spun to put her back up against the lumber pile beside the tramp who looked and talked and acted just like her father.

"Go on, my girl. Go on and run now."

"What?"

"Run, I said. Dammit! Run!"

Emma backed away from him, his acrid breath and vehemence

shoving against her chest. Behind her she heard a girl's voice cry out and then a scream. Eddie hollered and then Emma heard gunshots from two pistols. She moved to help, but felt her father's hand on her arm. She knew then that the tramp was her father. His touch, his grip was too familiar, too much like she remembered. As she stood there, frozen in memory, Eddie and Marta raced around the end of the lumber pile and came to stand with her, facing back the way they'd come.

Sounds of grisly violence came to them from their former hiding place and Marta sobbed in pitiable, wracking grief. Eddie put his arm around her and pulled her farther away, backing them into the corner beside Emma and her father. Emma watched all this happen and knew she should be doing something, but her father's hand on her arm kept her fixed where she stood. When finally he released her she almost toppled forward.

"Told you to run, Emma. You listen this time. You run, my girl. Run and don't stop."

Emma turned to regard her father, the tramp. Behind her the sounds of gore had gone silent and a steady, rasping breathing grew to take their place.

"You," her father said, looking at Eddie. "You take good care of her, boy. You do that, you hear?"

Eddie nodded and gritted his teeth. Emma's father trembled and muttered a feeble apology in Eddie's direction as he pushed past them all on his bicycle, moving straight for the growling and hissing sounds coming from around the lumber pile.

"Let's go, Lovebird."

Emma took Marta's hand and together they followed Eddie out of the lumber stacks and onto the bridge. Their gait was slow but quickened as they reached the middle of the crossing. A cry of terror pierced the night from within the stacked lumber and Eddie began to run. Emma tugged Marta along and pumped her legs with every ounce of strength she had.

CHAPTER 44

KEEPING TO A CROUCH, BRAND MOVED DOWN the street with Conroy trailing close at his heels. They passed shot up houses, and the sounds of battle came louder and harsher to Brand's ears as they neared Humboldt Park. At the end of the block, they pulled up against a shattered sedan. Brand risked a look around the fender and immediately jumped back a pace, nearly tumbling into Conroy as he caught up. A soldier was lying dead on the ground behind the car. The barrel of a Tommy gun poked out from beneath the body and a pistol still hung on the soldier's belt.

Brand dragged the body aside and lifted the Tommy gun. He struggled to balance it in his hands and settled for tucking it under his arm with his hand on the forward grip.

"You want a sidearm, Conroy?" he asked, noticing the kid's eyes were fixed on the still holstered pistol.

Conroy nodded, but his face said different, so Brand fished the pistol out and stuck it into his own pocket. The kid seemed to understand. His face fell, but Brand could see it was more from relief than shame.

A burst of gunfire sounded close by and they both tucked in tight against the ruined car. The park was across the street. Brand sneaked a glance around the sedan's grill and his eyes went misty with grief at the sight of soldiers and citizens fighting hand to hand on the wide open lawn of the park. Some of the people held shovels and other tools, anything that would serve as a weapon. Others had rifles or pistols and kept up a steady exchange with soldiers, trading shots from behind park benches and waste barrels.

Down the street to the right, buildings burned at the park's edge, casting an amber glow over the whole scene beneath the gray clouds above. To the left, a thick grove of trees extended empty branches into the wintery sky.

Tapping Conroy's shoulder to alert him, Brand edged back the way they'd come and raced for the trees. The kid followed close behind. At the tree line, Brand scurried up to a thick trunk and knelt down, looking out at the park. He motioned for Conroy to keep his eyes open and follow close. The kid nodded and followed Brand to the next set of trees. Silently hoping Conroy had it in him to stay alert if the bullets came their way, Brand lifted the mic off his belt and opened the channel.

· · ·

Aiden crouched behind his boss at the first tree, then followed him deeper into the grove. As they moved, Aiden thought he should ask Mr. Brand for the pistol he'd picked off the dead soldier. He should have reached out for it when it was offered instead of just nodding. Now his boss knew he was afraid of using a gun, that he couldn't be trusted.

Mr. Brand was taking them to where the soldiers and citizens fought like cats and dogs, only they did it with more than claws and teeth in the game. As he followed his boss through the trees, Aiden caught snapshots of action. He flinched when he saw a figure fall face down in grass out there. The guy had been holding a shovel and running. Then he just went limp and tumbled to the ground.

Aiden hoped they wouldn't have to shoot it out with anyone. If he got lucky, he'd only need to get pictures with his boss's camera box. He clutched it against his side, wrapping the heavy coat around it so it would be protected if he fell or had to drop down quickly. Mr. Brand waved a hand to get his attention and Aiden watched carefully as his boss used hand signs to communicate. Aiden knew enough from his scouting days to follow Mr. Brand's signals. He didn't know if he'd be able to keep up if the soldiers saw them and started shooting, but he told himself he'd do his best. He had to tell himself that with every step. It was that, or start bawling from fear that a bullet was already on its way to find him.

At the next set of trees, Mr. Brand lifted the microphone off his belt and reported about the scene in front of them. Aiden looked into the park again and had to clamp both hands over his mouth. Through the maze of trees, folks from the neighborhood locked horns with soldiers. Shovels and axes swung in the night air and were followed by cries of agony. Guns fired back and forth. Back of it all, the burning buildings made it look like hell had come up for a visit. Aiden had never imagined anything like it, even when Mr. Brand had told him, Digs, and Jenkins about the Great War, and he knew those stories were short versions of what really happened. Seeing it now, in front of him, Aiden knew why Mr. Brand had kept hush about things.

• • •

"Ladies and Gentlemen of Chicago City, this is Mitchell Brand reporting from the ground in Humboldt Park. Can you hear the gunfire? I'm going to hold the microphone up now. The battle will speak for itself. You'll hear voices mixed in with the shooting. Screaming, too. If any children are listening, this is a good time to get them out of the room."

Brand lifted the microphone away from his face and held it

facing out beside the tree. Gunfire and shouts echoed out of the fray, but they were indistinct. He had to get closer. Brand clipped the mic onto his belt again and got ready to move.

"Stay with me, Conroy. And stay down."

The kid nodded and kept flat. Brand crawled out from behind his tree and lifted the Tommy gun to ready position. With the gun up, he felt safer, ready to defend himself and Conroy if he needed to. But the weapon was like an unsteady dance partner in his hands, forcing him to contort his body in ways he never really had before. At the next tree he glanced back and saw Conroy was right behind him, at the tree they'd just passed. The kid made a motion with his hands, waving like Brand should come back to him. Then he lifted a hand with the forefinger extended and the thumb up. Brand fished the pistol out of his pocket. He looked back at Conroy and let his eyes ask the question.

The kid's face still hung heavy with fear, just like so many other young guys Brand had watched climb the trench walls. But Conroy's jaw tightened until his eyes said things were different this time. Brand tossed him the gun, nodded, and moved out.

• • •

Aiden tucked down as he caught the gun. He'd seen something in the corner of his eye, through the trees to their left. A dark shape moved out there in the shadows. Aiden whispered, trying to get Mr. Brand's attention, but his boss was focused on the fighting ahead of them.

Then Aiden heard a snarling and saw that his boss heard it, too. Mr. Brand whipped around to face into the grove, aiming the Tommy gun in the direction of the noise. Aiden rushed over to his boss's side, lying flat and pointing the pistol out into the darkness between the trees, watching for anything that moved, anything he might shoot at. He saw it then, a hulking dark shadowy figure crouched behind a stout tree about ten yards away. Its arms and legs seemed longer than normal, like it was some kind of circus freak maybe. But Aiden knew what he was looking at. He'd seen the same figure in Mr. Brand's camera box the night that Digs was killed.

Whispering through his fright, Aiden asked, "What is that, Mr. Brand?"

"Keep quiet," his boss whispered back as he raised up on his elbows to point the Tommy gun at the thing in the trees. Aiden heard a scraping sound, like a piece of steel raking along hard ground. Mr. Brand jerked as he fired the Tommy gun and Aiden pressed himself flat to the ground. The sound of the gunshots bounced against his ears and sent ripples of panic into his guts. The steel scraping sound became a rasping screeching roar and Aiden lifted his head up from the ground to get a look.

Mr. Brand kept firing until the shadowy figure disappeared deeper into the trees. Aiden had no doubt it was still alive. He'd seen it take the bullets, like a prize fighter would take a punch. It wobbled and stepped to one side like nothing had touched it at all.

Aiden's heart bulged into his throat. The punchy *chop-chop-chop* of the automatic gun echoed in his ears and he still felt the dull pressure of the shots in his stomach. He flipped around and drew his legs up, pressing his back against the tree. Mr. Brand grabbed his shoulder.

"We've got to get out of here. That thing doesn't take a powder."

"That's the thing killed Diggsy. What the hell is it?"

Mr. Brand didn't reply, but kept his eyes moving between the shadows in the trees. As they sat there, Aiden shivering and too frightened to move a muscle, a speaker crackled to life from overhead.

Looking up through the bare tree branches he saw the outline of an airship, dark gray against an even darker sky. The side of the ship glowed like it was on fire and Aiden wondered how it could be in the air still. Then the ship turned and Aiden saw an image flickering, like a cinema screen, on the side of the craft. The picture showed a soldier being shot down by two negroes whose faces were twisted up and angry as could be.

"What the blazes—?" Mr. Brand said and then cursed.

The speaker crackled again, and Aiden felt his stomach turn when he heard Jameson Crane's voice echoing out over the night.

. . .

Brand couldn't believe what he was hearing. Crane's voice cut through the sounds of battle from overhead and poured out a litany of nonsense.

"Ladies and Gentlemen, citizens of Chicago City, this is your Minister of Public Information, Jameson Crane. I'm afraid we've had quite a mix-up here at the Ministry offices, and I want to apologize for the inconvenience. There are reports of vandals and unruly behavior by certain savage segments of the population. These people are being led by fugitives, including known saboteur, Mitchell Brand. I assure you that officers from the Ministry of Safety and Security are working to correct and contain the damage caused to your city."

Brand lifted the microphone off his belt and then remembered the monster was nearby. He clipped it back on just in time to see Conroy whipping a glance around the tree.

"It's gone," the kid said. "I don't see it nowhere."

"It's not gone. I told you, that thing …." Brand remembered how it stepped out after taking Nitti apart, but leaving enough of him there to have a chat with the G-man who'd come in. The thing came back though, at the end.

"It'll be back. C'mon."

Brand moved them farther away from where the monster had been hiding, which put them closer to the fighting. He kept shooting glances over his shoulder, hunting the shadowy grove for signs of movement or hulking shapes hiding in wait. It was one of these times, as Brand turned to face forward again, that he tripped over the soldier lying in the dark.

The man groaned in pain behind him. Brand wheeled around on his knees and brought the chopper up, ready to fire. The kid had his pistol out, too, aimed at the soldier's face. Conroy's hands shook like mad and the gun fell from his grip to land in the dirt. Brand looked at the soldier and saw a dark stain spreading into the fabric of the man's uniform.

Lowering his gun, Brand turned the soldier's head as he coughed. Blood sprayed onto Brand's sleeve and wrist. He put both hands over the wound in the man's chest, pressing there, trying to stop the blood spilling out between his fingers.

"Conroy, help," Brand said, his eyes wide and his lips curled back. The kid froze for a second and Brand hollered at him until he jerked forward and added his hands to the task.

The soldier coughed again, his head rolling from side to side. He waved a hand in the air and said, through a gasp wet with blood, "Don't …." He was gone.

Brand sat back on his heels and looked at the dead man, his own pain lining his face and brow, curling his mouth into a frown of regret. Remembering the threat hiding in the trees, he stood, leaving the Tommy gun on the ground, and moved off to the tree line.

The kid caught up to him. "We tried to save the guy, Mr. Brand. I thought you were gonna shoot him, but—"

"I know," Brand said, rounding on the kid, who recoiled in fear. "Don't fool yourself, Conroy. It isn't easy shooting a man. Hell, just looking down the barrel at him is enough for most guys to call it a day. You should know that better than anybody now. And if you ever feel any different, I hope I'm there to remind you that life is worth more than the piece of lead that can end it."

CHAPTER 45

EMMA FOLLOWED EDDIE INTO THE NARROW space between two silos, pulling Marta in with her. Screams and animal snarls came across the night air, leaving a frigid regret in Emma's chest. She held tight to Marta's hand and wished she could free herself from the memory of her father's voice.

Run, my girl. Run!

"That wasn't no tramp, Lovebird. That was your daddy. Sure as I'm a black-skinned man, that was your daddy back there."

"I know. And now he's dead twice for me."

"Truth be told. That thing …."

"What was it, Eddie? What'd you see?"

"Didn't see nothin' but a shadow. Big and angry, like some kind of bear—"

"Is not bear!" Marta shrieked. "Is the monster. The rat. It kills my father, too. Like it kills anyone who goes against gods."

"What are you talking about?" Emma asked, flinching as Marta ripped her hand free and backed away from them both. "Marta, wait. Please!"

But the girl had already decided her path. She ran from their hiding place and down the wharf road, disappearing into the right.

"We should go after her," Emma said. "She'll get caught. Those soldiers—"

"They catch us, too. We go after her, we're good as nabbed and that's no lie. You know as well as I do. She's on her own now.'

Emma knew he was right, but for a different reason, she thought. Marta had lost her mother earlier in the day, and her father only moments before. She was just like Emma now. Alone in a city that had no room for her except in places she would never want to be. Emma said a silent prayer that the girl would find someplace safe for the night, even as she knew the cards were stacked against them all.

"Let's go, Eddie. That scrap yard is our ticket out of Chicago City."

"Probably our only one, hey?"

Emma didn't answer. She knew he was right and hated the fear inside that she might be wrong.

They moved low and quiet as they could, keeping to the line of silos and ducking into every hiding spot they found along the way. A jeep traveled in the opposite direction along the wharf road across the river. Emma watched its course, fearing that any second a searchlight would stab out at them. The vehicle turned down the bridge and the light did come on, but it stayed fixed on the abandoned jeep. A radio crackled to life back there, and Emma urged Eddie to keep moving. The soldiers would be occupied figuring out what happened to their comrades.

It took them nearly an hour to cross the five city blocks between the river and the marshaling area for the fair. They stayed south of Polk Street, following the narrow alleys and side streets around Dearborn Station. A light snow began to fall as they moved around the apartment blocks. Emma wished she'd had a chance to ask Marta or her father about tunnels on this side of the river. There must be some, but she had no idea where to begin looking. At the last intersection across from the fair site, Eddie pulled her into a doorway facing Michigan Avenue.

After their long journey through alleys and narrow side streets, the wide stretch of pavement seemed like part of another country. Emma peered across at the yard, a huge open space that extended from the street all the way to the lakeshore. Stacks of equipment and materials filled the yard. In amongst it all, digging machines stood ominous and menacing in the darkness, all angles and corners, jaws and augurs picked out by the Tesla lamps that lined the street.

Canvas tents filled the yard off to Emma's right, and stretched in a line to the lakeshore. At the far end of the tent line, Emma spied the billowy masses of airships bobbing in the night sky. A row of them hung there, clearly tethered to the shore below.

A few soldiers walked a shambling patrol around the tent perimeter at this end. Emma spotted at least three men with rifles plodding along in a circuit. As she watched them, a fourth came into view. This last one waved for another to join him and they left the patrol duties to the others. The two departing soldiers laughed and shared a flask between them. They stepped into a guard shack that stood across an open area between the tents and the piles of material and machinery. Emma waited until the soldiers closed the door to the shack before she spoke.

"What do you bet Nagy and the others are in those tents?"

"Sure enough, but what good we gonna be to them?"

"I don't know, but we've got to do something. There's only four soldiers that I can see. Did you spot any more than that?"

Eddie said he hadn't. Together, they moved down the street, away from the tents. They avoided the halos cast by the Tesla lamps and ducked into hiding as often as they could. Halfway down the length of the yard, Eddie drew them up in the mouth of an alley. Across the street a lone figure marched a steady beat along the edge of the yard. At the figure's side was an ironwork hound. Its piston-like legs thumping a threatening rhythm on the gravel and frozen ground. Emma and Eddie waited for the figure and metal dog to pass them by.

"I say we cross now," Eddie said, motioning at the shadowy

street in front of them. "Them fancy lamps don't spread far enough through here."

"Let's go then," Emma said and moved fast across the dark street. Eddie followed and soon overtook her. She came up behind him in between stacks of lumber and what looked like an enormous pile of jackstraws. Close up, Emma saw it was a mound of rakes and shovels. Nearby was a second pile and next to that a third that looked like furniture, all jumbled together.

"These must be things they took from the neighborhood. From the people's homes." Emma moved deeper into the yard through craggy collections of furniture intermingled with masses of old automatons and the little picture crabs the police used. She passed stacked up bed frames of iron and wood alike, dressers and highboys, end tables and parlor chairs. The pieces had been heaped together as though whoever had brought them here began with a plan of organizing the items but was soon overwhelmed and took to putting things wherever they fit or happened to land.

Emma examined the nearest chair lying on the ground. One of its legs was broken and an obvious trough in the dirt showed where it had skidded after being thrown from the back of a truck. The fabric on the chair was an older pattern, but the stitching was sound and the woodwork as good as anything she'd grown up with.

"All their lives are here, Eddie. Their homes were burned and their possessions looted for the fair. Anything worth taking, the soldiers brought it here."

Eddie pulled on her hand and put a finger to his lips. Emma darted her eyes around the piles and into every open space she could see. Finally she saw him, the figure from the edge of the yard, as he passed their hiding place from a few feet away and kept on through the yard. Emma wouldn't have spotted him if it weren't for the mechanical steps of the ironwork hound by his side. The man wasn't a soldier. Or if he was, he wasn't in the same uniform as the others. He wore a fedora and heavy coat and carried no rifle.

Emma hoped his metal dog didn't have a good sense of smell.

She and Eddie moved slow and careful, watching their steps

to avoid shuffling gravel when they came to it. After a short time moving through the yard, Emma realized the gravel had been laid down to make roadways. She and Eddie crossed one of the gravel paths and left the mounds of stolen possessions behind. On this side of the roadway were stacks of tools and rope, lumber, raw materials for building and painting the fair installations. In the nearest pile of material, they came across the tools that would allow them their escape. Emma spotted the box of flares first, but Eddie snapped them up and stuffed his pockets with them.

'We get a good blaze going, maybe some of that furniture.'

'No, Eddie. That's—" Emma wanted to protest, but she knew he was right. They had to make a diversion, something to get the soldiers and the lone watchman busy enough that they wouldn't notice two fugitives releasing the prisoners in the tents.

'You're right," she said, helping Eddie collect as many flares as they could carry. "If they can't have it in their homes, the Governor sure as hell won't get to decorate the fair with it."

• • •

They ran fast, with Emma following Eddie through the maze of materials and tools. The night closed in as they moved. Emma's worry grew with every pile they rounded, every turn down they took down this or that gravel path, winding through the yard on a crash course with who the hell knew what. When Eddie threw the first flare, a guard cried out from across the quite yard. Emma's worry exploded and she knew they were sunk. Then she saw Eddie's maniac grin and the thrill of revolution drowned her fears.

This was exactly what he'd wanted to do for so long, and seeing him enjoy the moment, Emma had to admit she'd wanted the same thing. Chicago City hadn't ever had space for her, except the places other people wanted her to be.

And what good is a cage when all you're looking for is a place to call home?

She struck a second flare on the chassis of an old automaton and hurled the burning wand into a pile of chairs and ottomans. Wood and fabric caught fire and flames spread throughout the tangle of furniture. More guards screamed and shouted around the yard, and Emma could hear them racing in her and Eddie's direction. He took off with his flares in hand, but Emma waited to catch her breath, and to enjoy the moment. It wasn't going to last that long anyway, and might be the last minute of happiness she'd have.

So why not use it up and wear it out?

Tears ran down Emma's face, but her cheeks lifted in a grin as she watched the fire grow. She let the glow warm her skin before racing off after Eddie to find the next pile.

He had already lit three more stacks before she caught up to him. Beds and highboys burned bright and harsh in the cold night and behind it all came the shouts and cries of the guards. Emma lit another flare and threw it into an open chest of drawers, enjoying the dance of flames that licked out at the chill air. Turning to the side, she spotted a painter's wagon. Its deck was laden with buckets and piles of rags.

"There's our ticket out of here, Eddie. That'll keep 'em busy while we get the people out of those tents."

"Yeah, okay," he said. "I'm out of flares, so you get the honors, Lovebird."

Emma lit her last flare and tossed it into the mound of cloth on the wagon.

Within seconds fire engulfed the wagon as the rags caught and the blaze spread. Emma and Eddie backed away, tucking themselves behind a mound of automatons and metal scrap. The paint wagon erupted in a ball of fire and cast embers in all directions. Moments later, with the shouts of soldiers drawing closer, the buckets of paint ignited and burnt a sickly orange, blue, and green. The containers spewed an acrid chemical smoke that made Emma gag. She and Eddie retreated further, moving ever closer to the lakeshore and the last row of tents.

Their path traced an arc out and away from the bonfires they created. As they moved, Emma saw the four soldiers racing in the direction of the flames. The fifth, the lone watchman, was still in the yard somewhere, and she feared he might have stayed behind to guard the prisoners.

At the last tent by the lakeshore, Eddie lifted the canvas flap aside and they ducked in. Cots filled the center of the space. They'd clearly been set up in ranks, but the people had moved them together around two iron stoves that kept the tent heated. The fires in the stove's bellies had nearly gone out, and the air at the edge of the tent was already chilled.

"They'd be lucky to get a week's work out of them," Emma said. "They'd be frozen after tonight."

Heads turned in their direction and Emma spied curious eyes in the dim glow from the stoves.

"We're not soldiers," she said as she stepped closer to the huddled prisoners. "We ... we're friends. Of Nagy and Biros. And—" Emma debated mentioning Peter and his daughter, Marta. Someone might ask what happened to them. The girl's mother might be among the crush of bodies piled together around the stoves.

"I know Nagy," a man said. "He drinks too much."

Someone else spoke in the language of the neighborhood and a third person chuckled. The man who first spoke translated.

"One says Nagy drinks too much, but still he makes best shoes in Chicago City."

A woman asked, "Why are you here? What is happening outside?"

Emma explained what they'd done. "We don't have much time. I'm sure they'll be back any minute. We've got to get out of here."

"How?" asked the first man.

"The airships. I can fly one, maybe some of you know how ...." The weak point in their plan now clear, Emma trailed off as her sense of failure deepened and red heat ran through her cheeks.

"How does woman who hides in shadows know to fly?" the man asked. Emma shuffled forward, not knowing what else to say but feeling she owed these people the truth. Eddie came with her and stood by her side. When they were both visible in the fire's feeble glow, the prisoners came alive with gasps and hushed comments.

"You are woman who helps us escape," a young voice said. Emma couldn't tell if it belonged to a boy or girl, she couldn't see the speaker, so she just nodded and said "Yes, that was me." She did her best to ignore the memories of her father, dressed as a tramp and making soldiers disappear as if by magic.

"I helped you before, and I wanted to help you again, get you out of this. Eddie and me, we both want to help. But—"

"But soldiers will stop us," the young voice said, and was echoed by others. Shouts from outside broke in on the scene and the prisoners as one retreated from the conversation. Many bundled themselves together around the stoves and pretended to sleep. Others left wary eyes aimed in Emma's and Eddie's direction, but were prepared to lie down again at the first sign of authority.

"Go," a voice hissed from within the mound of prisoners. Feeling an ache of shame and regret that she could barely control, Emma backed away and finally spun and fled the tent. She stood out of sight of the yard, behind the tent. The icy air blew off the lake and scraped against her face. Eddie came out of the tent and stood behind her, his hands on her shoulders. She wanted to shrug them away, just send the whole damn city off her back and away from her, let her crawl into a corner somewhere and forget trying to help people or trying to do anything.

"Ain't got time to stand around, Lovebird," Eddie said.

Shouts echoed across the open space between tents and the main portion of the yard. Angry voices called for the prisoners to awaken. Then, for the second time during the whole awful day's ordeal, Emma heard a name that magnified her thoughts of help-lessness. A soldier called out around the corner of the tent, shouting into the yard.

"Underminister Wynes, sir? I think we've found the saboteurs. They're in this tent here."

Emma's heart leaped into her throat when a familiar young voice cried out in protest.

"No! Is not me!"

CHAPTER 46

OVERHEAD, THE GOVERNOR'S AIRSHIPS continued to broadcast their hokum. Brand heard the bulletins echo across the city skies, sometimes coming from beyond the boundaries of the Village neighborhood.

"That sonofabitch Crane is running a citywide show," Brand said, worrying his lip as he stared at the fighting in the park. Soldiers and citizens had moved deeper into the night, away from the tree line and toward the houses at the edge of the open landscape. Those houses were still on fire, and the people fighting back would be trapped against them soon enough. Then it would just be a clean up job for the soldiers.

"Like fish in a barrel," Brand said. "C'mon, Conroy. We've got to get closer."

They moved out of the tree line and made their way through the park to where the fighting still raged. Along their path, they took shelter behind hedges and park benches. As they moved, Brand checked the grove behind them for signs of the monster. It hadn't shown again, but he had no doubt it would. Somehow he'd made himself prey for the beast. If it came down to it, he'd send Conroy off on his own and meet the thing alone. He hoped it wouldn't come to it, and with every step away from the trees he breathed a little easier. Still, the grove hissed terror in and out with every gust of wind that came through the park. Each burst of frigid air that moved the tree branches sounded like a rasping shriek, and the chill felt like a steel-sharp scrape against Brand's neck.

. . .

Aiden felt safer when he saw the fighting had moved farther away, past the ponds and now on the other side of the park. But his safety fell apart when he saw soldiers chasing citizens toward burning buildings. Mr. Brand seemed to be on a path that would go around the fighting, aiming at buildings that weren't burning as badly. Aiden knew they were there to get a story about what was happening, but he couldn't see any way to get that story to the people. Mr. Brand's microphone worked good enough, but the people still wouldn't see it. And if what Aiden saw on the side of the Governor's airships was being shown around the city, then even Mr. Brand's reports might not be enough.

They pulled up behind another hedge and waited while gunfire ripped into the ground not twenty feet from their position. A heavy hum sounded overhead and Aiden turned his gaze to the sky. An airship came into view. Its belly hung heavy with bullhorns and one side of the ship glowed with light, just like the other one Aiden had seen that showed pictures on a big screen. Aiden tried to focus on the image, but the ship flew across his vision at an angle and he couldn't get a good look at the screen. A burst of static came down to his ears and Aiden felt Mr. Brand tense up beside him.

. . .

"*Ladies and Gentlemen, this is Franklin Suttleby, with the … with the Ministry of Public Information. I'm, uh … I'm here to inform you* that the sounds you hear from the Old Town and Ukrainian Village neighborhoods, those are ... those are ruptured gas lines, damaged by vandals. We've, that is, the Ministry of Safety and Security has patrol ships combing the skies—"

"This is Mitchell Brand again, Ladies and Gentlemen. Don't believe that hogwash Suttleby is shoveling. It's not worth a plug nickel much less any of your time. The sounds you hear are explosions. Mortar fire. I'm here on the ground, watching it happen. Citizens fighting soldiers. And they're putting up a struggle. A good struggle. But I've seen first hand what happens when a small determined band goes up against odds like this. I saw it over there, at Amiens and Argonne.

"These people may not be here tomorrow to tell their story. It's up to you to ignore the lies that Crane and his toady are spilling into your ears. Ignore the pictures you're seeing on the Governor's airships. It's a rigged game, Ladies and Gentlemen."

Brand lifted his thumb from the mic and fastened the device to his belt again. He stared up at the airship sailing overhead, its envelope displaying a scene of citizens fighting soldiers, but the only images that appeared on the screen showed citizens with the upper hand. Pictures cycled like flickering film stills. Soldiers fell under blows from shovels and clubs. Citizens raised guns and fired. Brand stared at the ship with rage shaking his eyes out of focus.

Only one man in Chicago City could come up with a scheme like this, and it gave Brand an idea. The ship sailed on into the night, away from the battlefield and out over the neighborhoods. Brand watched it go with acid hatred burning in his mouth. Conroy was watching the airship, too, and spit into the grass as it left the area.

"They're trying to trick us. Make it look like what that Suttleby guy is saying is really true."

"And the longer we let them, the better it works. C'mon, Conroy. We've got to get closer. Get ready to give me that viewer, hey."

Conroy nodded and clutched the bulge in his coat tight.

Brand lifted the mic and kept his thumb on the switch as they moved. If he wasn't going to get any report of his own out, the least he could do was keep the channel open so the battle would be heard elsewhere. Shouts and gunshots bellowed out of the airship's bullhorns and then cut out as someone on board switched them off. Brand hoped the people in their homes kept the radio on. This battlefield report wouldn't be worth two helpings of bupkis if they didn't.

• • •

An explosion shook the park around him and Aiden went down in the mud. He landed on his side and watched his boss race ahead of him to hide beside a small stand of trees. They were getting closer to the edge of the park and the houses, and that meant the explosions were getting closer, too. Rolling onto his knees, Aiden made to hurry forward but another blast shattered the night and sent him to the ground. He let the dirt fall before he pushed himself up and went tearing through the mud to where his boss had found shelter behind the biggest of the trees. Aiden came up and leaned against a tree of his own, trying to squeeze behind it so he couldn't be seen by anyone out in the park.

"That was close, Conroy," Mr. Brand said. He had one hand on the tree and another on his side, like he was holding his guts in.

"You ain't hit, are you?" Aiden said, feeling his fear shake the words off his tongue.

"No, I'm not hit, Conroy. But that was too close at any rate. Dammit, I shouldn't have you out here doing this."

Aiden heard a tremor in his boss's voice now. It sounded to Aiden like a warning, like the man he'd known to be strong since he'd met him was really weak inside, and that weakness was fighting to get out.

"It's not your fault, Mr. Brand. I mean, it's the Governor behind all this, right?"

"Sure it is, but I could have sent you home. Sent you somewhere else, somewhere away from this. But I thought I'd do you a favor, finally give you that time on the mic I'd always been promising you and Jenkins and Gordon, too. I'm sorry, Conroy."

When no reply came to his tongue, Aiden sent his eyes around the park, looking for something else to talk about. All he could see was the reflected glow of the airships circling overhead, their envelopes ignited by scenes of fighting down below.

"How are those pictures up there?" he asked.

"Eh? Oh, probably the crabs. Crane must've sent them out here with his soldiers. Those ships are picking up images and broadcasting the ones they like. If we're lucky, we'll spot one of those crabs and then that'll be our ticket to the big time."

"How's that?"

"That viewer you're carrying. It works the same way as the image receivers in the G-man's ships."

With his boss sending his eyes this way and that, Aiden figured he should keep a watch, too, so he moved out from behind the tree to where he could see the fighting better. He searched the night for signs of the crabs, any little flash of light off of metal, anything that meant they could get a photo and get the hell out of the park.

"You're all right, Conroy," his boss said from behind him. "Taking the job like that. You keep a watch that side. I'll be over here."

Aiden caught the tremor his Mr. Brand's voice again, and it was worse this time, like the guy might cop the sneak to save his skin any minute. Aiden wondered how much longer they had before the game was up for them both. He had to keep the man talking. He knew that was the only way to make sure his boss didn't flub it and skip out, leaving him there in the mud to die.

"Where'd you get this thing, Mr. Brand? The photo viewer, I mean. And how's it going to help us out here?"

"Eh? How do you think I got the crime scene photo on Valentine's Day without ever setting foot on a scene? My pal used to work at Mr. Tesla's operation. Guy named Skippy. He carried a Springfield over there while I fired away with a Kodak."

Mr. Brand went quiet and his voice had lost the tremble Aiden heard before. But he wasn't ready to just wait in case Mr. Brand was crawling away.

"So what's the camera box do for us here?"

Mr. Brand answered slow. "We need a crab," he said. "Then we'll be set. We can show the people what's really happening down here. Not just ... not just tell them about it."

Mr. Brand's voice was all steady now, like it usually was over the airwaves. Aiden put his hands over the bulge in his coat. He felt the pressure to succeed sitting there against his belly and for a moment he let himself believe they'd do it. He and his boss would get the real story out to the people of Chicago City. He glanced up at the nearby buildings as a mortar round exploded a few streets away.

The ground rumbled and the air around them shook, making Aiden's eyes go blurry. The houses at the edge of the park shimmered and Aiden feared the fire had finally reached them. Before he realized his vision was fine, the city itself was being lifted aside and a tramp was emerging to stand beside the trees with a rusty bicycle propped up against his hip.

"Gotta hand it to you, Mitch. That's some hard news you're spitting," the tramp said. Aiden recognized the man's voice in that instant, and he felt the man's name rising only to freeze in his throat.

• • •

"Hey again, Chief," Brand said, standing up straight and reaching out to shake his friend's hand.

"Hey," Chief said, taking the offered hand and giving it a grip. "What's with Conroy joining on this? Didn't figure you'd want him anywhere near the action."

"Not my idea. He ended up here on his own. Isn't that right, Conroy?"

The kid made a feeble nod and kept his eyes fixed on Chief's face. Shock and worry danced across Conroy's eyes, and Brand feared he might think he was cracking up.

'It's okay, Conroy. Trust me. The things you and me have seen tonight, this isn't even close to the worst of 'em."

"How are you, Aiden?" Chief said, keeping his hands by his sides and inclining his gaze to look the kid in the eye.

'I'm … I'm okay. I'm a little scared is all."

"That's all right," Brand said. "A man should be scared in a war."

The kid's face picked up a bit and Brand went back to talking with Chief.

'I'm about to get the scoop on what's happening. Don't tell me you're here to get back into the news." Brand paused when he saw Chief's face droop. "Hey, I didn't … I mean, I'd sure like it if that was true, you know."

'Forget it, Mitch. I can't. And you should—"

'Help us fight them, Chief. It'll be like over there," Brand said and looked his friend in the eye. "You and me on the story, and with Conroy here, too. We'll get the scoop and report to the brass. Only this time we'll be telling it to the real people in charge. *The people!* Not the Governor or his soldiers, not Crane. The people will hear what we have to say; they're hungry for it. They need it, and we've got to give it to them."

Bullets peppered a wall nearby and the two men crouched beside the trees. Conroy stayed down behind them.

"It's now or never, Chief. You've got that machine with you. We can ride back there where it's safe and then pop out to get the news. Like we did when you were flying us over No-Man's Land in that two-seater jalopy they called an observation ship."

He waited for Chief's reply, but the man just shook his head, a frantic look racing across his face. He reached out and put a hand on Brand and Conroy's shoulders. Brand steadied the kid when the wisps of reality fluttered away and revealed the hidden landscape that Chief and the other Bicycle Men traveled in behind the city. Conroy stood on his own and stared at the world around them. Brand caught his eye and gave him a reassuring look before Chief piped up again.

"The boss'll do me a bad turn if I help you here, Mitch. *Propriety* isn't one to pass up a chance to show a man he's messed up and helping you like you say, that'd be messing up and how."

"How's about you tell me how? I don't see—"

"The gods aren't allowed to interfere with human affairs directly, not unless one of them finds a vessel to possess."

"You mean like Tesla and that fortune teller. They told me as much, but—"

"You've run into them? Then you already know more than I figured."

"You say. I'm not sure I know any more than I did the first time you brought me back here. What do they want? These gods, all of 'em."

"Aw hell, Mitch, I don't know. I hear them talk about influence, and I guess that's what it comes down to. If you've got influence, you've got power. And if you've got enough power, you can have the world by the balls."

"And that's why things go wrong. Why things like this happen. Because the gods can't agree on who gets to do the squeezing."

Chief nodded. "For my money, yeah. That's it. That war of ours was the last time they all got together and tried to sort it out."

"If you helped me with this story, they'd do something like that again? Is that it? How's that different than what's happening right now?"

"It's not that, Mitch. If I stick my neck out and help you here …. They'll make me a ratter."

Brand's memory flashed to the beast that killed Nitti and his boys, the monster that had chased him and would have torn him to pieces if Chief hadn't saved him. He knew it was the same beast that had killed Jenkins and Digs Gordon, too, and that's when it wasn't busy tearing up tramps across the city.

"So you'd be turned against the other Bicycle Men. Wouldn't that just make a mess of things anyway, you killing off your comrades? It'd disrupt the mail service like you said. Then the gods—"

"That's right."

The truth hit Brand square in the mouth and made him reel

away from his friend, but Chief kept a hand on his arm, holding him there behind the curtain in the bizarre landscape of memories.

"Somebody's already working that angle, Chief. That's the play, isn't it? Those two gods Tesla told me about. They're using the ratter to make things go south in a big way so they can waltz in and bring peace and prosperity to the poor unwashed masses who—" Brand cut himself off, mad as hell and unable to continue. Rage twisted his tongue and clenched his jaw.

"I don't know about Tesla. All I know is I wanted to warn you off, tell you to get home, get somewhere safe. And take Conroy with you, for Pete's sake."

"What about you?"

"Me? It's back to work for me. The longer I sit here flapping my gums with you, the more likely they'll send that ratter for me next." Chief paused. Before Brand could open his mouth to reply, his friend was talking again. "Part of me wants to let it come because it's the only way I can finally be at peace."

Brand gave his friend a confused stare that was halfway to an angry sneer.

"Can't kill a Bicycle Man, Mitch. We tried and it didn't work. Something the gods do to us when they make us their messengers. I've heard about guys taking shotgun blasts, getting hit by cars, run down by trains. They just stand up again a little while later. But that ratter ...."

"That one's for keeps."

Chief nodded and lifted his hands away, leaving Brand and Conroy alone in the dirt beside the trees with a light snow falling all around them. The sounds of war no longer echoed from across the park. Brand risked a look out of their hiding spot and saw the coast was clear for most of the way between them and where the citizens had made their stand.

"Let's go, Conroy. Now's our chance," Brand said, gripping the kid's shoulder and urging him along. They ran in a crouch along the line of houses. Flames licked up here and there within the buildings, but the real inferno was still up ahead. The glow of firelight picked out the crowd of citizens, their hands raised and their backs to the burning houses at the far end of the park. A half dozen soldiers faced the citizens with weapons trained on them. Brand feared the worst would happen and wanted nothing more than to stop it. But if he couldn't, then at least he'd get evidence of the crime and present it to a jury of the people.

As he and Conroy raced a dangerous path across the muddy soil, a sound came to Brand's ears, like the tromp of heavy booted feet on stone. A line of figures stepped from between two of the burning houses and formed a ring around the citizens, penning them in. The soldiers lowered their weapons and moved back. One lifted a bullhorn and spoke a command. What Brand saw next sent slivers of ice coursing through his chest.

The ring of figures were automatons that stepped with a lightness and force beyond anything Brand had ever seen a gearbox do before. He slowed his pace to avoid alerting the soldiers and Conroy drew up short alongside him.

"What are those?" the kid asked.

"They're the end for Stevie Five Sticks and his pals," Brand said. "Those are Tesla's new auto-men."

CHAPTER 47

EMMA FOUGHT THE URGE TO DASH OUT FROM hiding and stop Wynes and the soldiers from taking the youth away. She still had her father's gun, but what good would that be? She only had one shot left, and she'd probably hit the kid. Even if she did get Wynes or the soldier first, it'd be the guy she didn't shoot that'd gun her down. And then Eddie, and probably the kid and anyone else who made a noise.

She felt Eddie's hand on her shoulder and sent a look his way. He moved his head side to side real slow, and his face said what Emma knew his mouth wouldn't. Eddie knew what it meant to be innocent and need to hide from the police. This was all new territory for her, but even with all the noise of the people and soldiers shouting in front of the tent, Emma didn't dare make a whisper.

The soldiers kept up their racket and roused all the prisoners. Emma heard the people stumbling and pleading as they were dragged out of the tent and ordered to line up. Stepping away from Eddie's protecting grasp, Emma crouched and then got onto her knees. She moved around the rear of the tent until she could peer into the narrow gap between the first tent and the next.

In the open space at the other end of the gap she could see the prisoners, all bundled in their blankets. One soldier marched back and forth in front of them. Emma spotted Wynes then. He stood in the open space between the tents and the main yard. The fires in the yard still blazed in the night.

Wynes stepped forward and Emma could see his face clearly in the glow from the flames. His normal grimness was highlighted now by his eyes that spoke fury and hatred. He spoke to the prisoners in a low snarl, thick with malice. The words didn't reach Emma's ears, but she understood their meaning clear enough. Moments later, a young voice cried out and Emma's chest felt ready to burst from grief. The prisoners shuffled out of sight then, leaving only Wynes, the soldier, and the youth. The soldier moved away with his prisoner, but the youth protested still. Emma flinched when she heard the soldier's hand strike the kid's face.

"Have him clean up the mess he made," Wynes said. "And if he gets burned, that's too bad. The kid's got to learn not to play with fire."

The soldier replied with enthusiasm, making Emma's chest tighten further and her teeth grind together with impotent rage. She backed away from the gap, to rejoin Eddie, but he'd come after her and put a hand on her ankle, nearly sending her out of her skin with fright. Emma froze in place and waited for Wynes to come charging into the gap between the tents, but he'd disappeared.

"We've got to help that boy," Emma whispered.

"No more helping," Eddie replied. "We done enough damage, for them and us. Now it's time to get out."

Emma wasn't having any this time. She shook her head and set her jaw before pushing past Eddie and back around the tent. She heard him follow. At the far end of the tent, by the lakeshore, Emma paused and waited for Eddie to catch up. When he did, she stared into his eyes and dared him to protest or try to stop her. Even as she did this, Emma felt a part of her that wished Eddie would stop her.

Ever since the night she killed Archie Falco, her life had been one long storm, and she'd take any port to escape it. But Eddie knew better, or maybe he didn't. Maybe he just knew her too well.

"Go on then, girl. You lead the way."

Nodding and planting a short firm kiss on his mouth, Emma moved to leave the shelter behind the tent. She waited at the corner, listening. The only sounds came from within the yard, a banging and then the squeal of a pump handle. The soldiers had the boy drawing water to douse the fires. Emma drew her father's revolver from her pocket and darted a quick glance into the yard. The path was clear. She turned to look down the line of tents and her eyes locked with Wynes' glare. He stood about twenty feet away with the ironwork hound by his side. She felt herself running into the yard before his shouts reached her ears.

Emma heard Eddie behind her, and then the report of a gun. They raced into the maze of equipment and supplies, darting left and right around piles, all the while staying close to the lakeshore and the airships that held the promise of their escape. More gunshots sounded from behind them, and shouts came from both directions now. Emma pulled up beside a stack of furniture. It was all desks, chairs, and side tables in a mound, jumbled like matchsticks with some pieces broken from being thrown together. A hollow space at the center of the pile promised shelter, and Emma turned around to tug Eddie along with her.

He wasn't there.

"Eddie," she cried out. An airship motor hummed from the edge of the yard and Emma caught her breath as a searchlight lanced down. The light danced a staggering path around piles and machines. She saw the soldiers leading the boy along one of the gravel paths. Then she saw Wynes, standing still and rotating his gaze around the yard. Where was Eddie? The searchlight seemed to chase Emma, and she ducked into hiding in the hollow between a heavy writing desk and two parlor chairs. She pulled an ottoman into the space behind her and tucked herself under the desk as best she could.

What was she thinking? Why did she try to do this?

Even as the doubt came to her mind, it was replaced by the certainty that not doing anything wasn't an option. She and Eddie couldn't have survived, running with Peter and Marta, trying to get out of the city on a handcar and with no food or shelter against the cold. Where would they go? New Orleans was too far away, and she wouldn't know which track to take. But an airship meant freedom. Just like the fortune teller said.

She would fly out of Chicago City. If she could find Eddie and get one of the smaller airships untethered. She'd grown up sailing around the power plant with her father's repair crews. She could get herself and Eddie out of this fix.

If she could just find him.

The searchlight tracked an arc around a space not too far from Emma's hiding spot. With no overhead cover except for the desk, she felt like her knees and feet were exposed. She wanted to reach out, pull one of the chairs closer. It wasn't weighed down with much on top of it. She could drag it a few inches. But she knew if she moved the light would find her, like a flame seeking its moth.

As Emma sat on her heels, debating to run or stay put, Wynes' voice came from across the yard.

"Go on, boy! Tell her to come back. Tell her."

"Emma?"

Eddie!

"Lovebird, you gotta—," Eddie's voice cut short as he grunted in pain.

"Makes me sick," Wynes said. "Now go on. Tell her to get back here."

"Just run, Emma! Run—," his voice cut out again and he howled in pain.

Emma couldn't take it. She pushed out of her hiding place and bolted in the direction of Eddie's voice, the airship and its searchlight forgotten. Emma raced around a pile of rusted pipes, past a stack of tin siding. The searchlight continued its sweep of the yard, but had moved away, back to the tents. Emma tore around the tin and came up against a wall of barrels, stacked in twos. Peering between them she saw two soldiers shoving the young boy along. He carried a pail of water in each hand. The group tromped along the gravel and Emma waited until they'd gone out of hearing before she risked moving again.

She stepped along the line of barrels, keeping them to her right and using them as a fence while she cast her eyes around the yard to her left. Emma stopped still when Eddie grunted and cried out again. Now Emma could hear something hard hitting something soft. Eddie cried out again as another stick haunted the air and found his flesh.

"Stop it! Stop!" Emma shouted as she shot down the line of barrels and circled a mound of old automatons. Bits and pieces of the machines hung together, all in a tangle. She slowed and stepped softly, listening for some sign of which direction to go to reach Eddie. Another stick smacked against Eddie's skin and he howled. Just to her right. Emma darted forward and around another stack of furniture.

She could see Wynes now. He stood by a police van on one of the gravel paths with Eddie lying on the ground in front of him. Wynes held a bullhorn in one hand and a baton in the other. He jerked the baton up as if ready to bring it down on Eddie's body again. Emma watched in horror as Eddie cowered beneath the ugly grinning policeman above him.

Wynes let the baton come down to his side and lifted the bullhorn and turned away, leaving his back to Emma.

"Miss Farnsworth," he called, in a sing-song voice. "I got my gun back, and for that I have to thank you. But we're running out of time here." She was ready to shoot him when a rhythmic *thump-clark* sounded off to her right. Wynes' ironwork hound. It was close and getting closer. Emma sent her frightened eyes in every direction, but she couldn't see the machine.

She turned back to the van, hoping to see Wynes still had his back to her. He was gone.

Eddie lay on the gravel by the van, groaning and shivering.

Behind the van, a bramble of window sashes and door frames jutted into the air. Emma darted out a few steps as the *thump-clank* sounded again, and closer still.

Where the hell was Wynes? She'd have to find him before going to Eddie. If Wynes had simply hid out of sight, he'd be on them in a flash. He could gun her down and kill Eddie unless she got to him first. Emma tucked herself down by the pile of automatons. An arm hung at an awkward angle in front of her face. Empty eye lamps stared at her, mute and neutral to the atmosphere of terror in the yard.

Wynes' voice came to her from across the yard again.

"Miss Farnsworth. I'm running out of patience. If you keep this game up, I may have to change my mind about letting this nigger boy live."

Forcing herself to swallow the curse and words of rage on her tongue, Emma moved around the pile of automaton parts. The step of the ironwork hound repeated and then Wynes' voice came again, but lower.

"Go on then; go find her."

Emma didn't waste any time now. She moved out of hiding but kept low. Running in a crouch, she made it to the back of the van and tucked herself up against the pile of wood scrap. Wynes wasn't anywhere in sight and the *thump-clank* sounded from farther away. No soldiers came running out of the dark either. Saying a silent prayer for their safety, Emma went to Eddie and kissed his forehead, held him, and cried as she tried to cover all of his wounds with her free hand. He'd been badly beaten. His left eye was swollen shut and his lips and nose bled.

Emma's heart threatened to burst open inside her. Eddie was a mess. Her Eddie, and it was all her fault. If she'd only stayed with him that night, forgotten about Nitti, forgotten about revenge for a man who'd never treated her right.

"I'm so sorry, Eddie," she said through her grief, her tears falling onto Eddie's cheeks. She reached shaking fingers to wipe them, but

Eddie flinched and twisted his face away from her touch, sending the dagger of guilt deeper into her heart.

"Lovebird … you go—"

"No, Eddie. No. We're going together. I'm not leaving you here."

She tugged on his arm to help him sit up and he winced and let out a deep groan. His right hand went to his ribs and squeezed tight. Eddie's ravaged face twisted in agony and Emma had to let him slide back to the ground.

Her rage at Wynes grew and became a bomb in her chest, a falling menace that she meant to drop on the monster responsible for torturing the man she loved. Her heart beat with a hostility she'd never known before. She leaned down and kissed Eddie's brow again, tasting the salt and copper stains on his skin and then lifting him by the shoulders, ignoring his grunted agony.

"Eddie, you have to move now. We have to go together. Please, Eddie."

He tried twice before making it onto his knees, then got his feet under him. In the distance, Emma heard footsteps in the gravel. Wynes was coming back. Hobbling with Eddie, she got to the van and helped him into the cab. He slumped onto the seat and got himself upright with Emma's help. She went around to the driver's side and got in, putting the revolver on the seat beside her. Eddie slid down to lie across the seat with his head by her hip. She put a hand on his cheek and stomped on the starter, bringing the van to life.

Turning back to look out the windscreen, Emma let the engine stall. Wynes stood in the middle of the gravel path with a bullhorn in one hand. The other held a Tommy gun that he tucked against his ribs and aimed at the van.

CHAPTER 48

OVERHEAD, THE AIRSHIPS CONTINUED TO display images of violence on their screens, always showing citizens with the upper hand. Up against what Aiden saw in the park, the picture show nearly made him sick.

"That ain't right, Mr. Brand. Those screens up there, showing pictures that ain't true."

"They're true enough, Conroy. Even if they only tell half the story, what you see still happened."

"But it's not enough," Aiden said. "You and me know the whole story, what we're seeing down here. What'll folks think who only see those pictures and hear that Suttleby guy shilling for Crane?"

"You know exactly what they'll think. Don't you?" his boss said, giving Aiden a sober eye.

"I guess I do," Aiden said. "So that's why we're out here. To get the real story, like you said."

Mr. Brand nodded and turned his gaze to the airships above. Aiden followed with his eyes and watched the screens go dark in turn as the three heavy crafts sailed away over the neighborhood. Up ahead, those new auto-men marched one step closer to the crowd of people gathered in front of the burning buildings. The soldiers stood behind the machines with their rifles down.

"C'mon, Conroy," Mr. Brand said as he shuffled forward on his belly, scraping his hands and knees through the dirt and newly fallen snow. Aiden kept up, moving like his boss did, sliding like a snake in the snow and dirt. Slow and sure, they made their way down the line of shrubs. Aiden struggled to keep the camera box from digging into his ribs. At a gap in the bushes, Mr. Brand wiggled through and Aiden followed. Across the open space before him, a soldier lifted a bullhorn to his mouth.

"*You are all in violation of Civic Order one-one-three-eight, and EP four-two-one. You are therefore eligible for sequestration and internment.*"

Aiden felt his throat tighten. When the man next spoke, Aiden thought his throat might close shut forever.

"*Or, we could just shoot you right now as traitors.*"

Mr. Brand fidgeted and whipped a hand at the air. Aiden shrank back when his boss snarled.

"I'd kill 'em if I could. Dammit, why'd I leave that chopper back—"

Aiden waited while Mr. Brand breathed out his anger and tightened his face. "Nuts. Get that viewer out, and keep your eyes peeled for any crabs around here. We need …."

Mr. Brand's face drooped and he let his head hang so that his brow nearly rested on the frosty dirt.

"What do we need?" Aiden asked.

"A picture," his boss said. "Of whatever happens next."

Aiden followed Mr. Brand back down the line of shrubs, eyeing the scene of soldiers, prisoners, and auto-men. The opponents stood to Aiden's right, in the corner of an open lawn. A squat pile of bricks sat in the center of the open space. At the end of the bushes, a little ways up ahead, trees stood beside park benches in a line. The trees had seen a lot of years, Aiden could tell. Each was as big around as three men standing side by side.

Aiden kept his eyes on the brick pile while he followed his boss to the first tree and park bench ahead. After a long slow crawl across the cold dirt and snowmelt, they reached the tree. Aiden moved up beside his boss, still eyeing the pile of bricks. He figured it had to be an old well half tumbled over and was about to tell Mr. Brand when he heard a shuffling behind them and a woman's voice offering a cheerful hello.

. . .

"That you, Brand?" he heard a woman ask. "I thought you'd be around here."

Conroy jerked around and stared into the darkness behind them. "This is where the bullets are, Miss Reynolds," Brand said over his shoulder.

"Still can't get the name right, hey?" she said, crawling up to lie beside the tree. Conroy watched her come and kept his back to the tree.

"Conroy, meet Dana Reynolds. Dana, this is Aiden Conroy. He's one of my newsboys."

"Pleasure," she said, touching a finger to her brow. She'd tied her red locks back and wrapped a thick scarf around her neck.

"Don't suppose you've got anything other than that sword and scatter gun, do you?" Brand asked.

"Why? You decide to join the resistance after all, or are you just waiting around for the story to happen so you can take pictures after everyone's dead?"

Brand bristled at that and had a few words ready to go when Dana moved down the line of trees and benches and disappeared into the night.

. . .

The woman left them and Aiden went back to watching the soldiers and auto-men in the far corner of the park. He didn't know who she was, but something she'd said made him think there was more he could be doing.

"We ought to go after her, don't you think, Mr. Brand?"

"And do what, Conroy? Get our tails shot off? We're no good to those people in a fight. For one thing, we haven't got anything to fight with. And even if we did, do you really think you could pull the trigger? What if I'm lying there with my guts full of lead and you're face to face with the man who shot me? What then? Do you think you could pick up a gun and give it back to him?"

Aiden hadn't expected his boss to get so angry. He knew Mr. Brand had a rough time over there in the war. Hell, anybody who was over there had a rough time. Aiden went back to watching the soldiers and auto-men, and wondering what they were waiting for.

Why hadn't they killed the people already, like the one with the bullhorn said? The soldiers had spaced themselves apart a little more, standing behind the auto-men still. Aiden kept his eyes on the one with the bullhorn, expecting him at any minute to lift the cone and give the order that—

A shrill cry split the night and Aiden's eyes flashed to the soldier standing at the far end of the line. Only the soldier wasn't there anymore. The others reacted by lifting their weapons and facing out into the park. Aiden almost felt their eyes pass over his and Mr. Brand's position. Another scream ripped across the park and Aiden saw the next soldier fall. His chest crackled and glowed like an electric fire. The other four soldiers closed ranks now, moving into groups of two with their backs together. With two soldiers aiming their weapons at them now, the citizens moved closer together, too.

Aiden wanted to help them, to tell them to run or to rush the soldiers and take away their guns. At the same time, he knew what would happen if any of the citizens moved a muscle. Or … the auto-men still hadn't moved. Aiden had half a second to wonder why when the lead soldier with the bullhorn was cut down as he lifted the cone to his mouth. His partner spun around and stepped aside to avoid his comrade's falling body. A figure danced in the shadows and Aiden saw a glint of flame reflected off a long blade that whipped in the air and took the soldier's head clean off his shoulders.

. . .

Where six soldiers had once stood, only two remained. The auto-men hadn't moved, but the last two soldiers had. They now stood behind the line of machines. One with his back to them so he could cover the citizens with his chopper. He shouted some commands, or threats. Brand couldn't tell which. The soldier's partner stood directly behind one of the automatons, using it for cover while he aimed his Tommy gun into the darkness of the park. Brand couldn't help but keep his head down to avoid the searching muzzle.

"I hope she spelled their names right," he said.

"That lady who was here just now?" Conroy asked.

"Her name's Dana Reynolds, remember?"

"You say it like I should know her, but—"

"I'm just telling you so you get it right when you meet her again. Now keep quiet."

The kid hushed up and they watched the scene. The soldier facing the prisoners turned to look over his shoulder and that's when she struck, lancing out from a group of citizens to slice the man across his chest. Firelight reflected off the steel of her blade as it swept in a downward arc and then came back up to catch the other soldier at the back of his neck. His head toppled from his shoulders and his body dropped to the ground like a sack of lead covered in crawling arcs of electricity and fire.

Brand waited to see what the auto-men would do. When they just stood there, Brand shifted his weight to his knees and rose into a half-crouch.

"Let's go, Conroy. I think that's the all-clear."

The words died on his tongue and he pulled up short when he caught the hum of an airship motor. Three of the Governor's leviathans hove into view across the neighborhood, tracking a path to the park. The people scattered, running like frightened animals around the frozen auto-men and into the open lawn. Brand cast his eyes through the crowd, but the skirted figure of Dana Reynolds wasn't anywhere to be seen.

Tugging on Conroy's collar, Brand moved across the lawn at a trot. As they got closer, he could see that the auto-men were armed with pistol-like weapons. A citizen broke away from the fleeing group and grappled with one of the machines, yanking on its right arm. The man kept up his efforts, but the automaton wouldn't give up its grasp and no amount of pulling or wrenching seemed to help.

Brand heard the man cursing and bit back the laugh in his heart. It was Stevie Five Sticks.

Other men tried to disarm the machines as well, but their luck wasn't any better. The auto-men didn't fight back though. With the airships closing in, most of the citizens gave up trying to get a weapon and stampeded out of the cordoned area. Some knocked the auto-men aside, pushing them over onto the snow-crusted lawn. Some went a step further and jumped on the machines, trying to break them or just taking out their anger and aggression. Brand knew he had to stop them. Crabs crawled around the scene, darting around angry feet and falling automatons.

By the time he and Conroy got to the scene, most of the people had made it out of the cordon and formed into groups again. Those who had attacked the auto-men had given up, except for Five Sticks and two others who kept up their attempts to steal a weapon from the machines. From the assembled crowd came murmurs of what to do next. Brand wanted to go to them, tell them to clear out. But his attention stayed on the three men still wrestling with the machines.

"Let's go, Five Sticks! The smart ones are over there."

The gathered citizens watched Brand and Conroy approach. Five Sticks looked over at them, his face darkened with pitch and a cap snugged down tight over his head. The flames behind him cast a gory halo around his head. He was dressed like a cautious saboteur, but he looked every bit a maniac.

"That you, Brand? Glad you could join us. If you're in the

running mood, go on then. We've still got a few things to say to the Governor."

Five Sticks went back to wrestling with the automaton. His pals kept up their assaults, too, working on a single machine together now. One had his foot on the thing's chest while the other yanked on the arm with the gun in it. Brand cast a wary eye at the other machines. Tesla's terrors stood stock-still, mute and anonymous. Brand thought them almost humorous until he saw the pistols they held were smaller versions of the electric rifles.

The airships were overhead now. Two had gondolas hung heavy with gun turrets. The third was a broadcast ship, its screen aglow and megaphones blaring hokum over the streets. Brand watched them circle the corner of the park while Five Sticks and his pals did their worst to get the guns away from the automatons.

Brand opened his mouth to shout at the crazed gypsy. Instead, his tongue tasted ash and charcoal and he grabbed Conroy's shoulder. Five Sticks wrenched on the machine's arm and an electric bolt exploded from the weapon, burning a hole straight through the gypsy's chest. The crowd of citizens screamed and groaned, some running off into the night, others wailing grief and falling to the ground to pound their fists into the snow and dirt.

Five Sticks fell backwards and landed on top of a fallen automaton. Sparks and fire consumed the man's body, wrapping him in a shroud of lightning and burning him to a husk. Brand stood like a statue before the gruesome sight, his hand still on Conroy's shoulder, hoping it would help the kid keep his legs. Conroy wavered and shook, but he stayed up. Brand felt his own knees give when the remaining auto-men whirred to life and aimed their weapons at him and the kid.

CHAPTER 49

WYNES RAISED THE BULLHORN TO HIS mouth and Emma's ears bristled against the static of his voice. "Get out of the van."

Emma reached to set the parking brake and Wynes threw the bullhorn aside so he could jerk the Tommy gun up with both hands. Emma put her hands out on the windscreen and yelled. "The brake! I'm just setting the brake!"

"Do it slow," Wynes shouted back. He moved off to one side and kept the chopper on her. Emma pulled the lever back and felt the brakes take the weight of the van. Eddie stayed down on the seat, breathing slow and steady.

Emma whispered through lips that she kept thin and tight. "Stay here, Eddie. It's okay. It's—"

"Get out," Wynes said.

Emma cast one last frightened look at Eddie out the corner of her eye, praying Wynes wouldn't notice. He kept the gun on her and she felt his eyes drilling into her own. Emma opened the door to the cab and dropped a foot to the ground. She held the door with both hands and lowered herself down, letting go the door and pushing it closed. She kept her hands raised and moved to stand clear of the van, facing Wynes.

"That's more like it," he said. With one hand holding the Tommy gun on her, he fished a set of bracelets from the pocket of his great coat and tossed them into the gravel by her feet.

Emma picked them up and clasped them loose around her wrists. She let her voice run thick with venom. "You've done a fine job for the city tonight, Detective. I'm sure the Governor will reward you."

"Didn't you hear, Miss Farnsworth? It's *acting* Underminister of Safety and Security now. And you know, I think you're right. When I show up with a fugitive in tow, and a murderer at that ... well, I think that *acting* will vanish lickety-split."

Wynes came closer and gripped each of the cuffs in turn, latching them down tighter. "What about your dinge? You leave him back there, lying in the dirt?"

It took all her strength not to lash out at him. Emma set her jaw and let the rage shake through her shoulders. She'd meant to ride her feelings, just keep everything stuffed down so Wynes wouldn't know Eddie was in the van, but she couldn't keep it in.

"He couldn't move! You hit him too hard, and he couldn't ...." Without thinking, Emma whipped her head to the side to look at the van. She felt her stomach rising fast as Wynes chuckled.

"That's all right then. I'll have one of the boys pick him up," Wynes said. "You hear me, boy? Just stay in the van and wait."

Emma tried to look at Wynes with something like fury, but all she could manage was a look of sick as she gagged and spit up into the gravel at her feet.

"Well ain't that just charming?" Wynes said. "I guess you really do love him. Tell you what. I'll have the boys be real gentle with him. But let's hope he's got his legs back. Otherwise they'll have to drag him."

Wynes pushed her in front of him and marched her through the yard.

A few steps along, two soldiers came around a pile of smoldering furniture, leading the youth with two empty buckets in his hands. He didn't look at Emma. She wanted to apologize, make up for something, anything at all. But she figured it wouldn't be doing the boy any favors to speak to him now, so she stayed glum and hush and watched the heavy wooden buckets make trails in the gravel as the boy walked by.

Wines stopped her and told one of the soldiers to go back for Eddie. Emma nearly spit up whatever she had left inside, but the frantic heat in her chest had cooled. She couldn't do anything but stare straight ahead into the night.

They followed the gravel path to the far end of the yard, away from the tents. Off to the right, the line of tethered airships seemed to pass silent judgment on their progress, condoning and condemning at once, and Emma couldn't tell which she preferred. She'd done everything she could think of to make things right, but it had all turned out for the worst for everyone. The people who'd helped her ended up getting hurt.

Emma shivered in the growing cold and Wynes directed her to stay on the gravel. She hadn't noticed her path wavering and meandering into the dirt. Fatigue made stones of her legs and she sighed in relief when she saw their destination. A low roofed shed stood at the edge of the yard. The door was closed with a chain and padlock. A feeble light glimmered through a small window beside the door. Barrels stood in a row to the left of the shed. Beyond them were more piles and mounds of material, but here everything was stacked neatly, like it was ready for use. Raw lumber and coils of rope, lengths of chain and iron. A mound of gravel and one of sand. Beyond these Emma saw row after row of girders and two cranes standing nearby.

"Stand over by the barrels," Wynes said.

Emma stepped to the side, still looking at all the materials piled up for the fair project. Where had it all come from? Her eyes roamed the stacks and bundles until she spotted a familiar sign on one of the cranes and felt an emptiness in her gut like she'd felt the night she found her father in his office.

"You like the view, Miss Farnsworth?"

"Oh, sure, detect— I mean, Underminister. It's great to see my family's contribution to the fair project." The cranes had come from her father's plant. No doubt much of the raw materials had been brought from there, too. She hadn't known the plant was being demolished, but as she absorbed the scale of the fair project, taking in all the materials in the yard, the girders and chains and ropes became cast in a familiar hue. She closed her eyes and saw the mounded furniture, the filing cabinets, the desks. She saw the automatons all thrown in a heap and recognized them, like departed friends.

"It's a pretty sight, isn't it?" Wynes said from behind her. "Must warm your heart, knowing your old man—"

Emma rounded on him with a snarl and brought her cuffed hands up with her fingers ready to gouge his eyes out. Wynes got the Tommy gun up between them and she felt the muzzle jab her in the stomach.

"I wouldn't, Miss Farnsworth. I really wouldn't."

"I would," she said, her hands still up and her lips curled back. "But you'd like it too much, and I'll die before I ever do you a favor. Detective."

Emma stepped back a pace and Wynes opened the door to the shed. He motioned for her to go inside and she took a step, freezing mid-stride. Her eyes went to the bulk of the airship bobbing in the night air behind Wynes. Keeping the Tommy gun aimed at her navel, he whipped his gaze around and back.

"Oh, yeah. Thought you'd like the view this direction, too. You know what they say, Miss Farnsworth. The killer always returns to the scene of the crime. Now get in there."

Emma stepped slow and clumsy on numb feet and with legs that felt ready to collapse like straws. The shed was occupied. Two figures sat in the corners to Emma's left, framing a small pot belly stove that glowed warmth through the shed.

Wynes came in and unfastened one of Emma's hands. He passed the cuff around a pipe that was held to the wall by the door. She felt her knees shake and her teeth rattle when Wynes latched the cuff to her wrist again. As he stepped to the door, Emma slumped against the wall and slid down to rest on the earthen floor like the other two people in the shed.

"Play nice, everyone," Wynes said. "We'll have your dinge here in a moment, Miss Farnsworth." He stepped outside and closed the door. Emma heard him refastening the chain and padlock outside, the metal scraping against the wood of the shed door. She heard his footsteps crunch through the gravel. She heard the other prisoners murmuring and the weak fire crackling its quiet song in the stove. But all she could see was the back of Archie Falco's head silhouetted in the cockpit of the *Vigilance*.

CHAPTER 50

STATIC HISSED OUT OF THE BROADCAST SHIP above them and Aiden ducked without thinking. He was on his knees before he realized the auto-men still had their guns on him and Mr. Brand. The gypsy guy was dead on the ground, cooked like a sausage left on the fire. His pals had their hands up and stood face to face with two of the Tesla gearboxes. Off to the right, the crowd of people had thinned out, but a lot of folks were still there, standing eye to eye with the auto-men. Some folks seemed ready to bolt, and Aiden said a silent prayer that they wouldn't give the machines any reason to shoot.

Just don't move, Aiden thought. He breathed in and out and let his eyes move until he could see his boss.

Mr. Brand stood frozen, hands at his side and right in front of the lightning gun in an auto-man's grip. Aiden wanted to whisper. The machine in front of him hadn't fired when he ducked. On cue, the megaphones overhead crackled to life and Aiden flinched and went flat on the ground, waiting for an electric bolt to tear into his back.

"Citizens of Chicago City, this is Jameson Crane, your Minister of Safety and Security. It has come to my attention that the vandals and fugitives disrupting the peace have not confined their actions to the less well-tended neighborhoods of the city. Incidents have been reported in the Loop district, where savage members of the populace have taken it upon themselves to damage city property. They have destroyed an entire squad of new auto-men, which had been installed to ensure safety on your streets at night."

· · ·

Brand jerked when Conroy hit the dirt, but he didn't drop himself. He stood there, listening to the baloney spilling down from above and staring into the empty glass orbs in the auto-man's face. Brand was stunned by the broadcast, and grew dumbfounded as it continued, turning the scene of tyranny he'd just witnessed into perverse propaganda. He half expected a play like this. Hell, he cursed himself for not seeing it coming even sooner. But faced with the sickening reality ….

Brand fumbled with the microphone on his hip but didn't lift it. He fought through the fog in his mind, hunting for any response that would simultaneously prove the minister's statements false and reveal the truth. But nothing came.

"In addition to vandalizing city property, these savages have co-ordinated their efforts, like an army, weaving a storm of mayhem through the Ukrainian Village and Old Town. Both neighborhoods are in flames. Houses are burning and storefronts ransacked. Citizens are advised to remain indoors. These savage vandals have shown no respect for the property of other persons. We do not expect them to show regard for the safety of those persons themselves. I repeat, all citizens must stay indoors while officers from the Ministry of Safety and Security work to return a state of calm to the city. That is all."

Brand heard the megaphone cut out. A final hiss of static came through and then silence. The broadcast ship remained overhead, circling with its armed brethren. In front of him, the auto-man pivoted, rotating its weapon in an arc to Brand's left until it stood opposite the machine that Conroy had been facing. That machine turned as well, aiming its electric gun at its counterpart. The others did the same, squaring off by twos and aiming into each other's chassis.

"Get down, everybody!" Brand yelled, throwing himself to the ground and repeating his command. He hoped the people nearby would listen and he sent his pleading eyes in their direction. In the firelight, they looked like a crowd of terrified campers listening to the worst ghost story of their lives. Brand had a sickening feeling that's exactly what the night was about to become.

To Brand and Conroy's left, two auto-men fired their weapons, taking each other apart. The bolts seemed to ignite an inner source of fuel or destruction mechanism because the machines flew into pieces. Brand clamped his hands over his head and felt a stinging across his shoulders as a sliver of metal cut through his coat and sliced a furrow into his skin. Conroy shrieked beside him and Brand threw a glance at the kid to see where he'd been hit. He was fine, just scared out of his wits.

"Go, Conroy. Go!" Brand said, yanking on the kid's sleeve and pulling as he shuffled on his belly, sliding through the snow-melt and away from the walking bombs. Another pair did their self-destruct dance, sending more shrapnel flying into the night. The people ran and crawled away from the scene. Brand saw a woman fall face first with a smoking piece of metal jutting from her back. Grabbing Conroy's collar, Brand stood and hauled the kid up with him. He turned and ran like mad to the cover of the park benches and trees.

As they ran, a third pair of auto-men exploded. Brand shot a look over his shoulder. A group of people nearest the machines had fallen into the mud. Some clawed at their clothes, writhing in agony. Others lay dead on the ground.

Brand bit down hard as two more machines flew to pieces in a cloud of sparks and electric fire. Then it seemed that all the remaining auto-men blew apart at once. Detonations sounded throughout

the park, echoing into the night. It wasn't until Brand felt the tremors that he realized it was mortar fire coming down. The auto-men
had all done their bit. Now it was time for the cavalry to sweep
through.

. . .

Aiden held the tree and sent his eyes up above, wanting to look
at anything other than the dead people across the park with the
electricity burning their bodies apart.

"Mr. Brand, look," Aiden said, pointing at the airship above
them. His boss looked up and cursed a quiet mouthful and then
some. On the ship's screen was an image of the first man who died,
the one who was fighting with the automaton. That picture winked
out and was replaced by an image of the people knocking the frozen auto-men aside, pushing them over, and attempting to disarm
them. The images kept coming, a series of shots with Tesla's auto-men getting the business from the folks who Aiden knew were
lying on the ground over there, dead as can be. Finally, a picture
came of the ruined auto-men, their shattered chassis and limbs all
splayed out so they each looked like a drunk that got hit by a train.

Aiden felt his eyes go slack when he heard a whistling sound
from above. An explosion rocked the night and sent dirt raining
down across the park. Aiden watched the cloud billow out and listened to a low whistling until Mr. Brand grabbed him by the neck
and pushed his face to the ground. Aiden had just enough time to
see the houses at the edge of the park fly apart.

. . .

Brand clamped his hands down over his head and hoped Conroy
had sense to do the same. The kid seemed about two steps shy of
shellshock. When the dirt and splintered timbers stopped falling,
Brand lifted up and scanned the area for signs of the crabs. He
didn't see any, but he was relieved to see a group of people running

out of the park at the far end, by the trees where he and Conroy had first come in.

"Mr. Brand," Conroy said.

"What?" he snarled back and regretted it instantly. The kid shrank down tight against the base of the tree. "Sorry, Conroy. What is it?"

"The microphone. Why don't …."

Brand had been so absorbed by the theater of Crane's operation that he'd forgotten about the mic Tesla had given him. He unclipped it and brought it to his mouth, cutting in on the baloney spilling down from above.

"Ladies and Gentlemen," he started, casting a look at fleeing citizens. The last of them left his view, meaning he and Conroy were now alone in the park with Crane's dog and pony show.

As Brand opened his mouth to continue, another series of explosions hit in the middle of the burning houses in the corner of the park, throwing flaming debris in a wave over the ruins of the auto-men and fallen citizens. Brand kept his back to the tree until the shaking and pounding of the mortar rounds ceased. Then he clipped the mic back to his belt and grabbed the kid by the coat.

"It's now or never, Conroy. We've got to get out of here, and fast."

"But what about the story?"

"It's no good if we're dead when we get it. Those are mortar rounds coming down, big enough to take a man apart if they hit close enough. If they don't, they can still scramble your insides."

Brand pulled Conroy by the arm and made a beeline along the route the citizens had taken, aiming for the row of shrubs first. More eruptions came in, chewing up the park. Brand sent his worried eyes over his shoulder and watched the rounds fall in a path behind them. Explosions flung earth and stone and tree limbs into the air, and the shells kept coming as Brand and Conroy raced for shelter. Machine gun fire peppered the ground in front of them and they spun on their heels, Brand tugging Conroy like a rag doll and sending his panicked eyes in all directions looking for cover.

CHAPTER 51

THE COUPLE TO EMMA'S LEFT STAYED TUCKED into the corners around the stove. She curled up by the door, trying her damnedest to keep her body heat where it belonged. It wasn't doing any good though, even with the stove as close as it was.

"C— can you send the fire this way?" she said, not lifting her eyes.

The dirt floor showed tracks leading in and out from the door. Emma wondered how often prisoners were brought into the shed. A man to her left mumbled something to his neighbor across the shed floor. Then a woman's whispered voice broke the silence.

"It's her," the woman said.

"Can't be," said the man. "Look at the clothes. And the hair. Can't—"

"It is," Emma volunteered, letting her voice rise to a normal pitch. What was the point of secrecy now?

"Emma Farnsworth?" the man asked, still doubting her identity. She turned and looked him full in the face. The left half of his face stood out in the darkness of the shed, reflecting the glow from the stove. His round cheeks hung heavy with sadness and fatigue, but Emma couldn't feel anything like sympathy for him. His curiosity picked at her, like curious looks always had whenever she'd spent more than a minute in a public space. The whispers about the power plant owner's daughter. His single, unattached, unmarried twenty-five year old daughter. And the eyes that followed her into Macy's, around the sales floors, into the restaurants when she'd allowed some friend of her father's to wear her on his arm like a cufflink.

"Yes, I'm Emma Farnsworth. The woman who killed Archie Falco in the airship that's hanging outside. I'll be hanging soon enough, so get your looks while you can."

The man shivered, but Emma could tell his reaction was only from the cold of the shed and not the ice in her voice. She thought about giving him another helping. The woman saved her the trouble.

"I told you, Al. Hush up now, leave the poor thing be."

"Thing?" Emma rasped across the shed. "Save your sympathy for the animals, sister. I don't need anybody feeling the sap on my account."

"I only—"

"You only. Yeah, I know you only. Like everybody else in this city only." The woman squeezed herself into the corner to escape Emma's anger and the man called Al coughed up his own in protest.

"Hey, my wife ain't did nothing to you. She's just being nice is all, so how's about you do what the law man said and play nice, too?"

The mention of Wynes put Emma's thoughts back on what would happen to her next. Nothing that came to mind felt pretty or kind or nice, but she let her anger fade just the same.

"What'd you do to get Wynes on your tail anyway? How come you're in here?"

The man, Al, huffed out a breath. His wife nudged his foot with hers. "I don't know," Al said. "These G-men, they came into our house asking about our son, my boy, Aiden. He's out and about looking for work, I tell them. Got put off the job hawking papers, so—"

"They were rough," his wife said. "And they talked like gangsters. Like we didn't have any reason to worry but they'd give us one if we gave them any trouble. Then they shoved us into their car and drove us out here. Aiden's lucky he wasn't home," she finished, stifling a whimper.

Emma turned to face the other end of the shed. The glow from the stove was behind her now, and facing into the darkness made the chill air creep in again. She fought against a shiver that forced its way through her chest and down her legs. At the far end of the shed, a figure was wrapped in a tattered blanket or piece of canvas. His legs stuck out from beneath his covering like a pair of coat tails. She kept her eyes on him and asked the couple behind her, "Why is he down there?"

"He's a negro," the man said. "We don't know why he's here."

Emma felt heat in her veins that sent crimson through her cheeks as she turned to face Al and his wife. "I didn't ask why he's in here. I asked why he's *over there*." When neither Al nor his wife replied, Emma turned to the shivering figure. "Come over here. This fire's not getting any brighter."

At first the man didn't move. Then he shifted and slid across the floor a ways, but still not near enough to feel the heat from the stove. "All the way," Emma said. "Come on." After a long silence, the negro moved again. Emma saw he had an iron ball chained to his ankle. He dragged it behind him as he slid on his hip holding one arm against his side.

"How long have you kept him over there?" she demanded, sending an angry glare at Al and his wife. "The man's hurt and you don't have the heart to help him stay warm. Your son's lucky he wasn't home when the G-men came, sure he is. Now he doesn't have to live with a couple of monsters for—"

As the words left Emma's mouth, Al's wife gained her feet and had a hand raised in front of Emma's face. Al was up, too, and stepped halfway in front of the woman. She spat at Emma over her husband's shoulder.

"What the hell do you know about being a mother? You're nothing but a damn chippy! And a killer!"

Emma stared knives at the woman who towered above her. She had a mousy face made all the more unpleasant by the snarl on her lips and the venom that dripped from her angry eyes. Still, Emma was ready to give back as good as she got. Then Wynes' voice broke in on their shouting match.

"I said play nice in there, didn't I? Cool it, or you'll all be in cuffs, and gagged, too."

His feet marched away through the gravel and Emma watched Al coax his wife back to where she'd sat by the stove. She shrugged his hands off and moved to his corner instead. Al sat next to her, so he was now between her and where Emma sat.

"He can have that side," the woman said, flapping a hand to indicate the opposite corner.

"Awful kind of you," Emma said, feeling another shiver race through her legs. The negro moved forward and into the corner where he resumed his half-prone position, hunched and wrapped under the ratty piece of canvas. But Emma saw the man's shoulders relax as he felt the warmth from the stove.

Before he got fully settled, the man lifted his good hand and mumbled across the space to Emma. "M'obliged, Miss."

Al and his wife curled together in the corner, as if they feared the negro might somehow infect them. Emma felt a manic laugh building in her gut. She almost let it out to them, figuring why not show them the face of a crazy woman. Why not let the rage and sorrow turn into mania now when there really was nothing left in the world for her to lose? Emma yanked on her cuffs and grunted in pain when the metal rings cut into her wrists. She hunted the dark shed for anything she could use as a weapon or to help her get free. The dirt floor and bare wooden walls stared back, empty as a beggar's bowl.

CHAPTER 52

BULLETS SPIT UP TUFTS OF DIRT. MR. BRAND pulled them to a halt. He spun in a circle, all the while holding Aiden by the sleeve. A park bench they'd used earlier was the closest cover Aiden could see.

"The bench!" he yelled, but his boss didn't hear him. His eyes seemed blank and Aiden worried it was all over for them both. Then he spotted the old well, across the lawn. Fires from the nearest houses lit up the scene around the pile of bricks. A body was lying on the ground next to the well and another was draped over the lip, like the person had been trying to get into the well for cover.

A burst of gunfire came down, pattering into rooftops of houses that hadn't burned yet. The fires at the far end of the park grew bigger and brighter, and Aiden tasted the soot in his throat. He stared into his boss's frightened eyes once more and then ran for it, tearing his sleeve from Mr. Brand's grip.

His boss yelled after him. Aiden tore through the dirt and snow-melt, stumbling when he hit muddy ground. He went down on his stomach and crawled the last few feet to the bench. Mr. Brand came up behind him and seemed to snap out of his spell as they tucked under the bench.

Another mortar round came in close by, throwing dirt into the air. Another fell and then another. The last one hit close to the well. Aiden watched the smoke and dust rise through the soot-stained flurries of snow. After the haze cleared, he got a good look at where the well had been. Only a smoking hole remained.

· · ·

Brand saw the fields of No-Man's Land spread out before him. Gunfire broke him from his waking dream, but he held tight to the tendrils of memory leaving his mind. Brand steeled himself, clenched his jaw and fought back the urge to flee. He was here for the long haul, but that didn't mean he had to risk the kid's life, too.

"Conroy, I can't ask you to stay here anymore. This is on me."

"No funny stuff, okay, Mr. Brand? I'm in this now, same as you. Heck, what's left for me anyway? My folks are probably gone. If what we just saw is what's happening to people the Governor decides he doesn't like …."

"Okay, then—" Brand said, cutting himself off as more gunfire peppered the soil nearby. "They've got us pinned down here. I need to get a hold of a crab. There's nothing for it but to get one of those things and take it around with us, getting as many pictures as possible. Old Skippy would be laughing his tail off if he saw us here now, with that camera box the only thing standing between hell and the truth."

"Skippy? Who's—"

"Pal of mine. Forget it. Now, when I give the word—"

Conroy was already moving, rolling out from under the park bench and racing across the lawn. Bullets licked the night sky and picked up dirt and dusted snow. Brand tore after the kid, yelling his name, but Conroy kept on and made a beeline for the remains of the old well. He reached it and slid onto his belly beside the hole. Then he was down and vanished from sight.

Brand raced for the hole as more gunfire crackled into the night. He felt the pills of lead whipping by him and picking at the earth, telling him to run faster and harder. Then he saw the crab. The tiny automaton cantered around the ruined well, its little legs picking a path over cinder and shattered brick. Conroy must have spotted it and gone after it.

Mortar rounds whistled in again, taking apart the treeline and benches in the far corner of the park. Roots and branches flew in all directions amidst clouds of earth and rock. The night shook and Brand felt his legs turn to jelly. He went down just shy of the hole and crawled on his belly the rest of the way. Inside the hole, Brand saw the splintered end of a ladder; its timbers poked up from the darkness, all bent and shattered like a thousand knives. The kid shouted up from the bottom and Brand spun himself around. He felt his knee brush against something hard at the edge of the hole as he slid his legs over the edge and felt for the ladder with his feet. A mortar round whistled down and Brand dropped into the hole. His feet hit mud at the bottom just as the round came in, sending earth and rock down on top of them.

• • •

Bullets hissed their deadly whispers overhead and Brand shrank into the mud, retreating further from the opening above. Conroy hung onto the ladder beside him, eyes wide with shock. His back pressed against the damp earth of the shaft, dislodging clumps of soil that tumbled to the pile of rock and mud below. Brand lifted his feet from the muddy earth and clapped a hand on the kid's shoulder.

"Just keep your head down, okay? We'll get outta this."

Conroy nodded and lifted a finger to point up the ladder.

"The camera box. I—"

Brand followed the kid's finger upward and saw the torn leather strap of Skippy's box hung up on the broken post of the ladder. Hazy smoke wafted overhead in the glow of firelight from the burning neighborhood. Brand tasted ash and then the shaft closed in around his vision. The splintered ends of the ladder stood, jagged against the sky, like the fangs of a giant serpent that threatened to swallow him and Conroy whole. Brand's teeth chattered a cadence of terror. Conroy had a hand on his shoulder now, tugging or shaking. The kid's mouth hung open, then he worked his jaw like he was shouting.

All around Brand was silence except for the shelling and the zipping passage of lead over the hole. Another mortar round whistled in and fell nearby. The shaft shook and sloughed off another layer of soil as debris rained down from outside. The musty taste of soil mixed in Brand's mouth with the acrid flavor of gun smoke. Underneath it all, Brand caught the rich smell of burning wood.

Brand's gut turned and twisted into a ball of agony. He looked over at Conroy. The kid had his head tilted back, looking up and out of the hole. Brand followed his line of sight up the ladder to where the camera box got caught on the broken rungs at the top.

Conroy climbed the ladder and Brand shouted at him.

"Just leave it, Conroy. We can't go up there. We can't help anymore. We're sunk."

The kid was still moving. Brand lashed a hand upwards, grasping, frantic, and feeble.

"Conroy! Come back, Conroy! You'll get killed!"

. . .

Aiden threw himself up the ladder. He could hear Mr. Brand shouting at him, but the gunfire and explosions outside muffled the words. Just before he reached the top, Aiden looked down into his boss's face. He saw a man he'd never met. A twisted, terrified face stared up at him. Muddy streaks framed Mr. Brand's shuddering mouth.

"I'm all right!" Aiden shouted down.

Mr. Brand didn't seem to hear him. He was looking around the hole now, shaking and reaching out to touch the walls. When he looked back up at Aiden, his eyes were hollow, empty of everything but fear. Tearing his eyes away from that face, Aiden turned to the mouth of the hole. Clouds of oily smoke sailed overhead and bullets whipped at the air. Aiden's heart dropped into his shoes when he saw a leather strap hanging limp against the ladder.

The camera box had to be just beyond the shaft. If he kept down low, he could grab it and be back to safety inside of two seconds. Aiden looked down between his feet one last time. Mr. Brand's empty eyes stared up at him, seeing nothing. Hissing out a curse, Aiden tensed to climb from the hole. He waited for the gunfire to break and sprang up, dodging around the split timbers of the ladder. He dropped flat and strafed his gaze around the hole, looking for the box. He spotted it as another mortar round whistled in.

• • •

Brand's vision shook with the impact of the blast above. He clapped his hands to his head and tightened his guts. He looked up after the dirt stopped falling on him. The broken ladder extended from the mouth of the hole, but Conroy wasn't on it. Panic rushed through his arms and legs and he flung himself at the ladder only to tumble backwards into a heap in the mud.

He'd been left to die again. Alone. They'd all gone over the trench wall and left him. All the young men he'd talked to about homes and wives, their mother's cooking and their best girls waiting for them. Those boys never came back to the trench. They never showed up at Dearborn to meet him like they said. Never took him to meet their sisters or their wives' friends. And how could they? Almost every guy he'd talked to in the trenches had been killed.

Brand shook and felt a shivering start in the seat of his pants. He looked around him and saw he was ass down and up to his hips in mud. With a disgusted grunt he pulled himself free, clinging to the rungs of the ladder in the trench wall. An explosion sounded above him and he put a hand to his belly, holding himself together like he'd learned to do. Like every man who'd stood in a trench learned to do if he wanted to sleep in clean pants. Brand let himself chuckle at the irony.

Debris came down into the trench and he put a hand over his head. A shower of dirt fell into the hole. Then something heavy came down, striking his hand and sending a dull ache through his fingers and wrist.

"*Aggh!*" Brand shouted, shaking his numb hand and looking around for a sign of what hit him. Nestled into the mud at his feet was a square leather case. A single lens, smeared with mud, stared up at him from the top of the case.

"No good for taking pictures with a black eye like that."

Brand leaned down and scooped the case out of the mud. He rotated it and examined the metallic object held snug inside the worn leather jacket.

"What kind of dope makes a camera with no place for the film?"

A voice called down from the top of the trench in reply. "Did it break?"

Brand looked up, saw a kid's face peering down at him, streaked with mud and what looked like blood on one side.

"Aw hell," the kid said, his face bent around a frown.

"Conroy! Conroy, you're alive! Get down here!" Brand climbed with all his strength, skipping rungs until he came eye to eye with the kid.

• • •

"Conroy. What's it like out there? You made it back! Where'd you leave Jenkins and Gordon? Tell me they're all right."

"The camera box, Mr. Brand. I— Did it break?"

"What—" Aiden's boss shook his head and cast his eyes around him, down into the shaft, up into the smokey sky, and then back into Aiden's questioning face.

"Get in here you dunce!" Mr. Brand reached over Aiden's shoulder and grabbed the heavy coat, pulling him into the shaft head first. Aiden gripped the ladder and levered himself around his boss's back. He walked his feet down the side of the shaft for support until they were in their original position, two startled men hanging onto a broken ladder to nowhere in the middle of a battlefield.

"Mr. Brand? You all right?"

"Yeah, Conroy. I'm fine. I'm fine."

Aiden let his boss have a minute. Mr. Brand combed his fingers through his hair, scraping away dirt and splinters.

"How about that, Conroy? I thought—"

Aiden searched his boss's face, watched it slacken and shift away from the tortured fearful mask it had been a moment ago.

"Mr. Brand?"

"Eh? Yeah, Conroy. It's me. You did good getting this back for us," he said, hefting the camera box. "Sorry I ... I'm sorry, Conroy."

Aiden took the praise in stride and ignored the apology. He worried more about what came next.

"Does it still work? I didn't mean to drop it. Our good luck it wasn't blown to pieces and then I go and drop it."

"It works fine." Mr. Brand fiddled with dials on the box and it gave a low hum. Aiden flinched when his boss broke out in laughter and held the viewer out. Aiden took it and stared at the view screen. He saw himself in snowy black and white reaching for the viewer, his face set and determined as a soldier's.

"There's still a crab up there, Conroy. Now's our chance to show the people what's happening."

CHAPTER 53

THE SHELLING AND GUNFIRE HAD STOPPED. Brand went up the ladder. Over his shoulder he told Conroy to keep Skippy's camera box close.

"And stay down in the hole, Conroy. Let me scout around first."

At the top, Brand scanned the sky. The gunships were gone. Only the broadcast ship remained, still mocking the scene with its picture show and phony reports.

Brand cursed under his breath and edged up higher to look out from the mouth of the shaft. Desolate ground surrounded the old well. All around were bits of trees like bone fragments, hedges scattered like confetti, and pieces of rock mixed in with churned earth and mud. Around the park in every direction, flames stood out from rooftops, waving to Brand through the dark night. Haze and soot filled the air.

A clicking sound to Brand's right nearly sent him down the ladder in fright. He ducked and looked this way and that until he spotted the spindly legs of a crab. Brand lurched out of the hole to grab it, but he slid in the mud and overshot the little device, fetching up against a mound of rocks and earth.

Conroy came out of the hole after him, carrying the camera box against his chest. The crab turned toward the kid, then Brand, then back to Conory, flicking its single lens back and forth. A whirring sound came from the machine and a light shone out from a small port in its shell. Brand scurried around to its right and scooped the crab up in his hands. The single eye rotated left and right as Brand, still crouching, carried it over to Conroy. He aimed it at the ground as he approached and told the kid to get the viewer out. Conroy worked the lever and knobs. Soon enough the view screen showed an image of Brand lying on his belly, his face smeared with mud. The image moved then, showing Brand rising slightly onto his hands and knees, then crouching and coming forward, to the right edge of the image view. Then only his foot remained in the view screen.

"This thing gets more than one picture," Brand said, examining the crab. It was a new type he hadn't seen before. At the base of the little machine's shell, on the back, Brand saw the trademark of Tesla Electromagnetics.

"C'mon," he said, holding the crab with one hand over its lens. "This is our ticket to the truth." Brand set out at a march, dodging around fallen trees and the small craters that turned their course through the park into a trip backwards in time. Conroy slid in a mud puddle and nearly went down. Brand slowed their pace, but kept moving. If he stopped, he knew he'd find himself back in the trenches of memory.

"Let's get into the neighborhood," Brand said as the kid tagged along beside him, eyeing the crab like it was a box of candy. His face drooped at the mention of the neighborhood though.

"What're we after? I thought we needed pictures of what's happening."

"We do. I'd like to get some of the people who live around here. I just hope whoever we find can still do their own posing for a picture."

Brand veered them around a falled tree, hoping the kid didn't see the tangle of arms and legs and bloodied faces under the boughs.

• • •

Following his boss through the torn up park, Aiden darted his eyes in every direction, and waited for the sound of gunfire. They marched through the park, finally reaching a small grove of trees at the edge of the lawn. Mr. Brand stepped into the trees and made to crouch down among them, but he backed up and motioned for Aiden to follow him around the grove. As they moved on, Aiden looked for a reason for their detour and saw two bodies tumbled together in amongst the trees. Two dead soldiers. Their guns were missing and their boots, too. Their bloody faces told Aiden the men had been beaten up. Aiden looked at his own hands and remembered the soldier he and his boss tried to save in the trees earlier. He could still feel the sticky wetness of the man's blood on his palms.

Bringing his eyes up to level again, Aiden returned a half smile from his boss and then retreated into his thoughts as they paused by the last tree. He wanted to get somewhere safe and soon. The man who had died in the trees haunted Aiden's memory.

Don't, don't, don't.

Aiden heard the word and felt the weight of it like a command. He kept adding to the soldier's dying breath. *Don't kill me. Don't leave me here. Don't let me die.*

Mr. Brand was moving again, and Aiden made to follow. He stopped in his tracks when his boss gave a jerk and stood stock still in the night. Worried that Mr. Brand might be panicking again, Aiden went up and put a hand to his shoulder to jostle him. Instead, Aiden saw the city behind the curtain, and he saw who his boss really was.

• • •

Brand felt a hot piercing run from his guts up to his head. He shook his head and stiffened where he stood. The world around him split apart, fracturing like window glass around a bullet The trees flickered in and out of sight, and the nearby buildings did the same. Like when he'd been with Chief on the bike. He saw the world of memories behind the curtain, and he saw the city he knew, the real world around him with the grove and its gruesome secrets, the burning houses, and the blackness of night swelling from every shadow. Chicago City wavered and Brand struggled to focus on anything solid, anything that might tether him in place against the threatening nausea that made the world into a halo of memories that belonged to other people all mixed in with his own. He felt a touch on his shoulder and sensed Conroy trying to nudge him.

The sensation inside Brand shifted, from a burning insight to an expanding intimacy. Brand shook his head, unable to believe what he saw or deny what he felt. The sense of expansion filled his chest, like he'd taken a breath that could blow out every fire in the neighborhood. He felt his presence extend out into the city around him, touching everything and everyone in the space of the park He felt and saw Conroy, standing behind him and filled with a warm light that emanated trust, like the bond he'd felt with the boys in the trenches.

Brand felt the Governor's soldiers, too, still roaming the streets of the neighborhood. They appeared in Brand's mind as steel-gray automatons marching with a single purpose and no direction of their own. He saw the citizens fighting back. Some showed up as reddened husks, empty of anything but a desire for battle. They picked up weapons from fallen soldiers they had just beaten to death. The war-maddened fiends fired wildly at their enemies, furious with bloodlust. Others looked empty of everything but a need for vengeance, their will a black vortex, whirling them around the neighborhood and guiding them only to satisfy that single goal. Still others danced in and out of Brand's inner vision like extensions of himself; they seemed prepared to survive at any cost and moved away from the fighting and from a swelling sensation that Brand could only describe as the city's pain.

Brand saw these people in his mind's eye, saw them helping each other, fleeing and running and lending a hand to anyone they found along the way. Gypsies and negroes held each other as bullets flew overhead. Jews and Italians. German and Irish and Greek. They all held together like a net spread around the ruined parts of the city to catch anyone who might fall.

Brand felt the most intimately connected to these people, and he sent his gratitude out to them, and a promise that their work would not go unnoticed. In a flash, his every nerve flared with fire. Brand turned to Conroy. The kid leaned against a tree, his mouth open in shock, staring at Brand like he'd just done some kind of magic trick. Brand opened his mouth to tell the kid it was all right, even if he had no idea what all right meant anymore. As the first words hit his tongue, the tree Conroy leaned on quivered and seemed to ripple. The kid fell back as the air around the tree lifted aside, revealing a Bicycle Man. Brand had to smile when he saw his old friend again.

"You picked a fine time to give me the rest of story, Chief."

Chief's eyes didn't return the kindness Brand felt in his heart. "I've got something here for you, Mitch," Chief said, reaching into his satchel. He withdrew a slender metal object, like a cigar tube stopped by corks at both ends. Brand felt his smile drooping, but forced humor into his voice.

"Funny stuff from you, and at a time like this. That's rich, Chief. Now how about it?"

"It's a— It's a message. For you," Chief said.

Brand's smile crumbled then, straight into his shoes. He tucked the crab into his coat and held it trapped against his side. With his free hand, he swiped at the tube and plucked a cork out of one end. A scroll of paper slid out and uncurled in his hand.

Integrity,

I am pleased that you have joined us at last. The actions of Industry and Hubris cannot go unabated, and with your assistance we may see an end to their folly. Your memories will serve you. Please continue as you were. The people must be told. And shown.

Yours, Propriety

"What is this?" Brand asked, looking up at Chief, who had gone to looking sheepish, like a common bum confronted by a man of any station above his own.

"Did you have a reply?" Chief asked.

"Reply? So I'm a set of clothes for one of them, is that it?"

"Seems that way, Mitch. I mean—"

"No. Don't use that name. It isn't mine. If it's on me, then it's because he put it there, and he's welcome to it."

"Okay," Chief said. "I'll just be going then."

"Wait a minute," Brand said. He held the message face up and tapped it with his finger. "This bit about memories? What's that supposed to mean?"

"It's how you get around back there. If you need to get some-place, you just remember it and soon enough you're there."

Chief nodded and put a finger to his brow. "I'm sure I'll see you around again," he said and slipped out of sight. Brand shivered in the cold for a minute, staring at the space where his friend had just stood. At his left, Conroy fidgeted and tugged on his sleeve.

"Yeah, what is it, Conroy?"

"Mr. Brand," the kid said, looking past Brand and into the neighborhood. "There're some folks over there." Brand followed the kid's gaze. Sure enough, a group of people moved along the street, all in a furtive crouch. One of them held a weapon. Brand spotted a gun barrel jutting like a spine from the clutch of shadowy figures. They ducked in and out of hiding as they went, behind the ruins of wagons and fallen trees, past the odd jalopy that found its way into the neighborhood, never to leave. Brand reached out to the people, feeling for their intent. It came back as a flickering brightness amidst the dark terror of the night.

Another glimmer came from the next street away, and Brand shifted his focus. He found the source as the shots rang out. A steel-gray group of soldiers, moving like predators, wound their way to the people, firing as they came. And behind them, a pair of Tesla's auto-men, their weapons raised with bursts of electric fire shooting forth.

CHAPTER 54

A SHARP RAP ON THE SHED DOOR STIRRED Emma from a half-sleep. She remembered where she was and looked over at the Conroys. They were still glued together in their corner, keeping as much space as possible between their feet and the negro on the other side of the stove. The fire was nearly out now, and Emma's teeth chattered until she clamped her jaw together and tucked her chin into her collar.

Another knock on the shed door got the Conroys' attention. Emma heard the shuffling of a chain against a hasp and then the door opened. Two soldiers came in, one with a pistol that he kept trained on Emma. The other went to the prisoners with a rifle and menaced them before ordering them outside. The Conroys went first, hustling out ahead of the wounded negro. The two soldiers followed. When the shed was empty, Wynes came in with his Tommy gun. He tucked it under his arm and undid Emma's cuffs from around the pipe, then closed them again and led her out to join the others.

Outside, the prisoners had stayed apart. The ironwork hound stood in front of them, its bulky torso a tangle of tubes and pipes racing around the machine's core. Emma had only seen one this close at her father's plant, when he'd brought it in to watch the yard at night. She'd feared the thing then and felt no different now. Emma gave a sudden start when a jet of flame licked out of the hound's snout like a tongue tasting the night.

"He'll leave you be, Miss Farsnworth," Wynes said with a sneer. "Unless I tell him different."

She glanced at Wynes. In one hand he held a small box that he waggled in the air before pocketing it. Behind Wynes, Eddie stood in the open space before the shed, his hands raised to his shoulders and his right arm tucked in tight against his side where he'd been hit before. The soldier with the rifle looked at Wynes. Emma saw him jerk his chin up and down. The soldier swung his rifle around and hit Eddie in the back.

Eddie let out a deep angry groan and dropped to his knees, holding his injured side. Emma screamed when she saw him slump forward, collapsing into the dirt like he'd passed out from the pain. The soldier grinned and lifted a foot to kick Eddie. Emma flew forward past Wynes and knocked the man down, slamming her balled up fists onto his chest and arms. She caught him a good one on his chin and he reacted by bringing his rifle around to crack her in the side. Emma cried out and rolled off the man, curling up around her sore hip.

Wynes came over, followed by the ominous step of the ironwork hound. Emma tried to stay curled up, but a soldier grabbed her by the arm and pulled her to her feet. The other one came over and kept his rifle trained on her. She eyed her captors through a tear-filled glare, curling her lips back. Her bitterness and rage roiled until she felt her gaze drop on its own, down to Eddie. He breathed shallow and slow. Emma's guilt burned her cheeks crimson. She lifted her eyes to look out into the yard. The lakeshore was only a short distance away. The line of airships hung above the water, tethered on stout chains. Back to her left, past the *Vigilance* and behind the shed. a large tree offered shadows to hide in and protection from the bullets she knew would follow her.

She wouldn't make it. They'd shoot her, and then they'd shoot Eddie and probably the rest of these poor people around her. The couple here, the other negro. The people in the tents.

As if he sensed her thoughts, Wynes spoke up from behind her.

"Miss Farnsworth? I think we've had enough run around tonight, don't you?"

"Go to hell."

"With such a charming tongue, I don't know how you escaped attention on the dance floor all these years. Or maybe I do. Maybe it's because you were sloppy for a smoke."

Emma turned around and stared hard at Wynes. He'd slung the Tommy gun over his shoulder and was holding a coil of rope now. She let her eyes bore into his with all the rage she'd ever felt at how Chicago City had forced her to live.

"You think you know about me, Wynes? You'll never understand the real difference between Eddie and the guys I let take me onto the dance floor. The only reason I let them even touch me was because I had to. I played hard to get like any girl should, but I never played too hard. If I did, I knew someone would get their nose out of joint and start saying they smelled smoke. So I let them spin me around the floor because they thought it was their right to hold my hand. Just because I was a Farnsworth. Because I was from their set. Only they didn't know I'd given up on that set the minute I laid eyes on it.

"They'd never understand why I love Eddie, just like you'll never understand, and it's not my damn job to teach you anyway. I did what I was told when I had to. I did my best to keep my nose above the stink in this town. I lived the way I wanted to, and loved the man I wanted to. If that means I have to die tonight, I don't care. Just get on with it."

Wynes slapped her once, turning her face to the side. He lifted his other hand and Emma's eyes rounded in terror when she saw the coil of rope with a noose tied at one end.

"Oh, I'll be getting on with it, Miss Farnsworth."

. . .

Wynes frog-marched her around the shed, calling for the soldiers to bring the others along. Emma felt numb as she let him lead her to stand in a clearing around the tree. She turned to watch over her shoulder as the others followed. The Conroys stayed to the side. They stuck close together, and moved quick when commanded. Behind them, the soldier with the pistol threatened the injured negro and ordered him to get Eddie on his feet.

Emma's heart broke watching the two men staggering along, both upright but leaning on each other for support. Eddie held his side and grunted with each step. The man with the ball and chain on his ankle dragged his burden through the dirt and snowmelt. Emma could feel his bare feet chafing and freezing against the ground as he stepped a halting haggard path to his own execution. Wynes cursed under his breath and ordered the soldiers to hurry Eddie and the other man along.

"Get 'em over here already. We don't have all night to wait on a couple of dumb niggers."

Emma spun to holler at the man, but she still felt the sting of his hand on her cheek. The look in Wynes' eyes told her she'd be better off keeping quiet. So she pressed her lips together and bit her teeth down on the anger she felt. Wynes stepped over to the shed and lifted a post away from the wall and came to stand beside her. Emma brought her hands to her face when she realized it wasn't a post he held but a wooden cross.

"Hold this for me, will you, Miss Farnsworth?"

"Not on your life," she said, shaking her head and backing away. She came up against a soldier who shoved her to the side and went to assist Wynes in his grisly preparation. The soldier went to the shed and picked up a coil of wire and some stakes and a mallet.

"See, Miss Farnsworth? There are still men in Chicago City who know what's what. Guys like these two here. They remember the town that my father and his father made safe for the good people until the Dagos and Rigos and Jews and niggers moved in and turned it into a pit. That's what this city is now," he said, leaving the task of erecting the grim totem to the soldier.

Wynes stepped close to Emma, his breath reeking of drink and tobacco smoke and forcing her nose to the side. "This city, the place where men with the name of Wynes have walked a beat for nearly seventy years. Where the streets used to be safe and clean. It's nothing but a pit with greased walls, and all the good people are stuck fighting each other to get to the top. You want to hear about stink? It's gotten so bad you have to stick it to your neighbor if you want a chance to breathe good air again.

"I remember when Chicago City was a place a man could be proud of, a place you didn't mind hearing about in the news. Before Capone. Before the Micks came out of the Eastern Seaboard. Before the Chinamen rolled in on the rails from out west and the niggers came up river from New Orleans. That's the city I remember, Miss Farnsworth. And if I can't have it back the way it was, then I'll give my worst to the people to blame. People like your Eddie here," he said, grabbing Eddie by the shoulder and hauling him to the tree.

One of the soldiers grabbed the other negro and ordered him to stay still while they unlocked the shackle on his leg. Then they shoved him forward to join Eddie under the tree.

Emma screamed at the soldiers and roared her hatred at Wynes. The cross was in flames and the whole night seemed ablaze with angry firelight. Emma kept screaming, letting her rage tear at her throat. She whipped her head left and right as she shrieked, begging the night for help. She only saw the Conroys, who stayed against the shed, mute and still.

The ironwork hound marched a path in front of Emma, the spurt of flame licking from its snout. Emma shot her eyes back to the scene below the tree. A soldier held Eddie's arms behind his back and tied his wrists together before doing the same to the other man. He then moved to stand beside the metal dog and covered Emma with Wynes' chopper.

Emma shuddered as she watched Wynes lift the noose and toss it over a tree branch. He caught the menacing loop in his hands and draped it over Eddie's head. Emma shook with sobs. She felt so numb inside that she barely flinched when she heard a shot ring out from her right just before the night exploded in fire and pain.

CHAPTER 55

GUNSHOTS AND BURSTS FROM THE TESLA weapons came to Brand's ears. He and Conroy scooted down the street, finding cover behind a felled tree. Brand stooped low but kept his eyes over the fallen trunk, watching the dark streets for signs of soldiers or citizens, and hoping he'd only see the latter.

"*Good evening, Ladies and Gentlemen. This is Mitchell Brand ....*"

He let his voice trail off, not sure if the mic was working. How could tell if he was getting through?

Silence settled around the city and he felt it. Silence and stillness in the middle of a war. Across the street, the gunshots kept up, with the violent hum of the Tesla weapons as backdrop. A crackling as from a speaker sounded through the evening sky and Brand looked up to see the lights of a broadcast ship that hovered a few blocks away. The speaker crackled again and a faint voice croaked over the airwaves, spilling the stench of filthy hokum into the night air.

"*Good Evening, uh, Ladies and Gentleman of Chicago City.*

This— This is Franklin Suttleby reporting from the Ministry of Public Information."

Brand had the answer he needed and lifted the mic to his lips.

"Mitchell Brand here again. You've no doubt heard the explosions and gunfire tonight. You've been told the destruction and mayhem is the work of vandals. Members at the Ministry of Public Information have told us to ignore our suspicions, to sit complacent while the unpleasant truth burns like an inferno outside our window."

Brand cut off as nearby voices were raised in anger and gunfire followed. To his left he saw blasts from the auto-men's Tesla guns. Cries of alarm mixed with shouts of fury and Brand saw a group of figures running down a cross street. They were followed by the sure and unyielding step of two auto-men. A mound of bodies haunted the spot where the cross street let off the main stem. He pulled Conroy's sleeve and ran in a crouch, dodging and ducking behind any cover he could find as he made his way to the horrible truth that waited for them in the street. Overhead, the speaker buzzed and popped again before Suttleby's hammy voice returned.

"This is Franklin Suttleby again, Ladies and Gentlemen. Please disregard the transmission you just heard. Mitchell Brand—"

Brand thumbed the mic open. *"Mitchell Brand is on the ground, here in the streets with the people running for their lives while they're hunted down by the Governor's soldiers and those new auto-men you heard about only moments ago. They aren't here to keep the peace. They're here to kill, and that's a fact. I'll prove it in a moment. There's fighting nearby. I can hear gunshots. Someone screaming."*

· · ·

Mr. Brand cut himself off and dove for cover beside a delivery van lying on its side. They'd run right past the bodies, a whole pile of folks, all dead. At least half a dozen of them, just lying there. Aiden heaved his guts into the street as he came up beside his boss. Seconds later the night split open with an explosion in the next block. Mr. Brand gripped Aiden by the shoulder and shook him alert.

"You okay, Conroy? Nothing missing, hey?"

Aiden checked himself all over, feeling his joints, his limbs, his guts. It was all there. He nodded.

"Yeah. I'm— I'm all in one piece, Mr. Brand."

"Good. I need you on the mic, Conroy," his boss said, handing him the device and then taking the crab from his coat. Aiden grabbed the mic and forgot it was attached to his boss's belt. He almost pulled the cord out. A moment later, Aiden was strapping the microphone rig around his waist while Mr. Brand gave him the run down.

"The fighting's up ahead. Remember, you have to hold the button to transmit. Keep it open if you can; let the people hear what's going on. Even if you keep hush, it'll prevent Suttleby from gumming up the news."

Aiden nodded fast and lifted the mic to show his boss he had a thumb on the button. Mr. Brand smiled and it went all the way up to his eyes this time.

"You're on the air, Conroy. Let's go."

Aiden followed his boss down the street. The auto-men were up ahead, their heavy step echoing down the street like the steady beat of the old Brackston press at the Record. Sticking close to Mr. Brand, Aiden carried the mic in one hand and held the camera box to his chest with the other. They raced down the opposite side of the street and drew up against an overturned grocer's wagon, about a dozen feet back from the auto-men. The machines stood on the street in front of a house that wasn't burning yet.

Mr. Brand crept out from their hiding place and held the crab out in both hands. Aiden was worried the auto-men might hear them somehow, but this was their chance to get the crime scene photo. When he heard the whistling approach of a mortar Aiden forgot about the photos and dropped down to the ground. The night erupted with the heavy *thwump* of an explosion from a block away. The whole neighborhood shook and Aiden clasped his hands to his head as splintered timbers and earth and rock fell into the street behind him.

"Conroy," Mr. Brand said, shaking Aiden's shoulder. "Hey, make with the mic. The people need to hear that happening. They need to hear the shell whistling in. Crane has them believing it's gas lines blowing."

Aiden looked around for the auto-men and the soldiers The street was quiet except for the crackling of flames.

"Where'd they go?" he asked.

"Who? The bad guys? They're down the street doing their dirty work. Seems the Governor has teams on the street in case the artillery doesn't do the job. He's making sure the whole place goes up in smoke. And you need to tell the people about it."

"I just tell them?"

"You just tell them, Conroy. Like this," his boss said, lifting the kid's hand and pressing his thumb against the switch. Static hissed out of the broadcast ship that hovered a few streets away.

. . .

Another round came into the neighborhood, sending a cloud of flame and debris into the sky back by the park. Conroy and Brand shrank down and covered up until silence rolled out of the night. The kid shook his head like he was clearing away cobwebs and then got to his feet, holding the mic to his mouth.

"A— a bomb just fell nearby. That's what you heard, Ladies and Gentlemen. A bomb. Not a gas line. Gas lines don't whistle before they blow up." Conroy let off the mic and the channel went silent for half a second before Suttleby came back on.

"Franklin Suttleby here, Ladies and Gentlemen. Again, please disregard the interruptions this evening. Mitchell Brand is a known fugitive wanted for sabotage and assaulting a public official. He also appears to have convinced others to help him. Be assured, Mitchell Brand is a danger to society and a menace. He's—"

Brand felt his chest swell with pride and admiration when Conroy cut the fat man off.

"Mr. Brand is still here, Ladies and Gentlemen. Down here on the street. With me. I'm his newsboy, Aiden Conroy. I used to work with a couple of fellas named Ross Jenkins and Digs Gordon. They're dead now because, well, I don't know why, but I know they didn't die by any accident. Just like the folks in this neighborhood ain't dead by accident. We saw the soldiers just now, and them new gearboxes, too. Just bumping folks off left and right and burning up houses. It's war, Ladies and Gentlemen. The Governor brought war to our city."

Brand smiled at the kid then went back to work. He had the camera box in his hands and dialed in the images he got just before the last shells came in. He'd seen the soldiers tossing firebombs into the house and staying around to watch it catch flame. He'd held the crab out to get pictures of the crime.

Brand whooped and snapped his fingers when the first image came into focus on the viewer's screen.

"Get back on the mic, Conroy. Tell the people we've got proof!"

CHAPTER 56

W HILE CONROY TOLD THE STORY, BRAND dropped the crab in the street and smashed its lens under his heel. He knew the pictures he got would do the job. A final stomp and the crab was down for the count. The kid's face dropped as the little machine sparked and buzzed and went still.

Brand put a hand on Conroy's shoulder. "Crane can't use that one anymore, hey?"

"Oh, yeah. But what now, Mr. Brand? We're down here, but—"

Brand reached a hand up by his head and dug into the fabric of the night, feeling a tension like jelly that slipped around his fingers. He pulled and opened a path behind the city, bringing Conroy with him. The kid stiffened and startled, so Brand got them moving, flipping through his memories for an image of his old office at the Daily Record.

They reached the building, went into the lobby, and climbed the stairs to the fourth floor. At the broadcast booth, Brand stopped and lifted the curtain, letting Aiden step into the hallway first. The kid was shook up but good, so Brand slapped him on the back and made like his old sergeant with the attitude that nothing had changed.

"We'll get you on the mic, Conroy. The people need to be told to look for the pictures, otherwise this'll be a wash."

The kid snapped out of it, but still had a headful of questions. Brand gave him another slap on the back and Conroy nodded and slid the booth open. Flicking on the light, Brand took in the new equipment. Crane had brought in a wireless Tesla system, like the one the kid had on his belt.

"I'll be busy upstairs. Keep that mic rig around you in case you need to skip out of here. We need to keep the story on the air for as long as we can." Brand felt the essence of the god stirring inside him, buzzing beneath his skin. He had to get the pictures out to the people quickly.

Stepping out and into the sound engineer's cabinet, Brand fired up the board and set the levels. Conroy gave him a thumb up through the glass, standing and holding his coat open to reveal the mic rig around his waist. Brand gave the *OK* sign before whipping back into the booth.

"Take a minute and get some notes together. There's paper and a pencil in that drawer there," he said, pointing.

"What should I say, Mr. Brand?"

"Put out the story, like you did on the street just now. Tell the people what happened. I'll be upstairs in Crane's office. He's got to have something up there that's putting those images on the Governor's pigs."

Brand lifted a hand and peeled the curtain back again. He felt the pull of the god inside him, unbearable now. His feet left the floor and his body stretched into the space behind the city, flowing out and up and up.

. . .

Mr. Brand vanished, just winked out of sight. He said he'd be going upstairs, so maybe he just went. He could do that now, just disappear. Aiden shook off the spell of wonder and got a steno pad and pencil out of the desk. He scribbled a few lines, notes about what he'd seen, what Mr. Brand had paid attention to. Then he switched on the mic.

"Good, um … Good evening. Ladies and Gentlemen. This— this is Aiden Conroy at the Chicago Daily Record."

• • •

Brand's feet touched carpet in Chief's old office. He stood still for a moment, getting his bearings. The room had been rearranged and filled with all manner of equipment. Every wall was covered with gear Brand couldn't identify. The equipment partially covered the windows, too. Brand went to the glass and stared out into the night. He caught the muffled echo of Conroy's voice coming through the window from the bullhorns on the Governor's ships outside. Brand smiled and went to work.

Crane's desk was metal and covered in dials and levers, like a miniature soundboard. A thick collection of black cables connected a box set into the desk to a switchboard assembly on a cart next to the wall. Above that a small view screen, like the one on Skippy's camera box, was set into the wall beside a panel with two dials in it. The screen showed a cycle of the images appearing on the airships. The people shown as aggressors, firing guns, using tools as weapons, and killing soldiers or destroying auto-men in almost every image. Some images showed burning houses and storefronts, always with citizens running away, as if they were vandals and arsonists.

It took him a full cycle before Brand realized that most of the images were just the same picture shown from a different angle. Multiple crabs had captured the same incident, and Crane was using them to trot out his phony news. Brand followed the cables back from the switchboard to where they plugged into the desk. Beside each plug was an illuminated numbered switch. One switch was dark.

Brand took the plug from that switch. It came out with a scraping sound of metal on metal. Brand examined the plug, a stubby needle-like thing with a thin shroud around its base. He fit it up against the black port on the camera box and pushed it in. The screen on the wall showed the same set of images, but paused for a second on one of the Tesla men getting chopped down by citizens wielding shovels and rakes.

Then the screen flickered and the first of Brand's images came into focus. Soldiers throwing a firebomb into a house.

Brand set to unplugging all of the other cables. He had the first row of four disconnected when all the images he'd collected showed up in the rotation. He went for the next row and stopped cold when Crane's voice startled him.

"Returning to the scene of the crime, Brand? How convenient. How convenient, indeed."

Brand turned to face Crane and felt his face go slack. The G-man held a Tesla rifle and walked forward, forcing him away from the desk.

"I should kill you now, Brand, but I could still use a guy like you on my team. What do you say? Want to do the news in Chicago City again? We've got all new Tesla equipment, as you can see."

"That's real nice for you, Crane."

"I really wish you'd remember to address me with some respect. I have a problem with disrespect, Mr. Brand. It gets me right here," Crane said, stabbing a finger at his chest. "How can I encourage you to be more respectful, Mr. Brand? Maybe hold your feet to the fire?"

The words hit Brand in the gut. Then he felt them across his face, and pushing against the back of his head, forcing him face first into a burning crimson well of memories that he'd spent the past week struggling to forget.

"So you'd be the other one. *Hubris*, right?"

Even though the god wasn't wearing Nitti's face this time, Brand knew into whose eyes he stared. And with that knowledge came a sudden desire to fight back, to punish the offender by refusing to be cowed. The god inside Brand pushed the stifling resentment outward and filled him with a conviction to succeed. He kept up an outward appearance of strain, but felt the ease wash through him, softening his joints and leaving his muscles flexible, ready to act.

"You always were a quick one, Brand. Let's see how you handle this." Crane reached to a draw cord hanging next to the switchboard and pulled down a map of the city. The major neighborhoods were outlined in various colors, and Brand saw clearly that the devastated areas were all outlined in black.

"We'll be rebuilding, of course. It was my idea to call it New Camptown." Brand saw the name printed at the top of the map. He felt his jaw tighten and fought the urge to spit at Crane when the G-man chuckled. "Now, Brand … we're prepared to set you up with your own private mansion, right in the middle. All we need is for you to keep the people in line, keep them from doing anything foolish. Like rising up in revolt. Or protesting their treatment. You know, tell them a good story about what's happening in Chicago City."

"Or?"

"Or, well … We'd hate to have to kill all the negroes. The Dagos and gypsies. The Micks. Those damn kikes, too. Really. Can you imagine trying to explain that kind of bloodbath to the real people of Chicago City? My mind shudders at the thought of writing that story."

"That's your problem, Crane. You've forgotten. The negroes, the gypsies. Everyone else you're treating like livestock. They *are* real people!"

Crane snickered and shook his head. "Look, Brand. I don't have to ask for your help. I just need to make it so you'll want to help me.'

Crane thumbed a button on his desk and an intercom link crackled open.

"Suttleby? Will you bring the Conroy youth in here please?"

Suttleby's flabby voice mumbled something that sounded affirmative, but could just as well have been *nuts*. The door opened behind Brand, and he heard the kid's worried breathing along with Suttleby's lip-smacking toady routine. Brand turned halfway around as they came in. Conroy stepped into the room and Suttleby shuffled over to stand a few paces behind him. He held a revolver aimed at Conroy's back.

"You get the story out okay, Conroy?"

"Yeah. The channel's open."

Brand nearly gave the game away, but caught himself in time when he saw the kid's hand doing a slow dance by his hip. Crane snapped at them to clam up and Brand gave the G-man his attention.

"Like I was saying, I just need you to get the story to the people, Brand. Fair reporting is what we want here at the Ministry. A story that's balanced with all the important perspectives, and without those trifling details you liked to include so often."

Hoping to keep the G-man talking, Brand asked, "Which would those be?"

"Oh, you know, Brand. I believe you called it *the truth*. Well, the people don't need the truth really. They only need information, and as you know, I am the Minister of Public Information, so—" Crane cut off when he heard his own voice echoing his name back at him from outside. He kept the Tesla gun on Brand as he moved to the window.

"What have you done, Brand?" Crane said and then reeled away from the glass as his voice cascaded down from the bullhorns in the Governor's airships. Brand couldn't lunge for him because Crane still had the hellish weapon up and level with Brand's gut, but he had to keep the G-man's attention somehow, anything to stop him from gunning the kid down or sparing a thought to order Suttleby to do the same. Just when Brand was ready to chance it and grab for the Tesla gun, Crane yelled at his plushy pal. "Suttleby, he's got a mic on him."

· · ·

Aiden heard the G-man's words echo through the window glass, like he'd been talking into a drum. The fat guy came around and pointed the gun at Aiden's face.

"Just get the mic," Crane yelled, coming around his desk. Mr. Brand lunged and knocked the G-man's rifle to the side. It fired, sending a bolt of electricity into the ceiling. That's all Aiden saw because Suttleby shuffled forward, faster than Aiden thought a fat guy should be able to move.

Aiden lifted a hand to fend the big man off, but the guy was too much. He swarmed Aiden with his fat paws, using both hands to search for the mic. He still held the gun, but it dangled on his thick finger now while he dug into Aiden's coat pockets.

Mr. Brand's shouts mixed with Crane's. Aiden wanted to see that his boss was okay, but he had to keep his attention on the fat guy attacking him. Aiden used a hand to hold his coat closed and tried to grab the gun with the other. The big tub was in a frenzy, sliding his hands all over and poking into Aiden's collar, lifting the coat flaps and finally grabbing at the mic that hung on his belt underneath.

Suttleby tore at the belt, trying to rip it off. Aiden tried to close his coat with his left hand while he swatted at the revolver with his right, but Suttleby had a hold of his belt. Aiden batted at the gun once more and it slipped off the fat man's finger. The weapon hit the floor just as Suttleby ripped the mic off its cable. He spun around, showing Aiden his back, and shouted to Crane.

"I got it, Minister Crane. I got it."

Aiden heard the G-man yell back. "He's got your gun you—"

Suttleby turned back surprised and then dropped the mic and put both hands on the pistol. Aiden held on and grappled with the fat guy's thick fingers, trying to pry them loose. Suttleby was too strong for him and held tight to the gun. He pushed forward, trying to knock Aiden off balance as the gun waved left and right in between them. Aiden stepped backwards and Suttleby forced him off his feet. He came down on top of Aiden as his finger tightened on the trigger.

• • •

Brand had both hands on Crane's rifle, keeping it aimed away from him and from Conroy, too. The two men struggled in a dance across the office, coming up against the door. Crane pushed Brand away with a knee, but Brand side-stepped and sent a kick at the G-man's ankle, trying to hobble him. Crane kept his feet, but Brand knew he'd connected enough to hurt, and that gave Crane more reason to kill him.

They kept up their violent dance until Crane got the better hand and sent Brand reeling backwards with an elbow across his face. Brand came up against the desk and watched, horrified, as Conroy lifted Suttleby's gun off the floor. He wanted to shout *No* or *Stop*, but his tongue wouldn't work. He felt his will to speak and to act dissipate inside, and he knew it was the god, forcing him to remain silent, clamping his jaws shut around the words he felt rising from his throat and fixing his feet to the floor. So Brand stood mute and immobile, and terrified for Conroy's life.

The fat sonofabitch Suttleby spun around to show the gun to his boss. Crane roared back about the gun and Suttleby's face went from freakish grin to freakish grimace as he turned and saw the pistol in the kid's mitt. Brand's heart ached as he stood there, unable to do anything, powerless just like he always had been when young men went off to die. Brand felt the familiar agony watching Conroy fight with the heavier stronger man, but he didn't feel the sadness or the guilt. Then he did feel something, a lifting lightness that pushed against his chest from the inside.

This wasn't his fight, and it had never been his fight before. It had only been his job to tell the story about what happened. So he watched, and he wished that the story he would tell about Aiden Conroy would have a happy ending. When Suttleby pushed the kid off his pins and went down with him, Brand felt his gorge rising. Then a gunshot froze the scene in place. Brand's tongue came free, and his feet. No movement came from the pile that was Suttleby's fat body or the wiry limbs that stuck out underneath.

. . .

Aiden felt the gun fire in his hand and he saw the fat man's face twist up in shock. His thick lips and heavy cheeks wobbled and spit formed at the corners of his mouth as he jerked once and went limp on top of Aiden, pinning him to the floor. Mr. Brand's voice broke the silence first, asking if Aiden was okay. He wanted to reply, but he could barely take in enough air to keep breathing and he began to feel light-headed.

Somewhere in the room a cackling started. Was it Crane? Aiden didn't recognize the laugh, but he hadn't heard Crane laugh before had he? He couldn't remember and all he wanted was to take a breath, to just fill his lungs with air and free himself from the prison he'd made underneath the dead fat sonofabitch. Aiden's vision dimmed and he felt the light going out of the world as a heaviness began to fill his throat, weighing him down even more.

The laughter rolled across the floor to Aiden's ears as he passed out. The last thing he heard was the dull static-like blast of the Tesla gun followed by an angry roar and an electric crashing that filled the room with blazing light.

. . .

Brand let Crane's laughter go as he watched the bodies on the floor. He shouted the kid's name again, but nothing came back from the still figures. Crane kept up his chortling, gloating like he'd won the big hand, and that was the end of Brand's patience. He dove at the G-man, dodging to his left so Crane would have to swing the barrel across his body to hit Brand. As the Tesla gun let out a burst, Brand hollered and spun away from the weapon, pivoting on his heel so he stayed close to Crane. The G-man had to step back to get the gun lined up again, but Brand was already on him, his hands clamped down on Crane's shoulders and every bit of rage he'd ever felt at being stymied, shut down, silenced, forced to report less than the whole story, all of it surged out of him and into his fingertips that gouged into the G-man's flesh, nearly puncturing his skin through his shirt.

A blazing glow filled the room as they fought, and the air crackled with static and a violent thunder. Brand felt the presence of *Hubris* inside Crane, he saw the god flickering in and out of the world, struggling against the essence of *Integrity* within Brand's own being. He wrestled with Crane, shoved him to one side and brought a leg up to knock the Tesla rifle aside as Crane tried to bring it up between them. Brand felt himself roaring, loud and potent, straight into the G-man's face. Crane began to go slack in his grip and Brand let the sense of victory swell in his chest.

All around him, Brand felt the web of citizens who had stood up to defend themselves or just protect themselves and one another. The people of Chicago City who had always been ready to do right by the city, to keep it from being awash in the waste and graft of corrupt politicians and gangsters. The people who believed Chicago City was more than just a mound of steel and concrete and brick, who knew it was a place where people lived and loved and worked and died. Those people who were the city, they were with Brand now as he crashed against the G-man and drove him up against the window, slamming his head against the glass.

The electric gun fell to the floor at Brand's feet and Crane shook violently. Brand let him go and stood back, watching as a greasy mass of spidery blackness poured from Crane's eyes and mouth, forming a sphere in front of him. The mass swelled and moved as if to assault Brand, like it wanted to crash onto him, into him, taking away everything he was and leaving him an empty pitiable shell of a man.

Brand backed up a half step. The roiling inky mass pulsed and slipped out of sight, vanishing into the world behind the curtain. Brand was untouched, and alone with a weeping Jameson Crane.

"God damn you, Brand," the G-man said through his angry sobs. "This was the time. This was the decade we'd been waiting for," he went on, talking into the air beside his face, not even looking at Brand anymore. "Ever since the war. It's been aces up all over. Aces up for ten years straight."

Brand lifted the G-man's weapon and stood back. His eyes had seen enough lives ruined by men like Crane not to care that the G-man had been reduced to a whimpering child angry about losing his favorite toy. But Brand didn't find what he expected inside himself either. There was no joy at seeing Crane defeated. Only a sense of calm, a feeling that the world had lost something, but only something that it had not needed.

"Even a roar has to stop for a breath sometime, Crane." The G-man's face fell and he dropped his chin to his chest, sobbing his failure down his shirt.

Brand went to Conroy's limp form, still trapped under the dead weight of Suttleby. He shoved the fat man off and felt the kid's neck for a pulse. He had life in him still. It'd take a minute and fresh air would help. Going back to the switchboard, Brand went to finish unplugging the leads from the desk. He reached for the first cable and stopped. The screen now showed a rotation of images from around the city.

People huddled together in the dark beside the smoking ruins of a home or storefront. People ran from soldiers who followed with guns blazing. People fell before the blasts of electric fire from the auto-men. Whatever system Crane had set up to filter the crabs' pictures, it was broken now. Chicago City would see these images, and they would know Brand had been telling the truth. He was about to leave when an image from his nightmares filled the screen.

Two people stood face to face next to a shed. Brand recognized the place from a story he'd done on the World's Fair project. The Mayor had broken ground a year ago while standing in front of the shed. Capone had been there, too. Now, the low wooden structure stood witness to a different kind of travesty. One of the people in the image was Emma Farnsworth, though it looked like she had someone take a keyhole saw to her hair. The other person was Detective Wynes, his mouth twisted into a snarl of rage.

CHAPTER 57

B RAND HEFTED CONROY UP, HOLDING HIM around the waist, and then slipped behind the curtain, letting it fall on the scene of Jameson Crane crying into his lap. In a flash, Brand found his memories of the fair project story and moved behind the city to the yard by the lake. They emerged where he'd first set foot in the yard, only now they were surrounded by mounds of furniture and old automaton parts. A row of heavy canvas tents stood at their right, stretching from Michigan Avenue to the lakeshore. Two bodies were piled in a heap between the tents and the nearest scrap pile. Brand shuffled over to them with Conroy against his hip. Soldiers. One had been stabbed through the heart. The other had cuts under his collar. Little Red's handiwork.

"We'd have been in the way," Brand said to himself as Conroy came around. As he waited for the kid to get his feet under him, Brand reached out with his inner vision, seeking the presence of Emma and the other people near the tree. He found them and made a beeline across the yard. Smoke hung heavy in the air and small fires still burned in places. Whatever had happened here, it was nothing like the neighborhood Brand had left earlier.

Brand changed course and took them to the lakeshore. He and Conroy followed a path there around the mounds and stacks of scrap and raw materials. At their right, a row of concrete pylons ran the length of the shore. A line of airships hung above the pylons, tethered by chains. Brand kept his eyes peeled for the *Vigilance* and felt a stab in his chest when she came into view at the end of the line. Her bulk bobbed in the night air beside the empty branches of a wintered tree. A hushed sobbing came to Brand's ears on the wind, and he thought it was his own voice, broken in sadness at the sight of his ship chained to the earth.

"You son of a bitch," Emma sobbed from up ahead, her voice shaking around the words.

Brand motioned for Conroy to move slow and tucked against a stack of lumber. He crouched as he walked, moving closer to the *Vigilance* and the scene playing out in her shadow.

Beneath the ship, Emma Farnsworth stood illuminated by the flames of a burning cross at the edge of a clearing around a tall tree. In the middle of the space an ironwork hound walked a beat back and forth, the gas jet in its snout flickering in the chill night air. Two soldiers and Wynes stood beneath a tree with a pair of negroes. One of the soldiers tied the negros' hands and then lifted a Tommy gun from beside the tree. He moved to stand by the ironwork hound, which stopped its marching. The soldier faced Emma, holding the Tommy gun on her.

By the tree, Wynes stood in front of the closest of the two negroes with a noose in hands. He tossed it over a tree branch above and caught it. Brand felt his guts twist as Wynes slipped the noose around the first negro's neck.

A second passed and a gunshot sounded from behind Brand. He saw the ironwork hound explode and felt a wave of heat wash over him that knocked him backwards. Cries of pain and moans spread through the night air. Brand found his feet, looking for Conroy. The kid was up against the lumber pile, frightened but not hurt.

"Stay here, Conroy," Brand said and then raced forward to where Emma Farnsworth had been standing.

She was still there, but sat with her weight on one hip, sobbing and clutching her right arm above the elbow. Blood ran through a tear in the thick coat she wore. Another couple Brand hadn't seen held each other beside the shed. They kept their faces hidden as if to avoid looking at the scene.

The soldier who'd had a gun on Emma was now face down in the mud. Flames licked across his scalp like a halo. His helmet and the chopper had ended up a few feet away.

Back at the tree, the negroes slowly got to their feet. Brand recognized one of the men as Emma's lover, Eddie Collins. He and the other man leaned on each other and stooped to the side as they rose. The soldier who'd put the noose on Eddie was also down. He rolled side to side, hands to his neck. Brand rushed to him and saw a shard of metal had sliced into his neck. The soldier shook out his final breath as Brand, Eddie, and the other negro looked on.

Wynes had fared much better than the soldiers. At least, that's what Brand thought when he saw the man getting to his feet and holding a hand to his face.

"I think this is where we call it a draw, Wynes," Brand said.

Wynes didn't reply at first. He stood, holding his face and shuddering, and then turned to Brand and dropped his hand. Half of his cheek was missing, along with the eye above it. A bloody empty socket gaped between two shredded eyelids. Wynes roared and charged. A burst from a Tommy gun ripped through the scene and Wynes staggered and fell back. Emma Farnsworth stood and held the Tommy gun on Wynes' body. She squeezed the trigger a final time. The man jerked with each impact, but there was nothing left in him to kill.

CHAPTER 58

B RAND WATCHED THE TOMMY GUN SLIP FROM Emma's hands and land in the dirt. Eddie limped in her direction, reaching a hand to her shoulder and pulling her to him as she sobbed and wailed. Hurt though he was, Eddie still held Emma close and let her shake into his chest. Brand let them have their time and turned to the other negro.

"What happened there? With the hound?"

"Beats me. Ain't had my eyes on nothing but that rope 'round Eddie's neck. Where'd you come from?"

"Would you believe I'm a reporter that happened to be passing through?"

"No, sir, I wouldn't, but I seen plenty I didn't want to believe tonight. Name's Otis, by the way," the man said, extending his good hand. Brand shook and told the man his name.

"The radio man, hey? Ain't that something," Otis said before turning to pick up the fallen Tommy gun. Brand spun to see if Conroy had moved to join them. He had, and he wasn't alone.

A younger boy, maybe ten years old, stood next to Conroy. The second kid wore clothes like the gypsies had, thick gray wool and heavy shoes. He also held a revolver in his left hand.

"Conroy? You okay there?"

Behind him, Brand heard a rustling and then a woman's voice raised in fright. Footsteps raced in his direction, but Brand kept his eyes on the gun in the boy's grip. Conroy nodded and said he was fine. He was about to introduce the boy when a man and woman came tearing past Brand. The woman swept Conroy into her arms and covered him with a mother's affection. The man wrapped his arms around them both and they wept together, shivering by the lakeshore. Brand turned to the gypsy boy.

"Are you the reason we're out of the soup?"

The boy nodded and stared up at Brand with fearful eyes.

"It's okay, kid. You did … you did all right. How about the pea shooter?"

The boy held it out and Brand accepted it. He opened the cylinder and dumped the pills. Nothing but empty brass hit his palm.

"Lucky shot," he said to the kid. "What are you doing out here anyway, with a gun with one bullet and the know-how to plug an ironwork hound in its soft spot?"

"I was aiming for man. Soldier," the boy said as his eyes grew wet.

Brand pocketed the revolver and brought the kid close, letting him cry it out. Whatever got the young gypsy mixed up in this, Brand decided he would get the boy out okay. The Conroys stood at Brand's left as if waiting. Finally the mother interrupted to thank him for protecting her son.

"He did all right on his own, ma'am. Kid's a natural born newshawk."

"Well, thank you just the same, Mr. Brand," she said. The kid's father shook his hand and they moved away, leaving Brand with the gypsy boy.

"Where'd you get the gun?"

"Is dark man's. He leaves it in van." The boy told Brand about the tents, how he'd been taken prisoner with people from his neighborhood and brought here to work in the yard. He told Brand about the fires, how Emma and Eddie had come to help everyone get away, and how Wynes had his soldiers force the kid to put out the fires. They'd hit him a few times and worked him hard putting out the flames with buckets of water drawn from a pump.

"My father tells me. Man hits you, he should kill you. If he doesn't, you stand up, you kill him."

"Sounds like war to me," Brand said. "Maybe your old man has some good ideas, but I don't think that's one of them."

The boy sniffed at Brand's objection and got a faraway look. "When woman with sword comes to tent, I think is a dream. She is warrior from stories my father tells me. Woman who fought the Turks when they come."

"Where'd she go?" Brand said, sending his eyes through the night for signs of Dana Reynolds.

"She kills other soldiers, over there," the kid said, pointing down the lakeshore to the other end of the yard. "Then she leaves."

"What about the people? Those tents are empty now."

"They go with her. To railroad. But I found gun, and stay here. I should go now," the kid said and walked away into the yard. Brand watched him go and then raced to catch up, dropping the empty revolver as he went.

"Hang on. Where's this railroad? The one underground?"

The boy nodded. "That one. Yes."

Brand put a hand on the kid's shoulder and drew the city aside. The boy's eyes went wide, but he'd seen this trick before and held onto Brand's hand, clamping it to his shoulder with both of his own. They traveled through Brand's memories of the tunnels, the cellar in the curio shop, the cellar in the speak, and finally the underground system of rails and handcars that people had used to flee the burning city above.

They emerged next to a chain of flatcars with a handcar at the end. Gypsies mounted the cars and shuffled around in the weak light cast by lanterns almost burned out. Nobody seemed to notice the newsman and young boy who stepped out of the darkness. If they did, nobody said anything.

"You'll be okay?" Brand asked, helping the kid onto a flatcar. The boy nodded and smiled.

"Thank you," he said.

Brand reached back to grab the curtain for his return trip and paused when he heard his name.

"Good man, Brand," Dana said. "I knew we could count on you to help. Even if you did wait until the end."

"Better late than never, I guess," he said, sending his sneer across the dim space to where Dana stood by the opposite wall. "Be seeing you around, Miss Reynolds."

"Not likely. But stay tuned, hey?"

Brand had to smirk at that, and then laugh as he finished the line before stepping through the curtain and out of sight.

· · ·

Back at the yard, Brand hustled to join the group of people around the burning cross, stepping around the dead soldier in his path. He stopped and picked the pistol off the man's belt.

"What happens now?" Brand asked when he'd taken his place beside Emma. Eddie held her against him. Next to him was Otis. The Conroys stayed to the other side and Brand could tell the parents didn't have kind eyes for Emma's choice of company, or for the source of warmth that stood between them. Aiden seemed happy enough to be with his folks again and stayed wrapped up in his coat beside his mother.

Brand was about to break the silence when Emma spoke up.

"We're taking your ship, Brand. I'm going to fly us out of this city and to New Orleans."

"You?"

"Yes, me. I learned to fly out at the plant. Dad sent me up with his repair teams. He said I'd be excited by the view, but I think it just got me out of his hair."

"So you watched the pilots and helped the repair men, huh?"

She sniffed at his words. "They showed me how to work the ballast first. Then I asked if I could steer. By the end, they were playing cards and taking naps while I flew us around the plant in between jobs."

"Well that's you and yours settled then. What about the others here?" Brand asked, nodding at the Conroys.

"They can come with or they can stay here. I don't care," Emma said.

Brand looked through the flickering firelight. "You three up for a ride in that pig?" he said, lifting a finger to indicate the *Vigilance*. Her nose cone bobbed in a steady rhythm as she fought the chains that held her tethered to the pylons below.

Aiden's father spoke up. "We'll come along—"

"Al! We can't—"

"There's nothing left for us here, Alice. The neighborhood's burned up by now," the father said. "But I don't want my wife to be sharing no quarters with your friends there."

"You want to go back into the shed?" Emma spat across the frosty air.

Brand cut in to stop the pissing contest. "There's room enough for you to have your own space. You can take my bunk. These three can share the other room. It'll be cramped, but they don't seem to have a problem with that."

"What about you, Mr. Brand?" the kid asked.

"I'll camp out in the engine compartment. There's a mechanic's cot up there."

• • •

Emma got Eddie over to the airship with Brand and Otis' help. The Conroy kid joined them while his parents waited a few steps behind. Brand worked the catch that let the airship ladder unfold to reach ground level. He told the kid to go up first and dig the first aid kit out of the washroom. A minute later, the kid's face was at the cabin door and he dropped the kit down. Brand pulled out two lengths of bandages and worked up a quick and dirty sling for Eddie and another for Otis. Then he yelled up for the kid to throw down some bedding from one of the bunks.

With sheets tied around their ribs, and a pace slower than a snail's, Eddie and Otis managed the climb into the cabin. Emma followed, then Brand and finally the Conroys. Eddie and Otis went into the second bunk room to rest. The Conroys stayed together at the back of the cabin with their son.

Emma took the pilot's seat and fired the motors. They came to life with a coughing rhythm, finally settling into a steady churn that sent warm air through the heating vents and into the cabin.

Someone had cleaned the cockpit since the last time Emma had been in the ship. The ugly hole in the cockpit glass remained but Emma didn't pay it any mind. Her hands moved fast on the dials and levers. She only paused to swivel her head and tell Brand, "Get the damn cables loose or we're not going anywhere."

Brand nodded and palmed the pistol he'd nabbed from the dead soldier. He went to the door and dropped down the ladder. Emma watched through the cockpit glass as Brand pressed the muzzle up against the padlock on the first cable, turned his face aside, and squeezed off a shot. The lock split apart and the cable snapped away, narrowly missing Brand's head. He went to the second padlock and stood a few feet back this time. It took two shots before he hit the lock, setting the ship free.

Emma felt the craft buoy into the sky and she worked the ballast to keep her low while Brand raced to the ladder.

"You're pretty good with this pig, Miss Farnsworth," Brand said as he climbed in and began winching up the ladder.

"Don't call her a pig, Brand," Emma shot back. She brought the *Vigilance* up to altitude as they slowly left Chicago City behind and soared over the icy black water of Lake Michigan. Emma stared out at the lake, and the warmth she'd felt a moment ago turned cold. The loss of her old life, even if it was all a lie, reflected back to her like a thousand splinters of glass on the surface of the dark water.

CHAPTER 59

B RAND WENT TO HIS DESK AND RIFLED through the drawers before remembering Wynes had nabbed his bottle of hooch. He slumped into his chair and let his eyes roam the familiar cabin space. The wood panels, the brass and copper hand rails. All tarnished and scuffed. Brand put the pistol on his desk. Al Conroy eyed it and his wife gave him a look that seemed to put him of a better mind. Brand chuckled at their routine.

"You know, I wouldn't be here without the help of people like those two men in the back. A negro soldier covered me when I was over there. In the Great War. He took the shrapnel that would've put me in the ground."

"That's … that's terrible," Mrs. Conroy said. "I'm sorry." The woman didn't seem to know what else to say and her husband stuck to speaking with his eyes, flicking between Brand and the pistol.

Brand didn't feel up to arguing. If the guy wanted the gun, let him have it. Brand stood to go to the cockpit. He took one step from his desk and stopped mid-stride as the air beside him shook and a Bicycle Man stepped through the curtain into the space of the cabin. His rusty bike clattered to the floor. Emma spun around and shrieked, her face frantic with worry and fear. The Conroys shrank into the corner, the father covering his wife and son as best he could.

"It's okay," Brand said, putting a palm out in either direction and letting his face do the rest. "He's just here to deliver the mail. Ain't that right, pal?"

"I'm not your pal, Brand."

Feeling the cabin spin around him, Brand took a short step back. His heart hammered and his fists clenched and opened twice. Brand's spine worked a dance number that put his whole body into contortions. Then he felt the god leave him.

A swirling mist flew from Brand's eyes and mouth, formed a glowing orb that hung there in front of him and sank away, out of sight and behind the curtain once more.

Brand regained his sense in time to see the tramp advancing on the Conroys. Brand dodged in front of the man, but the tramp matched his movement, orienting on him now. Brand recognized the bird, or thought he did. The last time he'd seen him was outside an abandoned machine shop, the night Frank Nitti—

"So you'd be him then. The ratter."

The tramp nodded. Emma got into the act then. "Who is he, Brand? Why is he here and how—" The tramp cut her off.

"Ain't got time to tell the whole story, Miss Emma. Your daddy said farewell, I can tell you that. But that's all. I gotta make this quick, and I gotta say my piece first so Brand here knows I'm only doing this because I got no choice."

"*Hubris* put you up to this," Brand said. "Or was it the other one?"

"Other one. *Industry.* You spun his game every way from perfect and now he's gotta work double hard to have it come out how he wants. So this is payback. Shame, on account of you being kinda like a hero to me and some of the other fellas."

"How's that?" Brand put it together fast enough, but the tramp was already spilling it in his own way.

"Over there. Like I told you back on Valentine's Day. That's my story, Brand. One I been wanting to tell you all along. Them trees at Argonne. Three of us came out the other side. You, me, and Skip. Maybe with all our pieces on but something inside us dead and gone and never coming back on account of what we did in that forest." The tramp shook as he spoke, his thick lips blubbering around his words.

"What we did to them Germans and what we saw done to them. The friends we lost from our boys what didn't make it out with us. You told 'em about us, the people back home. You told 'em and they stopped the war. Didn't stop it soon enough for me and them others riding these bikes around this city, but you stopped it."

Brand stared at the tramp's grimy cheeks and huge bulb of a nose. The heavy eyebrows and scraggly beard, like rodent pelts pasted all over his face. The hairs moved and twisted, growing slowly in a thin coat to cover the tramp's neck and collar.

"Didn't want to do it like this, Brand. I liked my life okay as a Bicycle Man. But I messed up one time too much and they made me this. Sent me after my brothers. Now after you."

Brand stepped back, came up against the wall of the cabin and moved to the side, circling the center of the space. He kept moving so the tramp wouldn't take his attention off him.

"What's in it for you? Why not just call it a day? You did it once, so I don't see what's stopping you a second time."

'Dammit, Brand. Didn't your old pal tell you? I run into him earlier. He said he gave you the skinny on us fellas. We can't just take a powder."

"What about Chief? Did you do him like the others. Dammit, if you—"

"He's all right, Brand. For now anyway. They'll send me after him before too long though."

The tramp jerked and doubled over as hair spread and thickened across his chest and out his arms. He stood up and spoke through his puffy cracked lips as he walked a stumbling path toward Brand.

"It's awful bad you being around these other folks, Brand. I'd leave 'em be if I could, but once that thing takes over, I can't but know anything about what I'm doing. I can't stop it, Brand. I'm sorry—"

The tramps voice choked off as the greasy strings of hair spread over him completely, forming the beast that had haunted Brand's life since Valentine's Day. The monster twisted and stretched out of the tramp's face into a grotesque mask of a rodent with blood red eyes the size of silver dollars. Its long snout opened and knife-like teeth dripped spittle as it hissed. The monster's arms and chest rippled with sinew and it reared back on thickly muscled legs to let out an anguished squealing howl.

The Conroys screamed fright and terror in the corner. Brand heard Emma screaming from the cockpit. He stared at the beast until it had finished its display and settled onto its overly long hind feet. Its hands were held out to the sides, ready to grab at Brand if he moved in any direction. Behind the beast, Aiden Conroy twitched out from under his father's arm and reached for the pistol on Brand's desk. He raised it with a shaking hand.

"No, Conroy! Don't!" The kid let go of the shooter, throwing it over by Brand's feet.

Brand shook his head, stepping to the cabin door beside him. The monster followed his movement and rushed two steps closer before it drew up short and howled again. Brand took that moment to snatch up the pistol. Even though he'd been there when Nitti emptied a magazine into it, even though Brand had sent a burst of slugs from a Tommy gun into its hide, he had to try something. He had to protect the people around him somehow.

"Hey Larson," he hollered, firing two slugs at the beast. It roared and leaped at him, swiping with a clawed hand and tearing into Brand's heavy coat as he jumped backwards and turned into the strike. Shreds of wool hung from the thing's fingers. It shook the tatters aside and stalked Brand around the cabin again.

The monster gave Nitti a few spare moments before landing its final blows. Maybe Brand would have enough time, too. "Get us over the city, Emma," he shouted as he circled around the cabin, all the while keeping his eyes fixed on the monster and holding the pistol up between them. He felt the airship turning its course and kept one hand behind him as he slid along the cabin wall to the door.

Outside the cockpit glass, Brand saw the lights of radio beacons across Chicago City. A peppering of red dots lit up the darkness below. Tesla's radio towers sent signals through the night, no doubt still commanding the Governor's army of auto-men.

Brand felt his heart hammering as he unlatched the cabin door behind him. He got the story to the people, and he helped save people who would have been killed. Even if the Governor kept it up all night, the city knew what he was up to now. If he wanted them to play along, the man would have to put them all in chains, and where would that get him but nowhere fast?

In the cabin, the beast roared and stepped forward. Brand raised the pistol and fired into its face as it charged.

"Let's go, pal," he said, falling backwards through the unlatched door and plummeting to the city below. As tears filled his eyes, a grin creased his mouth.

The monster leaped from the cabin to follow him and the *Vigilance* sailed on through the dark skies over the city.

Thank you for reading! Can you take a moment to leave a review online?

Getting the word out through reviews is a great way to help independent authors, and is *really appreciated*!

To sweeten the pot, if you do leave a review, whether it's good, bad, or indifferent, please send me the link. I'll reply with a free e-copy of the sequel, ***Gods of New Orleans***, in your preferred format (.mobi, .epub, or .pdf).

You can send the link through the contact form on my website (www.ajsikes.com), or tweet the link and mention me @SikesAaron.

Want to keep up with the doings in and around Chicago City? Sign up for the Gods of Chicago newsletter (http://eepurl.com/LEYib). Monthly updates at most and never spammy.

ACKNOWLEDGEMENTS

Gods of Chicago would not exist without
the help, support, and encouragement of these wonderful people:

Beta and proofreading

Zoë Markham, John Paul Catton, John Monk, Horace Brickley,
Sarah Zama (Italian translations, too), Mike Harris, and Dover
Whitecliff

Readers of the initial serial release, to you, my eternal gratitude.
Writing a book is a process. Completing it, an objective. Sharing
it, a joy.

Thank you, readers!

Colin F. Barnes, for believing in the story and for your valuable
suggestions and improvements to the manuscript, my thanks!

Not to mention cover design, formatting, and publication of the
serial and omnibus/POD release through Anachron Press.

You're a top man, Colin.

ABOUT THE AUTHOR

I write and edit speculative fiction, primarily in the dark/ weird/thriller/sci-fi genres. In addition to Gods of Chicago, I've published multiple short stories and have co-edited two anthologies of Steampunk / Alternate-history fiction. When I'm not writing or editing (or picking up after the kids), I'm probably out in the woodshop making sawdust and chips with my grandfather's hand tools.

You can connect with me and find out more about my editing services on my website (http://www.ajsikes.com/). I'm also around the Twitterverse (http://www.twitter.com/SikesAaron), and I occasionally blog about woodworking, writing, and editing at Writing Joinery (http://writingjoinery.wordpress.com/).